Evolution took a strange path in a dark matter universe, refusing to reveal itself by any form of electromagnetic radiation, especially not visible light.

Although DNA was the basis of life on the planet Dokkheim, there was an uncharacteristic element in its structure. The DNA renewal mechanism resulted in near immortality of the sentient species, until their society began to disintegrate due to the side effects of that longevity.

Langur Skuggi, a Dokkheimien astro-cosmologist on that planet in the dark matter universe, is burdened with the task of finding a solution to the imminent extinction of his species.

His research leads him to a planet of Aliens who may be able to contribute to his theoretical solution. This is Vesimaa, the water world, known by its inhabitants as Earth.

The Alien, Tumma Varjo, a Finnish research scientist, gets caught up in the interaction between the two species. The solution that comes out of various complications is not what Langur planned, or could have foreseen.

Immortal

IMMORTAL

birologybooks.com.au

Cover design by Zsoall Robi, Birology Books.

Planet Dokkheim
In the Dark Matter Universe

Immortals

"Skuggi, I want you to lead the team at Temporality Nexus."

Commanded The Jarl, the supreme ruler of their planet Dokkheim, in his usual brusque manner. Myriad important matters demanded his immediate attention - always immediate attention. Well, they could all wait their turn as far as he was concerned. It was only because of the work of the pre-eminent astro-cosmologist, Langur Skuggi's discovery of the possible existence of 'light matter' that The Jarl ordered the short interview.

'Yes, Jarl Haakon." Langur debated with himself whether to raise the main problem on his mind.

"Why are you still standing there? Go. I have pressing issues to attend to!" The Jarl had very little patience for anything other than matters on his own agenda.

"Thank you, Jarl Haakon." Langur decided it was better to wait until he had more solid evidence to present.

It had been many hundreds of years since his appointment that Langur was able to dedicate any serious time to the major problem of his species; Immortality, or more accurately, an extraordinary longevity of life. It presented more challenges than benefits in the last few thousand years. When his home world, Dokkheim, originally coalesced out of dark super energy of the early universe, there was no indication of the problems future life would have to face on his planet.

The day started like hundreds of other days in the recent past. Langur wearily made his way to his office. He stopped in front of his office portal to contemplate the inscription on which the hopes of an entire civilisation rested – Langur Skuggi - Temporality Nexus Co-ordinator. His secondment to that section of the best cosmological research facility on the planet was made mandatory following his discovery. Perhaps he should have broached the subject of his concern at the time of his appointment. The Jarl must already have had some idea of the reason for the spreading unrest on Dokkheim to have chosen that name for the facility.

As quite a young man, some two thousand years ago, he had broken through an impasse that prevented their science from making any meaningful progress in the understanding of their universe. He had almost unlimited time on his hands to formulate and test theories. Gravity and its relationship to dark energy had been the key.

Langur had just been bonded at the time and looked forward to their first scion in the next few hundred years. His thoughts digressed to the eagerness with which he wanted to start a family early in his life. It wasn't the logical or most desirable thing to do given the circumstances, but this biological imperative dominated over his good sense; a common failing of his species.

Langur suddenly realised his mind had started to wander. Shaking off those happy thoughts he shambled through the portal towards his work platform. In many respects he was still considered to be a young man. One would not have thought it from his movements. The weight of responsibility can do that to a man. Sagging his vertical onto the energy connection he swivelled his visual receptors towards the window. It always helped him to organise the day's activities while gazing into their orb rise; one of the few pleasures he allowed himself to enjoy. True, he had seen it many thousands of times, but this particular morning the radiation was of an exceptionally high frequency. It made the landscape and its morning shadows almost discernible. Most unusual. The near yellow colours made him think of Leuhta's ornamentation, his mate, considered to be a most beautiful woman, and not only in his own estimation.

Langur heard a slight sound on the other side of the office and swivelled to see her waiting for him to notice her. "Leuhta! This is a nice surprise. What brings you to see me here at the office?" He unplugged to move forward to meet her half way.

Leuhta, a Linear Actuator specialising in biomechanical motion systems, visited Langur more often lately driven by her concern for him. "I can see there's something weighing heavily on your mind, Langur. Is it anything to do with us wanting a scion?"

"I was actually thinking about it when you arrived." As they met Leuhta flipped her vertical to the ground, raising her horizontal into the air and at the same time withdrawing her under-shield giving him full access to her private self. Langur also re-orientated and drew into close contact with her. Sometimes they would stay like that for half an hour, simply absorbed in each other.

"What have you decided we should do?" She asked after releasing him. Though not of an emotional extravert personality she used every opportunity to demonstrate her high regard for her mate.

"You know how much I would like to have a child Leuhta and I know you feel the same. But I've an overwhelming sense our species is coming to a turning point. Who knows what could happen in the near future."

"I understand," she replied in subdued tones, "we have time. We are both still young."

Langur had a deep affection for his mate. He greatly respected her knowledge and her dedication to her profession. She seemed to him to be a little more immune to their species' psychological disease, than most people. On many occasions she was able to jolt him out of his own deep depression. Not being of a particularly cheerful disposition to start with, he felt the overwhelming weight of issues facing his people. He often thought he'd be lost without her support. Unfortunately, he didn't express his appreciation to her as often as he should have. There was so much to be done and he keenly felt time running out.

"I'll leave you to your deliberations. I only came by to see how your day started."

Leuhta turned her slight figure slowly away from him, keeping her vertical in his view as long as possible. She knew he liked to see her amber-gold sheath glow in the faint morning light.

Langur retreated into his thoughts again. *I guess two thousand years old is still young compared to our Jarl's eight and a half.* Inevitably his thoughts came back to the problem threatening the annihilation of his species; Immortality. How could he resolve this problem? The process of natural selection, combined with the effects of a narrow spectrum of dark radiation emitted by their orb had a profound effect on the telomeres of their DNA. It wasn't really his field of study, but because of the theoretical existence of 'light' energy Langur had to become familiar with the repair and degeneration process of telomeres. It was that very process which had cemented into their evolution the longevity of their life span.

Dr.Raimo, his private systems engineer who checked his vertical to ensure all sensory receptors, energy networks and electron cloud data systems were functioning normally, interrupted the flow of his thoughts.

"Ah, Dr.Raimo, you arrived just at the right time. I need your input on an important matter."

"Of course, Langur, but let me do your diagnostic first."

Langur began talking as Dr.Raimo went about his checks. "I want to talk to you about our telomeres."

"You mean the caps on the end our DNA strands?"

"Yes. You know that their exposure to our dark radiation has altered their functioning, bringing about our extraordinary longevity. Perhaps other forms of radiation might have a different effect. What do you think?"

"Why would you want to interfere with that?" Dr.Raimo expressed surprised.

"I'm thinking that their evolution may have veered off course."

"Oh." Dr.Raimo didn't know where this line of thinking was going. "Perhaps. Our scientists have almost exhausted their experiments with the full spectrum of EMR available in our part of the universe. They've discovered some perplexing anomalies about it. It seems our planetary system, and indeed our whole region of the galaxy receives a range of frequencies not found in the rest of our universe. They don't know where those originated. They definitely have no concept of their connection with the evolution of our DNA."

"But what if there's another universe that's the source?" Langur ventured to ask.

"Well Langur my friend, there's nothing wrong with you – apart from some very strange ideas." I'll see you next time.

Dr.Raimo wasn't a lot of help, but he did bring Langur's thoughts out into the open. Immortality had its inherent problems. But in general they were not Langur's concerns. The greatest danger to the survival of their species was a specific psychological problem. Like himself, people had simply become weary of life. Although still a young man Langur had already succumbed to a deep ennui. The repetitive nature of existence, the lack of challenges and the slowness of change had a profound effect on his species, as it did on him.

Although not truly immortal, their lives were long enough to have many benefits, as well as many hidden problems. The acquisition and propagation of knowledge in an environment of substantially unlimited continuity had obvious benefits. Until in the recent few tens of thousands of years, no one considered the lack of 'fresh' insights and 'new' thinking to be any great hindrance. Interestingly it wasn't their scientists but their philosophers who came to the conclusion that obstacles had arisen.

Food resources became a more urgent consideration. Birth rates had not increased substantially. The normal gestation period of twenty-nine months for a scion had not altered in living memory. Death rates from natural causes or illness had fallen substantially.

Ageing was certainly not an issue. Anyone who managed to escape the normal hazards could expect to live for thousands of years.

On an entirely different level, life had become more burdensome due to their technological advancement having far outstripped their evolutionary physical development. It was becoming more and more 'inconvenient' to have a 'body' with both vertical and horizontal physical components. Langur understood all the forces that played a part in creating this characteristic over the last few million years. Gravity, dark radiation, electromagnetism all conspired to make life as difficult as possible on their world. Sometimes he had a fleeting idea they must be alien to a world where they had to undergone such a strange adaptation in order to survive. Surely an indigenous life form would have evolved a more 'efficient', a more 'natural' physical manifestation.

"Mr.Skuggi," his secretary reminded him, "Dr.Qilaq is on the way up to see you."

Langur had forgotten about the meeting as he ventured into the realm of fanciful ideas, ideas which had no place in his thinking when confronted with the future of his species. But then again he couldn't entirely neglect anything his augmented thought processors channelled into his consciousness. Langur made a mental note to bring his team together from time to time to engage in a bit of 'fanciful' thinking. If nothing else, from a psychological point of view it might help to alleviate some of the torpor hindering their progress.

Dr.Qilaq, the newly appointed psychologist on his team, entered without knocking. He and Langur had been friends as well as colleagues for many hundreds of years.

"We have no time to waste, my friend – come in – come in."

"What's so urgent, Langur. I'm heavily involved in my special project and prefer not to be interrupted."

"It is exactly your research into possible cures for our racial depression I'm particularly interested in."

"Yes, it's a most interesting discovery isn't it. Those people who've been diagnosed with various conditions have the common prognosis of a limited life span. Instead of becoming more depressed, they've started to behave in a most unexpected way."

Temporals

Langur had thought deeply about the forces of change, and the growing opposition to rumours associated with it. The light outside his window darkened to a deep cherry red. There were no emergencies during the day so far. That wasn't unusual. Everything got done extremely slowly on their world. The incredibly slow pace with which lassitude crept into the lives of his people became the very thing preventing them from recognising that a problem had arisen in the first place, a problem that threatened their existence.

"Dr.Qilaq, could you prepare a summary of your analysis, concentrating on the mental health of these terminally ill people and the range of activities your study sample engaged in. Let's meet again at the energy bar, this time next week."

"You are in a hurry. It won't be detailed, just a summary."

"That's all I need for now."

Whatever cures might be found for the racial depression was of interest to Langur. He certainly didn't guess at any specific connection between a universe of 'light' matter and the psychological health of the Dokkheimiens. There was a most compelling reason for Dr.Qilaq's inclusion in the research team. Almost all of his terminally ill patients, past and present, were generally less depressed than the rest of the planet's population.

Statistically, the more accurate the predicted life span of the individual, the more energized and motivated they became.

On the way home in the magnetrak, with his vertical folded down onto him, Langur felt ill at ease with many aspects of his existence. Why couldn't he just accept things like everyone else? Was it really so inconvenient to have two physicians examine him every time he had an ailment?

Dr.Raimo agreed with Langur about the inefficiencies of a split physicality. The harsh radiation environment, highly charged atmosphere and fluctuating magnetic fields made it necessary to protect the biological part of the organism by flattening it to lie in the horizontal plane. The evolution of a protective dark armour certainly shielded the body most effectively. However, it was necessary for sensory organs to function as well. So these evolved to a more mechanical, vertical component. Over time, through evolution and technology the vertical element gave up almost all of its biological components and became more like a robotic slave extension. It absorbed energy, collected data, provided mobility and possessed prehensile extensions to manipulate the physical environment. Dr.Aulis on the other hand, his biological physician, disagreed with Langur. He never tired of trying to convince Langur of the fantastic defensive mechanisms of their organism. The combination of the mechanical 'vertical' that could easily be repaired or replaced and the protective sheath of the biological 'horizontal' ensured their maximum survivability. Dr.Aulis believed that immortality was totally natural and had nothing to do with the severe depression of their species.

Langur lived only a couple of hours from his office. Leuhta always arrived home before Langur. She made sure all the energy tanks were well stocked with good spectrum ranges for their daily re-charge. Being newly bonded their greetings were still highly affectionate, which lightened his mood a little on arrival.

"Have you thought any more about our problem?" Leuhta came directly to the point because Langur seemed as preoccupied as earlier in the day.

"Our problem?" He wasn't sure whether she meant their aspirations for having a family, or the 'big' problem.

Generally, their conversations revolved around Langur's work and his special concerns. Leuhta became interested in the idea of how an organism could move if it only had a vertical aspect, without the stabilizing effect of a connected horizontal component. In fact, she was keen to discuss some of her latest thoughts on the matter rather than going over old ground, but he decided on the more sensitive subject between them first.

"You know how strongly I feel about creating our own scion. We have all the permissions for it, but my better judgement counsels against it."

"Like I said, I think we have plenty of time to decide." Leuhta was annoyed at having to deal with this again, especially when she wanted to discuss progress with her own work.

"Well … it's exactly the time element I'm concerned about. I think you understand by now how our long life spans could be the catalyst for the extinction of our species."

"Aren't you going a bit far with your theories?" Leuhta interrupted most uncharacteristically. Obviously this was something she was highly apprehensive about, or highly unconvinced about.

"It may have been just a theory when we first started the project. Now it seems an inevitable conclusion to the evolutionary path we are on. But … but … there is the slightest hope. You know about my ideas of 'light' matter and 'light' energy. If … and it's still a very big if … if there is another part to our universe, thought it may be very small, and if life existed in that universe, it might … a very slim chance that it might give us a clue to saving our species."

"That's too many 'ifs' and 'maybes'. Perhaps you're forgetting I'm a highly trained professional with a solid foundation in the physical sciences. I know you cannot base decisions and actions on a bunch of suppositions."

Langur listened patiently. She was very intelligent and extraordinarily competent in her field, in fact near the very top of what their scientific community could offer. Though they had differences of opinion on more than one occasion her input set him on fruitful paths of research. After some minutes of silence, he locked visual receptors with her and slowly put the question.

"Would you ever consider joining our team?" Deafening silence greeted the offer.

"Did I just hear you correctly! Knowing where I stand and my … let's say healthy scepticism … you want *me* to help you 'save' our species!"

"Yes. Most emphatically and urgently - Yes. I need someone who isn't convinced, someone who can clarify ideas through opposition and someone who has the skills you have. Outside of our team no one yet knows what I'm about to tell you. It is strictly confidential. Please understand I do not say this lightly."

Langur procrastinated for several minutes as if debating with himself about revealing his conclusion. Leuhta continued to hold his gaze encouragingly until Langur broke through the ice of his contemplation to quietly say to her, "I believe we have to overcome our immortality."

"What! Leuhta suddenly broke their connection to regard him from a distance.

Langur pressed on without pausing, "We have to become mortal with a much more limited life span - and we have to dramatically alter our genetic structure to achieve that."

"I cannot believe what you are saying! You want me to help you do this? No wonder you can't decide about having our scion. Your depression must be more than usually severe if you're contemplating such an extraordinarily dangerous course of action."

"I can tell you this much – from Dr.Qilaq's research into our terminally ill people, I'm convinced mortality could very well be our salvation."

"Is this another one of your 'if's' and 'maybe's'?"

"Please, just consider the situation Leuhta. I will give you as much information as you need when you're ready to think about it. But whatever you decide, we will have to postpone having a scion. I couldn't face the prospect of our child having to watch its whole existence destroyed in front of its eyes. What if something happened to the two of us, and it was left on its own?"

"Tell me about Dr.Qilaq's research." Though wound up by Langur's theories Leuhta had an open mind and was prepared at least hear him out.

"The essence of it is deceptively simple. When these people find out how long they have left to live it seems to boost their enthusiasm for life. Dr.Qilaq will present more details for me next week, but I've a fair idea what the conclusion will to be."

The conversation between Langur and Leuhta dwindled for the rest of the evening. Downtime was a welcome relief for Langur. The day had not turned out at all like he planned it. He lost a great deal of energy and needed a longer than normal rest period to re-energize. He left himself on a slow trickle charge and hoped that in the morning Leuhta would feel a little more positive. Sadly, she was also not immune to the general lethargy that had become a characteristic of their species.

A severe fermion storm hit Dokkheim that night. People inside their domiciles were safe enough except for interruptions to their communications. Vid records showed many of those caught outside were severely injured when they couldn't find shelter. Hospitals became seriously overcrowded. Spectacular as these rare storms were with their flashes of deep red and orange, sometimes outlining mountains in cornflower blue halos, one didn't wish to be found outside without double protective sheaths. Even their verticals were highly susceptible, particularly the visual sensors and their data processing systems.

As soon as Langur heard the news in the morning he contacted all the key members of his team to check their status. Any loss of personnel would have to be replaced immediately. Given the snail pace of their progress he couldn't afford any delays. Leuhta woke ahead of him, resting in a pensive mood.

Langur quietly asked, "Do you think it's natural that we should be so vulnerable to these storms? I mean - if this was really our natural world wouldn't you think our evolution might have taken a more practical and protective direction."

"And don't you think that if this was such a problem many others before you would have thought about it already and come up with solutions?" Leuhta responded.

Langur could sense Leuhta's agitation and kept the rest of the conversation neutral. "I've made an appointment with Dr.Qilaq for next week. I'm sure it will bring some clarity to our concerns." Leuhta flipped for the intimate contact, which Langur immediately reciprocated. All was well he surmised, and after a brief goodbye left in his private magnemini.

Yakiv – CEO

Langur's favourite energy bar, not far from the office, rested in a

more isolated area of their region overlooking deep Rift valleys. At least in his magnemini he had good protection against the elements and could let his sensors pick up the sights and sounds on the way. He arrived well before Dr.Qilaq and settled into an energy link to wait for him. They had not made a specific time for the meeting. It was enough to define the day. With so much time at their disposal punctuality became a fluid element.

Such a beautiful world, Langur considered as he let himself drift into contemplation, *I can't understand why our existence is so difficult on this planet.* He wasn't a pessimist by nature, rather the opposite. Yet the reality of his species' predicament filled him with dread and a sense of urgency at odds with their immortality.

In the dark amber-red light of the day, a meandering river at the base of the valley sparkled into life as it slowly flowed into the distance. Its ultra-smooth surface dimly reflected every geological feature giving potent presence to the shadows it carried, and flashed brilliant highlights of deep orange light along the curvature of its down-turned meniscus. Many rivers of mercury flowed from their volcanic sources into enormous pits to be swallowed by the planet, only to be recycled by the convection currents heating their large world.

Places of recreation and entertainment were often built in such areas where the wondrous behaviour of this liquid metal could be enjoyed. Langur rested, letting his mind meander with the flow of the river. Dr.Qilaq would bring it back to the present and its issues soon enough.

His thoughts were soon disturbed by a commotion behind him. He rotated his receptors at the last moment to see several tall, powerfully augmented verticals moving rapidly towards him. Langur barely had time to disengage himself from the energy link.

"Say nothing and don't struggle!" The closest to him warned. They were on him in a flash, folded and bound him, deactivating his visual receptors. Before the other guests realised exactly what was happening the kidnappers had him bundled into a magnetrans and speeding down the mountainside. There was nothing he could do. Langur wasn't what could be called a strong man nor particularly courageous in physical terms.

His strength lay in deep contemplation, patience and being able to see around corners of insurmountable problems. Being folded and blinded didn't present any immediate problems of course. They hadn't hurt him ... yet. Whatever the ulterior motives might have been he felt they weren't necessarily sinister because of the lack of brutality or absence of any desire to inflict pain.

"Welcome Mr.Skuggi," a silken voice greeted his arrival. A surprisingly short journey ended with a smooth unhurried stop. *Surely this isn't some elaborate hoax perpetrated by one of my colleagues. Sometimes they are prone to such things out of sheer boredom.* Two of the hefty abductors had removed him from the back of the magnetrans, careful not to inflict any injury and put him on a mobile platform. Although his visual sensors were dampened down he sensed they were in some kind of building heading deep underground. While still in motion he was unfolded, ushered into a room when the lift stopped and allowed to see his surroundings.

"The inconvenience is regrettable but essential. I only need your word at this stage that our interview and my identity will remain confidential." Langur didn't recognise the individual in front of him, but knew of his reputation. The symbols on his vertical were unmistakable. It was Yakiv, the CEO of Vertical Health. Un-arguably the most powerful and rich individual on the planet aside from their Jarl.

"So be it," Langur responded. Due to his unhesitating acquiescence his sensory dampers were completely removed. There was really no point in being aggressive or obstructionist at that stage of proceedings. *I'll hear him out. A man in his position wouldn't do anything to compromise himself.*

"I only know of your reputation – and – some rumours that I find somewhat uncomfortable." Yakiv gave Langur a few minutes to relax and to ease the threatening overtones of the meeting. Langur let Yakiv speak, giving himself a chance to study the man. "I fervently hope we can come to an understanding today Mr.Skuggi." Yakiv pronounced the name with a surprising degree of respect. No doubt he could afford to show some magnanimity under the circumstances. Langur began to feel quietly optimistic, at least of his continuing well-being. "Please - have some refreshment." The water his vertical channelled into him was cool and pure. A highly valued commodity on their world.

"What is it you need my humble understanding about – Yakiv?" With elegant self-assurance Langur posed his question as if it was the most natural thing in the world to ask.

"Without putting too fine a point on it Skuggi, I don't want to go out of business. Your project may have a critical bearing on that. I don't need to tell you that every individual on this planet can be thankful for the care we provide in the maintenance of their verticals. We are essential to their survival."

So, somebody's leaked information about Leuhta's re-engineering experiments, to transform our species from bi-folds to a single upright organism. Unfortunate. Perhaps if Yakiv saw the bigger picture ... "Yakiv – neither you nor I can afford to make decisions based on rumours," Langur said diplomatically, "or under – shall we say – pressure." Yakiv tilted his head in acknowledgement of the perhaps unnecessary 'abduction'.

"Our project is considerably more comprehensive than you may have been led to believe." Langur paused to let the full impact of his statement sink in. Yakiv said nothing, although his vertical fidgeted slightly while he engaged full security protocols for his office. "Perhaps there are more opportunities for an entrepreneur here than grounds for apprehension. I hope we may be able to work together." Yakiv's receptors twitched again. "I trust this friendly discussion will indeed remain confidential." Yakiv felt the balance of control shift slightly towards Langur.

"Our species is on the brink of extinction. We are working to prevent that." Langur said this slowly. Obviously Yakiv had not considered this, for it took some minutes of introspection for him to fully grasp the implications – if it was true. Langur could see he had Yakiv's full attention, so he continued.

"Immortality and its consequential problems will annihilate our species within the next few generations. This is not a theory. We are looking for solutions. We will need partners to implement those solutions. Now – if you would be so kind as to return me to the energy bar – I'm quite happy to discuss any thoughts you might have, but not today."

Yakin had the good business sense not to interrupt Langur until he finished, but then terminated the meeting rather abruptly. There was much he needed to think about. "Langur – may I call you Langur – I will impose on your time again, sometime in the very near future. We may indeed have some common ground." He remained connected while Langur was escorted out of the office.

Yakiv pondered the potential benefits of contributing to the welfare of his species in ways other than maintaining the people's personal hardware. He didn't panic, he didn't jump to conclusions, but most of all he didn't start thinking of solutions. He did however start channelling data to himself, and himself alone. In the next few weeks Yakiv engaged independent investigators, unknown to each other (he didn't want anyone accidentally putting the picture together from the jig-saw puzzle pieces), to gather information from a wide field of study; such background data as the evolutionary history of his species, behavioural trends of large masses of populations, death and birth rate trends over the last ten thousand years, trends in ailments, status of space faring technology and a number of other areas he felt might contribute to his understanding of the 'extinction' scenario. The next time he met with Langur, he didn't want to be caught on the back foot.

Dr.Qilaq's Report

Back at the energy bar Dr.Qilaq relaxed with an exotic energy boost while waiting for Langur. He arrived a little after Langur's abduction. Unaware of Langur's adventure he contentedly enjoyed the environment until Langur's arrival. Surprised to see Langur in a most pensive and distracted mood he remained silent.

"Things are beginning to move much faster than I anticipated my friend." Langur didn't even formally greet Dr.Qilaq before he launched into the discussion. "We will have a number of other people joining us in the next few months." Dr.Qilaq, more so than many of his close associates, was far more relaxed … perhaps saying he was in slow motion might be a better way to describe him. However, he was sufficiently astute to recognise the sense of genuine urgency in Langur's tone.

He let Langur finish, giving him an extra few minutes to unwind before contributing to the conversation. "Do you want to discuss what's bothering you or shall we get on with the review?"

"Someone is leaking information about our work. No – no need to panic. This may well work in our favour. What's just happened to me is an opportunity. The Jarl is taking an extremely long-term view of the problem and our associated project. I'm afraid we may not have five generations to find a solution. It has to be found in our life time and the implementation started."

Dr.Qilaq eagerly responded. "Well then, listen to this. As a peripheral finding to our specific area of research it seems there is an exponential increase in the effects of our racial ennui. Effects that may well escalate into large scale violence, reduced food production and gross neglect of all our infrastructure systems. In other words, if overpopulation doesn't kill us then the consequences of mass depression might well do the job." Thus began his report on a cheerful note.

Not what Langur wanted to hear – yet it was exactly what he needed to know. "The Jarl will have to be informed. Tell me about your study groups' data.

Dr.Qilaq's vertical rigidified itself and his sensors bristled and twitched with excitement. Obviously the man could barely contain himself having to listen to Langur going off at a tangent.

"If we hadn't bothered researching the phenomenon it would've completely escaped our attention. Now - you have to understand that the scope of our study included only those individuals who had a prognosis of highly predictable expiration dates. Some were quite short periods, up to twelve hundred years and some almost immediate – no more than seventy to a hundred years. We also considered both genders."

Langur had become agitated, his patience having almost exhausted itself at the meeting with Yakiv. "My dear Qilaq, I would be overwhelmed with joy to spend the rest of the day engrossed in all the intricate and elegant details of your work, but please keep it brief and to the point." Dr.Qilaq, taken aback by the uncharacteristic sudden interruption, slumped back into his energy connection.

"You have an outstanding reputation and the reliability of your work is unparalleled." Langur hastened to reassure his friend. "I've no doubt about the critical importance of your study to our project. But please get to the point. We can cover the details at another time."

Dr.Qilaq resumed with renewed enthusiasm, "The first indisputable fact coming out of hundreds of years of work was a correlation between life expectancy and degree of engagement in daily life. As life expectancy decreased, life fervour increased. The shorter the individual had to live, the more engaged he became in his everyday life, his work, his family, his leisure activities – and – the less prone he was to be seduced by the depression of those around him. Our research also examined those people who regularly came into contact with these Temporals."

"Go on!" As the tale unfolded Langur's excitement grew. *I have to run this by Leuhta.*

Rather than the Temporals becoming contaminated by the Depressives (the normal immortals), the Depressives experienced an increase in their enthusiasm levels – small but measurable changes according to Dr.Qilaq.

"The second astounding finding could not have been predicted by any of our advanced sciences. Because of the low percentage of the incidence of this phenomenon within the general population, it had slipped completely under the radar – up until now – until you asked me to look into it. In all the professional fields represented by the sample Temporals, we found they excelled above that of the corresponding professions amongst the Depressives. Not only was there a remarkable difference in achievement between them, but the greatest innovations in technology, philosophy, ethics and creativity in the last several generations have been made predominantly by Temporals!"

There it was, the proof Langur was looking for! *I can go to The Jarl with this!*

"We have spoken so many times about the uncertain effects of a reduced life span, and here we have extraordinary evidence that points us to a very positive aspect." Dr.Qilaq knew Langur wanted quick action from their Supreme Leader, but warned, "we will have a great deal of trouble convincing our Jarl to take decisive action in this direction."

"This is it my friend. You have provided me with indisputable proof. We must become mortal! A much shorter life span with only a small window of tolerance in duration is the only salvation for our species."

"It will be an extraordinarily daunting task to get acceptance for your theory and even greater improbability of action on a global scale."

"I believe you are right. I'm truly afraid that because of the general lethargy in the thinking of our people, and even of our honoured and wise leader we will need some form of leverage other than scientific proof to get action."

"Just one question Langur - How do you propose we become mortal?"

*

Langur became so fired up he couldn't contain himself. Early the following morning he was in his laboratory at the astro-cosmological research facility to continue work he'd already started on an implementation possibility, when Yakiv turned up unannounced. He may have been the one to abduct Langur, but it was Langur who'd hijacked Yakiv's thoughts with the lure of greater wealth.

The scientist was deeply absorbed in his calculations in support of his theory. 'Light matter' and 'light energy' must exist concurrently with the 'dark' universe. Their own dark universe could not account for the totality of mass and gravity in existence without the 'light matter' constituent. It only remained to be discovered. Their very own area of the cosmos was an anomaly. Nowhere else could they measure the same amount of infrared radiation. Where did that come from? The known EMR spectrum couldn't possibly have limitations. There must be frequencies they have not been able to detect so far.

Langur reasoned that their problem must be with their instrumentation; Either not sensitive enough, or too sensitive and unable to cope with the much higher frequencies. So he was in the process of developing sensors that could respond to EMR at previously unexpected high frequencies. Within days he hoped to explore the Void in search of the elusive phenomenon, driven by the conviction that their species should not have had to evolve extraordinary systems to protect themselves from all the dark radiation bombarding their planet. True, infrared gave them life and life support capabilities. But it was too expensive in evolutionary terms. What if life exists in another part of the universe, a universe where it was easier to survive? Perhaps a universe with a more benign EMR spectrum.

Yakiv's arrival made Langur angry. He should not have been disturbed at this critical stage of his research. However, he did acknowledge Yakiv could be a lynch pin in the overall plan.

"Oh, it's you." Langur was brief to the point of being abrasive. As previously, their conversation focused very quickly.

"Put me in the picture Skuggi. The big picture, not just words like 'mortality' to frighten people with."

"Talk to Dr.Qilaq. He'll give you facts. I can only give you theories. You'll have to put the puzzle together yourself. Your conclusion will be the same as mine though, if you're prepared to face the truth. The solution is up to us to work out – and if necessary, for us to implement. The timing is critical. If we wait for The Jarl to commit resources according to his own time scale then there'll be no species left to enjoy the solution. We – that is you and I - can either convince him to act sooner or we have to act independently."

What's your theory, Skuggi?"

"We have to modify our DNA to reduce our life spans. This cannot be done with our technology alone. It will require intervention from another life form with a similar DNA evolutionary history." Again Langur ambushed him.

"That's extraordinary. By another life form you don't mean anything existing on Dokkheim, do you?" Though incredulous Yakiv wanted to know where this would lead.

Instead of contradicting him Langur dropped the next surprise. "Well, here's a little something else. I believe we have to change our physical structure to accommodate our probable move to another location. By we, I mean our species; by another location, I mean either another planet in our universe, or at least a more benevolent EMR universe that will not damage our DNA." For a moment Yakiv looked like all his systems had shut down. "Ah! – Now you look like you don't believe me."

Yakiv just sat motionless in his connection, receptors focused on something on the ground, silent. After a while he looked up directly into Langur.

"And Dr.Qilaq?"

"He'll tell you mortality is better suited to our intrinsic nature."

"When do you expect to see The Jarl?"

"I'll let you know. Get yourself and Vertical Health ready."

"I see I've not misjudged the situation. I believe we can help each other. We'll need to define how exactly that will happen. Extinction is a very – terminal – kind of concept." Yakiv suggested.

"Permanent and inevitable - but it does not have to happen yet."

"Definitely not good for business," added Yakiv quietly.

"I'll be putting a special team together. You want in?"

*

Langur arrived home unusually later, though happy with the progress in the lab, and Yakiv. He surprised himself with that impromptu invitation. *Chances have to be taken – I have to trust my intuition at some point.* He was still ruminating about the consequences of the invitation as he entered. Despite being deep in thought he responded wholeheartedly to Leuhta's intimate greeting. *All seems well. I'll be able to tell her about today, and perhaps even ask her opinion about joining the team.*

Disengaging from the embrace Leuhta pre-empted him, "Yes, I'd like to join."

"Dare I ask ... " Langur ventured.

"Too much to lose if you're right and don't succeed."

"I think you will enjoy the challenge."

Although well past their re-charge time their energy reserves were not too low. They tuned into the magnevid before settling down for the rest of the night. Langur felt there was time enough to discuss his day's activities. Several mag-news streams broadcast continuously during the day and night. They selected one that covered their own city. Their attention immediately focused on images of violence broadcast from the other side of their metropolis. Verticals stood at odd angles, obviously badly damaged, their horizontals showing loss of fluids, and the city's security forces appeared to be completely out of their depth. Many magneminis were overturned and burning. With a shaking voice the reporter tried to get her message across.

25

"Nothing like this has happened within the living memory of even my parents! What could have gone wrong? No one seems to have an answer. Several people have already died, with many injured. Our Security is overwhelmed. One incredulous bystander described the scene to me earlier ..."

The noise behind and around her increased while Hospital Emergency response tried to gather up all the injured. Bio-fluids had to be saved as much as possible. One of the magneminis bumped the reporter as it was righted next to her. Some falling debris almost damaged her vertical. Leuhta gazed at the vid absolutely dumfounded. The reporter continued in a raised voice trying to make herself heard above the increasing noise of the gathering crowd.

"... The witness said a large group of people started to move down the street, when another group approached them from inside a building. I didn't think anything unusual about it until suddenly everyone was shouting and attacking each other. Just as suddenly both groups joined forces and started to destroy everything around them" –

"More news as it comes to hand," the reporter signed off.

The visuals ended abruptly followed by an immediate analysis of the riot. Leuhta was beside herself. When she looked at Langur she became even more alarmed. He didn't seem surprised at all. "No Temporal in Dr.Qilaq's sample study group was ever involved in anything like this," Langur said quietly more to himself than Leuhta. He immediately tight beamed Dr.Qilaq to make sure he checked all the rioters to see if any of them were Temporals.

Species Extinction Prevention Team

SEPT

It saddened Langur to see the violence. It exemplified the problem Dr.Qilaq alluded to.

"It's already happening."

Leuhta, hearing his comment, demanded an immediate explanation. "I need to know details, not just your theories.

As she listened to Langur explaining Dr.Qilaq's predictions, her earlier pleasant mood turned serious. "If our world's most notable psychologist's predictions are coming true already then we're facing an imminent crisis." Her resolve strengthened about having made the right decision to join the project.

Langur's choice of Dr.Tulok (Bio-Engineer), Dr.Qilaq (Psychologist), Ka-Ha-Sin (Anthropologist), Leuhta (Linear Actuator) and Yakiv (Vertical Health CEO), was supplemented by Dr.Qilaq's selection of a Temporal named Nostic (an Organisational Psychologist) to make up the SEPT.

Within a few weeks Langur had set up a gathering for the SEPT with the specific purpose of finding out if it was a group of energised, enthusiastic and creative individuals who could work cooperatively to produce results. He gave them a simple task to prepare for the event. "I want you all to find an answer to these propositions – Yes Yakiv, you as well." Yakiv wasn't used to being treated as anything but the CEO of his Company with all the due deference that entailed.

"These are you challenges,"

'Tell a short story about flames that have a mind.

Describe how to travel without moving your body.

Prepare a protocol to communicate with an Alien species.

Work out how to change the location of a planet.

Describe the most hostile environment for life.'

"I don't want 'reasonable' responses. Outlandish, unlikely, impossible and even silly, could all describe a good presentation from you."

As soon as Ka-Ha-Sin, the Anthropologist, arrived at the presentation venue she began complaining. Being somewhat of an agoraphobic she liked small, intimate spaces. Always happy to be ferreting about in a dark tomb or working in her over equipped and cramped laboratory. This place was enormous. Five thousand people couldn't have filled the area – and – it was empty. There was nothing there, not a table or chairs or any other furniture. Langur arrived ahead of them. He settled at the far end of the space waiting for everyone's arrival.

"THIS IS OUR FUTURE," he shouted to them as soon as they were all in the cavernous environment barely illuminated by the dim light. Dr.Qilaq caught on first. He was impressed. He knew Langur had an interesting way of thinking, but this really impressed him. There was nothing in the room, only the six of them. Their species had no future other than through these six people. They had to be focused, prepared for the unknown. Yes, he was most impressed.

Ka-Ha-Sin drew his attention as she pressed herself up against the wall inching her way towards Langur. Dr.Qilaq considered her reaction. What would it take to free her mind from the constrictions of her environment so she could feel comfortable in the dark unknown? Then he spotted Dr.Tulok, dithering. Obviously he'd no idea what to do, how to orientate himself in a space he couldn't connect with. It had no charts, no instruments, no documents and completely void of all the reassurances of their advanced technology. A complete absence of access to data! Dr.Tulok saw Ka-Ha-Sin moving away from the entrance, away from the small group. He shuffled towards her, keen to find a partner as he always did his best work in collaborations.

Dr.Qilaq remained where he was, watching Leuhta looking around taking a few random steps into the empty space. Her horizontal couldn't be seen at all in the near darkness. She appeared to be the most comfortable of everyone there. Her immediate concern was to familiarize herself with the enormous room. Good choice to pick her, he thought. Yakiv was the first to move about completely uninhibited. Dr.Qilaq didn't know him, but from his bearing and movements guessed he was someone used to being in control. Here, Yakiv was definitely not in control; there was no power base to claim as his throne, there were no subordinates to intimidate. He was just a single individual like everyone else, and he didn't like it. After agitating himself around the entrance area he'd just started to move towards Langur when Langur again shouted,

"STAND WHERE YOU ARE PLEASE." Then lowering his voice to just barely audible so they all had to strain to hear him, he said, "Look at where you are. You're lost. You're disorganised."

He waited a few minutes to let them think about it. Again it was Yakiv who started to move about. "If you must move, please make an equal space between each other and stand still. Spread right out away from the walls."

There seemed to be nothing else to do but follow Langur's directions. If anything, they were getting interested in the proceedings. Dr.Qilaq was extremely amused.

"What is this all about? Yakiv asked in a normal voice.

"Nothing … Exists ... To ... Prevent ... The Extinction ... of our Species ... Except ... Us." Langur responded giving each word equal measure. It has to be noted that no one at the meeting was generally given to rash and unconsidered vocalizations. Some minutes later Leuhta suggested they move a little closer together for ease of communication. Langur allowed them only a dozen steps. They were still far enough apart to make each of them feel isolated.

"What does survival look like?" Langur asked without delay. It was time to move the pace along.

"We are still too far apart", said Dr.Qilaq.

"Well then come closer together so we can have a discussion." Everyone moved closer together. They stopped about two manipulator lengths away from each other.

"Closer." They all took another step closer until each could see the other, and within touching distance. Ka-Ha-Sin visibly relaxed. Yakiv visibly become less comfortable. He liked a little buffer zone between himself and those beneath him. Next, Langur asked the strangest thing, which seemed to have absolutely nothing to do with the problem at hand.

"Please arrange yourselves in order of shortest to tallest." A humorous confusion ensued while they shuffled awkwardly around each other, actually having to touch one another for occasional support in order to achieve the requested formation. Leuhta turned out to be the shortest, Ka-Ha-Sin the tallest and Yakiv somewhere in the middle.

"What does survival look like?" Langur repeated.

No one knew how to respond to such a broad question. They stood silent, looking inquisitively at each other. Yakiv spoke first.

"My business continues and – thrives."

"Anyone else?" Prompted Langur.

Dr.Qilaq, "No depression in our people."

"Leuhta?" Langur prompted.

"Greater freedom of movement," she responded without seemingly having thought about it. A little momentum was building.

Ka-Ha-Sin said the obvious, "Our species continues to live and multiply."

Dr.Tulok offered, "Being off the planet – based on our most recent study."

Yakiv aimed one at Langur, "What about you Skuggi?"

"Without going into details – I agree with all of you, and would just like to add this – Mortality."

Nostic refrained from commenting, concentrating instead on listening to the other responses.

The only ones not completely taken by surprise by Langur's comment were Dr.Qilaq, and perhaps Leuhta. Until that moment Dr.Qilaq had not made a direct connection between his Temporals and Langur's mortality/survival theory. Suddenly he understood, or thought he did. *Does Langur propose to somehow limit peoples' lives? But how could that possibly work? How could he engineer such a thing? There would be planet-wide revolt.*

Leuhta could still not believe it. *He's actually serious about his idea that immortality is the cause of the imminent crisis. It is absolutely outlandish to actually consider forcing people to cut their lives short!*

Neither Leuhta or Dr.Qilaq said anything. The other three were just as incredulous. Even Yakiv only knew of Langur's idea that immortality was the big issue, apart from trying to re-engineer the species into a different physical form. The two didn't seem to be connected. He simply didn't know what to say at the moment. Ka-Ha-Sin and Dr.Tulok knew nothing of the latest developments in Langur's thinking. Their receptors bristled with agitation while they stood rooted to the spot. Ka-Ha-Sin wanted to sit somewhere but had to remain standing in close proximity to the group. She extended a manipulator to touch Dr.Tulok standing next to her. They regarded each other as if trying to work out if they were experiencing reality or some kind of strange dream.

"I believe each of you can have a critical input to the final solution, whatever you may think that is." Langur prepared the way for the next segment of his strategy. "Anything is possible and everything is permissible." He had no idea what the team would come up with. It didn't matter. What did matter was that they thought about the issues, that they didn't feel restricted in their responses and that they learn something about each other.

"What is the most hostile environment for life." Langur asked without giving a preamble.

Yakiv's response was in no measure tentative, "Anyone taking a position directly between myself and my desires." The group didn't know whether Yakiv was serious, or making a threat or just being perverse, until Langur let out a huge laugh. That elicited an applause from the others and broke the tension that had built up.

Langur added his own cheeky impromptu thought to help the proceedings flow smoothly, "Not choosing the right colour to match my vertical and using spotted dark magenta, in direct contradiction to her orders," indicating Leuhta.

Without letting the moment cool he continued, "How do you change the location of a planet?"

An impossible task, yet Nostic rose to the challenge, "Move the rest of the Orb system across a bit and leave the planet where it is." Until then Nostic had been so quiet that no one really took much notice of him, except perhaps Dr.Qilaq who'd volunteered him for the team. He also received good applause.

Langur was pleased with the progress. The next challenge wasn't at all frivolous and Langur was particularly interested in the response. "How would you communicate with an Alien species?"

Dr.Qilaq's eager contribution came quick off the mark. "Let the kids sort it out!" That would have to be an universal constant, thought Langur. Children can communicate with other children regardless of any obstacles. No doubt the secret resided in the lack of pre-conceptions with which youngsters approached most challenges. That was worth noting.

Leuhta promptly suggested, "Don't try too hard and use empathy." Trust her to get to the crux of the problem, Langur made a mental note of his partner's practical and probably the most valuable approach. By this stage he could see them all eagerly waiting for the next opportunity to have their say; even Yakiv thawed out and appeared to be enjoying himself.

"I hope you've put a lot of thought into this one," Langur warned, "How to travel without moving your body?"

Leuhta pounced on this one, "Put all your sensors in a box and magnetrak them."

Not to be outdone Ka-Ha-Sin elaborated, "Download your mind into the magnetic field. On world, off world, doesn't matter. As long as you can find your way back!" While the clapping settled Langur traded a look with Yakiv. 'Here's something worth following up', the glance seemed to say.

"Excellent!" Langur rewarded his team. Who is going to tell us about this las one, I wonder? – "The story of the flames."

A little hesitation preceded Nostic's small movement forward to turn and face the group. They must've all considered a contribution, but obviously Nostic was ready to make his. Flames were more greatly feared than any other phenomenon on their world; even more than the fermion storms. Those they had learnt to accept by their sheer predictability. Flames, the infrequent and uncontrollable eruptions in the flow of their magnetic fields, interacted with the lowest frequency infrared EMR. Visually these flames appeared as flashes of extreme brightness and extreme heat. People were often indiscriminately blinded or killed. Property was always damaged: Communications and transportation inevitably suffered, generally severely. If the flames were concentrated in any one area, they couldn't be contained at all. Scientists couldn't discover a way to prevent or forecast these events. What could possibly be worse than flames!

Nostic, a youngish man, looking quite healthy in spite of his limited life-span and with a sense of vitality about him, prepared himself. He waited a few minutes before starting his story in a low conversational tone. At first everyone had to strain to hear him.

"A very long time ago, from very, very far away, Eili came to our world. He was very frightened and lonely. He didn't want to come here, but he had no choice. His world had been destroyed. The only thing his parents could do was to try and give him a chance at life. So they put him in an electron cloud and sent him out into the void to be carried away by the cosmic winds."

All sensors were totally tuned to the man standing there, eager to hear him continue.

"For eons Eili traveled from one world to another, never meeting another intelligence until he came to Dokkheim. By then he had evolved into a mature and very powerful adult. He met no other life in the void, and was nourished by the cosmic rays of thousands of Orbs. Eili had also become very lonely. So when he arrived on our planet he was overjoyed that at last he found somewhere to live, somewhere where he could talk to people. But he soon realized that that was impossible. Eili had become such a strange creature of the universe that no one could see or even hear him.

One day, in utter frustration that nothing he tried could make him visible to us, he decided to try and end his life."

They all gasped at the unimaginable thought, even Langur in the grip of the moment. Nostic continued in a low, deliberate voice.

"No matter how long he lived, he could find no purpose to his existence. So he cast himself upon the only force he thought could end his unhappiness – our fatal magnetic fields." Langur knew this was only a fabrication, but he admired the ingenuity with which Nostic wove the essence of their conundrum into such a simple tale.

"The very moment he and the field touched a blinding flash erupted into flames and he thought it was the end at last. But life was cruel. He didn't die. He mutated into another form of existence. At first Eili was overcome by grief. How long must he endure? Even in the midst of these sad thoughts he saw people around him reacting to something. He looked around and realized it was himself, in his new manifestation, at the center of all the commotion. They were shouting and screaming and running away. He tried to keep up with them and flamed even higher. But the people just became even more frightened. 'At last,' he shouted, 'they can see me, they can hear me!' To this very day he's still trying to make friends with us."

No one made a sound, no one moved at the end of the story. Then to the sudden sound of applause, and by unanimous acclamation Langur invited Nostic to be a permanent member of the SEPT. Langur didn't need to think about the value of the Eili flame story. He definitely wanted this insightful, creative Temporal to join his team.

"Would you allow us to call you Eili in recognition of the valuable contribution you have already made today to the project?"

"Thank you, Langur - Everyone. There's no doubt that our predicament must be faced and a solution found."

Yakiv also recognized the value of a mind that could grasp such a monumental problem and express himself so effortlessly. "Would you consider joining Vertical Health to work with me?"

"Your invitation is most generous," Eili responded, "however, as you all know my life is not long enough to work for both of you. I chose the path that has more at stake."

"Good man," Langur said, "I already have a job for you. Weed out any deadwood from Temporality Nexus that might hold us back. Set up a workshop without delay. You have a free hand."

Zeal Workshop

Eili wasted no time in putting his ideas for a Zeal workshop into motion. He needed to find those with the greatest adaptability and enthusiasm in pursuit of an objective, and remove those most likely to be an hindrance. Langur, trusting in his highly innovative mindscape, gave him complete authority.

Up until a few days ago Eili had been silent. Then without any forewarning he dropped a little surprise on Langur.

"We will be ready in one week exactly," Eili advised. "The only thing I'll say about the event for now is that at the end of a single day that this will take, you will need to get rid of a few people and find new ones. Here's a list of Temporals, in a wide variety of fields, whom you should consider as replacements."

Langur couldn't help being surprised at the liberty taken by Eili. It must have shown because Eili quickly added, "I took as the guiding principle for my action the fact that in all probability our future is not on this planet, and the need for haste."

Hmm … this man has done his homework. He's taken the initiative to plan ahead, with very little to go on. I think we have chosen well.

Eili added, "The location is a secret. Everyone will have to take part, including yourself. You will be escorted with visual sensors dampened down to zero. The exact time and location for you to gather has already been disseminated."

Langur continued with his train of thought … *He's right, we have to look to the void.* Langur immediately went to see Yakiv.

"How do we get there Yakiv?" He came straight to the point without greeting or ceremony.

"There, where exactly?" Yakiv liked the brevity of his conversations with Langur.

"To the 'light' universe. There's no point exploring our own interstellar environment. There's nothing out here that can help us. But! … through the Rift … I'm convinced we will find something to work with."

"The Rift?"

Langur didn't want to elaborate yet, so he just added in an offhand, "Just something I discovered recently – to our joint advantage."

"Right - What about our ice barges?" Asked Yakiv, not fully latching onto the 'Rift' concept.

The ice barges, although complex examples of their technology, were slow, automated and highly specific in their limited function of netting ice meteors and bringing them down to their planet, providing their main source of water for the expanding population.

"We need something much faster. Almost as fast as the speed of light!" Langur stated.

"Why come to me?" Yakiv was perplexed.

"Opportunity. Near Light speed travel is the future. Without it we have no future. You have the infrastructure, the technology and the resources to make it happen. Vertical Health could be a thing of the past. Think what you could gain from truly fast space travel."

Langur stopped for a moment to let Yakiv take a mental breath. Yakiv said nothing. He'd been watching Langur intently for any sign of … hysteria, for want of a better word. He saw none. Yakiv's mind raced ahead, his thoughts moving faster than light. What was the single greatest innovation that Vertical Health had come up with that had put them ahead of everyone else? It was communication - communication between the vertical and horizontal components of their bodies. It had to be wireless and faster than microwaves. His mind was still racing when Langur cut in.

"I can see from your concentration you have some ideas. Well done. I knew I could count on you."

Yakiv let his annoyance show. *There it is again, damn it! That smooth mercury brain of Langur's, making me feel like I'm one step behind all the time. Damn.*

"So here it is in a nutshell, Yakiv. You come up with the means. I'll provide the destination, and the rest … well, between the two us I'm sure we'll work it out. Keep me in the loop."

With that Langur left. Whatever the solution was going to be, it would be far stranger than what they had up their sleeve at the moment. From barely a few months ago when Langur could hardly drag himself into his office, so much has happened. It was all moving literally at the speed of light in comparison with progress before. Just as well. Planetary civil unrest also increased exponentially. Temporality Nexus had to come up with a way forward - fast.

With all the passengers' dampeners connected and set to zero the convoy of maximagnetrans vehicles made their way to the workshop site. No one other than those specifically involved in the Temporality Nexus project were invited. Eili had already noted that about twenty-five individuals declined the invitation. Participation wasn't compulsory, intentionally. However, those twenty-five immediately lost their positions. Such an obvious lack of enthusiasm, even if it was just for an 'adventure', surely meant their contributions to the project would probably be mediocre at the best. More likely they would be a hindrance.

One individual, called Murha, recently recruited to the Interspecies Protocols Unit, made a considerable fuss about the visual dampening, though eventually gave in to peer pressure. Eili made a note of him as well, taking particular note of the person who managed to convince Murha to conform. It was a long trip, even by their time scale; as it was intended. Eili wanted them all to arrive in as much discomfort as possible and with depleted energy reserves.

Members of the SEPT, well dispersed throughout the convoy, had little possibility to communicate with each other. Again, all part of the plan. Langur trusted Eili, depending on him, yet had reservations about all the intrigue. But, he either trusted the Temporal or he didn't. Just as his own patience began thinning out, his vehicle stopped and with military precision everyone was herded into a long, cold tunnel.

Arriving at the end, a considerable distance from the entrance, the entire crowd found themselves in a totally dark enclosure which was sealed as soon as they were all ensconced in it. Eili slipped away to a secret compartment from which he could observe and issue directions. They had one objective.

"Your challenge is to GET OUT," he broadcast loud enough for all to hear clearly. Simultaneously he deactivated all their sensory dampeners. The pitch black enclosure immediately filled with discontented murmurs, thickening the already dark soup of apprehension they found themselves in.

"It is possible to escape within fifteen minutes. You will remain in there until you solve the problem." Eili said nothing else.

The Zeal Workshop had just started in earnest.

Within a few minutes one belligerent voice made itself heard above the rising din – Murha's. "What is the meaning of this!"

Murha was a Terminal – and a criminal with a suspended sentence. Dr.Qilaq selected him because of his superior intelligence, scientific qualifications and his unusual drive to involve himself in life. Murha's clonal servitude was suspended because of an illness which had already sentenced him to death ahead of his legal termination date. No one of any age was immune to those things that could truncate people's longevity. They lived in a hostile and unforgiving planetary environment.

"This is torture! We should not be subjected to this kind of treatment. Where's the respect due to us scientists!"

A few voices of agreement rose to align themselves with Murha. Yet there were many others who seemed prepared to take on the challenge. At first, friends found each other and discussed what the real point of the exercise was. Others, the great majority, went bumping into each other as they searched for an exit. It existed of course, but needed a particular trigger to activate it. Finding the trigger wasn't the aim of the exercise.

Instead of panic some diverse and interesting reactions emerged. A small discontented group formed around Murha. Another small group of 'fatalists' also banded together virtually on the spot where they had first entered the enclosure and did nothing. They folded themselves and waited, not even bothering to discuss the circumstances they found themselves in. While Murha and his gang built on their indignation with undignified outbursts, another group of people started to spread out against the walls, keeping physical contact with each other. They slowly shuffled along searching for anything that could give them a clue to the exit. Perhaps it was no surprise to Eili to see all the members of the SEPT dispersed along the wall, searching with the others.

Eili watched and recorded everything, making his own private notes. He kept a close watch on Murha's gang. At the first sign of violence he could illuminate the place with a brightness that would stop any activity. Murha may have been upset, even furious - but he was no fool. He'd heard some of the people shuffling along the wall.

So he picked his way through the crowd to get to the wall himself, abandoning the group gathered around him. The abandoned group just continued grumbling, without showing any initiative to find the escape solution.

Other noises emerged. Complaints of depleted energy levels, fatigue, microprocessor malfunctions and a variety of smaller ailments. It quickly became clear to Eili how the Temporality Nexus staff was polarizing. Good. He decided to push them a little further before releasing them. One of the walls could be mobilised. Eili engaged the motors, which everybody could hear start, moving the wall inwards. It had moved several small increments before somebody realised what was happening. They still couldn't see anything, but they did hear the quiet scraping of the moving wall.

"You are trying to kill all!" Murha shouted. He became uncontrollable to the point of having to be demobilized. The individual who took control of the situation didn't kill Murha, just drained most of his energy reserves into himself. Some of this he converted to a faint light source. Innovative and effective. A large group immediately converged on the light source.

"I have a little to spare," one of the people volunteered over the murmurings. So did many others almost immediately. Very soon scores of small lights illuminated the enclosure, allowing the crowd to take stock of their surroundings.

"There it is!" Someone exclaimed.

Like a castle made from a deck of cards some of the people who had been exploring the floor, built a pyramid to reach the "Exit" sign on one of the walls; it had a sensor next to it. Almost nobody thought of Murha as they filed out into the tunnel. Four younger females took pity on the malcontent, folded him and carried him out.

Eili meet them outside the enclosure. He wasn't surprised to hear many voices raised to query the very strange 'adventure'. Loudest of all were the group who had gathered around Murha. They had not even realized he'd abandoned them and they just as quickly abandoned him once out in the tunnel. A huge feast was prepared for the entire gathering, within sight of the exit of the enclosure. Discontent gave way to other more urgent business.

"There will be a debriefing after you have all recharged," Eili immediately put them at ease. He continued to watch and record. He wanted to see if the newly formed groups would consolidate. Langur and the other members of the SEPT took up positions near Eili's energy console.

"How could you possibly call this a …!" Langur almost shouted, but was cut off by Eili.

"Three words … Motivation, Initiative, Teamwork." Eili gave them a moment to absorb that before continuing, "Why is it only Dr.Tulok sought out one of you? What were the rest of you doing?" He looked at each person in turn, lingering a little longer on Yakiv and Langur.

Dr.Qilaq jumped into the gulf of silence. "Excellent!" So what are the results of your little game, and how do we use them."

"I gave you a list at the outset, Langur." Eili's response seemed impatient. "I'll give you another one shortly. You need to replace the people on the second list if you want this project to make any real progress."

"I appreciate your enthusiasm, but I'll need some solid reasons for dismissing members of my organisation." Yakiv nodded in support of Langur as Langur tried to resume control.

"You'll get a full report." Eili had to shout as the relief of escape permeated the crowd of freshly energised scientists and support staff. "But here is the crux of it. Do you have time for malcontents, dissidents, fatalists who give up before even trying anything at all? In short, can you afford to have anyone who does not have the initiative and motivation to find solutions?"

It had been almost twenty-four hours before everyone had returned to the main research centre. Leuhta travelled with Langur, Yakiv with Dr.Qilaq, Ka-Ha-Sin with Dr.Tulok and Eili with Murha.

A great many things were sorted out and decided during the return trip. Langur would find out later why Eili sat with Murha.

At a SEPT meeting after Eili's de-briefing with Langur, Langur launched directly into business without any preamble.

"I noticed a good many conversations took place on the way back from the workshop. I assume you have all been in contact with one another since, so I'll make this short. I propose the following teams and input projects to start with. If you have anything to add, tell me after. Otherwise liaise with others as much as you need. Yakiv and myself will visit The Jarl. Eili and Leuhta, please select the new recruits. Dr.Tulok, Leuhta and Ka-Ha-Sin – time to get serious with a solution to bi-ped locomotion please. Dr.Qilaq and Eili … here's a challenge for you – Alien communications protocol. There's no doubt that if we don't find others out there, our own future is bleak. Myself and Yakiv will work on how to deal with them after we find them."

Up until that day all the work carried out by Temporality Nexus had been essentially theoretical. Everyone now realised the theory had uncomfortably turned into reality. No one objected to the tasks assigned to them. A sense of enthusiasm and purpose pervaded the meeting. Eili remained behind afterwards to talk to Langur in private.

"Murha is unstable," he summarised, "but he's not the problem. The danger is that he attracts like-minded people. He should not be dismissed. Better to keep him close to us, under surveillance."

"I had an idea Murha's been the one leaking information. Fortuitously that brought Yakiv to us. But I still have grave misgivings about any contribution Murha could possibly make." Langur needed more convincing about Murha's value to the project.

"Fine. He can work with you and Dr.Qilaq. Watch him closely! Better not to get rid of him just yet."

Working in close collaboration with Dr.Tulok, Ka-Ha-Sin made an encouraging discovery. She found remnants from the evolution of their species. Many millions of years ago their kind were evolving towards a single vertical body structure. This discovery became important in the context of the project. She hadn't yet found the catalyst that had drastically changed the trend. The very idea that their genetics already contained the predisposition towards the vertical format was critical. She and Leuhta hoped that if a vertical biped life form existed somewhere out there, it would open up exciting possibilities; such as species re-engineering without having to continue their previously invasive genetic upgrades in order to just survive.

A Few Complications

Unrest continued to escalate as the months dragged on.

Whenever Langur tuned in to the news he saw further unrest in other parts of the planet as well.

"Leuhta," eventually people are going to look for a scapegoat. They need to channel their aggression."

"In that case you had better meet with Jarl Haakon soon, don't you think?"

"First I want to see how far Yakiv is going to commit himself and the resources of his organization to the project. He could provide the leverage I've been looking for to motivate The Jarl into decisive action."

Almost every night Leuhta and Langur scanned the magnevid for news of rioting. Examples of crowds out of control were reported with increased frequency. He felt the pressure for more positive action, more so than any of the others, except perhaps Leuhta. The entire team had been working hard with renewed effort over the last few months.

The Jarl had acted, but only against the rioters. Civil unrest had become so violent in some areas as to force Jarl Haakon to invoke almost the harshest penalty for some of the leaders; clonal servitude. Although society had evolved to a global community not all undesirable elements of their specie's psyche had been successfully purged. The range of penalties included clonal servitude among the harshest for aberrant behaviour. It became the most effective deterrent for most people. After immediate deactivation following sentencing, their life essence personalities were not allowed to dissipate into the great Void, but captured and uploaded into a slave clone. These clones worked in the most difficult occupations on the planet, without the luxury of self-determination. They were aware of their origins and had full control of their cognitive faculties, but their activities were pre-programmed. Not only did they have no choice in what they could do, but had to do it for several generations. The duration always depended on the severity of their transgressions. Suffice it to say, any normal Terminal who had the opportunity to give their existence meaning within a limited life span, didn't want to jeopardize that luxury, so it was rare for any Terminal to take part in the rioting.

It was a source of unending fascination for Dr.Qilaq that people would not choose to limit their own life spans voluntarily – in spite of their awareness of the seemingly improved quality of life of the Terminals. As advanced as he considered their civilization to be, he felt that such stubborn adherence to a throwback of evolutionary imperatives displayed a grossly primitive attitude. Admittedly, he too was one of the reluctant ones.

*

Another four months of research later Langur had made solid progress regarding the 'Rift'.

"It is only a light year away," he confided to Yakiv, "and it appears to be sufficiently open to allow some form of penetration, at least from our direction. What progress have you made with transportation?"

"It is promising, but we are lacking volunteers to test the process. We have devised a method to concentrate an individual's entire thought energy field into a tight light beam and transmit it over a long distance at light speed. Receiving the returning beam and reconstituting the individual into physical form has been slightly problematic. That's where we need volunteers who are prepared for the worst outcome. Clones are no good. We have to have uncompromised psyches to work with. There have been a few extreme short term temporals willing and available, and in some cases criminal individuals who preferred that experience to the alternative slave cloning reserved for them."

*

As time drifted, unnoticed by most people, Langur became increasingly restless. Dr.Qilaq visited his home trying to calm him.

"You have made an incredible discovery and Yakiv has almost perfected his transportation system for individuals. Instead of agonising over the rioting situation let's go and see The Jarl. I have all the information I need to convince him of the extent of the problem."

"You're probably right my friend."

Leuhta nodded in agreement as Langur accepted what his friend was saying. "But what if he's as stubborn as his reputation?'

"Don't underestimate him," Leuhta warned, "either in his willingness to act towards your preferred solution, or to prevent you from implementing it."

Within two more months Langur, Yakiv and Dr.Qilaq found themselves in the presence of their venerable leader. As one would expect of an individual who had the weight of responsibility for an entire species on his shoulders The Jarl was his usual brusque self.

"Why do you feel the need to disturb my peace?" He didn't appreciate any intrusion into his methods of ruling the planet. That process took time, much introspection, more time, a little input from his underlings, more time then many more decisions. One could not hurry these matters of state. Impatience already showed in his movements even though the audience had barely begun. The Jarl liked to take his time with some things, but never with crackpot theories about the annihilation of their species. Nevertheless, the fact that Langur had managed to get the interview, and in such incredibly short time, was a clear indication of Jarl Haakon's concern.

Langur knew of his leader's reputation. So he presented bare facts. "Rioting has increased by ninety-five percent in the last four years."

Dr.Qilaq explained. "The reason is depression, manic depression and a sense of helplessness with feelings of pointlessness."

Yakiv contributed from his perspective. "Manufacturing and infrastructure maintenance has diminished by over fifty-six percent. People just don't want to do the work anymore. They see no point. Nothing changes. Life has become boring and meaningless. They cannot find purpose, so business and life suffer."

The Jarl raised his hand for silence, remained seated at his energy console and scanned the wall high above the heads of his visitors, which displayed data feeding monitors. He sat silent and motionless for so long that Dr.Qilaq felt compelled to attend to the seemingly temporary paralysis of their Jarl. Just as he was about to move The Jarl waved at them to continue, transfixing each of them with a long hard scrutiny. They were actually being listened to, which encouraged Langur. However, he wasn't prepared to go into the details of the final solution they were advocating – that being 'mortality', which could have resulted their immediate promotion to slave clone status in a fit of rage from their leader.

Instead he indicated a solution for the rioting, the ennui and the breakdown of their industries and infrastructure. "We need to re-energize the population with a new challenge. We must find other life in the universe and make contact. We have to interact with them, bring more wealth and technology to our planet."

Again the long wait while the information was being digested. At the same time data poured directly into The Jarl from all parts of the planet, informing him of the veracity of the problems outlined by these three men.

Langur spoke again, without permission, and was quickly stopped by an overly armed attendant. On the appropriate signal from The Jarl Langur continue making his point. "We have three generations of leeway based on current trends, in which to solve the problems before complete breakdown of society."

"Must we be so hasty?" The Jarl asked with a semblance of boredom, even perhaps resigned disappointment at the haste being forced upon him. Yakiv started to say something. The Jarl snapped his attention to the intruding voice, immediately cutting it short. His pointing finger commanded Langur to continue.

"We have made considerable progress. And we beg your indulgence." Of course he could not, under any circumstances intimate what The Jarl should do. However, the supplication was sufficient to ensure the three of them would receive an audience with the ruler's personal assistant, Valokvantti, at the conclusion of the interview. He wasn't as indulgent as the Jarl.

"No. There will be no action taken against the general population! As for other assistance, remit your application and we will consider it in due time. Now leave."

They didn't even get a chance to put their case for an exploration through the Rift. Dr.Qilaq quietly voiced his disappointment as they made their way out of the place, "Not a satisfactory outcome at all. Yet, The Jarl has been primed. That may be of some value in the fullness of his time."

The three men left the royal premises, stunned; Langur was disappointed Yakiv didn't get the opportunity to make a bigger contribution. He hoped for some indication of serious commitment from the CEO to the project.

"Not at all satisfactory! He might be The Jarl, but I don't think he's a leader with wisdom or vision."

Yakiv said this quietly. They were still within the palace grounds. Such dissident talk could cost him his life – mandatory termination; a standard punishment for a standard crime, yet more boldly he added, "There's much to be gained here, for us at Vertical Health. Skuggi – I've set up a new division dedicated exclusively to intra-galactic travel. The Ice barge manufacturers can come up with leisure cruises on slow freighters, but we at Vertical Systems will revolutionize the transportation of our people in space."

The news made both Dr.Qilaq and Langur ecstatic, but neither showed it. That would have been bad form. They behaved as if Yakiv had already made the undertaking some time ago. So the two friends just quietly nodded their acknowledgement.

*

"Nothing came of the meeting. Nothing at all. Temporality Nexus is on its own," Langur updated everyone. "At least The Jarl's existing support hasn't been withdrawn, so we can continue our operations. He may think we are still concentrating on researching 'light energy' and the 'light mater universe' – and in a way that's exactly what we are doing – but with a much more focused agenda than just pure research. Surely he must know that by now."

They had stopped listening to Langur and were all staring at the magnevid screen. "There! That's him!" Called out Eili. He'd spotted Murha at the head of a large crowd being filmed in the middle of yet another riot in the inner city area. He looked wild. He and his followers were using all manner of implements to destroy anything in their path. Just as suddenly as the mayhem started, it dissipated well before the security forces arrived.

The reporter offered her opinion. "These rioters appear to have inside information. They always seem to get away before they can be detained. A leader had emerged amongst them. We are trying to get a clear picture of him. So far no one has been able to identify him," she shouted into the microphone.

"I know who it is!" Eili added.

"Are you sure its Murha?" Langur asked.

"Just look at his body language. He's taller than most people, and has very distinctive vocal characteristics. His vertical's markings are quite unique."

"He's your responsibility, Eili - What do we do with him?" asked Langur.

Yakiv nudged Langur and suggested a 'promotion' for the troublemaker. "Offer him a chance to become famous. Give him the recognition he obviously craves – but with responsibilities shall we say."

"You don't mean – Research - in the void, do you?"

"Exactly." Yakiv seemed very enthusiastic. "His got scientific training, and he's been working on Alien communications. I might just have the means to get him there – wherever that may be."

Yakiv's Starportation Systems department had almost perfected their travel system. They could tight beam an individual's full neural network and thoughts pattern with a new Concentrator, send it on a return journey to a remote ice barge in space and reconstitute him on his return - almost. With the process so well advanced it was worth testing more comprehensively on dispensable volunteers.

Langur didn't want to take unnecessary chances. "If you intend to use Murha, get it right. He's still a valuable asset in spite of his misguided actions."

*

Murha grinned quite happily, confidently – one might have thought, arrogantly - as he stood in the Concentrator chamber. He did of course realise his external activities had been discovered. *As soon as I get back with nothing to support Langur's theories, I'll be able to completely discredit him.* He thought this trip would help him destroy Langur's operations as recompense for his humiliating experience at the Zeal workshop.

"Let her rip!" He shouted. "I'll send you back the best data you've ever seen. I want full magnevid coverage on my return and full credit – thinking of course of his own public vindication.

49

Yakiv's chief scientist initiated the flux inside the chamber. Gradually Murha's image dulled in direct proportion to the increased illumination of his thought sphere. Each individual on the planet was surrounded by their personal data cloud. That data contained all the input received by the organism during its life span and all the simple and complex thought structures created by that individual. Their vertical components used the packets of the data to carry out further thought processing. The same processing had to be replicated to allow the energetic photon packets representing Murha to have full control. He wasn't aware of an added little complication. They were going to let him discover that for himself … a little bonus to the research if he actually succeeded in attaining control.

They focused Murha's cloud into a tight laser beam, with a processor packet tagged on. During the journey and on his arrival at a destination he could send newly gathered data back to Temporality Nexus. His processor packet would also enable him to return to his point of origin - hopefully. This was likely to be a long trip for Murha. His dull vertical and horizontal remained immobile inside the chamber as his essence was aimed directly at the Rift gateway in their cosmos.

"Will this solve both my problems, Yakiv?" Langur felt relieved to be finally taking some real action. His gratitude to Yakiv clearly visible as the two of them went off for a recharge while the technicians monitored the traveller's progress.

It Exists!

Data poured in from Murha. Unwittingly he was doing his species a great service. At first it was only images of the closer and more distant ice barges hauling the ice meteors towards their planet for their water supply. Six months out he started sending back readings of such light intensity that the receiving instruments needed to be re-calibrated to cope with the influx of the strong visible light spectrum emanating from the Rift. Murha was getting close to passing through the gateway.

Before his return, Yakiv's team had to finalise the re-constitution part the 'thought' transportation process. The remaining solution was to accurately and without damage to the incoming thought packets, put the person back into their own bi-fold body. Already Murha was on the verge of crossing the exit threshold of the Rift. In retrospect perhaps they should have sent an accompanying AI-Class-S cloud with him. What if his harvested data couldn't be streamed back through the Rift and all the interpretation and analysis had to be done at the remote location?

The SEPT gathered at Yakiv's research centre for the moment of Murha's crossing from their universe into the unknown. They waited in silent anticipation when all transmission ceased without warning. It had been continuous since Murha's departure – then suddenly nothing. Not even the background echoes of the creation of their universe could be heard.

Then, just as suddenly Murha's screaming voice burst into the room. Incoherent sounds of pain, which gradually diminished as Murha realised that the extreme light on the other side could no longer damage his sensors. They were left back on Dokkheim with his physical body mechanisms.

"I don't believe it! So much light! So incredibly bright! It's everywhere. Galaxies of swirling brilliance. Unfathomable numbers of Orbs and planets. I'm heading through dense clouds of cosmic dust bursting with luminescence," he transmitted. "Where should I go, Skuggi? What exactly am I looking for?"

The team was agape with wonder. They could not only hear his voice; they could see everything Murha saw. His transmission packets relayed not just his thoughts but also all his sensory inputs. The Dokkheimien vocabulary had no words with which to adequately describe, to try and comprehend the spectacle of this universe of light.

"It Exists!" Langur burst out. They were all overcome with the enormity of the discovery, with the unbelievable implications this Universe of Light presented to them. Hope! Their species had hope of survival!

"If only we could find Life somewhere in that chaotic spectrum of light,' Dr.Qilaq thought aloud.

Langur recovered sufficiently to direct Murha, "Just continue directly ahead. Search for any orb with orbiting planets in the habitable zone."

By the time Murha received the communication he was heading well into the outer extremities of the Orion arm of the galaxy he'd arrived in. There were billions of orbs, most he couldn't even see, let alone guess they existed. But they must exist. How else could there have been so much light?

Even as he raced myriad other shafts of light to destinations unknown, he'd decided this was a lonely place. So much could be seen, so incredibly overwhelming in its complexity. To stop himself from losing focus Murha concentrated on his home planet, and the reason he now found himself out there, alone.

'Perhaps the insurrection has succeeded by now and the planet is saved from the maniac Skuggi. But is Skuggi so mad? How did he know all this existed?' Murha debated with himself. *'He didn't know! He doesn't know what he's doing. He's putting our species at risk for some crazy idea about extinction because of immortality. You have to be immortal to be able to see all this. It would take many life times of immortality just to see a small corner of this place. What madness was it to make him think mortality is best for us? Skuggi is mad. I am the only sane one.'* It seemed he was wining the argument. *'I did the right thing to inform the people. Surely they must know by now what crazy changes Skuggi wants to impose on their lives.'* Murha convinced himself of the rightness of his actions to oppose Langur.

While his internal ramblings distracted him, he headed deeper and deeper into the outer reaches of the Orion Spur of the Milky Way, not realising all his thoughts were being relayed back to Langur. The latest image he transmitted was of a planet he'd just passed on his way towards a particularly bright yellow white orb. This was the most extraordinary planet he had seen so far. The other two were spectacular as well, but nothing like this one, surrounded by brightly coloured rings, casting a magnificent shadow directly on the equator of the planet.

*

"It's not going to work," Leuhta complained to Langur. "It's not that we can't reconfigure the format of our bodies. Our early evolution was headed in exactly that direction."

"The emissions from our Orb are too lethal to enable a purely biological, vertically oriented bi-ped organism to survive," added Ka-Ha-Sin. However, she wasn't one to give up easily; a necessary trait for a forensic anthropologist.

Leuhta elaborated on the difficulties they faced, "So far, we have had to introduce so much shielding that the vertical structure couldn't even support its own weight, let alone the extra protective layers. There's no doubt the genetic foundation still exists to enable the changes to be made. But they cannot be fully implemented on our planet."

That was both a severe blow to Langur and an important revelation confirming his initial theories. "What you say only confirms my idea - we must not only find an alternative location for our species, in this universe or the next, but we must crossbreed with a suitable species to ensure the changes would work."

"We haven't even attacked the problem of procreation. Scion budding is difficult as it is, without the encumbrances created by the realigned posture," Dr.Tulok rounded off the gist of their problems with an almost a defeatist tone of voice.

The verticalization process was creating more problems than solutions. "You have proved our species can stand on two feet.

There is no impediment other than our own Orb and our over-engineered genetics. And those circumstances may well come within our control. Well done both of you." Langur wasn't just mouthing platitudes. He meant every word. All the pieces of the jigsaw puzzle were falling into place. "Perfect the process as much as practicable, worry less about the shielding. We may not need it.

*

With Murha's disappearance public unrest had suddenly diminished. No one had an explanation. However, the lull didn't last long. In many global centres civil disobedience developed into a structured movement with dissident leaders emerging to organise the discontented masses. They had information, from unrevealed sources, that fuelled the dissatisfaction and growing anger. Murha may have been an extreme egoist, but he wasn't as big a fool as some thought. Before leaving he'd been leaking sensitive information to these emergent leaders about the project's progress and intent, adding his own little twists. Rumours started spreading fast.

When Langur heard Murha's thoughts about the insurrection and his intention to reveal to the populace his plan to make everyone mortal, he wasted no time. They needed to get to The Jarl again, immediately. Rumour must not be the basis of any of his decisions, not that he was prone to such unconsidered actions. They must get a chance to explain, in scientific terms and with proofs.

Leuhta received news that heightened their sense of urgency. "The media has latched onto rumours that you want to kill the people ahead of their normal lifespans. They're asking too many questions," she told Langur, "You have to come clean with The Jarl and tell him the people must give up their immortality. You have to tell him everything!"

"NO!" Came the unequivocal refusal from the royal representative. You have already seen The Jarl, only last year. Do you expect he has all the time in the world to entertain you whenever you want? NO!" Valokvantti didn't even let them into the palace grounds. Well, that was that. The people needed to know the truth - the first great error of judgement by Langur.

Yes they did need to know the truth, but not the way he proposed. As with all media, the news broadcaster chosen by Langur always made it a point to get the most out of any scrap of news; to milk every nuance of interest from a story. There really wasn't much happening on the planet for the last several millennia. So the current unrest and rumours represented media gold. Langur and Eili had no trouble at all to get immediate airtime.

The studio was sardine-packed with audience. At last they would see the man face to face – the man who threatened their very existence. There was no need to prime the spectators – they were eager and ready in their fear and indignation.

Meeri, the interviewer announced boldly to the viewers, "All those people who have been exhibiting what we might have felt to be totally unjustified violent behaviour, may have had a very firm foundation indeed for their actions!"

Sitting opposite her, Langur fidgeted and Eili looked extremely worried. The camera zoomed in on Langur's discomfort, setting the scene for Meeri's next inflammatory comment.

"We have here the very man, head of Temporality Nexus, who has finally decided we deserve an explanation!" Meeri turned a deceptively friendly smile towards Langur to ask, "What exactly is it you want to do to us?" She had managed to put Langur on the spot immediately. He wasn't ready to explain that straight away. He needed some sort of lead-in, now completely denied him.

"I don't actually – want – to do anything. Our race is facing extinction and ..."

Uproar erupted from the live audience. This was news to them and absolute gold for the cameras. Close ups of people shouting and hurling abuse created a wonderful scene of mayhem. This went on for minutes before Meeri could resume, ecstatic with the promise of more to come.

"That seems to be a bit unrealistic. What makes you think we are all going to die?"

"Immortality is going to kill us."

Angry interjections threatened to drown out his voice.

"People are suffering from extreme clinical depression."

Explosive shouting from the audience cut him off, making it impossible for him to continue. Langur was a scientist, not a public speaker. He didn't know how to get his point across. He actually thought if people heard a logical argument they would understand and behave in a reasonable, civilized way. He failed to take into consideration his misjudgement of people's good sense, and that it was their very depressive condition that contributed to their unreasonableness.

Eili stepped into the middle of the chaos Langur seemed to be intent on creating. "Perhaps we should take a step back and have a look at the bigger picture," he shouted above the noise. "You have a very good reason to feel frustrated and to feel the need to do something about it. But how do you know what you should be doing?"

A slight abatement of the noise level allowed him to go on. "You have all experienced the fermion storms, the fires and the many other problems of existence on this planet. Have you never wondered if this was all normal? If it was natural for us to go to such extreme efforts to protect ourselves against our own environment?"

Meeri introduced him to the cameras. "This is Eili. He's what Temporality Nexus calls a 'Temporal', a man with a limited lifespan. He's assisting Professor Skuggi."

She turned to confront Eili. "So you're saying our planet is going to kill us," she baited, intent on keeping the questions emotionally loaded. But Eili didn't bite. He remained focused and responded calmly.

"Many insurmountable problems have been created by a combination of forces from our Orb and our planet. The biggest of these occurred at a very early stage in our evolution and continues happening even now." Eili had everyone's attention, even Langur's. It was as if he was listening to the scenario for the first time, hearing it from a fresh perspective.

"Is that so? Why is it making people riot in the streets?" Meeri's turned cynical.

"It has to do with the way our genetic structure reproduces itself. The very efficient way it has been doing this is the reason our lives are so long. Such longevity has robbed many people of a meaningful existence. It has removed any sense of purpose to their lives."

He'd hit a nerve. Many in the audience could identify with that.

At this point Langur became excited by the listeners' receptive mood swing and felt it was time to lay out the bare facts. The live audience, and no doubt all the viewers were enthralled, quiet and listening intently. Before Eili could stop him, Langur dropped a bombshell. Meeri couldn't believe her luck. This crazy scientist just cemented the greatest success of her career.

"Our immortality is creating a worldwide depression, causing people to become violent, to neglect their jobs, their lives, their families… We have to become mortal!"

Stunned silence reverberated in the news studio to the revelation. Langur continued. "We will have to move to another planet, perhaps even another Universe. We will have to re-engineer our genetic structure to enable us to walk vertically with a body of a single vertical part."

He took a breath. Eili's sensors shook in disbelief – Meeri's grin couldn't control itself, and some of the audience began to laugh. Very quickly the laughter turned to fear and anger and shouting. The sentiment was echoed in many homes around the planet, and out in the streets. The lethargy seemed to have lifted. The latent energy of all the torpor turned destructive.

"Damn that man! I want him in front of me immediately! And send out the Forces to control those riots – NOW."

Valokvantti heard his furious master, heard the news transmission but was so dumbfounded he couldn't immediately react.

The news broadcast was an enormous success from a purely commercial perspective. Energy began to flow within the fluids of the Dokkheimiens again. But it was the wrong kind of energy. It couldn't be controlled.

Very soon Langur and Eili stood before The Jarl. People continued to riot, completely neglecting their everyday lives, their jobs, their responsibilities. They didn't know why they were rioting. They didn't know it was a sense of helpless pointlessness driving them to it. They thought it was the prospect of being forced to die unnaturally; being forced to abandon their planet, their home, being forced into some kind of freak monster shape by the removal of half their bodies.

Nothing Langur could say seemed to convince The Jarl that the possibility of their extinction wasn't only very real, but in many respects imminent.

"YOU are the cause of the infection and you will be removed."

No one had ever seen Jarl Haakon in such an agitated state. In an unnaturally short span of time The Jarl acted most uncharacteristically and most decisively. Langur was forthwith incarcerated, without even being allowed to go home. Leuhta and the other SEPT members were forced into secrecy about the project under pain of slave cloning. The threat included Yakiv even though he wasn't officially a member of Temporality Nexus.

Lack of shrewdness wasn't one of The Jarl's failings. He might have worked to a slow clock but he could see there was definitely something to take seriously in what Skuggi said, but the man had gone the wrong way about it. He appointed Leuhta as the new head of Temporality Nexus. It would have been Eili, except he had a limited lifespan. So the work continued, with no less enthusiasm from the team perhaps even a little more sense of urgency.

Although denied his freedom, Langur had access to news; ecstatic to learn Murha had located a planet not far from a yellow orb. It seemed to be a totally random serendipitous discovery. This new planet had a plethora of life. From close orbit Murha transmitted images of all manner of creatures that moved on many legs, four legs, two legs. Living things that flew through the air, and so much water that ice comets would never be needed on this planet. So much light that energy abounded in an unimaginable quantity. He called this third planet from its orb, Vesimaa; a land of water. Of all the animals that moved so freely in the abundant light, one particular species dominated. It walked on two legs, supporting a single vertical body.

Extraordinary! Langur could barely contain himself.

Vesimaa was a large planet, as large as theirs and it had much more habitable land. The two-legged aliens appeared to be a sentient, intelligent life form. They had dwellings and communications systems and mobility units able to carry them in their thick atmosphere and across the large expanses of water. But they presented as an aggressive species; fighting amongst themselves, killing other life forms, almost making a sport out of both activities. Life didn't appear to have any great value on this planet.

"These aliens seem remarkably similar to us in some respects," Murha reported. He had come upon the planet on its 'day' side, lit up by their orb. "The two-legged creatures walk about with a vertical body, with a dark, flat horizontal component attached at the base moving across the ground with it, mimicking all its movements." Later he discovered that the dark shape was a peculiar phenomenon created by all the light. The creatures' bodies created the strongly contrasting dark shapes by blocking out the passage of light, unlike the fermions which penetrated most objects on their own planet. Their own infrared was so weak in comparison that 'shadows' were essentially unknown. Dokkheimiens didn't even have a name for it.

Spurred on by such a momentous discovery, the whole team applied themselves to their given tasks with renewed effort. Leuhta, working with Yakiv immersed herself in developing the physical actualisation process once the focused tight bean of thought energy of an individual reached its destination. Murha couldn't do this yet. He would have to return home after transmitting sufficient data.

Meanwhile Langur languished in prison. He wasn't charged with any offence. The people on the planet settled down after news of Langur's incarceration, assured of their safety from the maniac. The Jarl had plans for Langur, which would come to fruition soon enough.

Langur is not a criminal. He just might be right about our future. If what he said is true, peace on Dokkheim will not last long. I will have a closer look at this water world.

An Alien's Dilemma

Right at that moment Tumma Varjo, a Finnish research scientist, with an ageing problem, hated his job. "How could I have been so careless, so stupid! Now I can't even go outside during daylight hours."

His colleagues sympathized with him. "This is a truly serious predicament," Jukka, one of his closest associates said to him. "But can't you see the funny side of it? Surely this is the first instance in the history of humanity that such a strange and hilarious thing has happened."

"No, I can't see why it should be so funny! How could anyone take a man seriously who'd lost his shadow!"

Being without a shadow had some strange effects, but one more serious than the others. The incident occurred just over thirty years ago. When it first happened, there seemed to be no injuries or side effects. So after the initial shock of the accident, Tumma took no notice at all – until the following morning as he prepared to go back to the laboratory.

It was a bright, sunny summer morning. Even in the summer shadows in Helsinki were longer than in most parts of the world. Tumma didn't have far to go. He generally walked to the Teknologian Tutkimuskeskus as he lived in a small apartment in Otaniemi, Espoo, within the Technology park complex. All the research buildings had sombre, dark red brick facades. Tumma hated the look of those walls. He generally walked with his head slightly bent towards the ground contemplating the forthcoming day's activities, oblivious to the many beautiful birch trees along the way.

Not even ten meters out of his unit Tumma began to feel dizzy. He stopped for a moment, leant against a birch, took a few deep breaths and tried to go on. Vertigo overtook him again so strongly that he felt compelled to return to his unit in case he fell and hurt himself.

Tumma staggered back to his home. Once inside, the sensation disappeared as quickly as it had come. He felt young, healthy and kept himself in good shape. Although not particularly gregarious, Tumma didn't shun opportunities to go out with friends to enjoy a coffee or a concert. He was always alert and steady on his feet. So he couldn't understand what just happened. He felt perfectly fine when he rose that morning. He wasn't taking any medications, had a good night's sleep in spite of the accident, and there was nothing outdoors he could think of that might have caused his unsteadiness. It was an exceptionally beautiful morning. He even noticed the shadows were a little longer than normal as he was ready at least half an hour earlier than usual and had time to take in the landscape.

Shadows …

Shadows … Tumma started thinking about the shadows. He was a qualified scientist trained to experiment, to analyse and above all, to observe. "Shadows! Oh my God!" He shouted as the realisation hit him. He rushed to the door and stepped outside. There were shadows everywhere. Shadows of the buildings, of cars, of the trees – of the people walking along the footpath – but nothing emanating from his feet. *Where is my shadow?* He dared not speak it allowed, even for his own ears to hear.

He barely managed to stagger back to his door, to fall inside onto the carpet. *I don't have a shadow!* It was unfathomable. *I must be dreaming! Did I dream the experiment? No – no - it was definitely real.* He turned his reading light on and stood in front of it. Again he staggered at the sight of a shadow that wasn't there. For days he couldn't go outside. Even in his flat he pulled the blinds closed during the day, and used minimum lighting in the evenings; anything in order to avoid a confrontation with a shadow he didn't have. Desperation almost forced him to call a friend. But who would understand? On the third day of his self-enforced quarantine an observer would have seen the blinds pulled back just a little, with a young man standing there, staring out at the pedestrians for hours.

Why should I be feeling so strange just because I can't see my shadow?

There was nothing physically wrong with him; no pain, no injuries. Why? What was suddenly so different in his life?

The accident definitely has something to do with this - nothing else has happened to me during the week. Tumma explored every angle trying to understand his predicament.

Eventually the observer would have seen him withdraw from the window, letting the blind drop back into place. One could imagine the darkness in his room, perhaps even the depression the young man must have felt. Could he have simply let himself drop onto a sofa and stare into space, mind blank?

Tumma was in fact sitting in his sofa. It faced the wall opposite the window. He'd let his eyes meander around the room, thinking of nothing in particular. Eventually his attention came to rest on a reproduction of Goya's 'Shootings of May Third'. The massacre matched his mood. The absolute reality of man's inhuman capability mixed with the incredible unreality of a victim finding himself facing a firing squad. So much darkness – so many dark shadows. He always had an introspective disposition, preferring to work things out by himself rather than seeking the help of others.

Tumma sat there staring unblinking at the painting for many minutes before getting out of the sofa with a deliberate motion and going outside. *I have to try!*

He stood there, on the solid pavement, looking down at the ground. And as he looked he realised he couldn't tell where his body ended and where the pavement began. His senses told him he was floating above the ground, suspended in space. He had lost contact with the solidity of the universe. Tumma felt like a man who'd been struck blind. He knew he existed – he knew the world existed – but he no longer felt connected. He no longer felt real. It was only with the sheer power of his will that he remained standing.

He took several slow tentative steps, concentrating on every footfall in order to make any progress. The sounds of his unsteady steps on the pavement gave him a little confidence. So he took several more deliberately heavy steps, this time trying not to look at the ground, instead concentrating on the sound of each footfall. Tumma didn't fall. He turned carefully and walked unsteadily back to his door.

The following day he faced the great challenge. *If I could just not look at the ground I might be able to make it.* He kept up the internal dialogue all the way to work.

Jukka greeted him first. "We're relieved to see you on your feet Tumma."

At the research centre his friends were happy to see their brilliant young scientist return to his Light experiments. Jukka didn't mention his missing shadow, and as no one else knew they didn't notice anything peculiar about him. After all, who goes around conscious of other peoples' shadows? "Did you enjoy your little holiday?" They bantered.

*

Thirty years later Tumma still looked and felt like a young, untroubled twenty-five-year old scientist. He found ways to deal with the shadow problem. Because he learnt to ignore the phenomenon and behave completely naturally nobody noticed his missing shadow. But now he had a much bigger problem and no amount of analysis could shed light on that mystery.

Back in 1998 Tumma had just started his first job. At university he studied optics. His fascination with light was very specific; visible light between 400 and 700 nanometer wavelengths. It could be argued that in a country with a 'light' deficiency problem, studying its behaviour could only lead to tangible benefits. At the research institute he was asked to examine the relationship between Seasonal Affective Disorder, a type of depression, and the effects of light deprivation during the long winter months. With a team of three other scientists he researched the eye's light receptivity; effects of light phase shifts on the Circadian rhythm and the reflection of light off solid objects. The last area of research became really only a curious by-product of their interest, not expected to produce any useful results.

However, within a couple of years all three in his team had joined together on the same area of research based on results from Tumma's initial experiments into reflectivity. Just why did light travel through transparent objects, translucent objects and opaque objects but not solid objects? What made the difference? All three realised the implications were staggering if they could get light to travel through a solid object. From a commercial perspective such a technology could have unlimited potential. Consequently, a good deal of money was allocated to his team, the latest equipment and as many staff as he needed.

"Stand clear!" "Stand clear!" "Stand clear!"

The repetitive warning put researchers in the direct vicinity of the equipment on alert, to take heed and move to safety. Not that it was a big issue. Essentially it was only light they were working with. The laboratory, situated in an enclosed area without any natural light, contained some equipment that shaped visible light in very specific ways. With the equipment they had devised Tumma could consolidate the scattered light waves with each other through constructive interferences. The process didn't result in high intensity laser beams, and was pretty much harmless - or so it was assumed.

"Today's the big day," Valokeila said to Tumma as they prepared to fire a modified beam at a one millimetre sheet of pure aluminium. "Good luck!" Valokeila had made significant contributions to getting the project to that stage. "If we could get at least a fifty percent penetration …" He left the rest unsaid as Tumma gave him an encouraging slap on the back. The two scientists were standing next to each other, beside the beam gun and its controls. Tumma then turned, intending to move over to the target apparatus. Valokeila, in control of the beam gun, did two things almost simultaneously at the moment when Tumma moved and fell.

He activated the firing mechanism, then almost immediately sounded the general alarm, which was used only in cases of accidents. Tumma had tripped on Volakeila's foot as he turned to move away. There was no physical barrier between the beam gun and the thin target sheet, only a demarcation tape, suspended about waist high. He fell directly into the path of the beam and with his flailing right arm knocked several of the controls on the equipment.

Tumma stood up almost immediately seemingly completely unharmed. By then the beam had been switched off, but not before he'd been fully exposed in its light, albeit only for a fraction of a second.

"From what I can see there's nothing wrong with you," the research centre doctor advised. "All you've had is a short 'light bath' – a lot less than five minutes of sunbathing. Other than the bruising on your hand and the initial shock, you're good as gold."

His team was naturally upset they had not taken adequate safety measures. The tripping couldn't be avoided. But falling into the path of the beam certainly could have been. No one had even remotely thought of the possibility of passing the modified light beam through living tissue, let alone a human being. Besides, it was only a diffuse beam of light, almost like shinning a torch at night. What possible harm could it do?

*

Interestingly, in that same year, the American 'Science' magazine published an article stating that telomerase was capable of expanding the life span of human cells. Initial experiments showed that at least theoretically it was possible to extend the life span of human somatic cells indefinitely. The effects of the visible light spectrum on telomeres had yet to be quantified. Of course Tumma didn't know this at the time, nor did any of his team. Their area of research wasn't even remotely connected with longevity experiments. They had no reason to read such an article.

*

By 2028 Tumma was fifty-five years old. His entire life style changed as a result of the accident. He was still single. He'd avoided human contact, always being extremely cautious because of his condition. The work he started at the Institute continued, achieving considerable success. They could now modify light to pass one hundred percent through translucent and opaque membranes. They could even get ninety percent penetration into aluminium leaf. Concurrent with that research Tumma tried to find the reason for a very startling characteristic about his body. The accident happened when he was just twenty-five years old. Now, at fifty-five, everybody remarked how young he looked … that he hardly changed at all during the passage of all those years.

They were right. He looked better and he felt better than colleagues of the same age, and he was healthier than any of them. Of course he'd changed his hair style and his clothes to styles more suited to his chronological age, but he still walked straighter than any of his ageing friends. To all intents and purposes, his body wasn't getting any older.

Murha's Report

"These aliens are obviously not primitive, as you can see from their technological development," Murha reported to Leuhta. "It amazes me to see them eating other creatures similar to themselves. They actually eat all manner of other living beings."

Murha had been in orbit for a number of years, constantly sending data back to Dokkheim about the aliens. At first just general observations about the planet, population densities in different areas, agricultural activity and the incredibly diverse energy intake of the dominant two-legged inhabitants. "They may be technologically developed, but they have no identifiable means of direct energy absorption to sustain their lives. Perhaps they'll be unsuitable for our use," he ventured to add.

He transmitted all the data back to Temporality Nexus. Some of his orbits took him over areas of the planet where it looked like ice meteors had crashed and not melted. There were aliens living even there, although in much less concentration. "I know what we are trying to do. If these aliens present a possible solution we had better act quickly. They are not only developing space flight capability but have started mapping the genome of their species. And listen to this," his voice sounded either elated or disappointed, depending on who was listening to him, "they're getting into genetic engineering in an incredibly primitive and ill-informed way."

Leuhta alerted Yakiv to the need of immediate action. "We may have been lucky to find aliens who have not messed about with their genetics, but from what Murha says we don't have much time before they do a lot of damage to themselves."

"We have the energy transfers for the identity clouds well tested and ready. All the test subjects whom we've reintegrated recently back into their physical forms are functioning normally." Yakiv felt very positive and pleased with himself. This wasn't only a magnificent achievement for his Company but a huge leap forward for future space exploration. "In that case let's put a team together and send them to get a closer look at this planet."

As preparations progressed on Dokkheim Murha located a suitable alien for scientific study. As he became more intimately involved in the project feeling he was making a valuable contribution, he spent less time thinking subversively. "I've found the perfect specimen for you, Leuhta," he was uncharacteristically enthusiastic with his discovery. "This alien is healthy and intelligent. It's one of their research scientists, so it should not be difficult to communicate with it. It seems to spend most of its time by itself when not working – so if we need to us it, it won't be missed."

"Sounds perfect. Anything else that might be helpful about this specimen?" asked Leuhta, overjoyed with Murha's discovery.

"Not sure. It does have one unique characteristic – and I mean absolutely unique. I haven't been able to find another one like it. You will not believe this - no other living organism on Vesimaa is like it – it has stopped ageing! And for some strange reason it doesn't have a horizontal component, like an extension to its vertical produced by their light."

Leuhta wasted no time in bringing the good news to Langur. Although still in prison he could have visitors. As long as he wasn't stirring up the whole planet's population with his theories The Jarl was unconcerned.

"It couldn't be more perfect!" Langur was elated. He'd forgotten all about his incarceration. What did it matter when they were on the threshold of success. "Put your team together, Temporals would be best. Get one of them to find a way to upload themselves into the alien's nervous system – develop a way to communicate with it. We have achieved so much in such a short time. I feel there is hope for us now Leuhta!"

"I'm pleased – for you and for our people Langur. You have done an outstanding thing for us. I'm proud of you." An interlude of intimacy later Leuhta hastened back to Yakiv's office.

Three volunteer Temporals came forward to go to Vesimaa as advance reconnaissance to learn as much as possible about this new planet and its universe. They could ill afford to come up against any nasty surprises in the future that could threaten their species in unexpected ways, especially not if they were to leave their own planet and set out for a new world. This watery world and its inhabitants showed great promise, but the Dokks only had one opportunity to get their strategy right.

Alien DNA

Prior to the Temporality Nexus Project there was no apparent practical application for one of their species greatest scientific developments. Dokk technology had created a method of looking into the past. They knew something about the evolution of their universe - knowledge that led Langur to theorise on the probable existence of a 'light' matter universe. And he was right. But they could not look into the past of the other universe as previously they couldn't get access to it.

If the reconnaissance team was to get the maximum benefit out of the highly risky expedition they had to be well prepared. Yakiv visited Langur to get his thoughts on an aspect of exploration that Leuhta wasn't familiar with – Past Time Exploration (PTE).

"Would there be any value in examining the origins of this alien species?" As usual Yakiv went directly to the reason for his visit.

"Once we have a sample of their DNA it may not be necessary – but there may be hidden factors related to its evolution." Langur thought aloud. "We've learnt a great deal about our cosmos, in spite of the lack of information encoded in 'dark matter'. Perhaps in a 'light matter' universe we may be able to discover much more."

Encouraged by Langurs response Yakiv continued, "Leuhta has three Temporal volunteers studying all the information Murha's sent back. I'll make sure they become familiar with the PTE technology. We'll keep you up to date with all developments." Then as an after though he added, "I like Leuhta. She's a highly competent professional, but I still consider you as the head of the Project."

Odd thing for Yakiv to say, Langur thought, "I appreciate your confidence. Just don't forget – we all need each other on this one."

PTE was relatively uncomplicated in its capacity to read the energy signature fluctuations inherent in all matter, and how those energy levels changed over time. Recording such fluctuations from the past required the ability to capture residual information carried by energy waves still rippling through the cosmos from past super eons. The team's training consisted on how to interpret the data captured and convert it into useful information.

Leuhta made her final farewells to the three scientists. "You all know it's highly unlikely any of you will be able to return. The contribution you are about to make to your people is without precedent in our history. Live your life well."

Asvor, the leader, scanned her two companions. "We would rather die in space on this fantastic adventure than suffer our remaining years surrounded by depression and riots." Boi and Class, the two men nodded agreement. Their expected termination was about forty-two years, so none of them would have to endure a long period of solitude at the end.

Boi expressed his feelings succinctly, "If only you Immortals could experience the joy of purpose each of us feels."

Neither Langur nor Jarl Haakon attended their unceremonious departure. Nevertheless, they were in good spirits. Asvor, the communications expert, a chatter box and a trained philosopher, kept the two men entertained with her constant conversation on their way to the Rift. They liked that. It kept them from thinking too much about all the unknowns waiting for them in that strange brilliantly lit universe.

The Rift was the obvious place to start their investigation, but they were too close to it. Three energy bundles made their way towards the yellow orb's co-ordinates. Asvor led her team to a point several Astronomical Units above the plain of orbits of the planets. From there they could scan both the Rift and the blue/green planet. Embedded within each of their energy complexes the scanners were already at work, absorbing and filtering data out of the cosmic soup of information. Asvor's task was to decode the data and relay the findings back to Leuhta.

"Bois, I want you to work on the Rift. Claas, get as much as you can on Vesimaa." Asvor put her team to work independent of each other. There was still the faint chance of something going amiss with all the new technology being put to the ultimate test. While they calibrated for time-span indicators and fine-tuned to block out extraneous early creation noise, Asvor went down closer to the planet to intersect with Murha.

"You've done your job, Murha – you've gathered an impressive amount of information. It's going to be invaluable for the Project."

"And don't forget about the alien I found," Murha quickly add.

"Your efforts have already been acknowledged at home. It's time for you to return. I'm going to help you recharge, but there's still the chance you won't get much beyond the Rift once you're back in our dark matter universe. There's not enough available energy there to keep your beam focused."

"I know." Murha seemed matter-of-fact about it. *I wonder what it's going to be like to diffuse into the darkness?* He mused to himself.

"You don't seem upset," Asvor commented, surprised.

"No. I knew what to expect." Although he'd harboured hopes of vindication at the outset for his insurrection, he'd come to understand some realities, aided by time, his discoveries and his contemplative solitude during the years in space. *Langur was right. He was right about everything; this universe of light, our depression and probably about the ultimate solution.*

"Live your life well," Murha bade farewell to Asvor as he headed for home, hopeful but resigned.

Asvor took over the surveillance of the target alien, Tumma Varjo.

It looks like a healthy organism, although it's area of research is extremely elementary; her first impression not particularly encouraging. At Tumma's research centre she made a thorough study of alien physiology. She had an idea which focused her study with particular emphasis on retinal and optic nerve functioning. She found exactly what she was looking for; a way to infiltrate the alien's nervous system. Her next concern was its DNA profile. She needed to reassure herself it was indeed free of artificial genetic mutations.

This is surprising! Asvor thought, *"there seems to be some superficial DNA similarities between our two species. I'll let Langur sort out if there's sufficient compatibility for the alien DNA to accept integration with our own.*

Several months passed before Claas began streaming clean data to Asvor. It needed formatting into information, mathematical and visual before relaying it back to Dokkheim. Asvor's astonishment grew as she watched images of the past.

About three billion years ago this orb system was anything but stable. She never imagined there could be so many asteroids crossing the paths of the planets. Multitudes of them didn't cross at all, they simply smashed into anything in their way. Vesimaa received an abundant shower of planet builders. Her analysis indicated not only myriad ice comets, but also many containing metals, carbon dioxide, nitrogen and hydrogen; all the constituents of life they knew of up till then. *It's fortunate we're not getting caught in the cosmic play of jousting dust trails and ion tails now,* Asvor thought and had a flitting idea, *Could life possibly have existed on any of those comets, as well as on the planets they were pulverising into submission?* Decidedly she was witnessing a war of worlds, where only the largest and strongest could hope to survive.

She continued to watch this drama unfold hoping to see anything useful to their endeavour. It was necessary to skip great gulfs of time to get any idea of the rate of progress. Eventually those relentless forces eased allowing the heaving Vesimaa to settle a little, her opportunity to look for signs of early life. Tiny multi-celled organisms flourished in the seas created by those generous ice comets. They survived even the onslaught of the volcanic indigestion suffered by this extraordinary water world. They flourished because they could multiply. Their molecular structure contained just the right combination of proteins and amino acids. *Wow! That looks like primitive DNA!* Without even examining the genome she sent all the information home. *They will be overjoyed. Langur will be vindicated!* Although Asvor had studied their own DNA extensively and was able to recognise some similarities to what she saw, she didn't immediately realise she'd made a critical discovery.

Bois had been scanning the Rift to try to determine its origins. For surely it would hold the key to many mysteries discovered so far and many yet to come. He'd managed to pinpoint the exact period of its naissance, an incredible event that joined their two universes. Not only did it solve the conundrum of the missing mass of their dark matter universe, it was in fact the very reason for the existence of their species.

"Asvor, I've found out what made the Rift. Have a look at this." Bois sent his data to Asvor to analyse more fully. As soon as Asvor realised what created the Rift she examined Boi's data more closely.

"Are you sure about this data, Bois?"

"Yes, no doubt about it. It was caused by energy generated from an impact on Vesimaa," He replied without hesitation.

Asvor watched the events unfold and even flinched automatically as she witnessed the last great comet of the superepoch strike Vesimaa. The cataclysmic event threatened to destroy not just life on the planet, but the planet itself. The great comet came hurtling past the giant gas planet. Its altered trajectory put it on a collision course with Vesimaa. She could almost feel the planet shudder under the force of the impact. Massive amounts of ejecta hurtled into space. She thought perhaps a large chunk of the world had been dislodged and ejected into the void. She witnessed the great energy shock generated by the massive explosion. The resultant wave was so powerful it tore open the fabric of space, about a light year from the planet.

The devastating force of the energy that opened a Rift into the dark matter universe continued its destructive path, carrying with it much flotsam, changing the universe of macho's and wimp's and all manner of dark matter particles before it eventually dissipated itself in the immensity before it.

"Bois, can you send me more detail on the moment the Rift opened?" Asvor had a suspicion and decided to follow her intuition. *With all that meteoric matter coming towards Vesimaa, and all the stuff blown away from it, surely there could be ...* she let the thought dissipate until she found evidence.

Tracking forward again in the data she discovered the planet had undergone monumental changes. The moon-sized meteor had struck in the northern hemisphere of the planet, changing the behaviour of its tectonic plates, tilting the axis and changing the direction of rotation. Whatever evolutionary path Vesimaa was destined for, it no longer exited. It had a completely new future. In spite of the cataclysm, life survived.

Ok – now let's have a closer look at the period just before the formation of the Rift … She saw the dramatic changes that had taken place to life that did survive, becoming stronger and more robust for the cosmic intervention.

She was intrigued and wanted to find the exact period when the critical changes took place to the DNA. So she went back over the data again only to discover what seemed impossible. "It's just not possible!" She told Bois, as much as to try convincing herself. She dared not voice her thoughts, *The discovery will shatter all our beliefs about the origins of life on Dokkheim!*

'Ka-Ha-Sin must know of this." Asvor told Bois, "and The Jarl! But we'd better be absolutely certain before telling them. Dr.Tulok won't believe this."

Unknown to Asvor she had discovered the late RNA period, the Last Universal Cellular Ancestor (LUCA) of the alien genome. Still the mystery of a possible similarity in the DNA of the two species eluded Asvor.

"Re-scan the Rift for me please Bois," She asked, "and the space between the Rift and the planet. There has to be something there."

He'd seen the initial data as well and formed his own hypothesis which he too wanted to check. "It's going to be difficult. From the moment of impact very little time elapsed between the generation of energy fields and the opening up of the Rift," Bois informed Asvor. "The ejecta was moving at the same speed as the energy waves, causing a great deal of interference in the data I'm trying to sift through."

"You can't ignore all the flying matter just because of the noise." Asvor was impatient to know more. The answer might just be contained in the gigatons of debris flying in space.

"Right. Don't be so anxious. I know what I'm doing. I'll check out the particulate contents being carried in the rock fragments. Happy?"

"Just don't waste any time. I want to know the results as soon as you have them," Asvor urged.

He didn't need to be told. He was just as excited as Asvor. It seemed his entire life had been a preparation for this moment of enlightenment. Until he was diagnosed with a terminal illness, drifted in a sea of ennui like everyone else. If he hadn't immersed himself in a serious study of Cosmic Microwave Background Radiation, he probably wouldn't have been accepted as a volunteer for the mission. Bois' proficiency with linear time focusing gave him the skills with which to look in detail at exactly what was going through the Rift in the past.

Within hours Asvor heard his elated voice, "This is unbelievable, Asvor! Just listen to this … the larger rock debris was carrying life!"

"What!" She was silent for a few minutes trying to absorb the impact of that simple fact. "You mean – dead – organisms?"

"No. I mean living multicellular life with the DNA capacity to reproduce, drifting through the opening of the Rift!"

"NO!" She was overwhelmed.

"I have to follow the trail," Bois shouted back to Asvor, "I have to find out where they went."

Asvor was almost too excited to think straight. She knew he might not survive without the strong EMR energy source. "Please initiate continuous information transmission to myself and Temporality Nexus … just in case … you strike some difficulty. Thank you for your help. You are magnificent! Live your life well."

Bois didn't survive. Asvor and Leuhta received the following information simultaneously, several months after Bois passed through the Rift …

… "I'm half way to Dokkheim, on a direct trajectory home. There isn't enough energy left to get me there. I have been following the path signature of the waves that came through the Rift at the time of its opening. Much of the ejecta was swallowed up by dark matter, but much more survived and headed directly for Dokkheim."

The last image he sent was of a strand of DNA from a live organism he discovered cocooned in one of the rocks on a collision course with Dokkheim.

That was the past. Millions of years in the past, multiple millions of years of history. The obvious conclusion couldn't be ignored. It was just possible – remotely possible, that they and these aliens were related.

First Contact

Asvor knew exactly what was involved in the entire process of their own reproductive system, from inception to final growth management. As part of her preparation for the trip Langur insisted she undertake a comprehensive study of the basic genetic structure of their species. She was well qualified to recognise the alien's superficial DNA similarity to their own.

Because of the impact of her incredible discovery Asvor needed to know a great deal more; enough to ensure the subsequent phases of the Project would bear fruit. She needed to know how the alien species reproduced: How their DNA strands combined and what brought the cells containing them into contact with one another? What was the success rate? How was the offspring grown, and how was it removed from the parent? All critical questions. Not least of all, how the population managed to survive with such a bombardment of high energy EMR from their orb with so little personal protection.

Asvor and Claas's renewed their efforts as a result of Bois' evidence. "I cannot believe that these primitive creatures, who have barely emerged from the Stone Age, could possibly have a common ancestral beginning with us.

"If you could get a sample of their DNA," Class volunteered, "I'll try to get back home with it."

"You know how dangerous that could be, don't you?" She warned Claas.

"I'll stop all transmissions after the Rift, and if you could give me an energy boost I just might make it." Asvor knew he was being optimistic, but it just might work.

There was no easy way to get those DNA samples. Ethically she had an imperative not to harm these creatures unnecessarily. But the survival of her own species took precedence over the aliens' welfare, particularly over such a warlike species who actually took pleasure in harming its own kind. That was one characteristic she couldn't accommodate in her schema of what constituted an advanced, civilised life form.

Leaving Tumma till later, as she considered him to be a valuable asset, Asvor sought out a terminally ill individual languishing in what looked like a medical centre. At least she assumed it was from the general look of the occupants. The procedures being carried out didn't seem to Asvor to be entirely adequate for successful curative results. The middle aged alien female appeared to be in good spirits, although those around her were depressed. Asvor knew those symptoms all too well. Being in a confined space presented no issue for Asvor, however her energy field did produce a little enhanced illumination in the top corner of the ceiling where she waited, which the patient noticed as soon as Asvor arrived.

"Mother … can you see the light?" Of course her old parents couldn't. Partly because they were so distraught and partly because of the failing eyesight at their advanced age.

"It's been there for a while now. I've been watching it move about. What do you think it is?" She asked quite cheerfully.

Both parents burst into tears. The end must be near for their precious daughter. Realising the creature could detect something of her presence, out of curiosity Asvor increased her intensity just a little.

"Daddy! It's getting brighter." With the patient's increased heart rate, alarms went off prompting an immediate response from the medical staff.

"How are you going Hoshie? Let's have a look at you," the doctor insisted. Hoshie resented the intrusion. She wanted to concentrate on the light. Asvor watched the other alien in the white garment shine a strong light into the patient's eyes. She didn't understand what was happening, but she did understand that the patient's 'eyes' were her visual receptors. She could also see that the shining light didn't cause her any distress. Asvor recalled from her study of their biology that the aliens' eyes had a direct link with their main CPU.

There's no point waiting, she thought, and aimed herself directly into Hoshie's eyes when the examining doctor had moved aside.

"It's coming to me! Oh, she's so beautiful! I want to go with her … Mother – I want to…"

The alarms went off again. Hoshie's heart had stopped beating. Her mother and father looked at her, saw the look of rapture on their daughter's face.

"Let her go, it's her time," the father said.

"Hoshie is happy now," her mother sighed between tears. As the doctor walked out, the mother looked up into the corner of the room and saw the room lighting was just a little brighter there. She couldn't possibly know what it was, but she smiled her gratitude towards it. Asvor had harvested what she needed.

It was a facial gesture on the old woman that Asvor came to recognise as expressing some kind of pleasure. It made no sense. She was directly responsible for the death of the scion. Still, she'd got what she wanted … and more. The death was regrettable. The creature's condition most probably caused its termination, but undoubtedly her intrusion may well have hastened it. *Regrettable.* Perhaps a feeling of empathy brought something out in Asvor.

Immediately upon contact with the pupil Asvor felt the impact of the eye's clear gel before being stopped by the retina. It occasioned a moments concern about being able to get back out, but it had no effect on her wavelength. The optic nerve carried her signal directly into the alien's central processing area, exactly where she wanted to be. She immediately extracted all the details of the DNA, encoded it and made her way back out through the optic nerve.

The impact of such a concentrated bundle of energy stimulated the majority of the patient's neurons to fire simultaneously. The surge interpreted as a thing of exquisite beauty by the alien's brain, before the energy overload effectively shorted out her network. Asvor had in her possession probably the most valuable item ever to be possessed by any single individual of her species since they came into existence. She also knew now the specific intensity with which the Alien brain could be infiltrated without causing it to overload.

Asvor proceed to the next task. There were four other racial types to harvest from. She had to be cautious as mistakes were not an option. A second attempt at communication with a Negroid failed completely. Asvor's choice appeared to have no fixed domicile. On the creature's continent a nomadic homelessness was the preferred way of existence. Infiltrating its brain mass went smoothly. Asvor made adjustments to her energy emanations to reduce the effects of the immediate impact. However, the alien still became hyperactive. As it settled, Asvor stimulated the visual cortex with images of her own home. As far as the native shaman was concerned they were just more hallucinations he would have to interpret to the tribe. Asvor harvest the DNA but achieved very little else.

The fact the shaman remained alive after her visitation emboldened her for the next subject, and of course it also reacted to the images. So Asvor concluded it was indeed possible to interact directly with the aliens' central nervous system.

She didn't want to experiment on their target subject, Tumma, so she devised a method to get visual messages across to a Native American and the Australian aboriginal without causing them distress. The aboriginal was most receptive. It wasn't exactly the kind of communication she was hoping for, but at least the interaction provided a basis for training the primitive brain to respond in a meaningful way to a range of stimuli. She passed her new knowledge onto Class.

"There, you've got it all. No need to wait. I can send the rest directly to Leuhta." She accompanied Claas to the edge of the Rift, giving him a boost as they agreed, hoping he would make it home safely.

"With all those DNA samples Ka-Ha-Sin should be able to determine if in fact there is any kinship between our two species. What a strange situation," he commented as he left for Dokkheim.

Asvor streamed back to Vesimaa for her last assignment.

At sixty years of age, Tumma prepared for retirement. He still looked like a young man and felt as healthy as one, except for recent problems with his eyes. He'd started seeing bright flashes of light. Without any pain or effect on his eyesight the phenomenon didn't worry him as much as the sight of his friends getting old. He'd learnt to cope with the shadowless-ness issue by becoming a recluse. Even though he'd continued his experiments to alter the behaviour of light he had not found any clue as to why he had no shadow and why the accident suppressed the aging process in his body. He became what his colleagues termed 'eccentric' mostly because he'd developed the habit of talking to himself. In itself that wasn't so unusual. However, having arguments with yourself definitely was.

After obtaining Tumma's DNA sample, Asvor spent time in his company. She would pop in and out of his neural network, trying to familiarize herself with the complications of this alien's neural patterning. Eventually she was able to come and go through its optical receptors without having to adjust her intensity. Those were the instances when Tumma experienced the flashes. Recently, on more than one occasion he'd been sent home from the Research centre because of his lack of concentration. His co-workers had become used to his self-generated chatter, but daydreaming on the job was dangerous.

Perhaps it was his ageing mind causing him to have more frequent images of the countryside while sitting in the local cafe or hyper-realistic images of people he had met. On those occasions he would respond as if they were actual occurring events. Tumma would greet these people as if they had just walked up to him.

It was only Asvor trying out her ability to manipulate his mind. At home in his unit Tumma would start up a conversation with himself. It was comforting, even reassuring to know exactly what responses he would get. Even the outcome of arguments with himself were a foregone conclusion. Yet one day he heard something extremely odd in his mind; an interruption to his personal, predictable and amiable dialogue.

"No, I don't want you to do that." It was a simple enough response to a simple enough thought. He'd proposed to himself, *"Let's go out and get something to eat."* To which his normal answer was, *"OK. Where should we go?"* And he would reply to himself, *"The usual place, maybe we'll meet a nice girl."* Then he would laugh as he walked out the door. He might have chosen a more reclusive life, because of his peculiar circumstances, but he wasn't innately anti-social.

This time he didn't get the usual agreement. This time he definitely heard, *"No, I don't want you to do that."*

"What!" He shouted at the unexpected statement. Asvor didn't respond. It was enough for her to know she had mastered the language sufficiently for the alien to understand her. More specifically, she had mastered a technique for stimulating its audio centre cerebrally. With a little more time she could no doubt navigate around its entire brain with ease.

After the disturbing episode Tumma had no more immediate surprises. His daydreaming images suddenly stopped and he'd ceased talking to himself for fear of the response he may receive. Asvor had left him for a while. She went out of the solar system, up to near the Rift and transmitted a wealth of information back to Leuhta. Between the three of them, the reconnaissance team had achieved far more than Langur could possibly have hoped for.

Departure from Dokkheim

Synty, the artificial moon created by the Dokkheimiens, was unique in one respect. The aliens would live in the hollow interior set up to replicate their ecosystem. The Dokks had their own dedicated environment in the thick shell of the craft. Synty had one primary function; to get a Dokk contingent to Vesimaa in order to harvest alien specimens for their experiments.

"You should call it 'Earth' and get used to it. You're going to have to communicate with the aliens, so you may as well do it with words they understand." Leuhta was quite adamant Langur should learn their language before he went rushing over there.

True, urgency certainly existed, but they still had time. The facts that came to light indicated they were probably on the right track. Besides, the alien Langur particularly wasn't growing older. Class did return home, but in a bad shape and terminated soon afterwards. His contribution became the foundation on which the expedition could build success. All the DNA data arrived undamaged. Yakiv, Leuhta and Eili went to see The Jarl with the results of Ka-Ha-Sin's latest research.

Jarl Haakon already knew the Temporality Nexus team were making great strides and reluctantly granted the 'revolutionaries', as he now called them, an audience.

"Be brief, I'm a busy man. There's a species to save."

That came from The Jarl as a complete surprise. Obviously their illustrious leader had recognised the inevitability of the situation and took it upon himself to assume supreme control of the history about to be made.

"We are related to the Aliens," Leuhta stated in a matter of fact voice. "The details are in the report. Their species may have the solution to our problem. An expedition can be organised …"

The Jarl stopped Leuhta before she could elaborate, without reacting to the stupendous revelation.

Instead he barked, "I don't want details. I want results!"

Unfortunately, he wasn't yet aware of the final solution – mortality for his species. It is true that after Langur's imprisonment and Murha's disappearance from the scene everything settled down for a few years. The Jarl would have liked it to stay that way. But the unrest resumed – with serious consequences to the population at large. He had put his own team of investigators onto the situation and found, to his considerable distaste, that the Skuggi character may very well have been right. As much as he disliked the ideas Langur put forward he conceded the man was on the right track. He called his security chief, then turned abruptly back to Leuhta.

"Take Skuggi with you on your way out. Report to me in six years," ordered The Jarl. That was barely enough to get another team out to Vesimaa and back. Somehow every interview with The Jarl took the same course. They would just get started and end up being dismissed within minutes. However, this time they got everything they wanted. Implied in The Jarl's command was his total support for their project.

The billions of people on Dokkheim were being controlled while the Temporality Nexus team carried on with its work. Every instigator of a riot was captured and terminated. The majority of the rioters themselves were slave cloned. They became the workers in the factories run by the State, producing bulk intra-stellar transport carriers after completing Synty. The technology came from Vertical Systems, making Yakiv extremely wealthy. The materials, factories, storage facilities, testing laboratories and labour were provided by the State, as was the security keeping these activities hidden from the people they were working to save.

Langur had been kept informed of developments whilst in prison and Leuhta remained the nominal leader of Temporality Nexus. After his release he was to head the expedition to the alien planet. "Are you happy with this arrangement?" Leuhta asked him, knowing that her mate liked to be in full control.

"Yes, I have complete faith in you. But if you're asking if I'm happy because my theories have proved correct so far about a universe of light matter and the existence of a compatible alien species, then I'd have to say – No. I'm focused. I have a mission in my immortal life with a deadline but I cannot take eternity to succeed. I will do everything and anything to achieve the salvation of my people and may a river of mercury take anyone who dares to oppose me!"

Leuhta had known her mate for countless number of centuries. She had never seen him so vehement about anything. She may not have agreed with him on every aspect, yet she did greatly respect his dedication and motives.

"I can see only two options," he went on to explain now that Leuhta had opened the floodgates of his thoughts, "my preference is to colonise another planet."

"Do you mean Vesimaa?" Leuhta asked.

"That's my second option. It does not sit well with my ethics to contemplate how that would be achieved."

"A species that enjoys killing and consumes living beings to fulfil their energy requirements has little or no moral claim to continued existence, be they related or not to Dokkheimiens, in my opinion," Leuhta countered.

"If there was absolutely no other alternative and their existence had to be cut short for us to survive, then I would come to terms with it." His voice trailed away into silence.

Leuhta tried to get him onto another track. "Tell me about this alien who calls himself Tumma."

"Well – it's a most interesting case," Langur brightened a little. "Somehow it's bridged the gap between its mortality and immortality. Most interesting. And another thing – the telomeres of its DNA seem to have become as robust as ours. What an amazing development."

"Wouldn't that mean he can't be used as a source of reproduction?"

"It doesn't matter. It's the reason behind his mutation that makes him valuable. Are you aware of his other problem?" Langur asked rhetorically and continued, "we can use the restoration of his shadow as a bargaining tool to get him to cooperate with us."

"That's a bit devious. I didn't think you were like that." Leuhta suggested.

"Like I said – I'll do anything and everything."

*

The entire scientific contingent of the expeditionary community had been briefed with all the data received from Murha and the surveillance team. Strategies were formulated, with contingencies for emergent situations. Similarly, the ship's technical crew and defence personnel were ready for embarkation by the time Langur became proficient in the alien language. Of the original SEPT only Langur, Eili, Tulok and Dr.Qilaq were going. The other sixty-two members of the crew consisted mostly of Temporals. Their initiative and dedication were ranked well above that of the immortals. Both Dr.Qilaq and Eili insisted on the arrangement in order to create the optimum probability of achieving their goals. This was, after all, the first major space mission for the Dokks.

"How long is it going to take us to get to this Earth, Yakiv?" Langur wanted a reassurance he would be back in time to report to The Jarl.

"At least twice as long as sending you all along as individual tight beams. But it wouldn't work in this case. You still need to transport the specimens back to us. A round trip should take no more than several years. You will of course have the landing crafts and the Concentrator with you. Use it to infiltrate and make contact. You should be back in plenty of time to make your report."

Langur voiced his deeper thoughts, "That's not what's worrying me. I don't want the aliens to expire prematurely because of an extended voyage. We have all the time we need. Their resilience is an unknown factor."

"If you feel so concerned, then just bring extra specimens. We equipped Synty with everything you will need for yourselves, as well as the aliens either conscious or in stasis. There's fully equipped bio-labs just in case you need to carry out experiments or adjustments on the aliens." Yakiv was confident in the craft's capacity to sustain both life forms for extended periods. "We have built for you a bio-sphere giving you complete self-sufficiency – you and the aliens."

"Leuhta … you've been very quiet. Can you foresee any problems?" Langur asked. He was apprehensive about how she would take a separation from him, albeit quite short. She was the one person who couldn't join them on the trip; essential she stay behind to maintain control as head of Temporality Nexus.

"No, I don't have any personal issues. Dr.Qilaq had some concerns about the effects on you of being inside the alien central nervous system for an extended period; how your interaction with it could adversely affect you - a kind of psychic contamination. There's another problem; how would we know if it had occurred."

"Yes, I'd considered that. Take a scan of my pattern before I leave here. In fact, do all of us on board then re-scan everyone before we leave Vesimaa. If there are any aberrations our software surgeons can't deal with it ... even termination if that becomes necessary." Langur may have developed a single minded attitude to the project, but Leuhta didn't feel as maniacally dedicated ... and said so, especially when it concerned her mate's wellbeing.

As the departing armada of shuttle craft neared the extended mooring docks, nobody could see Synty. It was large enough to blot out the background void from their vantage point and the shuttles were like dust specks on a ball. The structure, composed of dark matter of a dark matter universe, absorbed all infrared light emanating from their orb and the small amount of visible light infiltrating through the Rift. Camouflage was important considering the surveillance capabilities of the aliens, and their progress towards achieving true space flight. The craft needed line-of-sight communications so they wouldn't be able to hide behind one of the neighbouring planets of the yellow orb system. Presently it was parked in geosynchronous orbit around Dokkheim.

As the shuttles began docking procedures the expectant crew and breeding volunteers waited, watching the area directly above them as a deep red glow slowly grew into a large round aperture. It was as if one of the artificial craters had opened up to release its trapped energy. A long tubular escalator extruded from the open crater towards them. Silent excitement engulfed the entire scene.

For Langur it was a defining moment for all the hundreds and hundreds of years of research and the successful culmination of all the challenges he had to overcome in the recent past. All was forgotten during the magic transition of the embarkation.

Captain Valokvantti and his immediate crew were already on board directing the operation. Langur had no prior advice who the

Captain would be. Yakiv knew, but kept it to himself because of Valokvantti's status as The Jarl's personal assistant.

After settling in to his new accommodation, which consisted of little more than a resting platform, Magnevid, comms, and personal energy supply point, Langur went directly to the control centre, meeting Dr.Qilaq on the way.

"I thought the day would never come." He said as the two of them accessed the control centre from the back corridor of the private enclosures. Neither could immediately recognise anyone.

"Captain?" Langur queried as they approached a figure from behind who appeared to be in charge. Valokvantti heard the two individuals approaching and on turning was almost facing them as Langur called out in utter surprise, "What! … Why! … Who gave you … that is!" He stopped because the Captain addressed him, taking absolutely no notice of the fact he was completely thrown off guard.

"Ah, Skuggi - The Jarl felt it important that the investment in the future of his people should have maximum opportunity to succeed. I am the most highly trained pilot suitable for this mission." Valokvantti turned back to his console to continue preparations for the launch sequence, then addressed the crew, "There will be a full briefing in three hours from myself and the head of the scientific team." That didn't leave a great deal of room for Langur to engage the Captain in further conversation. He and Dr.Qilaq left the control centre.

"We have to call an immediate meeting of our team," Dr.Qilaq suggested and proceeded to do it even before Langur could concur.

Their thirty members crowded into one of the conference enclosures not expecting to be called upon so soon, and consequently vocalised their discontented thoughts to one another. They were completely unaccustomed to doing anything in a hurry. They'd not even had a chance to fully settle in.

"I'll be brief," Langur began, "but make no mistake, what I'm about to say is critical."

"Is there a problem?" Eili called out from the back of the group, voicing everyone's immediate question.

"No. You need to know that our Captain Valokvantti, and I'm sure he is the best and most qualified individual for the job, is also our Jarl's private assistant." He let that sink in as murmurs surfed around the enclosure. "It is only fitting he should keep our Jarl informed of our progress as we make our way towards achieving our goal. I lead the scientific contingent of this project. You will take direction from me. In any life-threatening situation I'm sure Captain Valokvantti will carry out his mandate to protect us. That is all. No questions."

"Good." Eili and Dr.Qilaq agreed it was a straightforward, factual presentation of the situation. It left no doubt for people to understand they were constantly under scrutiny ... not that they needed to worry about it, but Langur did worry. *This lack of trust in myself and my team is unjustified. Surely there are other highly qualified pilots!* - a thought Langur wasn't prepared to express openly.

At the appointed time the crew assembled in one of the larger conferencing enclosures. With all the scientific personnel, the sizeable defence crew, eight control room staff and thirty-six techs and engineers combined, as well as the large contingent of breeding volunteers it became a crowd of many hundreds. Langur and Valokvantti had equal status on the podium. To set the correct hierarchy of authority from the start Valokvantti began the proceedings.

"I am Captain Valokvantti. Except for the scientific group under Mr. Skuggi's direction you will take orders from me. Any deviation from our strategy, which may put us in danger, will result in one authority only on board this vessel; myself. Our Jarl has placed a great deal of trust in you. I will reassure him regularly that the trust is well founded. No questions." There should be none, as far as he was concerned.

Langur felt momentarily at a loss to say anything else, however it was politic he also address the crowd. "You are all well briefed and well trained for this project. You know who I am, and now you know our Captain. Just one further thing. When we have the aliens aboard I expect everyone," he cast a quick glance in the Captain's direction, "to treat them with respect regardless of how we may need to enlist their aid, or what lengths we may have to resort to, to get it. Clearly understand this … They are related to us."

"That is all. We leave in exactly one hour," Valokvantti announced, ensuring he had the last word.

Eili took Dr.Qilaq aside afterwards for a quick word before their departure. "I don't like it," he said confidentially.

"Whatever do you mean?" The layback, take-it-easy psychologist feigned.

"This business about Valokvantti being The Jarl's spy. And especially not about the obvious tension between him and Langur."

It made Dr.Qilaq ponder the situation. Of course he'd noticed the strained vibes between their two commanders, but thought it to be mostly Langur's doing. Still, Eili was a very astute student of personal interactions. "Hmmm …" Dr.Qilaq murmured and left it at that.

At the same time as Eili and Dr.Qilaq were having their 'word', Langur and Valokvantti had theirs. The Captain was in his quarters, so had no reason to be 'brief' with Langur.

"I know exactly what my task is Captain. That can only be carried out if you get me there and back with the specimens, safely," Langur asserted.

"Why do you feel the need to tell me this?" Valokvantti bristled.

"There may be occasions where we may need to work more closely together than simply as co-operative joint leaders. I wanted to express my openness about that to you."

"No need." That's all Valokvantti said while scanning Langur with his visual receptors. As Langur decided not to add anything else, after a brief pause Valokvantti ushered Langur out and headed to the control centre himself.

Ten minutes later the warning sounded for their imminent departure. Disengagement from the space dock was effortlessly gentle with no sensation of movement at all. The vessel had few visual ports to the outside cosmos, relying on many magnevids throughout to give the crew a view. Not that there was going to be very much to see for the first few months. After the initial excitement of watching their sombre deep red orb slowly disappear behind them, there was nothing to see, their planet being all but invisible. Other celestial bodies, of which few existed in their near vicinity, were well camouflaged in a dark matter universe with little or no light. They trained sensors and imaginations towards their first destination; the Rift.

Through the Rift

The Captain's crew and Langur's team made their independent preparations to cross from their known universe into the unknown one of light energy and light matter – and aliens.

Routine maintenance became the most consuming part of their existence. Langur held many sessions with his two bio-engineers going over the data received from Vesimaa. Their immediate concern; to find a way to reinstate the target alien's shadow, obviously the one single aspect of his life that seemed to dominate a good deal of his thoughts and his behaviour. Being without their shadow wasn't a normal condition for the aliens. Only one out of all the billions of them had the peculiar affliction.

Claas had concentrated on the evolutionary timelines of this primitive species. His initial findings were good but not sufficiently targeted. Subsequent, more focused linear time-line data analysis revealed the exact moment at which the unfortunate event took place for the alien who called himself Tumma. It was important to understand the cause/effect scenario partly to satisfy their own scientific curiosity, and partly because Dr.Tulok thought they might be able to reverse the effect.

He had a worthwhile suggestion, "If I could re-engineer the alien's cellular structure there's every chance his shadow would return… but … It must know that we are doing it, and it should understand that an appropriately useful expression of gratitude will be expected."

"Your deviousness surprises me Qilaq. Oh – and please don't refer to him as 'It'."

"No my friend, it's not deviousness. We need to seek the path of least resistance to solve our problem before resorting to inevitable measures."

Langur knew exactly what he alluded to. "So the point is to blackmail the alien using his own wellbeing. What if he isn't intelligent enough to understand our 'benevolence'?" Langur put the rhetorical question.

"There's more at stake here than just harvesting DNA and cross pollinating the two species. We are on the threshold of having to consider the possible annihilation of an entire sentient life form. Their planet may not be suitable for us. But what if it is?" Dr.Qilaq felt it important to state the case openly. They were not on an ambassadorial good will mission.

Langur listened. There was no need to make hard decisions just yet and certainly no need to involve the Captain in these little details for the time being. "By the way, you and Tulok are scheduled for visual sensor adjustment in the next few days. We are getting closer to the Rift. It's actually visible now without magnification. The entire crew must be done to prevent permanent damage from the high frequency EMR. I'll ask you both to come to Tulok's lab immediately after, and bring Eili of course. I want to go over the shadow problem with you in more detail." Langur didn't want to think about genocide.

It was a long voyage. In many respects Langur had too much time on his hands. Almost every contingency had been worked to fine detail. Hundreds of Vesimiaan private environmental enclosures had been set up in the Shell. Fine tuning the conditions in the belly of the craft could be carried out as soon as they arrived at the planet and had specific soil/air/water data and alien samples to work with. Fortunately, gravity requirement for the two species was similar.

All Langur could do in the interim was practice the new language and think of all the demons that could haunt their enterprise.

His visual sensor adjustment felt extremely strange for a little while. Gradually the vessels' internal lighting was increased to acclimatize them to the changes in the environment outside their spacecraft. It made it difficult for him to navigate his way to Tulok's laboratory because everything was so bright and blurred, like trying to see your reflection in a moving stream of mercury at noon.

By the time Langur arrived everyone in his immediate command group was there ready to view images of the alien. Thankfully Tulok had dimmed the lighting considerably to make it easier for them to follow his presentation. Langur still marvelled at the extraordinary technology that allowed them to 'look' into the passage of time and isolate virtually any recent event with comparative clarity. He didn't understand the science behind it, but certainly appreciated its benefits. They started watching the accident unfold on the magnevid.

Tumma, for they agreed to call the target alien by the name it used to refer to itself, appeared to be discussing something with one of his workers. The two of them were standing by some primitive looking fairly clunky machinery as a bright reddish light began flashing on a wall opposite to them. Various passing aliens moved away from the equipment, except for one who controlled the laboratory apparatus. Even Tumma turned to walk away when they saw him suddenly fall backwards into the area between the machinery and a flat plate placed a short distance away. Obviously the machine and the plate had some sort of relationship. At the instant Tumma fell, a flash of varying intensity bluish light came out of the machinery and completely lit up Tumma's body.

"In case any of you had forgotten, Tumma was experimenting with passing visible spectrum EMR through solid objects, with a little measure of success I might add. So he must be reasonably intelligent", Langur commented.

"There is hope for us yet." Tulok couldn't resist adding.

"But how is this accident related to the loss of his shadow?" Eili seemed to be more curious and more impatient than the others.

"Watch carefully. I'll show you the sequence again. Keep your sensors on his manipulator." This time they could see Tumma's arm fly out sideways in an effort to balance himself. In the process he hit several of the levers on the machine, which controlled the light beam.

"Did you see his manipulator hit the levers? Now watch again … look at the indicator next to the lever." And as they watched they saw the dial suddenly jerk well out of position before springing back to its previous setting.

Tulok summed it up. "That's how it happened. We have examined the information available about the machine. One lever was intended to modify the photon properties of the particular light frequency they were using in an attempt to 'squeeze' it through the inter-cellular spaces of the flat piece of material. He also moved the other lever, which ended up slightly changing the light frequency. Both instruments returned to their initial settings immediately after the disturbance. So there was no possible way Tumma could have discovered the cause of his condition." Tulok enjoyed his moment of discovery, and the obvious respect directed at him through the silent anticipation of his small audience.

"I can see you want to know exactly what happened. Tumma's body changed dramatically in two ways. The changes caused by adjusting the frequency and photon density cauterized every telomere of every DNA strand of every cell in his body, stopping them from deteriorating after each subsequent replication. You can probably guess what that meant. All subsequent cellular reproduction proceeded without any damage to his telomeres. Does this sound familiar? I should think so. He's now very much like any one of us in that respect."

Knowledgeable Ahhs and Oohs and Hmms followed the last statement. Tulok beamed and continued. "Then we investigated the anomaly of the missing shadow - a little more difficult to understand this phenomenon. We had to minutely examine the physiology and anatomy of a standard alien. Claas provided excellent base line data. Nevertheless, we will still need to re-examine this when we have a physical specimen on board. Now, as I was saying ... Tumma had managed to get his inter-cellular spaces modified to such an extent, virtually rearranging each cells' positioning, that much of their orb's normal visible EMR could now pass through those spaces." Tulok paused for dramatic effect and received the expected compliments. "Tumma still cast a shadow, but it was so greatly dispersed as to seem non-existent. Despite what happened Tumma remained visible as a substantial quantity of light still reflected off his body, particularly its external coverings."

Pragmatic as always Eili interrupted the congratulations, "And the solution, Dr.Tulok?"

Tulok took a moment to refocus before continuing. 'Ah, yes ... the solution. Those spaces between the cells quickly filled with a clear aqueous, slightly saline solution; just like the material in their visual sense organs. The light had no problem at all passing through it. I propose to 'dry' out the solution and let the cellular structures resume their original configurations."

"What if it doesn't work?" Dr.Qilaq always found it fun to seek discomfort in others. It was his duty as a keen psychologist to observe reactions, and his pleasure to do so.

"Then Tumma is stuck with the problem. Perhaps he might not even survive the process." That made Langur wince. It was not a good answer. They needed this alien ... alive.

"What if I could make him think he's got his shadow back?" Langur offered, without expecting an answer. "I think we'll try that first. What about his immortality?"

"That's as much a problem for him as ours is to us. We could do a bit of engineering. There's a chance it could work. The alien system is still pristine clean of any long-term DNA interference, unlike ours. But perhaps there's another way."

"Work on it my friend, but don't hurry," Langur suggested. "In the meantime it's an attribute definitely working in our favour, and I'd like to keep it that way for a while."

More weeks and months passed as the light of the Rift came closer with each hour. Their acceleration had been constant for some time, and their velocity nearing a tenth the speed of normal light. Gradually the crew got to know one another and became more comfortable being together in the spaces allocated to them, which were by no means cramped. Their craft, having been manufactured to simulate the appearance of a small moon, had the dimensions of a small moon. One could easily get oneself lost in any of the myriad passages of the thick hull. Restrictions had to be imposed on some of the more adventurous crew. With little to do, curiosity became too much of a temptation for the Temporals.

Inevitably Valokvantti thawed out a little with time. Langur made sure of it. He wasn't convinced their Captain's dedication to the project was of equal measure to that of his dedication to The Jarl. Both were important of course, and there needed to be good rapport between the Captain and the man responsible for the future of their race. So Langur made sure he fed regular updates to Valokvantti, personally, engaging him in every-day conversation and finding other opportunities to help out in small ways. It was much easier to seduce the CEO of Vertical Systems than Valokvantti. Yakiv had only one loyalty – to wealth. As long as Langur could help him amass more of it, he was Langur's friend. Valokvantti was different. He had ideals and ambitions; ambitions of power. He only invested his time and attention in matters and people who had similar ideals and who could progress his personal ambitions. With anyone else his impatience dominated, much like The Jarl's.

Langur's strategy worked to some degree. The more Valokvantti knew about the details of the mission, the more he could see possibilities of harvesting acclaim for himself. Just one problem … he had to get along with Langur Skuggi. At first the Captain pretended a modicum of friendship, but as Langur drew him closer into the project that gradually changed.

"Ah, Skuggi, there you are. We'll be coming to the Rift within days. Approximately one week, two days, six hours, seventeen minutes, one hundred and thirty-six seconds." Valokvantti said, and gave one of his grudgingly friendly motions. Skuggi wasn't so bad really, just a bit tiresome with his constant pleasantries. He was trying to be funny, which Langur didn't immediately recognise, yet soon enough to react appropriately so Valokvantti wouldn't be disappointed. "Ha!" they exclaimed simultaneously.

"So how are you going to squeeze us through it, Captain?"

"The tear in the cosmic fabric isn't as small as you would think. I don't think we'll touch the sides." The friendly banter continued for several minutes, until one of the female technical crew came and stood by Valokvantti. They'd obviously become an item. The Captain's recent good moods had nothing to do with Langur's efforts at all, nevertheless he resolved to continue with his relationship strategy with the man.

As the gateway to the light matter universe grew closer, activity on the vessel increased in direct proportion. Each crew member had full body scans, concentrating on their telomere characteristics to establish bases line data against possible alteration by exposure to visible EMR; though unlikely as the craft's dark matter substance didn't interact with visible light photons and presumably didn't allow penetration. However, some of the crew would eventually have to shuttle down to Vesimaa's surface to harvest alien specimens.

Precautionary backups were made of each individual's complete software profile; partly to ensure any reconstituted individuals from tight beam concentrations would have backup data for recovery in case of any problems. The two Concentrators received full diagnostic checks and several dry runs and all other systems were made fully operational. Perhaps some of these activities were premature as the Rift still had to be crossed. But no one aboard the vessel knew exactly what was going to happen on crossing the threshold in such a large hollow object like their planetoid spacecraft.

They were certainly not prepared for the difficulty they were about to have during the actual entry into the Rift. Problems began a week out from the threshold as the craft headed directly into the light cascading through the Rift. Of course many people watched, some of whom risked going to the few observation ports to see the phenomenon directly and not via their internal magnevid screens. Although adjustments had been made to their visual sensors, most spectators experienced severe light impact trauma, effectively blinding them temporarily.

What more natural thing is there than for a small moon to be hurtling through space, albeit at phenomenal speeds? Perfectly normal, except this moon was made of dark matter wimps. Because of their lack of electromagnetic interaction with normal matter, wimps would be dark and invisible to normal electromagnetic observations. Because of their large mass, they would be relatively slow moving and therefore cold. In the case of the unique vessel designed by Yakiv & Co. this space craft's constituent parts were modified to the point where they could no longer be accurately described as made from wimps. They were more like wisps, weakly interactive small particles, though neither weakly interactive, nor cold and certainly capable of moving at more than a quarter the speed of EMR.

The torrent of visible light impacting on the vessel had a cumulative effect. Because there was such a concentrated stream it heated the shell of the craft enough to worry the Captain.

"Langur, you'd better come up to the control center. We have a problem." Valokvantti wasted no time in alerting Langur as soon as the temperature increase was verified. Without turning to the scientist Valokvantti stated the problem succinctly. "Our hull temperature is increasing - and we don't know why."

"What's our tolerance?" Langur really didn't know much about such things but he didn't want to be excluded from the interaction.

"At this rate we have another few days before we, and our systems fry." Valokvantti's reply was subdued, only loud enough for Langur to hear.

"How long before we're through the Rift?"

"I know what you're getting at, but there's no way to know if the situation is going to change on the other side."

In his ignorance Langur said the first thing that came to mind, and immediately regretted it as being a stupid thing to say, "Could it be the intensity of the EMR coming through the Rift?" Langur had said this loud enough for the chief scientific advisor to hear, who immediately checked the instrumentation. It was simple enough to verify the suspicion, and there it was. The heat had spread from the front of the craft, from every part of the surface area which had direct contact with the concentrated light. Everywhere else, away from direct light, was perfectly cool.

"Yes," the scientist confirmed, laconic to the point of preempting anxiety.

"Solution?" asked Valokvantti immediately.

"Reduced concentration. The light hitting our surface tangentially is producing only minimal temperature increase."

"We'll increase speed and get through the Rift lens in time." The vessel still had booster and breaking power in spite of their accumulated speed.

"Captain, I suggest we reduce speed. Increased speed increases the heating."

"I haven't given the order yet helmsman, why did you reduce speed?" Valokvantti snapped. He was losing patience and getting more concerned by the minute. Langur could only stand by and watch the drama unfold.

"I didn't alter speed Captain. The vessel is being slowed down by something else!"

"Light pressure," again the briefest statement from the chief scientific advisor. "I strongly suggest we reduce speed. It will lower the rate of temperature rise, and will reduce the light pressure. The combined action will give us time to get through the light lens effect without damage. There should be a dispersion of light on the other side."

"Should be?" Valokvantti didn't want to hear suppositions.

"What's there to lose when there's no alternative?" Langur ventured the fatalist point of view.

Valokvantti fixed his visual sensors on Langur for several moments, and acquiesced to the suggestion with silence. The temperature gradient did ease as their speed dropped incrementally with each AU as they approached the aperture. By the end of the tenth day they had passed through, 'without touching the sides' as the Captain had quipped. The vessel had reached the limit of its tolerance, and so had the crew. Their personal maximum temperature endurance of thirty-five degrees severely tested, well beyond anything they would have experienced at home. It was however an excellent test for some of the extremes they may encounter on the alien planet.

The nature of space on the other side of the Rift could not have been imagined by any Dokkheimien. In their cosmos space was dark. Here there was light; absolute, colorful all-pervading light. In front of them lay the Milky Way with its billions of suns. So much light and so much color the effect became mesmeric. A dark matter universe planet possessed next to no color. The advance team neglected to report on all the color on the other side. Perhaps they didn't actually perceive it in their tight beam state. What the mind cannot conceive of, it may not even be able to comprehend when seen through its external senses.

Every available magnevid to the spiral spectacle became crowded. They could barely tear themselves away even to recharge. Looking beyond the spiral they saw what no other member of their race could possibly have ever seen, even in their immortal life spans – a universe filled with light – and therefore with the probability of life. The very idea of other sentient life filled them with awe, yet to find a species so close to them, maybe even related to them, seemed inconceivable. Perhaps it was wrong to think of them as being alien.

Langur dwelt on such thoughts for many days, as did Valokvantti and the other key members of the expedition. It created a conundrum for Langur. Whereas before he could think coldly, clinically about the other species and consider them as no more than a means to their own survival – now it became more difficult. How far would he be prepared to go in his treatment of them? Ethics wasn't a part of the equation before. Such immense considerations brought Langur and Valokvantti closer together, for Valokvantti, in spite of his hard exterior wasn't immune to the sacredness of life, whatever form it might take.

*

Deceleration started within months of leaving the immediate vicinity of the Rift. Although nearly a year away from their objective the yellow orb was beginning to take up a more prominent spot in their field of vision. All the members of the limited landing party were required to spend time in the light acclimatization chamber; a major concern being EMR at such high frequencies. Fine tuning of their visual sensors took time. The other sensory receptors, particularly the sense of touch would be essential to have well under control when handling beings who were so soft and fragile. It would be much too easy to damage them with manipulators accustomed to dealing with mostly solid objects. Microbial shields, which had been developed on board, posed another problem. They couldn't be assessed and adjusted until there was actual alien atmosphere and soil available to analyze and test.

The original plan was to concentrate Langur's and Dr.Qilaq's patterns and tight beam them to the target alien after they had achieved Vesimiaan orbit, which now seemed to be an unnecessary delay. There was no obvious reason why they couldn't go immediately. In their altered state biological and atmospheric agents were immaterial.

"Welcome aboard Asvor," Langur was keen to get the latest information.

She boarded Synty soon after it emerged from the Rift, after transmitting all her data from the Rift to ensure its integrity on arrival back at Temporality Nexus. Langur made sure her hardware was with them and ready to receive her. "When can you be ready to report?"

"I've been monitoring Tumma without interfering further with his mind. He's not altered since you left home," she reassured Langur. "There's no immediate need to hasten your initial plans to interact with him."

"Settle in and meet us in the Captain's office."

Asvor, as keen as Langur, arrived within the hour. After introductions she went directly to the heart of the situation.

"They are not completely primitive and they are not exactly savages … but they are dangerous." Langur glanced at Valokvantti. This was an aspect they had not considered before. "Technologically this species is just in the process of waking up. Unfortunately, their technology has already advanced well beyond their ethical capacity to control it for the benefit of their species. Their two main problems are uncontrolled reproduction and the indiscriminate use of their finite resources. If nothing changes in their consciousness, or if we decided not to intervene, this species is on a direct path of self-annihilation. So before I talk about the alien Tumma, I want to present to you a viable solution scenario regarding our own problem." Langur expected a professional analytical report from Asvor. But the initiative she showed was commendable.

"Go ahead, Asvor. You've been here a while, so your analysis is most welcome."

She acknowledged the show of confidence and continued. "The time scale of their probable extinction is well within the scope of our SEPT plan projection. This could work very well for us in two ways. It gives us ample time to carry out the DNA re-engineering, including bi-pedal locomotion development, and with a little patience provide us with a useful planet to colonize unhindered by this sentient species, which will have exterminated itself by then."

The cold, hard facts surfaced again. This was welcome news for Langur, or would have been some time ago before his ethics got in the way of his thinking. Now there was another choice to be made. The unwelcome thought crept into Langur's mind – *Would we, should we, help them prevent destroying themselves? Perhaps that could be considered as an appropriate way to maintain balance in the cosmos, in return for their help (willing or otherwise) in saving us from a very different extinction process, though just as terminal.*

Asvor paused a moment seeing Langur's introspection, "Psychologically, their greatest attribute is initiative; their greatest strength the desire for knowledge, and their greatest enemy; themselves. There is no global depression. They do not, collectively or individually, present any serious threat to us at this time. They are much too divided amongst themselves to unite against a common enemy." This sharpened Valokvantti's interest in Asvor's presentation.

"Everywhere you look this species is fighting and killing its own kind. In my opinion there is no reason for us not to treat them exactly the same way as they treat their own kind. Viewed from a purely entomological perspective, this species is in plague proportions on its own planet and willfully, systematically destroying it."

"This could make our task much easier," Valokvantti suggested to Langur, who didn't immediately concur with the sentiment, and winced as Asvor further unfolded her thoughts.

"If we should consider this planet as a viable option for our resettlement, I believe we should prevent its inhabitants from destroying it further. It may mean hastening their self-annihilation."

Asvor stopped to allow her audience to consider the repercussions of her latest statements. All five, Valokvantti, Langur, Dr.Qilaq, Eili and Dr.Tulok were taken aback by her frank proposition.

"How would you suggest we prevent them from destroying their planet?" Langur quietly put the question to her. He didn't entirely like the direction being explored.

"Take what we need from them to ensure our own survival, then slave clone the rest to work at making the planet suitable for us, regenerating what they have so far destroyed." Asvor answered dispassionately.

There were no immediate noises of approval for the last suggestion, and Langur became apprehensive about taking such a train of thought past its initial expression. Surely the aliens cannot all be the same, with the same despicable attitude to other life on their own world, to each other and to their resources.

"Thank you Asvor for all the data you gathered and your thoughts."

Langur decided he needed to take a very firm leading role in future events. The group faced each other across the Captain's table and after allowing a moments contemplation Langur felt the question had to be put. "Does anyone else feel the same as Asvor?" He received no immediate response from anyone.

"Captain?" Langur prompted.

"Seems perhaps to be a premature direction to take until we examine more of their kind." Valokvantti finally said, and as the others didn't disagree Langur gave Asvor explicit directions.

"Asvor, I'd like you to take a small team back to the planet and concentrate on determining the 'racial mind-set'. Take particular note of their leaders, their scholars and their scientists. Report to me in four weeks. We will then review future strategy."

After the others left, Langur asked as an aside to Valokvantti, "Would it be appropriate for your report to The Jarl to be postponed until we've had our deliberations?" The Captain responded with a silent affirmative nod.

Vesimaa, The Planet of Aliens

Synty continued to decelerate past the outermost planets, traveling at speeds that now allowed the crew to enjoy the splendor of the giant gas planet, and to marvel at the extraordinary spectacle of the ringed planet. Without exception, they all felt that to have a cosmic garden such as they were witnessing could not fail to humble any sentient species living in it. Yet it seems that wasn't the case with the aliens, according to Asvor. Perhaps it was for the best. It would make Dokkheimien transition to a new home much easier.

By the time Valokvantti maneuvered Synty past the orbits of the closer planets and parked it in orbit behind the Earth's moon, Asvor had completed the assignment and was ready to report back. Preambles were not necessary. Langur wanted to get on with it as expediently as possible knowing their Jarl was in the process of making some critical decisions.

Asvor's second report began on a somewhat sour note. "Scientists and scholars co-operate, leaders do not. The leaders are elected, generally, by the people, so they would presumably accurately reflect the racial character and mind-set of the people. They do not."

Langur didn't like the direction her information was taking. "We can assume you approached the assignment with an open mind," he said quietly.

Instead of responding Asvor went directly to the brutal point. "This species is inhabiting large land-mass segments, each with its own leaders. In some instances, even the populations on the same landmass have segregated societies, with their own individual leaders. These leaders cannot co-operate with one another and have an essentially combative relationship. There is no central governing body or ruling individual for the species. They do not even have a global common language."

Asvor made every effort to be professional without passing any value judgments, although it was plain to see she was less than impressed with this alien species. "The divergent populations elect their leaders. Peculiarly they do this at regular intervals as if they were not satisfied with the previous ones they chose. In fact, in many cases they will actively oppose their leaders, once elected, and even go to extraordinary lengths to depose them; sometimes by brutal force and at the considerable loss of life." Langur and the others looked at each other in disbelief.

"This is not making a whole lot of sense!" Valokvantti wanted to hear clear-cut simple information he could act on without undue hesitation, without scruples getting in the way.

Asvor continued. "My full report is much more comprehensive. These are only the essentials I'm giving you. It would seem they are not just primitive, but in fact barbaric. In evolutionary terms they have made very little progress. Chronologically they may have been on the evolutionary path for several hundreds of thousands of their years, but in achievement terms they appear not have advanced past the first few centuries. Their energy requirements are extensive, which they acquire by depleting the planet's natural resources. The finite nature of those resources does not seem to concern them. They refuse to harness other energies available within the current state of their technologies … However," here she paused. Obviously something important was to come.

"Just when I thought it was getting clearer," Valokvantti expressed disappointment. Langur remained quiet so far, deep in thought.

"… However … There have been and there still are outstanding individuals who seem to carry the conscience of the species forward. More often than not, these individuals become outcasts, but not before they make a little progress in raising the general level of species consciousness. Tumma is not one of these individuals, although he is working to increase the sum of knowledge of his people. There is even an occasional rare leader who does not appear to have a warlord mentality."

"So what are you telling us?" Interjected Valokvantti.

Asvor replied in a more considered tone. "I'm saying that the situation isn't as clear in my mind as it was previously. I'm saying - that in consideration of our findings, and the fact that biologically we have a common ancestry with these aliens, our recommendation to The Jarl should present a case that is more balanced."

"Do we need to debate? Langur finally spoke up.

"Perhaps not," Dr.Qilaq suggested. "I would like to consider Asvor's full report first." They all agreed to do likewise.

"We will meet back here tomorrow." Langur directed.

"I've no illusions about this matter, Skuggi." Valokvantti made himself quite clear.

"Have you already made up your mind what you're going to report?"

"No, but I know our Jarl, and I know he's already made up his mind as to what should happen; and it does not look good for these people." Valokvantti's reply was frank and pragmatic.

"So - I take it you have – contemplated – a contrary opinion?" Langur ventured to question.

"We'll see tomorrow after I've read the full report. In either case your work should continue as planned. Make sure you and Dr.Qilaq are ready to leave after our decision." Valokvantti's reply suggested he may not have been as resolute about his position as at the outset of the venture.

It didn't take long for Langur to scan the document and pick out the salient aspects. The rest of the day he spent in front of his magnevid watching Vesimaa in all its splendour rotating its dark face towards the warmth of its yellow orb. He also watched its peoples going about their lives, some in peace; the majority engaged in conflict. It did cross his mind, several revolutions back, that by 'melding' with these aliens they were giving them an extraordinary opportunity to evolve out of the rut the species seems to have dug for itself.

The following day Valokvantti addressed the team in even, measured tones. "Our first obligation is to our own species. The optimum survivability of our race cannot be assured by occupying a planet with severely depleted natural resources. Nor would it be possible to totally integrate the two species, if for no other reason than the unsustainable size of the resultant population. It is however imperative we carry out our initial plans. I'm convinced by Langur's proposition that in order to survive we have to change, and that we must find a new home. If we could prevent the destruction of Earth by its current inhabitants, and perhaps initiate some other measures, then this planet could be eminently suitable. We would be coming home!"

Langur didn't expect that last statement from Valokvantti. *I wonder what he meant by 'other' measures?*

Dr.Qilaq had his own slant on the issue. "There is also the psychological aspect of course. I believe we, as a people in crisis, a crisis of self-preservation struggling to find reasons to exist, would not survive the guilt of genocide of another sentient species; especially not a species with whom we share a common birth place."

Tulok's comment ran along similar lines. "We have severe laws to deal with our own undesirable social elements. It seems we have at least that much in common with the people of this water world."

The statement occasioned a pause in the proceedings. It pointed out that although there were obvious and major differences between themselves and the aliens, there was also much they had in common. Everyone was expected to contribute, because the fate of the people of an entire planet depended to a large degree on the decision of these six individuals. The Jarl would most likely act on their recommendation, though not guaranteed to do so.

After having read the report Eili pointed out what none of them seemed to have considered. "We do not yet know how compatible the two species could potentially be. Consequently, the possibility does exist we could come together for our joint benefit." His contribution became critical as future events unfolded.

"What about you Asvor?" Langur prompted.

"I didn't think my position in the scope of this project warranted any special consideration being given to my opinion. Data gathering is simply that. Decision making is beyond my mandate."

Langur encouraged her, pleased with her self-imposed neutrality. "Good. Based on that attitude and the fact you've been in the most intimate contact with them you are the one most qualified to express a learned opinion."

"Very well. I've no doubt we were once very much like them in some respects. An incredibly difficult environment has shaped our future, leading us to this point. It has brought us to the situation where we have been given the chance to come face to face with our relatives. They are not alien to us. In the past we had diverged. In the future we could converge."

"Well said Asvor. Is there anything else anyone needs to add? ... Good ... There appears to be a consensus, please correct me if I'm wrong. They can help us, we can help them, and let the future take care of itself – Captain?" Langur prepared to listen to dissenting voices.

"So be it. However, whatever course of action is decided its outcomes should be more in our favor. Do you want The Jarl to impose his own solutions, or would you like to seed his thinking?" A most surprising question coming from Valokvantti.

Langur voiced his thoughts. "I believe he's already decided on the migration, perhaps not the destination. The ships have been under construction for some time. You might like to suggest an appropriate location for our new home." Langur was sure the Captain could make alternative viable propositions to Vesimaa for settlement.

With that vote of confidence, Valokvantti went to prepare his report and recommendations to The Jarl. Slowly but surely Langur drew the Captain's loyalties towards a deeper understanding of the project's ramifications. To be given the trust and authority to select a location for their species' future amounted to a considerable validation for Valokvantti. He didn't always have to be commanded, as The Jarl invariably had the habit to do with him.

Langur, Dr.Qilaq and Dr.Tulok went to the Concentrator with Asvor. She would accompany them for a while as a guide. Langur would infiltrate Tumma's central nervous system, with Dr.Qilaq as back-up from the outside. Fortunately, the expeditionary force didn't need to unduly burden itself with the big decisions. They could concentrate on the single most important and critical aspect of the overall plan; would their DNA be sufficiently compatible with that of the aliens to achieve the mortality they were seeking so desperately?

All four beamed directly to Tumma Varjo's enclosure. He wasn't yet home from the laboratory. This gave Asvor a chance to ensure Langur had his infiltration parameters correctly set, and to reinforce the precautions he needed to take so as not to burn out Tumma's central nervous system. The four of them waited in the darkened main room. Tumma always had the curtains drawn so the space took on a dull glow emanating from their combined energy fields. Langur had been made fully aware of the alien's history except for the last period while Asvor reported aboard Synty. Consequently none of them were aware Tumma's only friend had died of old age, well after retirement. Tumma remained as healthy as a twenty-five-year old and still looked like it.

Langur Makes Contact

On that winter's day darkness had already descended in Otaniemi, Finland by half past three. Tumma didn't leave work till quarter past four arriving home in the dark, cold and depressed. Without bothering to put the lights on he went directly to his bedroom, not even noticing the unnatural glow in the front room. It had been a particularly bad day. Inevitably some of his colleagues brought up the very sore point of his youthfulness while everyone else around him aged, retired and died. He'd thrown off his coat and winter ankle boots, fell into bed, pulled the doona over his head and closed his eyes. After years and years of experimentation he was no closer to resolving the two big problems in life; shadowless-ness and continuous youth. There was only one thing he hadn't tried, although lately it had been in his thoughts more and more often.

Langur became most annoyed. He wanted to upload without delay. Unfortunately, he needed full access to both of Tumma's open eyes to do so. They had to wait several hours before hunger and cold forced Tumma out of bed and into the kitchen for hot coffee. A moment after he turned the lights on Langur beamed directly onto the alien's retinas routing immediately into his central brain mass. Tumma flinched from the sudden burst of light, thinking it was the lighting in the room after having his eyes closed in a dark bedroom. He thought nothing more of it as the moment passed almost immediately.

Having thoroughly absorbed everything Asvor had taught him Langur had no trouble getting his bearings. First he established his own center of operations in the frontal lobe, and set up a direct pathway to the occipital lobe. Dr.Qilaq stayed with Tumma in the room while Asvor and Dr.Tulok went in search of suitable male and female specimens for their experiments.

Before Langur could explore Tumma's cognitive environment, a storm of activity buffeted his awareness. Tumma sat quietly in his armchair planning the alternative; a painless means of committing suicide. An astounded Langur couldn't believe what he was picking up and immediately transmitted it to Dr.Qilaq. He had never been so glad of his friend's presence. Here was a creature actually capable of considering the termination of its own life force; a concept unheard of on Dokkheim. He couldn't even convince his people to shorten their life spans, let alone consider voluntary euthanasia.

After an urgent discussion with Dr.Qilaq Langur took immediate action. There wasn't time for him to get the 'feel' of his host and ease into some form of introductory dialogue. So he short circuited one of Tumma's thought pathways and seeded it with one of Tumma's own past thoughts.

Let's go out and get something to eat. Maybe we'll meet a nice girl.

"Where the hell did that come from!" Tumma exclaimed aloud. He hadn't been thinking of going out that late and especially not under the current circumstances of his friend's death.

Langur triggered another one of Tumma's well used thoughts.

I'm hungry and I damn well don't feel like cooking after the day I've had.

Langur achieved what he had hoped, even though he didn't get the thought sequence quite right. Despite his somber mood, Tumma stopped thinking about suicide. Langur wondered how long Tumma could be distracted and realized he might have to hurry things along. His first attempt to exercise control over Tumma's thoughts worked. Langur was elated. *I'll have to stabilize his psychological state before I can do anything else. Perhaps sex will be a strong enough urge to divert Tumma's thoughts away from suicide.* Langur remembered Asvor saying that the aliens in Finland engaged in casual sex fairly regularly. Apparently the pleasurable activity had something to do with their reproductive process, without necessarily achieving reproduction.

In his current condition Tumma decided his idea had merit. It didn't take him long to walk to the Café near his place. The walk lightened his mood helped a little by the warm, friendly place with a strong aroma of coffee. The small intimate place catered largely to young couples. He spied several single females enjoying the ambiance as he entered. The possibility of having a casual liaison dawned on Tumma as he glanced around the room. Langur noted Tumma's strongest response to a female in the far back dimly lit corner.

Why don't you go over there – to that one – and see if you can sit at her table, Tumma heard himself say to himself. It had been some time since he'd engaged in a flirtatious conversation, or any conversation with a girl. Normally he would not have been so forward. He walked over casually and stopped at the table. "Hei, mind if I join you?"

The female looked up slowly, letting her eye meander leisurely upwards along his long torso, obviously deciding in the affirmative.

"Hei - Sure." The length of her scrutiny was much longer than a fifth of a second to decide if he was right for her. The instantaneous rapport between the two individuals surprised Langur. Tumma's thoughts no longer dwelt on suicide.

Langur had nothing else to do for the next few hours, indeed for the rest of the night other than to marvel at the most peculiar interaction he could ever have imagined. As it turns out it was an essential bit of education about the species for his future plans.

Early in the morning Tumma prepared to go back to work. He was even a bit early for the eight o'clock start. Bouncing out of bed, getting through his morning routine took no time at all; not at all like the normal drag on other dark winter mornings, except for one really odd little thing.

Tumma's routine gave Langur a chance to put the second part of his plan into action. He subtly activated a small area of neurons in the occipital lobe. As a result, Tumma misplaced his foot each time he tried to put it in the ankle boot. He became so exasperated with himself that he pulled them on rather than to keep trying to slip his feet into them.

"Damn! How very odd," he said aloud, "perhaps my eyesight is going ... if only!"

Langur had manufactured an image for the location of his boots to be just slightly different to where they were actually situated. With the test successful, Langur could activate his plan to make Tumma think he had his shadow back.

While Tumma concentrated on getting to the lab, Langur created the image of a very slight, almost imperceptible 'synthetic' shadow in Tumma's mind. But Tumma took no notice of it. He was still thinking about the girl from the Café. During his lunch break he decided to go back to the Café and see if she was there by any chance. As he stepped out into the sunlight he did a double take. *What's that!* Tumma stared at the ground in front of him. *No – it's not possible!*

That can't be my shadow. Tumma glanced behind himself briefly to see his assistant a step away from behind him. A wave of relief washed over Tumma as he continued to the Café.

Langur monitored every reaction. Another success. He decided to gradually increase the intensity of the shadow over the next couple of weeks, being careful to calibrate it to the available lighting conditions. That turned out to be a complex procedure, requiring the activation of a wide range of neurons to fire in a specific sequence within an accurately calculated time span.

The girl wasn't there. Tumma surprised himself with how disappointed he felt. *I'll try again tonight.* Quite a natural though under the circumstances but somewhat uncharacteristic of Tumma. He was after all over sixty-five years old, and living a mostly reclusive life.

Ok. Tumma thought. *There it is. I'm talking to myself again.* Suddenly the old fear surfaced. *What if I hear something I don't want to hear?*

Relax. The internal voice said. By then Tumma had arrived back at work and busied his mind with more scientific matters. He forgot about his internal conversationalist. He forgot about the shadow he thought he saw earlier. The rest of the day flew by. It was dark before he realized it and time to go home; too dark to think about shadows – instead - the Café.

A quick shower and change, then you can go, he heard the voice say.

"Yes, you're right. It was hot at the lab today." Once again he responded aloud to the suggestion, which was a perfectly normal one. Anyone would have thought the same thing in the same situation.

Dr.Qilaq interrupted Langur just for a moment. "That was a good strategy. Try generating some more challenging thoughts; something he would not normally think himself."

Langur decided to observe events unfold for a little while. The Café expedition proved successful with another assignation between the two aliens.

Several days later Tumma found himself in exceptionally high spirits. He'd met the girl again, they had coffee and arranged to meet on the weekend. He was also having the oddest feelings that had eluded him since the accident; a sense of being connected, of somehow being anchored and in touch with the earth: Nothing he could quite put his finger on, but he was looking forward to going out in the light of the day again.

"I think I'll take her to the Forces of Light Festival."

No, not a good idea. Too many people. Langur took the opportunity to generate one of those challenging thoughts to dissuade Tumma from going there.

"Of course it's a good … What!" He'd started to say aloud when he suddenly stopped. *There it is again! That voice, telling me what to do!*

Langur decided to press the point.

I only meant you might prefer something a little more – intimate. Tumma's mind went blank. His pupils dilated and all the lights went out inside his head and he fell into his armchair in a near faint. The realization he wasn't just talking to himself but some invading entity finally hit home. The cerebral reaction gave Langur quite a start.

"I think you'd better ease up and let him let him come to terms with what's happening." Dr.Qilaq suggested. "He's not yet consciously aware of the re-emergence of his shadow, albeit it's illusionary. I think he needs time to reassert his sanity, that he's not going mad."

"What do you suggest?" Langur invited direction from an expert.

"Ask some subtle questions and let him work out that something other than himself exists in his consciousness." Dr.Qilaq felt they were very close to the tipping point with this alien. That's exactly what he was there to prevent. Langur took this expert psychologist's advice leaving Tumma alone for a day.

Thursday night:
Tumma's narrowed eyes darting from side to side, his head slumped forward and his breathing slowed. He broke out in a cold sweat while on the way to the Café for another chance meeting. The street lighting cast everything into high contrast to the snow-white background of the park he had to pass on the way. There was no one walking near him. There was no one in the park.

What is happening to me!

Langur could clearly see the anguish change Tumma's heart rate and body temperature. His head bent further down until the only thing in his sight was the pavement. There, starting at a little distance in front of him, the beginnings of a human shadow extended itself towards him. His eyes followed its darkness back until it joined his boots.

That evening, Langur took the chance and gave the imaginary shadow its full grey toning to synchronize with the street lighting. Tumma had not noticed it until then. The thought of Lilli had put all else out of mind. Now the image of the shadow consumed his entire being. The voice inside his head had disappeared, and his shadow reappeared. A soft whimper escaped from his lips. He looked around for a bench. Fear gripped him and he froze before he could take a step towards it.

What if I'm only imagining the shad … ?

Don't be afraid. Of course it's your shadow. It has come back. Langur said to him.

He'd become expert at simulating the shadow in Tumma's mind, making it appear to be quite real. He began lifting his left foot, watching the shadow intently, afraid to breathe. Tumma concentrated so hard he though the shadow hadn't moved, but just as he was about to implode his dark grey companion slowly withdrew as the foot gained height. It stopped, then came towards him again as the left foot came back down towards the pavement. The two met and touched intimately at the point of landing. A sense of joy and relief washed over him.

How is this possible?

While Langur continued with 'priming' the alien, Asvor and Tulok located the specimens they needed.

"Langur, are you set?" They waiting for Langur to have Tumma ready for transport aboard Synty.

'No. I want to spend more time with the alien, to develop some kind of rapport, perhaps even enlist his willing co-operation. I've made a lot of progress in the last few days in spite of Tumma being near his limits on several occasions."

Tumma took a few tentative steps, then started running towards the Café, bursting in the door and making every patron turn towards him. "Lilli!" He almost fell over a table in front of him in his eagerness to get to her. She sat alone. "Hei Lilli."

"Hei Tumma, sit." He just nodded, out of breath for the moment, sat and stared at her. *Yea … she's here!* Lilli smiled, delighted to see him and waited.

And she's happy to see you, he heard himself saying to himself. A big smile spread across his face that she reciprocated with just as much enthusiasm. He's heart raced again and he was much too pre-occupied with her welcoming smile to notice the subtle change in Langur's statement from the word 'me' to the word 'you'.

Tumma couldn't contain himself and blurted out without any preamble, "Would you like to come with me to the Forces of Light Festival?"

"Joo," Lilli responded, accompanied by smiling eyes.

Langur relaxed for the rest of the evening giving Tumma time to consolidate his thoughts about the 'inner voice' and the return of his shadow … if he could spare a thought for anything other than Lilli.

The weekend came and went, much too quickly in Tumma's opinion. He had a great time with Lilli, but there were a few anxious moments. As with all budding relationships in the process of getting to know one another there's always a bit of weaving back and forth. Some information about himself he volunteered freely, other bits not so freely. His birthplace, not a problem: his age, definitely a problem. Lilli wanted to meet his friends … but they were all so much older looking than him. They all looked like they were in their sixties whereas Tumma still had the face and body of a twenty-five-year-old. He certainly moved like one!

Sunday night after the festival:

At home alone, Tumma had time to think things over. *Just how am I going to manage this?*

You can't keep it a secret forever, he heard his inner voice say. *She would never believe you.*

"No she wouldn't". Tumma responded aloud.

Would you tell her about your shadow?

"Definitely not. She'll think I'm a complete looney."

He suddenly realized the conversation didn't sound like a person talking to himself at all and became silent. This time Tumma's mind didn't go blank. He was a scientist. He was supposed to have an open mind. *"What is going on here?"* he asked himself.

Langur took the chance - it was now or never. It's just two people having a conversation.

Silence.

"Lucky I'm at home. They'd lock me up on the spot."

Perhaps not, but you need to be careful. Langur tried to reassure him.

"What are you? Where are you?" The words came tumbling out of him almost like a manic plea for his life.

I know you've had an accident, which left you with two big problems.

"Are you ... the ... the third problem?"

No. Well not exactly. Perhaps you could think of me as the solution to the other two.

"What do you mean ... 'not exactly'. If I'm going crazy - so be it. If not, then don't speak in riddles!" Another loud plea from Tumma.

I don't know what I can do to make you believe what I'm about to say.

"Just say it!" He was almost shouting by this stage.

Watch your shadow. It hasn't exactly come back to you ... But I can fix that if you want.

Langur gave him a few moments to comprehend. Then he started fading out Tumma's shadow as Tumma watched utterly disbelieving.

"What! ... How?" He yelled as his shadow disappeared, then a moment later returned. "Did you do that?"

Yes.

"Did you take away my shadow?"

No. It was the accident, but I know how to fix it.

"Wait. Wait. Stop! Don't say anything else! … I have to think."

Minutes passed. Tumma sat down, got up, then sat down again. Then got up again to get himself a coffee. Anything, just to have something 'normal' happening. Then he sat down again.

"Right. Answer me straight! What are you? Who are you? WHAT ARE YOU DOING INSIDE MY HEAD? Answer me!"

My name is Langur.

"I don't believe this."

I said you wouldn't believe me.

"It's just a figure of speech."

A figure of what? What does that mean?

"You don't know? This is getting weirder and weirder." The longer the conversation continued the more Tumma regained his composure. Langur could see Tumma settling from his neural activity. He decided to keep progressing the situation.

Call me Langur. First, let me tell you about your accident. When you fell in front of the light beam of your apparatus, your arm hit two levers changing the settings. The change to the characteristics of your already altered EMR caused your two problems. I can fix both of them. But not here.

"What do you mean not here? … Not in my unit? … Not … Aaah … just go on." Tumma decided it was best to hear the whole story before he tried to unravel what he was going through.

Secondly, I am not you. I am - another entity - shall we say. I have a physical manifestation as well as an energetic one.

"Great. I'm talking to a spook."

I don't understand some of these words you're using.

"Why not? Just Who are you?"

All this time Dr.Qilaq watched, silent in the background, letting Langur control the situation. He was doing extremely well. But Dr.Qilaq had a small suggestion. "Langur, tell him about me."

Langur thought for a moment how to best approach the introduction. *Tumma, you work with light and have done so all your life. It has been a secret project very few of your people know about. But we know about it.*

"We?"

We know you're trying to get high frequency EMR to pass through solid objects, and that you have achieved some measure of success. Which, by the way, would be much higher if you had been able to work out what happened to you during your accident.

"You know about my work?" Langur now had Tumma's full attention. "What do you know about the properties of light?" He was genuinely interested, forgetting he was talking to some strange manifestation in his own head.

Turn the light down and watch.

"Dr.Qilaq, would you mind giving your energy field a little buzz." Langur let Tumma hear his request.

"Who's Dr.Qilaq?"

You keep asking all these questions. Patience. Just watch.

As the lights dimmed to darkness, Dr.Qilaq made himself glow a little more than usual.

That's Dr.Qilaq, in his energized photon configuration. He can't communicate with you because he isn't connected into your neural network.

"Jumalauta! Goddamn! Now you're talking my language!"

He could talk with you but his physical form is back on the spacecraft, just as mine is.

"Stop it. You have to stop now. I need to think. Where is my real shadow?"

We can discuss that tomorrow. His tone was dismissive, making Tumma aware of the end of the conversation.

Tumma wandered around the room, his thoughts in turmoil. *This is too incredible. How could it be true? How could it possibly be true? But they know about my research. They know about my accident. He can even control my damn shadow!*

Langur needed to have a conference with his staff. The project was moving ahead more or less as planned. They had achieved a major breakthrough in making contact with the alien; his mind not as primitive as Asvor's report led them to believe. They just might be able to work with this individual, and possibly with the other specimens of the species. While Tumma slept and dreamt strange science fiction dreams, Langur and Dr.Qilaq returned to the vessel. It was a relief to be back in their own bodies. Amazing as the experience had been, Langur felt the strain of his out-of-body experience. The team gathered in Valokvantti's office. Asvor and Tulok had made their selection of suitable specimens, but had not yet harvested them.

Langur made a very confident statement to the group. "This alien called Tumma will definitely be suitable. He has a good mind. He's intelligent and resilient to new experiences. He can communicate in three of their languages. Asvor, it is imperative the other specimens you choose are be able to speak at least one of the known languages of Tumma. So review the specimens you have selected, and find new ones if necessary." Langur wanted to keep the conference short and get back to his alien without delay.

"Valokvantti, have you found a suitable planet?"

"Yes. The Jarl has my report. Two possibilities. Vesimaa and another one. A new vessel is being prepared to explore the suggested location. It's a planet in the Tau Ceti system; the fifth planet of that orb. Considerable work needs to be done to make it habitable, but it is in the habitable zone, for both our species. We could make it work. Time may be a prohibitive factor. However, the planet is large enough, about one point five time the size of Vesimaa, sorry, Earth. The Jarl is prepared to consider more data before making his final selection."

Langur acknowledged the Captain's efforts and continued without digressing, "I expect everyone at Temporality Nexus including Yakiv, are being kept advised of developments. Once we have the aliens on board we have to be ready to proceed. They have a very limited life span. Tulok, my friend, please prepare the equipment to restore my alien's shadow. We may need it quite soon."

Many other matters had to be dealt with before Langur and Dr.Qilaq could return to Earth. Not least The Jarl's indecisiveness about the target planet. Most unusual for him. It couldn't possibly be due to ethical considerations. A leader in his position does not have the luxury of ethics to guide his decisions.

Tumma Meets Saija

Monday morning:

Saija Kevat was a thirty-two year old nurse; single, Scandinavian, attractive with mousy-grey hair bordering on blond. She trained at the Keropudas Hospital in Tornio, Finland's premier institution for alternative treatment of psychoses such as schizophrenia. The Open Dialogue approach appealed to her from the first moment she read about it. She was on duty in Otaniemi when Tumma had a near breakdown at work.

Tumma slept fitfully through the night, so wakefulness was slow to claim him. His dreams mixed with memories and he wasn't clear about anything. The remembered experience was much too disturbing. There were no strange voices greeting him that morning. *It must all have been one hell of a dream ... and my shadow. My shadow!* Everything came to a screeching halt in his mind. "My Shadow! Voi Luoja! Oh God!" He shouted in sudden panic.

Still warm under the doona he reached out a hand to turn on the lights. He lifted the doona off himself, sat up, swung his legs over the side of the bed, barely having the courage to breathe. He thought of closing his eyes but couldn't. Tumma stood up.

"Ahhh!" His shadow was gone again.

"LANGUR!" He screamed, but there was no answer.

"LANGUR!" He screamed again. Silence.

What is happening to me! Was everything in the last few weeks a dream, a great long hallucination. Frantic and confused, he only partly dressed before rushing out the door. All Tumma could think of was getting to work – it was a Monday morning. He didn't notice it was cold, or that it was still dark. Tumma ran all the way to work, arriving late.

Everyone was already there preparing for the day's activities when a disheveled young man burst into the cafeteria, his hair wild, half dressed and mumbling incoherent words between breaths he could barely gulp down.

"Hei, isn't that Tumma?" Jukka called, rushing to him. "Come, give me a hand somebody." Several of his colleagues took him by the arm and sat him down. Tumma's eyes wouldn't focus. He didn't hear what they were saying to him. It took a good half hour to settle him. By then the ambulance had arrived.

Tumma continued mumbling disconnected words … "my shadow … accident … energized photons … he's in my head" - and he kept calling out a name nobody knew while being led to the ambulance.

"Well, what can you expect, some of the onlookers were commenting. "He's been strange since his accident all those years ago."

Langur didn't expect to be aboard Synty for so long. On his return he was surprised to see Tumma in the foyer of the building being led towards the entrance by several people. He was even more surprised at Tumma's condition, so he wasted no time in reconnecting with him. Before alerting Tumma to his presence, he 'switched' Tumma's shadow back on in his mind.

It was a dangerous situation. The alien actually had no shadow. If the other people realized it, the whole thing Langur was trying to keep 'clandestine' could suddenly be exposed. Very dangerous indeed. The Vesimiaans were not ready for an open encounter with an off-world species.

"Dr.Qilaq, take control of the other alien and get him to walk directly behind Tumma to block the incident light from behind him."

Miraculously a faint shadow emerged in front of Tumma as they all made their way outside to the ambulance.

Tumma. It's me. Sorry I wasn't with you this morning.

"LANGUR!" Tumma shouted. The attendants tightened their grip on Tumma's arms. "Where the hell have you been!" Then he tried to reassure the attendants, "It's alright. Everything's all right. You can let me go now. I'm fine. My shadow is back. It was all just a little misunderstanding."

They didn't let him go. He was put in the back of the ambulance while one of them called the Health House at Otaniemi. They took Tumma back to his apartment instead of the hospital. A Health Worker already waited for him when they arrived. There was still the problem of a man talking to an imaginary person, which he persisted in continuing to do while traveling in the ambulance. Saija, from the Health House, was a fully trained Open Dialogue specialist, dealing with mental health issues.

"Langur, are you here?" Tumma asked. "You gave me one hell of a fright."

Sorry. You better stop talking and listen to the female.

Saija settled Tumma on his couch, brewed him a mug of light roast coffee, then sat in front of him waiting until Tumma focused on her face.

"My name is Saija. Can we talk?"

"Sure. I'm alright now."

"Would you like to tell me why you were so upset this morning?"

"My shadow … this will sound crazy to you … I had an accident years ago which – er - affected - my shadow. The experiments I was working on are classified so I can't tell you anymore."

"Yes. That's fine. Who is Langur?"

"He's – he's – well – I often talk to myself. I don't get out much." Tumma was starting to dislike the direction of the conversation.

"That's fine. Let me tell you about myself and what I do," Saija volunteered. Tumma relaxed a little, sipped his coffee and listened. So did Langur and Dr.Qilaq. Tumma in full control of his faculties by then had no problem catching the drift of what Saija was getting at. Yes, he had a problem … yes, perhaps he could use a little help … no, he would not like to go to the Health House and see what they do … and so on.

In effect the institution wanted to put him under surveillance isolated from his normal environment. There were obviously some triggers setting off his aberrant behavior. Saija's suggestion didn't suit Tumma at all, nor Langur. They might end up losing this alien and have to start again with a new specimen.

"So - I'll come and visit you again in a couple of days and see how you're getting on." Saija sounded relaxed, sympathetic and not too pushy.

"Yes, yes - that's good." His voice was perfectly normal now. He'd finished his coffee, and just wanted to finish dressing. "I'm feeling a bit awkward half dressed like this."

Saija took that as a good sign of normality and made her way to the front door. Just by chance she glanced down at the floor, as we all do unconsciously before stepping outside. Tumma watched her get into her car and drive away.

Not until she turned a corner did Tumma dare say anything to Langur. "So what am I supposed to do now?"

Listen carefully to what I'm going to say. This is all real. I am real, so is my friend Dr.Qilaq. We come from a different place. None of it is a dream. We can restore your shadow. But we need your help in return.

"Who is 'we' exactly?"

Dr.Qilaq, who is currently a photon energy manifestation, myself and the rest of our people.

"This sounds like you're going to bend my mind again."

We cannot help you here. You need to come with us.

"No. I don't think so. Why can't I see you, or this Dr.Qilaq?"

You will, soon. I promise. You don't have many alternatives. The female wants to restrict your freedom. She cannot help you but we can. We can also help with your other problem.

"Yes. Well this ongoing 'youth' business does make things difficult. How would it work out with Lilli? I really like Lilli."

Langur ignored the girl. There were other things far more important. *Will you let me show you something? You don't have to go anywhere. I can show your mind images; A little like I made you see your shadow, which isn't really there – yet. But these other images are real. I would like to take you on a little journey.*

"You could really fix - give me back ... that is make everything normal again?"

Yes. Are you ready? All you need to do is close your eyes.

Monday afternoon:

Langur took Tumma into himself, to see the greater reality of the cosmos in which he lived, all the while talking to him, explaining everything, letting him ask questions and answering all of them. The journey took the rest of the day, and most of the night.

Keep your eyes closed. First, I'm going to show you your room and the front door. Then we'll go out the door.

As soon as Langur activated Tumma's visual cortex with the internal images Tumma immediately saw his room and squinted his eyes tightly shut. For a moment he thought he'd opened them. Everything seemed so vivid, so real. As he watched the front door getting closer it felt as if he was actually walking towards it ... down the couple of steps and out into the street.

"How does it feel? Are you feeling safe? I promise, nothing can happen to you. You are still in your room."

"It's a bit like when I first had to walk without my shadow. I feel like I'm floating and not connected to the ground."

"Good. Because we are going to leave the ground shortly and go higher."

The look on Tumma's face would have seemed to anyone watching him like he was having a thoroughly delightful experience.

Langur could sense Tumma's excitement mixed with anticipation. So they went a little higher. His mind fluttered for a second, but Langur reassured him.

"How is this possible?" Tumma asked. They hovered over the Research Centre, before rising vertically until he could no longer even see Finland's coastline. Langur gave him a little while to get used to the feeling. Tumma's eyes moved from side to side under his closed eyelids, as if he was in REM sleep. He was looking at the Earth and Sun and the Moon and all the incredible brightness of the stars around him. He gave himself over totally to the experience, fascinated, as a little boy would be - as the scientist in him was.

Would you like to see what my people look like?" Tumma didn't answer, he was too immersed in wonder. "We are going inside our spacecraft."

Several crew members were busy at the instruments in the main control room. One of them moved to another console. Tumma watched these strange beings with odd elongated bodies supporting a variety of extension, all with very dark, almost black shadows following them everywhere. He was sensitive to the concept of shadows and couldn't fail to notice that those were quite thick; like several centimeters thick black rubber mats. Langur sensed the question about to be asked.

"This is what we look like. We have a vertical part and a horizontal part. The horizontal part is our biological aspect. The other is bionic."

"Where are your faces?"

Langur didn't want to get into too much detail too soon and changed the subject. "I want to show you the gateway through which we came to your world." He sensed acquiescence, and so continued outwards past the solar system.

Tumma watched in awe all the images of the great planets. He recalled everything he'd learnt about Mars and Jupiter and Saturn. They were magnificent beyond any photographs he'd ever seen of them … and a thought flashed into his head –

I want this!

He wanted to be a part of the greater cosmos. His small flat in a cold, sun starved country couldn't possibly satisfy him anymore; not even his experiments, not even the prospect of a future with Lilli. Many things went through his mind, all of which Langur could see. But Langur didn't interfere, overjoyed at the alien's malleability. They would have no trouble convincing him to go with them and help them.

Langur took Tumma well out past the solar system, going above the plane of the Milky Way. It was almost more than Tumma could cope with. He couldn't even entertain a lucid thought - he just stared, mesmerized. To use even a single adjective to describe the spectacle would destroy the magnificence of that Galactic miracle.

This is my world!

"Look over there … there, at that brightness." Langur directed Tumma's attention to an area of space that appeared to be gathering light; light of every intensity and every perceivable color. "That's the gateway we came through. My world is on the other side. It is a dark world." Without even thinking, Langur voiced his own immediate concern, "My people are all going to die, if I don't find a way to help them." And as Langur told Tumma about his world, he took Tumma through the rift and into the universe of dark matter. He could feel Tumma shrink into himself. Tumma could see nothing but darkness; absolute solid, infinite blackness. His eyes were not sensitive enough to pick up the light of Dokkheim's deep red sun. He couldn't see the planet's feeble reflection of that light.

"I want to go home". Even for a scientist the experience pushed the man's capacity to comprehend such things to the absolute limit.

Back on the couch in his room Tumma had pulled his body into itself, raising his knees and wrapping his arms about them. Langur took Tumma's mind back slowly the way they had gone. In quick succession Tumma saw again the solar system from a great distance, then the planets one by one. Mars … he marveled at Mars. He couldn't remember seeing it on the way out. Then they were back above white Finland, down his road to the front door and inside his small apartment.

Keep your eyes closed for a little while. Think about your room, and where everything is, your table and chairs, the light switch, the door to your bedroom. Now, slowly, slowly open your eyes.

Curled up on his couch Tumma felt exhausted. He just wanted to sleep. His body felt heavy as he dragged it into the bedroom. He woke late the following day to the sound of an insistent door bell. It was that woman, Saija from the Health House. He remembered her – she was nice. Then he remembered what she planned to do to him. Disheveled from a turbulent night's dreaming, in his slippers and old dressing gown so late in the day he went to answer the door.

Saija Kevat

Tuesday morning:

"Come in."

"Good morning Tumma."

Her first impression wasn't encouraging. Saija returned sooner than she had anticipated and saw again the same unkempt, albeit attractive man she interviewed only a day ago. As Tumma walked towards his kitchen Saija took a long critical woman's look at him. There was something about the man that attracted her. She decided she could be quite interested in Tumma despite his 'minor' problem. Then she looked down at the floor near him. Just as she thought. She wasn't mistaken. Saija couldn't imagine how it could be possible for a man not to have a shadow, but there it was ... no - there it wasn't!

I'm still here, Langur reassured.

"Coffee?" Tumma asked Saija.

"Yes please. How are you today?" *Hmm, quite a handsome man. But I shouldn't be thinking like this, it's most unprofessional:* She chastised herself.

"Much better than when you first saw me. Sleep. That's all I needed; some good sleep." He was determined to say nothing about his problems, especially not about his new 'friend'. *Well ... that's an interesting thought ... friend,* Tumma said to himself. Langur heard the 'thought' of course. Good. Very good. He didn't want to admit it to himself, but reluctantly he had to recognize he'd actually developed some kind of rapport with this alien. The differences between the species seemed to be shrinking little by little.

Saija looked up from her mug of coffee, explored Tumma through his eyes for a moment before asking conversationally, "How is Langur?" She needed to maintain her professionalism in spite of the attraction she felt for him. That bombshell didn't faze Tumma.

He pretended ignorance. "Who?"

"The person you were calling out to yesterday."

"Oh that. Must have been someone I met the other day at the Café. He was there with Lilli, my new girlfriend. I kind of wish he wasn't there," he said while looking into his mug. For some reason he didn't want to look at Saija's eyes … into her eyes; and it wasn't because he was lying to her.

"I see." A pause - another sip of coffee. *A girlfriend. Somehow, I don't buy it.* Saija was skeptical about that. She prided herself on being a good judge of character and Tumma didn't seem the sort to have a casual girlfriend. She remained unconvinced.

"I'm a little worried about the other morning. I think it would be wise to do a couple of tests; just to rule out any possible biological infection. There are a few nasty bugs around at the moment. Would you mind coming down to the Health House with me?"

"No - that is Yes. I don't think it's necessary. I'm feeling fine. I should really be back at work."

Saija finished her mug while talking pleasantries, both of them avoiding the subject of Tumma's peculiar behaviour. She didn't want to go yet. He didn't want her to go either, but the conversation died out, choked by all the unspoken things said only to themselves and not to each other.

"Well, alright then. I'll come back to check on you again in a few days … perhaps sooner."

She had every intention of coming back with reinforcements to take Tumma by force if necessary, although reluctantly. There was definitely something about this man that caught her attention. Whatever the specific nature of his ailment he definitely needed urgent care. Tumma's colleagues confirmed the accident to her, confirmed the loss of his shadow, and they made a particular point about something else; his age. Saija couldn't believe Tumma was over sixty-five years old. *He doesn't look a day over an attractive thirty, even in his disheveled state. He certainly doesn't move like an old man. This is not a mental health issue. Perhaps the military should get involved.* She felt unreasonably torn between what she felt she had to do, and what she wanted to do.

You know what she's going to do, don't you? Langur asked Tumma rhetorically.

"Yes. But I don't think she wants to. I just have this feeling."

She may not want to, yet she will. I think she's genuinely concerned for you. Do you want to end up as an experiment yourself? Langur prompted. It was an odd thing for him to say considering that was exactly what he had in mind to do with Tumma. He'd already alerted their shuttlecraft crew to be ready for a pick up. They were waiting in a nearby park, one of many in the locality, some with secluded areas perfectly suitable for a landing - and an abduction.

"I'll tell you what I want!! I want my shadow back and I want to be my age. But what I mostly want is … to be … out there! And he looked up towards the ceiling. You knew exactly what you were doing when you showed me what is beyond the realms of our current knowledge! You knew I wouldn't be able to resist. You said I could help you. How could I possible help you? I don't know how, but I want to try if it means being a part of all you've shown me."

Tumma finished his little outburst, barely able to contain his excitement at the possibilities before him. Dr.Qilaq and Langur listened without interruption. There was nothing else to say. They now had what they came for. It was time to go.

Quickly pack a few things. You don't need much. We have to go. They will be back soon. Today probably. Do you have a mobility unit … a … vehicle?

Within the hour they were on the way. Tumma had just turned onto the road out of his garage when a 'Polis" vehicle and another black sedan appeared at the end of his street.

Go at normal speed till you turn the corner, then move very fast to the Nuuksio National Park. There is an entrance not far from here, Langur said.

The pursuers didn't immediately follow, not until they discovered the apartment was empty. Tumma had time to get through the park gate, abandon the car and run in the direction Langur showed him.

There! You can just see the shuttle crew past the trees.

Modified biped slave clones already waited to take him on board. Tumma ran like the young man he was, not even out of breath when he arrived at the shuttle ramp. The Polis and the military were several hundred meters behind and closing fast. That in itself wasn't a problem. The craft with the fugitive had ample time to lift off. What they didn't want was for the aliens to see them.

Still an hundred meters from the craft the pursuers stopped dead in their tracks. They were not prepared for what they saw.

"Whatever you are seeing or not seeing, you are not seeing it! This is classified," barked the Military Polis Major.

"What I'm not seeing is the trees. Something is blocking them," responded the Sergeant.

They couldn't actually see the craft, only an absence of the background where the trees were supposed to have been. Light didn't respond to the fabric of the dark matter shuttle.

"And what I'm seeing and not believing is that young guy walking up into the air. There's nothing there to support him!" added the Sergeant.

Tumma had ascended the invisible ramp and disappeared into a hole in the air. They also saw several shimmering indistinct objects follow the man into the hole before it closed. These simmering apparitions were perhaps half a meter taller than the man himself.

The five officials and Saija remained where they had stopped. It was hard enough to comprehend what their eyes were telling them, let alone attempt to apprehend the fugitive. Within minutes of the hole closing, the background began to reappear, from the bottom up, gradually revealing the full height of the trees. Whatever was blocking them was large enough to hide the length of four full sized tourist buses, and at least three times their height. There was no sign of Tumma.

"Search!' barked the Major. They searched the area of the trees and all around the vicinity, finding nothing.

The Finnish authorities decided there were only three possibilities. The Russians were trying out some new technology and Tumma was a Russian agent: Or extraterrestrials were abducting the man while he was under some sort of drug: Or there was no abduction, only a pick up, and Tumma was definitely one of Them. The first option seemed the most likely, or at the least the most comfortable for the military minds to cope with. Saija was sworn to secrecy. But she didn't need to keep the incident to herself for too long.

They can't see us, but they do see you. Most unfortunate, Langur commented just as Tumma stepped into the craft, turning around for a moment to wave to Saija. Mesmerized by the spectacle Saija remained absolutely still watching him disappear until her arm automatically waved back even before she realized she was doing it. *Saija is nice, in spite of her profession,* Tumma made a mental note. Langur also saw her waving and formed the same opinion. He knew she was aware of all of Tumma's problems.

After her second visit, when she realized he was communicating with an invisible entity, which sounded so very familiar to her, and that Tumma didn't have a shadow, she was confronted with a dilemma. This was no ordinary extraordinary situation. If she didn't alert the appropriate authorities and the whole thing became 'complicated', she could again be facing a turning point in her career, one that would definitely not be to her advantage. *What should I do? I don't know this man. He's very attractive, but he's a stranger … a complete stranger. He could be a homicidal maniac for all I know!*

During the second interview Saija tried to let him know he could be 'detained'. If he was as smart as she thought he was, he would do something about it.

Oh God, I hope he's not home!

When arriving in his street on the third occasion she could only think about protecting him. *Perhaps he might contact me later,* she allowed herself to hope.

As she proceeded towards his unit with the Military Polis she saw a car in front of his place slowly move off. The military authorities of course had no reason to connect that vehicle with the man they came for. Saija guessed it might have been Tumma's as they got a little closer. By then his car was moving well away from them. She made a sudden and totally irrational decision. Firstly, she didn't alert them to the departing car, then she acted as if he was at home, hoping to delay them.

"I saw him just a few hours ago – he should still be here."

All the would-be captors crowded around Tumma's front door as Saija rang the bell. No answer. She rang again. Still no answer.

"Yesterday I had to ring several times. He was still asleep." She tried to sound casual, then rang the bell a third time. The Major decided it was enough.

"Sergeant, let's get in there – NOW!"

Backing up a little the Sergeant kicked the door in with a well-practiced boot aimed exactly at the position of the lock.

Complete silence greeted the intruders.

"He's gone."

All reason escaped out the back door of Saija's mind. She knew it was foolish to try and help him, but she couldn't stop herself. She even managed to trip over in front of the Sergeant as he came rushing out of Tumma's bedroom, tripping him in the process. Every little delay might help Tumma.

The Major realized the car they saw moving away from the apartment must have been that of their man.

"Did you recognize the car?" He shouted at her.

"NO!" Saija was pleased to be able to answer back truthfully – at least part truthfully.

By then they couldn't see Tumma's vehicle, but as they came to the next intersection it was spotted speeding down the road to the left, towards the park entrance. It only took a minute to almost catch up to it. The pursuers all jumped out of the car before it had fully stopped and went running after Tumma, with Saija following in the rear. There was nothing she could do now to help him. She had tried everything; everything she dared. Then suddenly they all stopped. There was Tumma, about a hundred meters ahead, walking up into the air, unsupported.

It can't be! Saija's mind screamed. Even as she denied herself the reality of what she was looking at her arm lifted automatically into the air and moved in response to Tumma waving at the group - at her. Fortunately, she was at the back of the spectators. They were too focused on Tumma disappearing into a hole in the air to notice what she was doing anyway.

They didn't see her broad smile and the blush on her cheek as she waved back to the man. Saija knew instinctively she'd witnessed something she wasn't supposed to. Undoubtedly they would try to censor her in some way. She didn't care. The only thing she could think about at that moment was that Tumma got away. It was only later, the following day, after the authorities had gagged her to silence on pain of being charged with treason, that she even dared to contemplate where he could possibly have gone. *Will I ever see him again? Do I want to see him again?* It all become too complicated and confusing much too fast.

*

Inevitably Saija recalled a previous liaison, from a time before she began her training.

He was a bit odd also. Perhaps she just liked people who were not ordinary. Saija could never quite work out why she was attracted to a man who claimed to have been abducted by extra-terrestrial visitors. She wasn't at all convinced about Uneksija's story, but she gave him the benefit of the doubt at the time.

Uneksija wasn't just strange because of his story. She recalled that this young man almost floated above the ground, so out of touch he seemed with everyday reality.

"I just want to explore the stars – I don't care about anything else," he had said to her one day.

"Would you take me with you?"

His enthusiasm infected her with a desire to know more about reality, more than what she experienced on her little planet in her everyday life of routine. Perhaps it was inevitable Uneksija should die young as a result of a most bizarre accident. Saija was at the hospital at the time, in her final year of study, when news of his death reached her.

It even appeared in the Pohjolan Sanomat, a broadsheet newspaper published in Kemi.

The Polis records indicated that several witnesses traveling in the train claimed to have seen a young man climb up onto the handrail at the Finnish end of the bridge across the Torne river in Tornio. That in itself wasn't so unusual because the area was restricted for safety reasons. Credibility of the witnesses was seriously questioned, even though several of them from different carriages said they saw the same event. One passenger in particular had a good recall of the incident.

"I swear to you – this guy stood on the handrail and reached out into the air, as if he was trying to hold onto something. But I saw nothing there! You're not going to believe this! He then stepped off the handrail and began walking up what would have been an upward sloping surface, like a ramp … as if it *was* actually there. But I'm telling you – It wasn't there!"

His friend corroborated, adding, "No one saw anything other than the man virtually suspended in the air. He'd let go of the imaginary handrail with both hands. His feet must have been at least five meters above the water. He just floated in mid-air!"

Understandably the Polis and the press were more than dubious by that aspect of the corroborated story. What happened next would be totally understandable, if someone was trying to commit suicide by jumping off the handrail into the water. Everyone saw the man advance a little further into the air, before suddenly falling as if whatever he was walking on had stopped supporting him.

When the Polis eventually recovered the body, they also found its exact entry point into the water. A piece of the man's shirt had caught on an overhanging branch. He didn't drown. He died from a severe trauma to the head when it hit a rock near the water's edge. Again nothing extraordinary - except the rock was so far away from the handrail of the bridge that it would not have been possible for a human being to jump so far out.

Saija tried to tell her friends what really happened. "As far as the Polis were concerned, it was a simple suicide. They didn't believe any of the witnesses, but they were right."

"Didn't you say he was a bit of a nutter?" One of her friends reminded her.

"No, not really. Sure, Uneksija was unusual in many ways, perhaps even a little unbalanced mentally. But he was certainly not suicidal. There was too much he wanted to discover, too much of the universe he wanted to see."

When Uneksija first told her about his special experience, she thought he was just having a joke with her. But he seemed so earnest and so genuinely excited. It was obvious that at the very least he did have some kind of exciting and extraordinary experience. Then, as he unfolded the story with all the incredible detail, all she could do was to file it away in her mind. If anything the whole episode drew her closer to him. It excited her imagination and her innate sense of adventure.

While reading the details of the accident in the newspaper she recalled everything Uneksija had said to her. Reluctantly Saija could come to only one conclusion; which she didn't like at all. Perhaps her own mind was partly off its hinges. She learnt enough about mental disorders by then to know that to be a distinct possibility. She came to the firm belief that her boyfriend had somehow managed to make contact with his extra-terrestrial friends again, who at the last moment must have changed their minds about taking him off the planet. In all likelihood they may not have realized that withdrawing their access ramp would lead to his death.

Polis interviewed Saija several times. The newspaper wanted to know intimate details about their relationship. Her consoling friends wanted to tease out all the entertaining facets of her liaison with such an interesting person. She couldn't tell them about Uneksija's past experiences. She would have been laughed at, ridiculed for being so opportunistic of exploiting the situation for some instant fame. *How could I explain my own conclusions about what had happened to him? I would have become an immediate candidate for some serious Open Dialogue intervention myself, not to mention probably putting an end to my career.*

So Saija said nothing. She completed her training and became highly proficient in Open Dialogue techniques, perhaps aided by her own peculiar experiences. In all probability her capacity to tolerate the uncertainties raised by different clients and her ability to listen non-judgmentally contributed to her success.

Eventually Saija was assigned to the Health House from which she was called out to respond to an urgent situation; to attend to a young man, acting very strangely, who had burst into his work place half dressed, calling out to imaginary people. It sounded vaguely familiar to her. She felt an immediate attraction to Tumma the first time she saw him getting out of the ambulance. She even chided herself for the silly feeling.

Saija had put her past behind her. Her life was again normal – until she met Tumma. Here was somebody definitely enigmatic ...

and handsome, and educated - hopefully not too unusual, but he undoubtedly had a problem.

Aboard Synty

Synty rested, motionless behind Earth's moon waiting to depart

with a treasure not yet loaded. It looked just like a smaller version of the moon, pock marked by meteor strikes, with nothing to betray her as being the cocoon of sentient life of two distantly related species.

The First abduction

What are we going to do with her? Langur asked Tumma. He was still inside the alien's head. The female was a little detail that needed sorting out before they left Vesimaa.

"Who? ... Ah, you mean Saija. Let me go and talk to her, alone. Don't worry, I'll come back - I want this!" Langur didn't doubt his sincerity. He could read every thought, every intention, every deception in him. There was no deception.

You are presently in a special Earth atmosphere enclosure. While in your current alien body you will have to stay in that environment.

"What exactly does that mean? Are you calling *me* an alien?"

There's no easy way to say some things to you, so you will just have to trust me. He felt that trust immediately, as a bunch of Tumma's neurons responded with appropriate fireworks around him.

We may arrange another manifestation for you, compatible with our environment. In the next few days you will be able to go and meet with Saija. Dr.Qilaq tells me she's 'suitable'. So if you wish her to come, or if she wants to come, she is welcome. But it must happen soon. Langur said exactly what was in Tumma's mind, even before he had articulated it to himself.

At first Tumma took no notice of the space he was in. There were too many other things happening around him; especially these extremely strange, tall creatures bustling from place to place. He'd had time to adjust to the way they looked, from his first introductory view of them when Langur took him on a virtual tour. It would take him quite some time to see them as an highly evolved life form. *What a strange evolutionary path they must have followed to arrive at that peculiar dual-planar orientation,* he thought. *It's odd to think of Langur actually being one of them, and not just a voice inside my head.*

Then his thoughts returned to Saija for a while. He hadn't realized the impact she had on him until then. He hadn't considered Lilli from the Café at all. Obviously it must have been no more than a temporary flirtation. Saija on the other hand occupied his thoughts on a much more serious level. He'd been very much alone all his working life. Not that he'd wanted it that way. Circumstances simply corralled him into that lifestyle. Then the accident and all the complications that came with it. But now ... well, now he might be free. Perhaps his life was only just beginning. A great adventure, and he realized he didn't want to go on that journey alone.

Destiny seems to have placed this enigmatic woman in his path. I have to see her again, not as her potential patient, but perhaps a potential partner. There, I've said it - I think I would definitely like to be with Saija. Then he waited for a response. He'd got used to Langur's voice being a part of the conversations he'd been having with himself. But Langur was no longer there. It felt very strange to be 'alone'. Remarkable how quickly he'd become accustomed to the companionship. It gave a whole new meaning to having an 'inner voice'. Tumma almost wished Langur was still with him.

As these thoughts vagabonded around in his mind his eyes roamed around the enclosure, having become accustomed to the dim lighting. It wasn't really so strange. More accurately, it seemed surreal. There are times when the messages received by the brain via the senses just do not correlate with expectations. This was definitely one of those times. The room didn't feel like part of a spaceship capable of crossing the vast expanse of the universe, just a room devoid of all science fiction décor. There was no incomprehensible alien equipment of any kind in sight. For a moment he felt the same fear he had when he woke up several mornings ago and found Langur gone. Was everything that just happened another dream?

No, not a dream. This was … his room … unquestionably! He was standing in front of the sitting room window looking out onto the street. Except there were no vehicles and there were no people out there. Tumma stepped over to his front door and tried to turn the door handle. It would not move.

"Langur? … Langur?" There was no immediate response. Heart beat spike!

"Yes Tumma, I can hear you."

"Where am I?"

"You're aboard our spacecraft."

"What is this room?"

"It is your enclosure. We re-created it for you. It is a long way to where we are going. We wanted to make you feel at home."

Tumma thought for a moment, then tried the light switch on the wall on the left-hand side, where it always was, almost level with the door handle. The full lighting came on. *This is just too weird!*

"When do I get to see Saija?"

"Tomorrow. It isn't a working day for her. I left her a message from you, to meet you at your Café."

"What about Lilli?"

"We have made sure she would not be there."

"What did you do?" Tumma asked, just the slightest bit apprehensive.

"*Nothing bad. We arranged for her to win a - what you call - 'holiday'. She will be away for two weeks.*"

"Nice."

"*Examine your enclosure. Tell me if anything is not satisfactory.*"

Tumma explored his 'apartment'. The furniture was a slightly different colour, but all in the same place as before. Both bedrooms were there and all his own clothes in the cupboard of his room. The other room had all his books and papers and various odd bits of equipment. They brought it all aboard or perhaps recreated it. It was a luxurious apartment from the Finnish point of view. Few had two bedrooms. But he was an important scientist with considerable status.

The narrow, short corridor between the two bedrooms led to a back door. Tumma was undecided whether to open it or not. Surely, they wouldn't have recreated my small backyard. His curiosity won out. Instead of the small garden there was a much bigger surprise. A long, wide, well-lit corridor with images of a Birch tree lined street, floor to ceiling on both side walls. Intermittently between the trees, a door, each door with a name on it. About the fifth or sixth door stopped him dead in his tracks. There on a name plate in clear, small letters – 'Saija Kevat.'

Tumma didn't know her last name, but that was really beside the point. *What do these people know that I don't? Have they already contacted Saija? Has she already made up her mind? Have they drugged her?* He walked on, thinking things well out of the realms of reasonableness. Other avenues led off the main one, also with many doors and names. Some of those names were not Finnish. It still didn't feel like a spaceship, or look like the one he saw on the virtual tour. Turning back to his own rooms he wondered what these Beings really had in mind. *Mass abductions?*

Inevitably, the day's activities and excitement caught up with him. His bed looked awfully good. Just before falling asleep, he thought the most ordinary thing, as minds tend to do when under extreme stress ... *so nice to have new clean sheets.*

Immediately on waking Tumma first thought of his rendezvous with Saija. The sky could be falling, but important things must come first - coffee. Without even thinking, he went to his kitchenette, reached into the cupboard, up to the usual place, for his jar of coffee. It was there. Every detail had been reproduced perfectly. Water even flowed from the tap. Tumma didn't think about any of that until he was dressed and had automatically gone to open his front door, finding it locked. His mind had still not fully processed the fact he was on a spacecraft about to go out into the greater universe with some very strange creatures.

"Langur?"

"Langur?"

"Good morning Tumma." It wasn't Langur's voice. "I'm Dr.Qilaq. I think you remember me. Langur is busy. How can I can help?" Suddenly Tumma didn't feel so comfortable. He'd not spoken with Dr.Qilaq before.

"Are you in my head?"

"No. There are sensors in your enclosure. We can always see and hear you. How can I help you?"

"I have to meet Saija today."

"Yes I know. I suggested to Langur it was a good idea. Go out your back door, and follow the wide corridor to the end. Go through the door there. The shuttle is waiting for you."

Tumma found the shuttle, and the small cubicle inside it with the Earth atmosphere. Within three hours they were back in the same park, but in another section. He had to walk for fifteen minutes before reaching the park entrance to a waiting taxi.

They are well organized! He wasn't surprised.

Another ten minutes later he walked into the Café. At eleven thirty people were already filling up the place. It was cold, but still pleasant outside, and the sun was out. So he found a table with two chairs near the entrance. He needed privacy. If she came he wanted to be sure not to miss her.

The appointed time came and went. Ten minutes, fifteen minutes, twenty minutes and he still sat there by himself.

She won't come. Why should she? There is nothing between us. We haven't even had a decent conversation other than those mad hours in my apartment.

Tumma just sat there, head bent, trying to think logically about an impossible situation. *I've completely misread her.* Tumma started sliding down a snow covered, damp disappointment slope when he looked up for no particular reason.

There she stood, smiling at him. He couldn't think of a single thing to say. Saija chose to say nothing. He sat there and she stood there, on the opposite side of the table. His eyes found her eyes. Saija was asking him the question he was most afraid to answer. Words would not find their way to his lips, but his eyes didn't betray him. Saija's smile widened, spreading to embrace him. Tumma was standing now. His body was moving towards her, trying to catch up with his emotions.

"Are you coming with ..." he'd just started to ask when she cut in,

"Yes."

Saija had arrived at the Café early, her emotions fighting with her good sense. Tumma wasn't there yet. She walked up and down the pavement for a few minutes, wrestling with her thoughts.

This is crazy. What am I doing? He's ... he's ... disappeared into thin air for heaven's sake! I don't even know him. A delusional total stranger!

Her internal argument still squirmed when he arrived. She had moved across to the other side of the street from where she could clearly see him. She watched him arrive and hesitated going over. She saw Tumma expectantly looking around and watching every arrival. Saija let the minutes pass without realizing she was already quarter of an hour late. She watched as his face changed and his head slowly bent towards the ground. Saija made her decision at that instant, and within moments found herself standing beside his table looking down at him. She saw a head with a mass of luxurious hair. *Sixty-five years old? ... Not possible!* Then he was looking at her. There was only one question she wanted to hear.

It seemed like a long time before she heard herself say yes, and get into a taxi with him. They didn't embrace, or share a kiss or even hold hands. Each sat on their side of the back seat. Their hands touching lightly, and their eyes exploring each other deeply.

Ten minutes of eternity later they stood on the wet grass at the park entrance, with the taxi already gone.

"We can never return," he said.

"Yes, I know," Saija's reply was quiet and confident.

The taxi left and the two aliens walked, hand in hand to the distant copse of trees.

In the shuttle, while watching the Earth recede, Tumma asked, "Why?"

"Why am I coming? Or why I am with you?"

To Tumma there was no distinction between the two. But now that she had expressed it that way, it made sense.

"Why are you with me?"

"Because I belong with you, and I have to do whatever you're doing."

They were still hand-in-hand when Tumma lead her off the shuttle and into the wide corridor. First he showed her his door, and his apartment. Saija had to do a double take. Didn't she just watch the Earth disappear from under her feet? Didn't she just board an alien spacecraft parked beside their Moon? Then Tumma took her back down the corridor to the door with her name on it. Saija just looked from the door to him and back at the door, uncomprehending.

"Well, aren't you going in?"

Afraid to open the door, not daring to think what to expect she put her hand on the handle and hesitated. Turning the handle felt like the ultimate gesture of leaving her past life behind. *I've made my choice!*

Tumma watched her back straighten a little, noticed the slight clenching of her jaws and color come to her cheeks as she turned the handle. In those few seconds he knew her, he knew her as he knew himself. Saija stepped into the room without any further hesitation, stunned as she looked around. "Unbelievable! This is my home. This is exactly like my home! How could they do this?" After a moment's reflection Saija said, "Come in … come in," with a slight pause and change of inflection between the two invitations.

As soon as she said it the second time she realized that the invitation wasn't for him to come into her home, it was her unreserved invitation for Tumma to come into her life. Again the blush rose in her cheeks. In the times ahead Tumma came to love that warm flush on her face.

Saija walked briskly over to her kitchenette. There was a jar on the top shelf of the cabinet, in the right-hand corner. She lifted it down and opened the cork lid. The money was there, to the very last euro.

"How did they do it? Where are we?" She had to ask. Tumma just raised his eyebrows.

Saija jumped suddenly from the sound of an unexpected voice in her sitting room.

"Please take a little while to acquaint yourselves with your enclosures before we invite you to a meeting." Dr.Qilaq used his most polite voice wanting not to alarm his new guests. To Tumma's great surprise Saija remained composed after the initial reaction.

"Your place or mine," he asked.

"This will do. I know where everything is. Coffee?"

Even the coffee was there, exactly the same light roast she liked, exactly where she liked to keep it. A little tentative now that the exhilaration of the departure had waned, they settled on opposite ends of Saija's three-seater couch. Although the foundations of their relationship had already been established, they still had to follow at least a semblance of getting to know each another in a more traditional, on a more personal level.

"I need truth, absolute honesty." This wasn't a request from Saija. She stated it as an essential prerequisite for a relationship the two of them could build on.

"Truth and reality have been my life long search." Tumma answered matter-of-factly.

"Just how long has your life long search been?"

Not that it worried her particularly, but she didn't like unnecessary mysteries. Tumma knew instantly what Saija was getting at. So instead of stating the duration of his professional life he gave what she wanted.

"Sixty-seven."

He paused. Other than a slight raising of her eyebrows Saija remained silent, so Tumma went on to the heart of the issue.

"Langur says my problem can be fixed. The chronological age isn't the problem. My body's refusal to accept that reality is the issue. It seems that physically I'm not ageing."

With the last statement he expected something confrontational to come from Saija. It would have been natural from any normal person faced with such an incomprehensible revelation. Instead she asked with a cheeky grin,

"Can I have some of what you're having?"

Whether it was her past training or just her sense of humor, the question broke the tension between them. Somehow, in the process of smiling and laughing the couch seemed to shrink and they found themselves sitting much closer to each other. Tumma visibly relaxed, relieved to be able to explore the subject with her.

"They seem to know how it happened to me, and claim they can do something about it. So ... you're not serious ... Are you?"

"We have only two choices. Either you start ageing right now, or I stop at thirty-two."

Perhaps it was fortuitous that Dr.Qilaq's voice interrupted them again. "Please go to the enclosure marked 'Conference".

It was situated at the center of the main avenue, quite a large area with a three-hundred-person capacity. Chairs and tables were laid out in an informal pattern. One of the walls displayed an incredibly unusual scene of intense darkness broken by a meandering river, reflective like the surface of shiny metal. Tumma could have sworn it was a river of mercury because of the meniscus, but he knew it was impossible for such a river to exist. As the two of them approached the scene, part of it folded open and two individuals stepped through from the other side. They both had a peculiar attachment to their vertical components, which must have been breathing apparatus.

"Please have a seat. This will take a while. Hello Saija. I'm Langur and this is my friend, Dr.Qilaq. He's a psychologist. As I said to Tumma previously, there's no easy way to get to know one another. So we will start at the beginning. What you're about to see is real. We have an advanced technology well ahead of yours, with which we are able to look into the past. It would be too complicated to explain the technical details. Instead we will show you our evolutionary history."

"Thank you for my … apartment." Saija managed to say before the wall changed again to reveal a mostly orange planet in great turmoil, with many little green land masses. Great swirling white clouds parted as meteors suicided onto its surface regularly. One such strike was greater than all the others. Saija watched fascinated as the planet shuddered under the impact moments before an incredible explosion hurtled great masses of it into space.

"What is that place?" Saija asked.

"I think it is Earth, from the past." Tumma said. The view moved quickly away from the shuddering planet, past its moon and followed the chaos out of the yellow sun system.

Langur added quietly, "It is the planet on which our evolution began."

Saija moved her chair closer to Tumma and hooked her arm into his, totally absorbed in the drama. She didn't seem to have registered Langur's comment. He deliberately showed them images of the other planets of their sun, which, although in the early stages of their development were nevertheless recognizable to them. The perspective moved above the plane of the Milky Way. Their view followed the progress of the debris as if it was carried on the back of an astronomical tsunami, with myriad shafts of light following in its wake. They witnessed another explosion with brilliant flashes of multicolored light causing their eyes to snap shut involuntarily. When they looked again the debris was all but gone through something that looked like torn black velvet cloth, with streams of light continuing to push their way through it.

"We are now coming to our world," commented Dr.Qilaq, leaving them to piece the story together so far for themselves. But they saw nothing when the view passed through the rift. Dr.Qilaq had to point out the area of the image where his planet was located, a deep, deep red/black disc all but invisible to the aliens. They watched as gravity pulled large amounts of the debris onto the planet. Supereons later the planet surface changed and they saw faint images of the remains of strange creatures emerge. Surprisingly they appeared not unlike the very early ancestors of the living organisms which eventually gave rise to homo sapiens on Earth.

"This is about your evolution, right?" Tumma asked as he and Saija looked at each other, both realizing at the same time what story was unfolding. Langur, ever alert to his guests stopped the show.

"Yes it is, and you are probably no less surprised than we were until very recently. The evidence is undeniable. We share a common origin. Earth was once our home too. Organisms which contained the original DNA blueprint foundation of our species were transported to this planet where those organisms continued to evolve." There was nothing the two could say, other than gaze in bewilderment at Langur standing in front of the wall.

"Why have you come back to the Earth?" Tumma asked first, followed immediately by Saija,

"Why do you need us? What do you want from us?"

"I have already told you Tumma; you can help us. We have a problem very similar to your personal one. We can help you but unfortunately we cannot help ourselves the same way."

Langur moved aside and the wall animated again with new images. A very large, strange looking city with odd shaped buildings and even more oddly shaped entrances occupied all of the walls. Chaos and destruction seemed to be the only motivation of its citizenry. City after city showed the same upheaval. It seemed even worse to Langur and Dr.Qilaq than when they left. Some order was restored here and there but the unrest and destruction had spread.

"Is it always like this on your world?" Tumma questioned, appearing to take the whole incredible scenario in his stride.

It may have been his scientific background enabling him to observe with some degree of detachment. Not so with Saija. She had pressed up close to Tumma unable to force her mind into meaningful channels of comprehension, suffering from an overload of impossibilities.

"No, not always. It's been getting worse in the recent past, in the last few thousand years ... because of a debilitating condition that has developed in our people - mass depression. It has become so widespread that the only release they can find for it now is through violence. But there is a solution, and it is with that solution we need your help. Well, not just yours personally, but your species in general; not all of your people, just a good sampling of specimens." Langur realized the choice of his last few words wasn't entirely diplomatic. Perhaps he should not have referred to them collectively as specimens.

The conversation had taken a turn with which even Tumma was having difficulty. His mind started to go blank. He and Saija had become uncommunicative. Langur realized they'd probably been pushed a little too far, too soon.

"Please go back to your enclosures and have a rest." Langur suggested before turning to leave.

"Before you go …," Tumma interrupted his departure.

Although Tumma and Saija had open minds they found it almost impossible to relate to many of the things they were learning. It needed an extraordinary stretch of the imagination to even begin to think of Langur and Dr.Qilaq as 'distant cousins'.

"Being told to go to our enclosures makes me feel like I'm some kind of trained pet animal." Saija seemed quite upset as she made the point to Tumma … and he to Langur. For he also felt strange about that, adding quite forcefully,

"Nor do we take kindly to our people being referred to as specimens."

Langur acknowledged the communication without responding, and left anyway.

The First Harvest

On the way to their rooms Saija expressed her feelings openly.

"Perhaps I'm being a little too sensitive, but how are we supposed to cope with traveling into the cosmos with extraterrestrials who want to use us for experiments. What do you think they want to do to us?" A straight forward simple question which Tumma felt to be a little too direct, too close to the mark.

In spite of all the excitement of the escape, the romantic rendezvous and the momentous revelations, both slept well in their own familiar surroundings. Saija woke first and went over to Tumma's place. The door opened before Saija had a chance to knock, for Tumma was just on his way out to see her. The immediacy of the moment overcame previous inhibitions. The two locked into an intimate embrace right there at Tumma's back door. Eventually they released each other, making their way back to Tumma's sitting room. Needing some distraction, Saija prepared the coffee while Tumma just watched and smiled. She smiled also; a wide, very personal smile, just for him. He never saw her use that smile for anyone else.

"What did you mean?" Tumma asked when Saija asked about the extraterrestrial's intentions again.

"Do you think they want to dissect us, study our brains and perhaps feed us to their pets?" She asked half seriously, now sitting close beside Tumma.

"I've been with Langur long enough, that is to say he's been in my head long enough I think, to know that's probably not their method of operation."

A knocking at the back door broke their flow of thought. Tumma jumped up to open it when he heard Dr.Qilaq's voice.

"Pardon for interrupting. I'm not at your portal. I just wanted to get your attention. Could you both please go to the Conference enclosure again. Tumma, we need to discuss your cure process."

"Well at least they're polite." Saija quipped.

Tumma tried setting some base line protocols. "Before we go any further, we have a simple request. Please refer to the enclosures as 'rooms', the portals as 'doors' and the other members of our race as 'people'. We feel there's a demeaning connotation in the words you use."

Tumma tried to sound authoritative without being demanding. Dr.Qilaq didn't respond to the request, putting Tumma and Saija into a particularly unreceptive mood.

"Tumma," began Langur at the conference center, "We can start to reinstate your shadow today. It will take many days. It will be necessary for you to retain your current physiological age - Not permanently, but perhaps for a considerable time. Saija, you have a choice. We can delay your ageing if you wish and synchronize you with Tumma later. If you do not choose this, the difference in your biological manifestations will become more obvious as time passes. I should warn you that much time, as you think of it, will pass during this project. Although our plans are on schedule we cannot be complacent and will have to imminently start finding suitable specim ... people to join us. Do you need time to decide which alternative would suit you better Saija?

Langur correcting himself didn't go unnoticed. The decision was easy for Saija. She didn't want Tumma watching her grow old while he remained unchanged. Neither of them should have that disturbing experience.

The two responses came almost immediately and in unison. "Yes," and "Yes."

Dr.Tulok, in charge of the procedures for the two aliens, had re-created Tumma's equipment which had caused his cellular changes and set it up in a room adjacent to Saija's bedroom. The Doctor decided it was best to re-enact Tumma's accident, using Saija as the recipient of the modified EMR, theorizing that the same effect would ensue. The two of them could then go through the re-shadowing process together. Dr.Qilaq arranged for the 'accident' to happen without Saija's knowledge, and to inform her of the result afterwards.

Before the meeting ended Dr.Tulok, Eili and Captain Valokvantti introduced themselves from the other side of the screen. Tulok explained the re-shadowing procedure; involving the drying out of the intercellular fluid so the body's cells could resume their normally packed configurations.

Eili introduced himself and spoke up with unusual excitement. "I'm known as a Temporal because I have a limited life span not unlike the inhabitants of Vesimaa, sorry – your Earth. It is considered to be an unfortunate condition by the Immortals.

"Until now ..." Langur very quickly prevented him from continuing. The aliens still had not been informed of the critical aspects of the project that they were going to be forcibly encouraged to participate in. He steered the discussion in another direction.

"Perhaps it is time for you to know a little more about us. Amongst our people there are two essentially different conditions. The Temporals have had their life spans severely curtailed by a variety of causes. The rest of us, who have the potential for an unlimited life span, are suffering the consequences of that longevity in the form of extreme personal and racial depression."

"What exactly do you mean by 'unlimited' life span. Is it in any way related to my condition?" Tumma asked. Saija became extremely alert at this point in the discussion.

"Unless some form of physical intervention occurs to our wellbeing we have the potential to live almost indefinitely. As it happens, on our world such disruptions are not uncommon."

Saija turned to Eili. "So how long do you expect to live Mr. Eili?"

"Please, just call me Eili. About three hundred years. It is one of the shorter life spans for a Temporal." Tumma and Saija glanced at each other not really knowing where to go from there. It was all getting stranger and stranger by the minute. Three hundred years almost equated to immortality from the human perspective.

Captain Valokvantti couldn't contain himself any longer. All this tiptoeing around the critical issue wound him up into his usual gruff, short tempered self.

"You have to understand that our species is going to become extinct unless we become like your people Tumma; unless we become mortal with a much shorter, definable life span."

"Captain, perhaps we should give our – guests – a little time to …" Langur suggested.

"NO. We don't need any more time for anything!" Cut in Tumma. "Langur, if we are going to help you – willingly that is – we need to know exactly what your plan is. Otherwise this whole thing could become most unpleasant. No doubt we would be more useful to you as willing participants, then as – shall we say, uncooperative specimens." Saija squeezed his arm. Exactly what she was thinking.

She knew she could trust her instincts about this man. He may not have a shadow, but he certainly had a backbone.

Langur turned away from them to confer with his small group. They arrived at a consensus very quickly. He said to Tumma and Saija, "I see it is time to be candid. We have to re-engineer our DNA, using a natural process, to change the way our telomeres function. As our two species are so closely related, we think our respective DNAs will be compatible and we will be able to achieve mortality as a result, and consequently stop the extinction of our species. But that isn't the end of the problem."

Langur had come this far and could see no reason not to lay it all out. "We also have to move our entire population to a more benign planet, where circumstances would not continue working against our chances of long-term survival as a modified species." He paused for a moment, partly to let them assimilate what he'd just said and partly to steel himself against the next statement he had to make. "In short, we have to colonize another planet. Here again we need the help of our related species. Captain Valokvantti has already found a couple of possibly suitable locations. They are known to your scientists as well as ours."

"For a moment there I thought you were going to say Earth was that planet. We have to go and talk about this." Tumma had heard enough for alarm bells to start clamoring. On the way back to their area, neither spoke for a few minutes. "Can you believe any of this?" Tumma asked Saija.

"Why not. We are in space, parked beside the Moon, talking to aliens from another part of the universe who say they are related to us, wanting to breed with us perhaps – and maybe even live with us. What is there not to believe? Come to my place," she added with her special smile.

As they walked into her sitting room, she turned the lights on, and there was a momentary bright blue flash. Neither of them took much notice, there were too many strange things happening to occupy their attention. She made them a mug of coffee, and they settled on her couch.

"Good. Excellent. It worked exactly as I thought," commented Tulok. Saija's couch had been implanted with sensors to detect any changes to her cellular structure. It now matched Tumma's exactly. Not only had she become immortal, but also lost her shadow. The process was as quick and as painless as it had been for Tumma. All that remained was for Saija to be told about it.

"So what are we going to do?" She asked Tumma, completely oblivious of what had just happened to her.

"First we finish the discussion, then the coffee, then we're going to warm your bed," Tumma suggested. He needed to do something familiar, something comforting to settle their tumultuous thoughts. There came that special smile again as Saija stood and pulled him to his feet. "Why delay the inevitable?" She led Tumma to her bedroom, feeling no less concerned but not yet ready to voice those misgivings.

Langur wasn't at all sure if they should be watching what was about to happen. Surveillance of the two aliens had been continuous since their embarkation.

*

Valokvantti turned away from the monitor. "From what they're doing it seems obvious to me they didn't comprehend a single thing you said. If we cannot work cooperatively with them, we'll just have to use them as we see fit. It will make no difference to the final outcome. As you said, we don't have the luxury of unlimited time to put the rest of the plan into operation. We've already harvested a thousand of them without any difficulty."

"And you had no opposition at all?" Langur asked.

"Only minor. It seems their greed outweighs their fear. We promised them a new life, adventure, wealth – they all responded well to that."

"Do you intend to keep those promises?"

"That is immaterial. They're already on board."

Langur became a little alarmed at the change in the Captain's mood. He didn't want reports to go back to The Jarl indicating this species was hostile in any way or that they were going to try to oppose their project. "Eili, what is your opinion?"

Since the introductions and explanations Eili had watched the two aliens intently. He had already proved his expertise in being able to detect 'unsuitable' personnel at Temporality Nexus. Perhaps his skill would extend to assessing their distant cousins. He didn't respond immediately. The fact he'd been thinking along the same lines as Valokvantti added bias to his opinion, which he didn't want to reveal or emphasize.

"As much as we may or may not be related to these - let's face it, mostly primitive beings - our primary responsibility is to our own people."

Valokvantti felt vindicated by the position Eili took, which showed clearly in his body language. When he drew himself up to full height, he presented a truly formidable force to recon with; as one would expect of a person in his dual positions of responsibility. Eili noted the change in the Captain's posture and continued.

"Assuming our strategy of DNA cross-fertilization is going to work a hybrid organism is going to emerge over a number of generations, which is going to consider itself 'independent' of its dual ancestry ... that's both us and these aliens. We have to ensure their loyalty *us*. We will not get that if the new scions feel their parents have been – let's say for the sake of discussion - badly treated. In the short term it may well be more expedient, for experimental purposes, to treat the Vesimiaans as specimens and use them without their co-operation. That could be very easily achieved. Their mental faculty is obviously highly susceptible to manipulation. However, that strategy may not serve us well in the long term."

"Dr.Tulok, any thoughts?" Langur asked.

Tulok had listened patiently, ready now to contribute. He'd already considered the situation of three Peoples trying to co-exist in harmony. "We may end up with three planets with three different civilizations, at least for a time. Not everyone on Dokkheim is going to want to migrate, nor will everyone on Earth want to come with us. They may prove to be much more reticent than our people. After all, they seem quite content to fight one another and completely unconcerned about exhausting their non-renewable resources. The inevitability of their own extinction does not seem to concern them at all. Doubtless with time they will need to secure their own future off Vesimaa once they have completely depleted her. I think our most prudent course of action is to always seek co-operation between the three potential civilizations. That starts here and now, with these specimens… people."

The good sense demonstrated by both Dr.Tulok and Eili was obvious, now that it came out in open discussion. Valokvantti just nodded in his rather terse manner and went off somewhere to carry on with his duties. More to himself than the others he mumbled, "We must harvest many more specimens." Langur heard that but chose not to react.

"Eili, would you take on the role of Vesimiaan Liaison?" As far as Captain Valokvantti was concerned Langur had no doubt he would make an important contribution in the future. For one thing, should anything happen to their Jarl, Valokvantti would be the successor - probably.

While their two guests became more intimately acquainted Eili went through a minor transformation. Tulok's team had fashioned a clone slave facsimile body whilst in transit from Dokkheim, partly resembling their own vertical component and partly the Vesimiaan body type. It was a bi-ped, a little taller than the Vesimiaans, could breathe their atmosphere and with visual sensors fashioned along the lines of the Vesimiaans' eyes. All that remained was for Tulok to 'concentrate' Eili's essence and load it up into the clone's CPU, situated in its quasi-cranial area.

Eili waited at Saija's door to greet them when their rest period ended, knocking after they had completed their customary energy intake ritual.

"Coming" came Saija's happy voice. She showed only mild surprise at seeing the clone body, for she remembered the guards at the boarding of the shuttle. "Yes?"

"I'm Eili."

"You don't look like the Eili we saw before."

"May I come in?"

"Tumma, it's Eili," she called back into the room. After a courteous greeting Eili explained about his bionic carrier, which was developed so he could interact with them more directly. Tumma only took superficial notice of the transformation because of the many other thoughts claiming his attention.

"I will be the main liaison for you, between your species and the rest of us. But first, today we start the procedures for both of you. Langur didn't want to tell you this just yet Saija, but I think you should know. You have already been 'treated', just like Tumma was, to make your telomeres robust."

"You mean, the ageing suppression?"

"Yes. So now you don't generate a shadow either. The process to give back your shadows can start for both of you. There will be many treatments. All painless, and it must be done gradually as we are attempting to re-arrange the configuration of every cell in your bodies."

"When did you – zap – me?"

"It was the flash you saw when you arrived back in your enclosu ... sorry apartment. Today, after your first treatment you will confer with the first group of your people who have come aboard. They will meet with you before seeing anyone else. Tell them what you wish. Anybody who doesn't want to come will be returned home. I would like to add that it is important for them to know that their primary function is procreation; interbreeding with us."

Tumma and Saija were taken aback. Not that they didn't guess at that reality from all they'd been told, but they somehow thought it would all be very scientific; a test-tube sort of process.

"So exactly how is it going to happen?" Saija wanted to know the mechanics of the procedure."

"I am personally not aware of the details other than that DNA samples will be taken and tested, then a voluntary program of fertilization will begin. Our own volunteers are already aboard. The entire operation must begin while on the way back to our planet."

"How are we supposed to tell them all that without having a riot on our hands?" Saija asked.

"Your people have been carefully chosen. We have examined their pre-disposition to extraterrestrial experience. I think you will be surprised by their reactions. Please come with me now for your first treatment."

Walking down the long corridor leading to the laboratory they passed several internal windows, one of which showed a view towards the interior of the ship. Up until then they had no comprehension of the size of the vessel. Even then, seeing the vast space between the center and the 'shell' they were in, failed to give an appreciation of the capacity of the craft. It was like being inside an immense hollow sphere with a very thick crust. They couldn't actually see the center because it shone so brightly, almost like a sun. Arranged in immense terraces around the interior surface of the shell were fields of various crops, and groves of trees, with pastures populated with all manner of grazing animals that appeared like tiny ants in the landscape. Rivers and lakes provided ample fresh water. The entire scene faded into the internal curved distance. One g generated by Synty's slow rotation kept everything in place; ideal for the aliens.

"What is all that about?" Tumma asked Eili.

"As we explained to you, it is going to be a long trip and unlikely any of you will return to your planet once the journey has started. We have created a compatible ecosystem for your peoples' energy resource. It will be their responsibility to develop and maintain it; perhaps for several generations."

The enormity of the enterprise was just starting to scratch the surface of their minds. Further on, which seemed like a flat passage, but in fact was curved like the outer surface of the artificial moon, another window revealed a throng of humans gathered on the other side of the passage.

"Are they our volunteers?"

"Yes. The first of several loads. We expect some will want to return."

"And they actually came willingly?" Saija sounded just a little skeptical.

"Not entirely, but once aboard the shuttles people from each group had the opportunity to return to their homes immediately, following some minor memory adjustments. The second of three choices are to follow after you have both spoken to them. There are several hundred in there at the moment."

"How many in total?" Tumma finally came out of himself to try and get a mental grasp of the scope of what they had got themselves into.

"A thousand. Subsequent missions will harv ... collect ... that is, invite - a few more thousand more if necessary."

"You meant to say harvest, didn't you!" Saija interjected quicker than Eili could apologize. "Do you realize that kind of terminology could very easily alienate every one of us? Not just alienate, but initiate open rebellion! It makes it sound like you consider us to be no better than animals - even less than that!"

"Can I assure you, Saija, it is only our lack of understanding of your language. We are related. It is difficult to absorb such an idea, but we are trying to express respect. However, be warned, there are those among us who would prefer a more scientific, shall we say – a more rigorous approach to the project."

Perhaps Eili didn't mean to sound a warning but it was in his nature to be more conciliatory than the Captain. Neither Tumma nor Saija pursued that line of conversation. Eili continued, "More information has been made available to your people in there. They will be asked to choose soon after your presentation."

The room Tumma and Saija entered for their first treatment looked like most operating theatres on Earth. Perhaps the instrumentation and technology were far superior, yet the environment betrayed its function. At one end of the room two cocoons had been prepared. Once encased inside them, a mask for air attached itself to the immediate area of the nose and mouth, allowing them to breath and absorb a sedative. A purplish jelly like substance flooded each cocoon as they started to slowly rotate. Picking up speed, they spun continuously for ten minutes while both of them were unconscious. As the jelly slowly turned green the mechanism slowed, with Saija and Tumma regaining consciousness. The green jelly drained away leaving them completely dry.

Somewhat disoriented but otherwise feeling no different, they listened to Eili explaining the process. "The purple jelly has the concentration necessary for the intra-cellular fluid that had distended the space between the cells of your bodies, to travel by an osmosis-like process from between your cells, into the purple jelly. The change in color indicated saturation level for the jelly. It would be many such treatments before your bodies again completely 'block' normal light."

Eili took them from there directly to the auditorium with hundreds of humans milling about. A hush came over the crowd. There were no children, only breeding age adults between the ages of twenty and twenty-five. They all looked healthy, alert and eager to hear what the two people on the podium had to say. Some murmured uncertainties about the third strange looking individual standing beside Tumma and Saija. They gathered around the three on the raised platform in front of the wall near the entrance.

"My name is Tumma Varjo, this is my - a slight pause while he looked and smiled at Saija - partner." Turning to the person on his other side he introduced Eili. "Eili is a representative of our hosts for the duration of the journey. Saija and myself are from Finland. The only difference between you and the two of us is that we arrived on board a little before you. Apparently, the only difference between all of us and Eili is – well – evolutionary. It seems we all began at the same place, on Earth." The crowd remained expectantly quiet. All murmurings stopped as hundreds of scrutinizing eyes turned on Eili.

"It is unlikely we know more than you do about this adventure. We will all get more detailed introductions later. For now, I want to emphasize a few important facts. Our region of the universe has not experienced history as we are about to make together." Tumma held a little pause to let the idea sink in. People turned to one another with quiet questions, uncertainties and insignificancies. "Secondly, you have to understand that there is absolutely no guarantee you will ever return to Earth if you decide to continue. Some people, who were initially asked, declined to come on board. They have been returned to their homes. That was choice level One. Today is choice level Two. You have read all the information made available to you. If you have not – Do So – because you will have only one more opportunity after this to decline the adventure of your life!"

"WHY ARE WE GOING?" Someone shouted out from somewhere in the crowd. Others noisily supported the question.

"Briefly, it is to save a relative of the human species from extinction. They originated from the Earth and had evolved on another planet not far from us. Eili is one of those people."

"HOW DO WE KNOW THAT'S TRUE!" It sounded like the same voice. Tumma was feeling relaxed about these questions. They needed to be asked and they had to be answered.

"You will be shown the evidence when you progress to the third choice level. Many of you will have doubts. That is the healthiest state of mind to have. Always doubt, and always question everything. Saija and I have committed ourselves to this enterprise." Saija nodded confirmation as he looked at her, though both kept their reservations unsaid.

"You will now have two hours to make your second choice. The door behind you leads to another area. It is a one-way door. When you go through there, you will have made your Second level choice. Please wait on the other side until your name is indicated. Those of you who make the final decision to continue will be shown your residences while we are in space. Please, READ all the information presented to you, and discuss it amongst yourselves. You can speak with us at any time."

Of course there were more questions, but none of which couldn't be answered if they'd bothered to read the literature presented to them. The three ambassadors left the way they came.

Eili was most impressed with Tumma. "I think we will be able to work very well together," he said to Tumma.

"Only if you always tell us the complete truth," Tumma shot back immediately.

Eili may have been a Dokk, with a very clear understanding of what had to be done to save his species. Some of those actions, if they had to be implemented, may not be in the best interests of Tumma and his people. However, he couldn't help but like this alien. Whatever evidence past history may have shown about their relatedness, it was behavior such as he had just witnessed, from both Tumma and the crowd, that made him feel not so distant from the Vesimiaans.

Tumma found himself in a particularly introspective mood. Outwardly he seemed nothing but confident to the first batch of people. Now, as they headed back to their own apartments, little worrying procedural details started to emerge into his consciousness. His years as a research scientist were beginning to assert themselves. Just how was their genetic compatibility going to be tested? Were there going to be 'experimental' children born of the two races? What will happen to 'unsuccessful' children, those who are deformed or mentally impaired?

Known only to the Dokks, no alien from the first harvest was returned to their homes, the unwilling being 'stored' for future use.

Integrating Dokks and Aliens

Tumma was so immersed in his thoughts he didn't notice Eili steering them towards a small transport bubble. It took them an hour at a substantial speed to arrive at a Dokkheimien habitation zone. They had to stay inside their bubble as the air wasn't suitable for Tumma and Saija. They saw a group of individuals working on something that looked very much like farm equipment. The oddity of that didn't consciously register. Even though Tumma had seen their natural dual-plane form in his 'mind-trip', he still found it difficult to understand how they could manage with such an awkward configuration.

One of the group turned towards them, and called many others to follow him. Eili acted as interpreter. These individuals were volunteer breeding stock, who had only recently learnt the Vesimiaan language.

"Are all you people so small?" It was an odd question to ask. One would have thought them to be more interested in how children were made. "How old are you?" That was more to the point. They were incredulous at the Vesimiaans' youth, making comments which Eili translated as ... "How is it that such young scions are allowed to be part of such an important project?"

Saija commented to Eili, "It's surprising these volunteers are not better informed."

He made a mental note. *It was remiss of Langur not to have initiated a much more comprehensive orientation program. Inevitably the two races of volunteers will have to come into contact with one another. They must both be made suitably ready for that encounter.*

The parting was friendly enough with the universal waving of hands and manipulators that everyone understood. On the way back Eili had a chance to think. Tumma and Saija talked animatedly as they observed the Dokk habitation environments.

Eili withdrew into his own thoughts - *Perhaps the slave clones could be adapted for use by both us and them. It would allow us all to congregate in common areas and interact freely.*

By the time they arrived back at the human habitation zone of the shell, Tumma had again withdrawn into himself, probably catalyzed this time by the meeting with the Dokk volunteers. *They are so totally strange. How could there possibly be any common ground between us?*

"Come to my place," Saija suggested. "We could cook up a nice meal." Tumma didn't object, although his mind was off at a tangent. Saija noticed his distraction.

"Our ailments; immortality and shadow-less-ness seem so insignificant in the context of a whole planet of beings on the verge of extinction."

"Do you mean them or us?" Saija couldn't help herself saying that. She was worried.

*

The first batch of human volunteers lost just a few individuals, with most of them choosing to go through to the third vetting stage. At the same time, a second contingent arrived on board and about to go through the same set of procedures. It was left to the final vetting stage to announce the most critical piece of information; one expected to significantly reduce their numbers - Procreation.

Tumma spoke to the stage three people. "The two races will need to interbred to create hybrid beings, both Dokk and Vesimiaan and yet neither, with view to colonizing another planet." About twenty percent of them immediately decided to return to Earth.

"I'm not surprised. This whole enterprise stretches the boundaries of reality." Leuhta commented.

"They could have at least asked about the methodologies of such a process. They must have been frightened out of their wits."

The others went through to their holding enclosures to prepare their release into the alien habitation zone in the internal shell of Synty, The Great Valley. The two ambassadors were not told what actually became of the dissenting twenty percent.

*

Even as aliens were being harvested on Vesimaa other plans were progressing back on Dokkheim. Yakiv turned out to be as visionary as he was ambitions. By giving his total co-operation to The Jarl and Temporality Nexus the backup plan to terraform Tau Ceti-E advanced satisfactorily. There was no reason why they should not adopt Captain Valokvantti's recommendation, at least as a safeguard. An armada of sophisticated ice barges were built and Bio-Dome constructions initiated, as well as a wide range of other initiatives put into action. The primary plan, Plan A, wasn't openly available for scrutiny. It concerned Vesimaa and what had to be done to make it suitable as the new home for the Dokks. On this issue Yakiv was taken into The Jarl's confidence, but not the rest of Temporality Nexus. They didn't need to know about Plan A – yet.

Langur didn't want to be burdened with the details of getting Tau Ceti-E ready. Of more immediate concern to him was Eili's suggestion to use the modified slave-clones as an intermediary means to facilitate the co-mingling of the two species. Dr.Qilaq expressed his thoughts to Langur and the rest of the project group about that very matter.

"After seeing what they look like and their general psychology I've no doubts the greatest differences between us are our physical appearances. I've been studying the behavior of our first two aliens and the first harvest of breeding specimens. Remarkable as it may seem, their neural patterning shows few deviations from ours, which means their cognitive and emotional landscapes are incredibly similar to ours. There is one odd phenomenon though, which I would like to explore with Tumma."

"So you see no objections to using Eili's suggestion of the upright slave-clone interfacing approach?" Langur asked.

"None from me," interjected Valokvantti, "unless the similarities between us raise the same issues we are having with our own people - like emotional upheavals, riotous behavior, mutiny; just to mention a few."

"Duly noted. Most valid observations." Thank you Captain. Langur made a point of recognizing his contribution. For indeed it was a consideration that had not surfaced during his own deliberations. "Tulok, my friend, how long would it take you to prepare enough slave-clones for our initial two volunteer populations – say at least a hundred?"

The limited alien life spans meant the scientific crew of the ship had to work at an extraordinarily fast pace to make the first part of the plan come to fruition. Within a few months some upright biped Dokk slave-clones were ready to receive Dokk psyches. Concurrently the aliens were introduced to their life support habitation zone in the interior of the planetoid-craft and were able to begin implementing systems in order to sustain their own life energy requirements; which meant building dwellings, setting up farms and so on.

A sampling of the biped slave-clones fully loaded with Dokkheimien personae were soon ready to be tested. In an enclosure designed to suit both species as much as possible, the clones and the aliens were introduced to each other, much as one would make introductions at a large party.

Valokvantti and the other leaders gathered to watch the first interactions. Although these clones had been engineered with a few rudimentary surface characteristics of the aliens, and although they had a good command of the alien languages, the 'party' turned out a complete failure.

"I doubt if we can make this work," commented Dr.Tulok. "The physical differences are still too great to overcome the 'social' barriers. You saw how many of the aliens became openly hostile to the clones."

The fiasco resulted in innumerable questions from the Vesimiaans about the actual procedures involved in the cross breeding process. Inevitably some of them harbored secret sexual fantasies. These were destined to be unfulfilled. Normal alien sexual practices could continue unhindered amongst themselves until pregnancies were to be initiated. The logistics of setting up parental bonding partners was yet to be determined.

"It is obviously too much to ask these aliens to find slender metallic looking slabs with grotesque flat features, attractive." Langur could empathize.

Similarly, the Dokkheimien mentality could not immediately cope with small, floppy, pinkish creatures who looked like they were going to fall over at each step they took. After removing the hostile elements from the sample group; there being as many clones as aliens in that category, the others received further 'orientation' with the hope of eventually establishing a foundation to enable some degree of rapport to develop between them.

Dr.Qilaq, not satisfied with just the one attempt to get the species to mingle, devised two more social opportunities for a few of the individuals in the two test groups. One group of clones was to work cooperatively with the aliens in their 'fields' planting crops, tending their protein animals and helping to construct dwellings. With the exception of a handful of couples, the cultural differences were still too great for the clones to be able to comprehend much of what the aliens were trying to achieve by digging in dirt, or extracting the white animal body fluid for energy intake. The act of killing an animal, stripping it of its skin then burning it before attempting to eat it, sent some of the witnessing clones into catatonic fits. This second experiment proved to be another comprehensive failure.

"Don't beat yourself up over it, Dr.Qilaq. I understand the difficulties our clones are having trying to make friends with these primitive creatures. I also cannot reconcile myself to what I've come to know of Tumma and Saija, and the behaviour of others of their species," Langur said in support of his friend.

Dr.Qilaq, undaunted, had another idea. " ... A competition, like challenges more suited for pairs participation."

This alternative scenario yielded a slightly better result. The engagement rate of both species was about equal. More interestingly, a few individuals had actually 'paired up' driven by their competitive drive to achieve distinction. That behaviour exhibited by the Dokkheimien mentality was a big boost to Langur's diminishing confidence. He had not witnessed such enthusiasm even in the special challenges he had set for his people at Temporality Nexus. *Perhaps these aliens have more to offer than just their pure genetics. The foundations are definitely there to bring our species together, but the physical appearances barrier has to be overcome.*

The clone barrier was too much of a deterrent to both branches of the species. So much attention being given to superficiality by both groups was perhaps just another indicator that their mentalities were not too distant from each another.

Dr.Qilaq, Dr.Tulok and Eili came up with a radical new proposition which Dr.Qilaq presented to Langur and Valokvantti.

"Have you consulted any of our volunteers to find out their willingness to participate in this new plan of yours?"

Valokvantti made no secret of his potential opposition to such an outlandish concept. It meant putting many of his own people at risk just to make life a bit easier for the aliens. He could see no advantage in that. In fact, he could foresee many unnecessary complications.

"I'm more than willing to be the first," Eili responded without any hesitation. "And there are enough others of us Temporals who are also willing to try."

"This means we'll have to return to Vesimaa to collect many more specimens as receptacles for the neural transfers. Would you go along with that Langur?" Langur let others do the talking before responding to the Captain's obvious reluctance. *I don't like this. This new procedure represents the first stage of an highly intrusive coercion.* Yet the most important thing couldn't be ignored because of 'convenience' or friendly regard for the aliens. He had to do whatever was going to best succeed in saving his race. There was no choice and in his response Langur made that quite clear.

"Captain, this is the most obvious course of action in order to achieve our primary goal. This was always going to be a 'fluid' process. I can see that by using some aliens as physical receptacles, and uploading our own peoples' psyches into them is the process most likely to succeed in overcoming the physical disparity problem." The insights Langur and Dr.Qilaq had gained whilst resident in Tumma's neural network clearly showed the efficacy of building on that knowledge.

Dr.Qilaq counselled caution. "It would be counter-productive if a rumor started that 'live' specimens' were to be used as hosts for Dokkheimien volunteers. The aliens will have to be told that only 'bodies' of their people who had recently expired would be used as the carrier shells. I also think it is imperative that our Dokks in the simulacrum bodies have a very prominent physical identifier to set them apart from the aliens, otherwise we will not be able to identify our own people."

Neither Langur or Valokvantti objected and Dr.Qilaq continued with a suggestion. "They should be given a light amber pigmentation to their skin. This visual difference is critical not just for their own psychology, but also to ensure there's no confusion generated in the minds of the aliens. Each new hybrid generation between the aliens and the hybrids should have a deeper amber/red pigmentation."

Always with a mind to practicalities Eili brought up another minor detail. "I take it each subsequent generation will be strictly monitored to ensure that most aspects of the alien contribution are diluted. All this is assuming of course that the desired changes are taking place to the telomeres and the functioning of telomerase."

"Yes, absolutely." Tulok responded emphatically.

"How soon could you have Vesimiaan host bodies and sanitized minds ready?" Langur asked.

"One month. We can start with some that are already in storage, but we'll need many more," Tulok replied.

"We'll turn back immediately," Valokvantti said. Evidently he'd realized the virtue of the new radical approach. He certainly had no qualms about using such a primitive race in any way possible to save their own species, be they related or not.

Langur wasn't as sanguine about the new plan. Initially the seeming lack of respect for other sentient beings troubled his ethics. On the other hand, although the technique was substantially invasive, it offered the aliens as well as his own people a much greater opportunity to live a better life on a better world. He had no doubt the aliens were engineering their own extinction with the accompanying complete desecration of their world. He could see no other outcome for their behaviour as things stood at that moment in their history.

"So what is your opinion?" Eili asked Tumma and Saija. He'd told them about the proposed use of deceased Vesimiaan bodies as neural receptacles for Dokkheimien psyches, but not about 'diluting' the alien genetic contribution to subsequent generations.

"That is bizarre and absolutely appalling!" Saija shouted. "Our volunteers will never accept such a thing! Turning the bodies of our dead into freak zombies! It's very obvious to me you know nothing about us. No one is going to agree to that!"

Tumma's scientific background gave him the clarity with which to assess the proposition more objectively.

"Medically it might work. Have you considered using terminally ill individuals instead? Perhaps that would be more palatable. In either case it has to be crystal clear from the start who is who and there is a very careful introductory protocol."

Saija was much more concerned about the people's reactions to establishing relationships with zombies, as well as the callous disrespect for the bodies of those who are destined to be used for these simulacrums. She would have rebelled at the outset if she'd known the real truth at the outset.

"I will not allow the desecration of our dead! Giving our dying people another chance at life I could accept. Though the whole thing is bizarre!

"As for our people, although the bodies will not be their own, they will retain their selfhood. So the simulacrums will look exactly like someone from Vessi … Earth, but they will be essentially different people. No doubt they will have some difficulty with the concept Saija, just the same as your people even if we use Tumma's suggestion." Eili concluded.

"Hmm." Saija responded guardedly. In her mind she still had great reservations. Something didn't feel right. *Can we trust that they'll only use end-of-lifers?*

The Primary Plan

Harvesting a diverse range of live specimens began as soon as the ship arrived back at Vesimaa. About three thousand people were taken aboard. Many more were harvested than immediately needed, and the excess stored for future use - not necessarily only as future simulacrum shells. Neither Tumma or Saija or the other aliens for that matter were involved in the process. The new alien 'volunteers' were not told their true destiny. They would remain 'intact' whilst in storage, but their minds purged prior to the neural transfers.

The Dokks realised cadavers would not work. Dead flesh devoid of life force could never be reincarnated. Neither did they take up Tumma's suggestion. All their 'enforced' volunteers were live and healthy specimens. It was expected that no part of their own minds would remain after the purging and prior to the uploading of the Dokkheimien psyches. It would be necessary to also reload the alien customs and all general Vesimiaan background knowledge into the neural shells as well as the new Dokk 'minds.'

*

"Your job Yakiv, is to succeed with our Primary Plan. I don't want to know the details. Report back to me when the process is well under way." The Jarl was brief and to the point as always. "Be advised … What you're about to do is not for general knowledge! Am I perfectly clear!"

Yakiv couldn't even tell Leuhta. He would have welcomed her assistance on such a monumental undertaking. Before even beginning the procedure he had to ensure the advance party was well away from Vesimaa and ahead of launching the other armada to Tau Ceti-E (TC-E). They were not to know about the primary plan just yet. He almost felt like a traitor to Langur. The longer he stayed with the project, the more he felt drawn into circumstances making him feel decidedly uncomfortable. There was no logical reason for it. He was after all only contributing to the survival of his species - or so he tried to convince himself.

As soon as The Jarl received the latest report from Valokvantti he'd made up his mind on the best course of action. The TC-E option became Plan B. Very time consuming, expensive, complicated and with a much lower probability of success than the Primary Plan. He could also discern the subtle changes in

177

Valokvantti's reports. His developing bias towards the wellbeing of the aliens didn't impress The Jarl. He'd taken careful note of all the characteristics of these primitive aliens, be they related or not, and their disregard not only for their own lives, but that of the planet which gave them life. In Haakon's opinion they deserved neither a future, nor their planet which they treated with such contempt. *The solution couldn't be simpler; we will adapt our people to live on Vesimaa, remove the existing inhabitants and rehabilitate the planet before migrating there.* The only thing he had to be careful of was to ensure the cooperation of Langur and Valokvantti, so as to minimize any likelihood of a revolt; a distinct possibility if they got caught up in the ethics of genocide.

Jarl Haakon paid Yakiv handsomely to come up with a strategy to achieve Plan A and to make the extinction of the aliens look like a natural, inevitable process. It was really quite simple. They'd already done most of the job. It only needed a little creative input from the Dokks to hasten the inevitable - and it could be achieved within the right timeframe.

Yakiv set up several independent companies, referring to them only as Company A, Company B and Company C, rather than by their functions; for reasons of security.

He briefed Company A with scrupulous clarity:

"Your primary objective is to develop and implement a strategy to take control of the world leaders on Vesimaa in order to influence their political agendas. We must achieve population downsizing conflicts between their nations.

Your second objective is to bring about a higher level of passivity in the populations, making them more susceptible to propaganda. A compliant population was essential. Ensure an exponential increase in the use of fluoride in drinking water. A compliant population is essential."

At an undisclosed location he commanded Company B's responsibilities:

"Increase the levels of male and female infertility. This should ensure planet-wide negative population growth to the point of a species extinction event within five alien generations.

Make it undesirable for them to have children until the females are over 35 Vesimaa years of age, reducing natural conception: Re-invigorate the habit of smoking tobacco, thereby damaging ovaries and interfering with the body's ability to produce their ovulation regulating estrogen: Promote a more sexually promiscuous society with the attendant increase in STDs: Promote obesity as a more desirable body condition. Too much body fat causes production of too much estrogen, and the body reacts as if it was on birth control. Both the smoking and the obesity approaches will work equally well on the male of the species, thus reducing the viability of their sperm. As a fail-safe strategy, introduce a virulent STD pandemic."

This Company was Yakiv's favorite. All the processes involved were so 'natural' that there could be no possible suspicion of manipulation by outside agencies.

Company C had the 'benign' role:

"I want you to rehabilitate Vesimaa's ecology, species diversity, air and water quality.

This will ensure our maximum survivability. Although the planet is habitable immediately, the long-term prospects of any sentient species, or in fact any life form at all, would depend on the success of your efforts. You may begin the process even before the aliens are eliminated."

The Jarl was quite content to fully support all the work being done by Langur to adapt their species to another environment away from their dark universe. It may yet turn out that Tau Ceti-E would be the best option. In the meantime, as they were traveling in its direction, some twelve light years from Vesimaa, there was time enough to progress the species adaptation sufficiently to assess its viability. All the while Vesimaa would be undergoing a 'natural', albeit accelerated change towards the inevitable.

Establishing a transient population on Tau Ceti-E gave The Jarl an opportunity to consider a number of factors associated with the colonization of Vesimaa, not least of which was developing a procedure to pre-select those Dokks who would be suitable as 'colonists'. That couldn't be left up to chance or individuals' preferences. Seeing the latest behaviour of his people it became obvious they couldn't be trusted with their own futures.

Tau Ceti–E, A Temporary Home

An armada of ships left Dokkheim fully equipped with personnel and the technology to establish a long-term colony on Tau Ceti-E. Only a limited number of bio-domes were needed to ensure the 'evolution' of the hybrid species which would eventually colonize Vesimaa. By that stage all critical characteristics of alien DNA would have been expunged from the hybrid species, leaving the best of Dokkheim to step onto a new benign world.

The ice comet barges left some time earlier to drag enough water onto TC-E to start modifying its climate, essentially for creating an atmosphere to protect the planets biosphere. It was also important to give the impression to Langur's expedition that TC-E was indeed the primary destination of their enterprise.

Captain Valokvantti received an update on the progress of the planet's modifications, with the added good news that the luminosity of its sun was only 55% of Vesimaa's yellow orb. From The Jarl's point of view that made the transition of his people much easier. They would not immediately have to cope with the extreme brightness of the yellow orb system or all of the undesirable effects of the full spectrum of visible EMR. Little was known of TC-E apart from it being in the planetary habitable zone. New data from a reconnaissance team showed that the planet was too hot, surface temperature being around 70 degrees centigrade and that its gravity required further DNA modifications to their hybrids – yet life was possible there. An extensive dust cloud ring, which, because it appeared to have no direct impact on planetary weather was considered to be an asset. Once gathered it could be used to build soil layers on some of the more exposed rocky surfaces of the planet, particularly under the proposed bio-domes.

*

Complications always arise when one least expects them. Progress on board Synty was slow, taking considerable time to get the Vesimiaan shells ready. And they had another small issue to deal with. The aliens had already started to form pair bonds with each another; a rather worrying though not altogether unforeseen eventuality. As a precautionary measure Langur decided they would not be allowed to have progeny. He had enough problems to deal with on the craft without also having to co-ordinate his activities with Yakiv. The project had gained considerable momentum and to maintain it required careful co-operation between its contributing participants, including Leuhta. His discussion with Leuhta, still back on Dokkheim, didn't pan out quite as he'd expected.

"So what do you expect me to do now?" Leuhta seemed at a loss regarding her activities now that it was no longer necessary to engineer a fully functional bio-mechanical biped shell. She was still the nominal coordinator of Temporality Nexus in Langur's absence, but felt she was being sidelined. "I agree that the 'simulacrum' approach has considerable merit and I've already postponed all further work on the biped bio-mechanicals. It would've been nice to be included in the decision making rather than be told afterwards. And another thing … What is Yakiv up to? He's become secretive about his progress, spending a great deal of time on something other than our TC-E project. I can't seem to drag any information out of him!"

"Come and join us - here," Langur invited. Stunned silence greeted his invitation.

"Why? So I can feel useless there?"

"I need you with me as a Vesimiaan Simulacrum. We need to represent both our genders to these aliens in order to gain their full cooperation," Langur explained without going into too much detail. "And, what do you think about the light amber color?"

He left her to think about it while he contacted Yakiv. He fully expected to have the usual brief conversation and was surprised at the loquacious reception he received.

"Langur! Good, good – good, good - Good! I should have briefed you sooner! The ice barges are well on the way to TC-E. All equipment, personnel, bio-domes etc. are in transit. We should have a base set up for you when you arrive. It'll take time to work on the habitability of the planet but we'll get that … "

At this point Langur cut in, he'd twigged something extra was going on that Leuhta had eluded to. Yakiv had never been so talkative. Something or someone must have been tweaking his receptors or doping his energy supply. "What are you not telling me Yakiv?" Langur prodded in a confidential tone.

Yakiv immediately realized his mistake of fluffing about instead of getting to the point. He made the same old error of underestimating Langur. He couldn't lie, or at least not completely lie - not to that man.

"I've had some meetings with The Jarl." Yakiv said tentatively.

So, he's had Some meetings with The Jarl - Some meetings. Not many people get to have 'some' meetings with the leader of our world. I had better be a little circumspect. Langur got the ball rolling … "Right, right. You know what we've decided at our end. We believe the Simulacrums are the best way to go. The process is also more efficient in terms of transporting our people. We only need their full psyches beamed to us, without their physical bodies. Are you able to do that en-mass?" Langur then made a quick change of subject to throw Yakiv off guard. "Give me some details about the modifications to TC-E."

Yakiv also realized their historic laconic conversations were a thing of the past. There was a lot of pussy footing going on, and he had to be particularly careful how much he revealed to Langur.

"The Jarl is working on a contingency plan," he said.

"That is wisdom personified," Langur responded candidly.

Silence.

Then Yakiv uncomfortably broke the silence, "Yes, yes … just in case … just in case we need a contingency plan."

The man is blubbering. This must be serious. Langur remained quiet in an attempt to draw more out of him.

"… Just in case the climatisation of the planet does not work … and we may need to colonize another planet."

Ah! So that's it!

Langur didn't feel it was the best time to confront The Jarl about the contingency plan of 'invading' Vesimaa, for he guessed immediately that that was the primary plan. The Jarl had actually dispatched all the necessaries to do what needed to be done on TC-E. The question was, how far would he go with the process. *I have to discuss this with Leuhta.*

"So you think Jarl Haakon has only one plan in mind. Why would he go to all the trouble and expense to set up TC-E? Perhaps you misunderstood." Leuhta wasn't as sensitive about it.

Amber Simulacrums

Three years out from Vesimaa saw many changes on board Synty.

Their craft travelled at near one tenth light speed. Amber Simulacrums were working the fields and tending the animals with the Vesimiaans. There were no hybrid children yet.

Of the three thousand Vesimiaans initially harvested, only one hundred were used as simulacrums to start with, their light amber colored skin attractive to both the Dokks and the aliens. There were a few losses during the neural cleansings and psyche transfers. Vesimiaan individuals with particularly resilient persona required a more rigorous neural scrub resulting in permanent damage to many of their bodies' survival functions. The Dokk scientists entrusted with the neural bleaching carried out their work with precision and indifference to the specimens concerned, which to them were nothing more than receptacles with vital life signatures on the sensors. They certainly looked nothing like thinking, intelligent beings to the scientists. They were after all, only primitive aliens.

An altogether independent team loaded and rebooted the sanitized Vesimiaans into Simulacrums; naming them AmbSims – amber coloured alien bodies with Dokkheimien minds. From the very beginning Valokvantti wanted to ensure no interference with the project, either from his own species' ethical qualms, or from the aliens. On a vessel the size of a small moon it wasn't difficult to establish highly secret locations to house all the experimental laboratories, to which only the leadership and the scientific staff specifically involved in experiments had access, or any knowledge of their existence. Even fewer knew the storage locations for the unused aliens, where those who chose to return to their planet were also deposited.

Langur established independent laboratories aboard the craft to deal with the different aspects of species re-engineering. In the initial stages it all worked well. The AmbSims received their Dokkheimien psyches, were uploaded with Vesimiaan languages and given some historical and cultural data as a foundation to assist in their assimilation with the guests.

"It's taking us too long to integrate our AmbSims with the Vesimiaans," complained Valokvantti. "They've already created a rudimentary social structure even in the short interval since leaving their planet. Do you realize many of them have formed pair bonds?" he said to Langur. "I'm ordering immediate temporary sterilization of all the male aliens. It is not their function to procreate with their own kind!"

"I agree. They are certainly not on a romantic pleasure cruise. But perhaps the sterilization is a bit drastic. I'll speak with Saija, she may be able to help with the assimilation."

"Do that. In any case the sterilization is going ahead."

"I have something to ask of you and to tell you Saija. I've asked Eili to join us."

They met in Saija's place. Tumma also joined them. Langur seemed a little less comfortable than usual. They waited for him to open the conversation.

"It's time to get our respective peoples together, wouldn't you agree?"

"How do you propose to do that? With the 'zombies' you've been working on?" Saija still couldn't reconcile herself to the Dokk's outrageous plan.

"That's not quite correct." Langur remained calm though he could see the storm gathering in Saija's eyes. "We have listened to your concerns. There is an alternative. It is the best solution we have."

Saija waited to hear what other unconscionable idea they'd come up with.

"Instead of using cadavers or terminally ill people we have used healthy individuals. It has been possible to inhabit their minds with the minds of our own people without causing harm to anyone. You can meet some of them soon."

Tumma and Saija exchanged a long look, both dubious about the extent to which they could trust the Dokks. Saija waited for Langur to continue.

'In fact, I would like to ask you to facilitate the introductions and assimilation between the aliens and the AmbSims – that's what we've called our volunteers."

"Do I have a choice?"

"Of course you do. But you know your people better than we do. You and Tumma are a key element in the entire enterprise. It is only with your help we have the best chance of success."

*

Between them Tumma and Saija realised this gave them the only option to have some degree of control over the extraordinary circumstances they found themselves in. Saija became the primary liaison between the Dokks and Vesimiaans; between the AmbSims and Vesimiaans, taking over from Eili.

She arranged for small groups of AmbSims and her own people to come together at intervals. To the aliens these Simulacrums were not at all unpleasant to look at; their light amber coloring almost like an early summer suntan. They spoke the same language and they looked human like themselves. So apart from being told these were not the true physical forms of their Dokk hosts there was nothing to be uncomfortable about. Friendships soon developed and both species were to be seen working the fields and participating in a communal life. Langur made a special effort to better prepare his people for the culture shock of Vesimiaan life, resulting in fewer dissidents in spite of having to kill animals for food consumption.

Unfortunately for Saija the position also carried with it the burden of having to listen to all the inevitable complaints that arose.

"We've been on board this vessel now for over three years and we haven't been able to have any children," complained one of the Vesimiaan women to Saija. "And the AmbSims amongst us behave as if they've been told to break up our partnerships. What is going on? It's not just me and my human partner, but many others are having the same problems!"

Saija could only listen. She had no answers. But she could sympathize with the apparent bareness of her people. She'd also wondered why she had not become pregnant. For three years she and Tumma had been living together. She knew she could bear children and Tumma wasn't impotent. In the absence of Dr.Qilaq, Langur, Eili and even her new 'friend' Leuhta, who had all returned to visit The Jarl on Dokkheim, she had to deal directly with Captain Valokvantti.

"Have you done something to prevent us from having children?" Saija confronted Valokvantti. "I've been getting far too many complaints about our apparent sterility, not to mention the behaviour of your AmbSims."

"That is not your concern," he snapped back.

Not only was he under pressure having been left without support to control the mixed population, but his own inner turmoil complicated his capacity to rule aboard Synty with authority and empathy.

"I'm the Captain of the vessel, not a social psychologist." With the next statement he betrayed his unbending position regarding the ultimate goal of the project. "Scions will only be allowed between mixed species bondings."

"You cannot do this. There will be trouble, which I may not be able to control." Saija left having no doubt their Captain wasn't the sort of person prepared to entertain any compromises.

The public announcement of this edict almost caused a riot among the Vesimiaan people. Even the way it was worded ruffled many feathers. It took all of Saija's diplomacy to explain the situation to them at a public gathering without inciting a revolution. They all knew why they were aboard. The reality of that situation wasn't as readily accepted as the theory.

"You have all undertaken an unprecedented adventure in the history of Humankind into the unknown. Unknown even in the history of our hosts. This is not a fancy holiday. This is the greatest thing any human being has ever been asked to do. You have agreed to help save a species, a relative of the Human Race, from extinction. You have agreed to do this by having children who are both ours and theirs."

As much as Saija found it distasteful dealing with Valokvantti she had to inform him of the developing instability.

"Our people know why they're here. Everyone at the meetings understood the situation. But not everyone liked it. Dissent has started simmering. What friendly relations with the AmbSims exists is being strained. And as far as they're concerned – well – they're not entirely happy either. Some of them have formed strong relationships with our people and resent being treated like laboratory animals implied by your proclamation."

The Captain listened and perhaps softened his attitude on hearing everything Saija had to say. "Tell your people to report to the fertility clinics."

No more needed to be said. Saija left the interview without showing any gratitude for Valokvantti's largesse. Why should she? Perhaps with a little more tact and a little more patience from the Captain the very goal the Project was working towards could have continued as an unencumbered reality.

At least Saija managed to get the child bearing 'interference policy' suspended for a period. Saija spent a good deal more of her time amongst the people doing her best to settle feelings, often accompanied by Tumma. His reluctance to engage in conversations, perhaps fearing voicing some of his suspicions, didn't sit well with her. It became a background tension in their private relationship.

Time, the great healer, even amongst alien species, produced some quietude as the people went about the routine of their lives. Eili showed great foresight ensuring the Vesimiaans were responsible for their own livelihood. The activity ameliorated the simmering unrest that had begun to show itself. That, and the very great size of the vessel gave people at least some sense of being separate from their masters. They lived and farmed a self-sufficient existence within the belly of the great craft, well separated from those living in the shell. It even helped them a little to forget the Dokks existed. Eventually, many months later, the crying of a few infants could be heard in some residences. After each birth the babies were taken from their parents for a day, returned seemingly unharmed or unchanged. Understandably a new discontentment arose.

"Why are they taking our children away from us!"

The mothers complained to Saija. She'd been spending so much more time dealing with the people and with the AmbSims that she came to be seen as their leader, by them as well as by Valokvantti. It didn't sweeten his mood, and his relationship with her further deteriorated; as did her relationship with Tumma. She couldn't understand why Tumma didn't take a more active role in representing the welfare of his people. He didn't even try to contribute to solving the various issues of discontent. In fact, Tumma had become secretive, not just with Saija but in all his interactions with everyone.

She told him about the forthcoming meeting with The Captain.

"I know what's going to happen," he said to her, "just a battle of words and wills, which you will surely loose. Nothing's going to change until Langur returns."

Nevertheless, she had to try.

The meeting didn't go well.

"I see they've sent their leader with more grievances I presume. Make this short."

In the absence of both Langur and Eili, Valokvantti reverted to his authoritarian methodology to maintain discipline and keep the Project on track. He'd spent too much time in the The Jarl's office to have any real sense of connection with people.

"I'm not their leader, only their voice." Saija countered, already in a bad mood because Tumma refused to accompany her. "They want open communications with the Dokkheimien leadership." Saija tried not to be personal, "and they want a voice in the decision making process that affects their future."

"These are not democratic circumstances!" Valokvantti growled back at her. "This is not about your future but ours." *Democracy has no part to play in the execution of the aims of this Project. As far as I'm concerned, these Vesimiaans - these aliens - are nothing more than a convenient and necessary means to a great and noble cause. What could be more important than the preservation of our own species!*

"You aliens will have to do as you're told." With that resolve he calmed down enough to make his decision clear to her. "Be quite clear about this; Single species pairs will be sterilized - Mixed species pairs are required to breed after attending the seeding clinic - All mixed couples will be monitored - All scions will be monitored - All teachers will be AmbSims."

"I don't think he even listened to me," Saija complained to Tumma. "He'd already made up his mind what he was going to do before I even had a chance to talk to him."

Tumma refrained from commenting. He knew how it was going to end. By the time Saija returned to her cabin, the new 'orders' were already in full view at every possible vantage point throughout the interior of the spacecraft. Using such measures was the only way Valokvantti felt he could ensure Dokkheimien DNA was present in fertilized eggs; that defective scions were weeded out and that successful progeny were instructed in the full spectrum of their own culture, not alien culture.

Valokvantti didn't get to see his desired outcomes but he did get some idea of where the loyalties of his AmbSims lay, and he wasn't impressed. His edicts resulted in impromptu riots. Therefore he ordered more AmbSims to be added to the society of the aliens. *Why fight them if you can overcome them by sheer numbers.*

The riots had not been planned. Disorganized flash mobs of people and AmbSims came together to vent their anger at the barefaced audacity of their Captain's unreasonable proclamations. Although only several hundred turned out, one outstanding element to the composition of the mobs was the large number of AmbSims who participated. There were as many of them in support of their Vesimiaan partners as there were Vesimiaans.

Vesimaa Begins to Change

Dr.Qilaq, Langur, Leuhta and Eili had left quite some time ago to beam back to Dokkheim for a meeting with The Jarl and Yakiv. The Project had advanced to an exciting stage with great prospects of success.

Langur and Dr.Qilaq had many discussions about operational matters, their hopes and fears, and the progress of the latest procedures. They had been friends for a very long time and knew each other well. Yet Langur always became guarded when the subject of future planning and contingencies came up in their conversations. Sometimes he felt he'd said a little more than he should have. None of this reticence was lost on Dr.Qilaq. Apart from being a friend, he was an accomplished psychologist who could read people well.

Pondering upon the things Langur had said, as much as on what he didn't say, Dr.Qilaq realized a few things. *We have backed ourselves into an ethical dilemma regarding the Vesimiaans.* He was, unfortunately, a being with a conscience. The idea of species re-engineering worked well in theory. The methodology appeared to be highly practical and efficient in many respects; other than reservations about possible DNA incompatibilities. *We, the AmbSims, the Vesimiaans and future Hybrids will all have to come to terms with the highly intrusive interference in the lives of another species - especially because we are so closely related.* Foremost in his mind was a growing suspicion that another plan may have originated from their Jarl. *I'm extremely worried about the future of the Vesimiaans on their own planet.*

Perhaps he should only have concerned himself with the welfare of his own species - but surely these aliens deserved some consideration. He guardedly brought up the matter with Langur.

"You're troubled my friend. I know you and I can see you're battling with something in your mind. Would you care to share?"

"Why would you think that? Everything is going well, apart from a little unrest, but that's to be expected." Langur began, being a little evasive.

"It's something more. You get a fading look in your receptors and you shut off. This is a great enterprise we have embarked on. We need to support each other. Come on - out with it."

Langur often used a moment of silence either when he was slightly unsure of himself, or if he felt totally in control of a situation.

"Get me started. What are your thoughts Qilaq?" He prompted.

"There's something else going on you're not happy about. Will that do?"

"I'm concerned about the aliens' future on Vesimaa. We both know they are a truly primitive species who are bringing about their own destruction. They have little regard for each other or their world. I ask myself why we should care about them. But I do. I would not like to see any serious harm come to them. Not that I know there is such a thing about to happen, but I have my suspicions."

"What suspicions?" Dr.Qilaq quietly asked.

"Well - I've had a conversation with Yakiv and he was very strange. He's had several meetings with The Jarl. 'Several' meetings mind you …"

Dr.Qilaq jiggled his visual receptors in recognition of the unprecedented nature of that eventuality.

"… about a contingency plan. Do you know about any contingency plan? A plan to colonize another planet, other than TC-E … just in case. Just in case of what, I ask myself. Are they expecting TC-E not to work perhaps? Or are they thinking another planet would be far more suitable? Maybe Vesimaa? And what about the aliens already there? Wouldn't that be extremely complicated to have two species on the same planet trying to coexist? Surely there would be too many for the planet to support!" By the end if his monologue Langur had become quite agitated.

"So you feel the real plan is to remove the existing inhabitants to make room for us?" Dr.Qilaq voiced Langur's greatest fear.

"Yes. It's the only logical conclusion. And why have we not been taken into confidence about this?" They both became silent and introspective for a while.

Eventually Langur spoke quietly and with assurance, after having calmed himself. "We can assume Valokvantti doesn't know about this. He wouldn't be able to hide it from me. We can also assume that if there were such a plan then there would already be some evidence of it in action on Vesimaa. Before we do anything else we should send a reconnaissance team back there to review the situation." They took Leuhta and Eili into their confidence, and arranged for two recon personnel to investigate Vesimaa.

While he was away from Synty Langur had several operational matters to deal with: He was to ensure the fetuses of the mixed couples contained Dokkheimien DNA. It didn't matter whether the females were AmbSims or Vesimiaans, but it was essential that all the progeny had the appropriate color coding in their skins. He left the details up to the Captain and the scientists on board. Next, he needed to deal with the unrest amongst breeding couples.

Prior to the meeting with The Jarl their frank discussion did nothing to ease Langur's mood.

"I had no choice but to leave Valokvantti in charge of the Project. You can see from his report there's some unrest."

"You could not have foreseen any major problems," added Dr.Qilaq, "there was no reason for you to think he would become difficult and confrontational in dealing with the people. Nevertheless, our AmbSims appear to be assimilating well into the alien society. This is an encouraging sign, don't you think?"

Eili's insight didn't provide much comfort for Langur either. "We didn't take into consideration the extraordinarily fast rate of change that occurs in a species that is modified and required to assimilate into the lives of another species that has a body with a very limited life span. Having only fifty to eighty years of biological life means our AmbSims have to immerse themselves in all of their life's functions much more intensely, much more quickly than an immortal species. Consequently it is not unreasonable that the unrest we've been alerted to should have arrived sooner than expected."

"Granted, we may have underestimated some things. But how do you explain the recon teams' findings back on Vesimaa?" asked Langur. "As far as I'm concerned they have clearly confirmed my suspicions about what's happening there."

Eili didn't try to evade the problem. "Yes, we are interfering with the planet and with its people – that is – our Jarl is, although there appears to be no obvious visible change to the ecology of the planet so far. However, the population attrition rate has shown signs of increasing, and similarly birth rates appear to have started to level out. The findings are also clear about their Governments. The leaders of the major countries appeared to have altered the pattern of their behavior. In particular, the 'peace' peddling nations softened their peace initiatives with a corresponding increase in the production of weapons of war."

As difficult as Eili found it to connect these trends to a direct link between themselves and their cousin species Langur had firsthand experience with infiltrating the mind of an alien, and how easily they could be influenced. He knew it was possible to direct their thinking and consequently their actions.

Dr.Qilaq was under no illusions on that score. "I remember quite well how you took control of Tumma's thoughts. There's no doubt the phenomenon witnessed by the scouting party is an example of the more widely spread use of your 'mind control' technique. We have more than enough cause to have a candid audience with Jarl Haakon.

The meeting with The Jarl proceeded as unpredictably as always. He made no attempt to hide his displeasure either at being interrupted in his routine of maintaining a semblance of control over a planet of people who had become 'troublesome', nor at being 'held-to-account' for his decisions about the fate of the alien species.

"I have no time for this confrontation. I've made my decision. It is a decision on information *you* provided!"

The accusing glare directed at Langur held annoyance mixed with a goodly dose of threat.

Yakiv avoided any interaction with Langur, standing to one side, nearer to The Jarl than Langur's group. *Why am I feeling like a traitor to Langur? absolutely no reason for this.* Yakiv did his best to justify himself in his own eyes. *I'm only doing what is best for my people. I am following my Jarl's directives.* Langur had taken only a cursory glance in Yakiv's direction, so the man must have been feeling particularly guilty about something.

"What do you want!" The Jarl barked in their general direction, while looking busy with other matters.

195

Langur, being the head of the project on the vessel replied calmly, "Firstly, to report that all is going …"

"Yes, yes! I know all that. You didn't come here just to tell me that! Get on with it!"

With great self-composure, expending considerable effort to achieve that state of mind particularly after the previous disquieting conversation with his team, he replied, "For the purpose of ensuring all our efforts are coordinated towards the single desirable goal, it would be expedient for us to be assured there *is* only one desirable goal."

"Why are you prancing about with your words Skuggi? The survival of our species! That is our goal! Surely you have not deviated from that! Out with it man, my patience is limited!"

"I," this time Langur turned the focus on himself, "… I have the feeling that our respective methods may have deviated somewhat from each other." Langur tried to get his point across about the hidden agenda without sounding confrontational.

"Why should that be a problem for you? You know exactly what you have to achieve before getting to TC-E. The rest is not your concern." The Jarl pronounced the last few words with considerable emphasis, conveying with them an implied dismissal.

Leuhta, Dr. Dr.Qilaq and Eili remained silent during the conversation, all apprehensive to some degree with only Eili feeling he really had nothing to lose. He was after all a Temporal, becoming more temporary with each passing year. Perhaps that's what gave him the courage to interrupt.

"Please allow me to explain something, on behalf of all of us here and perhaps on behalf of all of those on board Synty who have already dedicated their lives to the Project."

The Jarl and Yakiv both turned their attention in his direction. Neither spoke. This man, who, from their point of reference had not much longer to live, carried an air of assurance and an aura of authority somehow lacking in Langur. After a brief moment Eili continued.

"There may be a second plan, of which we have not been officially advised. Rumours of this plan are causing considerable unrest among the aliens and among the AmbSims who have now integrated themselves into the alien society." The Jarl regarded him intensely, still not commenting. "That unrest has the potential to jeopardize the entire Project." Although Eili wasn't exactly telling the whole truth of the matter he did manage to shed light on their focus of concern.

At this point The Jarl and Yakiv looked at one another again before The Jarl responded.

"Why?"

Now, the interesting thing about the question was that The Jarl didn't refute the statement about the second plan. Eili kept his gaze on his Jarl. The passive support of Eili by the others didn't go unnoticed by The Jarl.

"Because, if there is a full scale rebellion, perhaps even escalating to a mutiny, then the entire effort will be lost," Eili answered.

Perhaps The Jarl took that as a personal affront to his plan to colonize Vesimaa and exterminate its existing inhabitants. Perhaps he took it as a threat to his position as the leader. Perhaps he might even have taken it as a vote of no confidence in his dedication to preserving his own species from extinction. In any case his response was unequivocal and not open for discussion.

"Be aware – *fully* aware … Vesimaa *will* be rehabilitated … Superfluous alien population *will* be eliminated … Tau Ceti-E will only be a *temporary* facility … We *will* colonize Vesimaa."

It became abundantly clear The Jarl had no qualms about the extermination of a primitive species already doing a good job of it themselves. This time Leuhta found the courage to speak her mind. For indeed it took courage to engage the absolute and omnipotent leader of their species in any form of discussion which involved questioning his decisions, the details of those decisions or perhaps even his judgment. Her only chance of getting away with her audacity was the firm belief that The Jarl knew the only chance his species had rested on the success of the Project currently well advanced under Langur's leadership.

"Who amongst the aliens would not be considered superfluous?"

She asked this outwardly calm, inwardly trembling. If she were to be seen as a threat to the Project The Jarl would immediately terminate her existence. Immediately meant just that. She would not be able to move another muscle or utter another syllable. Every person in the chamber was registered in the sights of a weapon of ultimate convenience, which could be activated by a simple neural command from The Jarl. So the very fact that several seconds after her question she was still alive meant she was correct in her assessment of the situation. Langur dared not move, nor any of the others, including Yakiv. The Jarl turned extremely slowly to fix his visual sensors directly on hers.

"You have a compromise solution in mind?"

That came out more as a command for Leuhta to elaborate, than as a question. This augmented bio-mechanical unit, embodied in the presence of their leader had no trouble keeping several jumps ahead of any intellectual interchange. Langur could barely believe his bonded mate could be – so impersonal – so unemotional – so devoid of empathy, so completely unethical with her suggestion, yet be so courageous. As he listened to her unfold her thoughts he realized that amongst all of them, it was only Leuhta and The Jarl who had a clear focus on the very problem and its solution he himself had proposed so tentatively in the first place.

"Harvest more aliens, selecting only those who meet your specific criteria of suitability, and eliminate the others. In addition, allow the hybrid progeny to develop to an advanced pre-determined stage before subjecting them to critical examination. Failure in the examination would mean immediate termination for the infant, regardless of which species had become dominant in the individual. Similarly, use only the most suitable of our own people for the AmbSim program, those who eventually want to migrate to TC-E.

The rest of the population would remain here. When the hybrid population on TC-E has reached its desired span of mortality, then and only then transport them to Vesimaa."

She took courage because The Jarl had not interrupted her long soliloquy and she ventured to round off her thoughts. "Of course the rehabilitation of Vesimaa should continue as scheduled."

"We have your permission do we!"

That unprecedented jovial comment brought about a slight, only a very slight, easing of the tension in the chamber. Jarl Haakon then addressed Langur directly.

"Resolve the conflicts to our satisfaction."

The order and the embedded dismissal came from The Jarl almost as an afterthought. He had already assimilated the compromise solution, found it to have merit and had already set his mind to plan accordingly.

The notion that appealed to him most was the expediency with which his own species could be dealt with. The proposed concept would allow him to solve a major problem. He could obviously not take all of his people off Dokkheim. There were just too many of them. Then again, a goodly number were in fact unsuitable genetic stock material for a large variety of reasons. There would be those in any case who would not want to engage in the Project at all and those who could simply not come to terms with the idea of voluntarily limiting the life-spans of their scions. Immortality was the natural order of life for these people and anything else was inconceivable. The Jarl reflected that all the unrest occurring in every corner of their world was because their longevity would be taken away from them. The lethargy, the depression, the ennui, it all seemed so distant when faced with the alternative of living almost only for a moment. How could they possibly achieve anything if they only lived for a 'moment'. With such thoughts and with feelings of helplessness the only outlet his people could see was to resort to violence.

Well, this was a chance to pacify them. The perfect solution to keep Langur and his crowd under control and to take another step towards the survival of his species. Of course the suggested compromise plan would need a few minor adjustments. In the meantime, Vesimaa's rehabilitation and species 'cleansing' could continue exactly as devised by Yakiv. The Jarl instructed him accordingly.

Trouble Aboard Synty

Tumma and Saija had shadows again. Enough time had elapsed for their bodies' cellular structure to realign itself exactly as Langur predicted. However, they were still not mortal. Given the general state of affairs when Langur and his team arrived back on the vessel, that little matter became low priority.

The riot that broke out soon after Langur departed, left normality aboard Synty in tatters. Restrictions on who could breed, abduction of children by the Dokks and then the outrageous edicts announced by Valokvantti almost tipped the scales of tolerance. After thirty years of cohabitation between the AmbSims and Vesimiaans it became inevitable that the AmbSims who formed pair bonds with the Vesimiaans, being the vast majority, would begin to identify more strongly with their partners and their offspring than with the 'ruling' powers aboard the vessel - That was only natural since they spent each day of their lives with their new families engaging in the normal routine of life in the belly of the hollow moon like ants in a giant terrarium, to the exclusion of all contact with the Dokks.

The trip to TC-E was taking too long. Predictably, a leader emerged amongst them to represent the four thousand strong mixed race people who considered the artificial moon to be their home; not just a transport vehicle, but their permanent place of existence.

This leader was Lefe; an AmbSim soon to have a scion of her own, Vesimiaan style. Lefe was tall for a woman, with ample proportions. One could say she was good breeding stock. Her Vesimiaan shell originated from somewhere in the South Pacific Islands. Lefe had a pleasant disposition, although amongst her friends she had a reputation of being forceful and outspoken if a situation required it.

Being taken against her will certainly fueled her sense of outrage initially, which abated after her transformative neural cleansing. Apart from making room for the Dokkheimien personality, she was also subjected to other biological procedures to ensure her fertility with Dokk eggs. This individual exuding agitation, confronting Saija, was in fact neither from one species, nor another … rather an amalgam of both.

"I don't know who I am anymore!" She almost shouted at Saija.

Over the last few years the two women had become close friend; close enough for Lefe to vent her frustrations openly in front of a pure Vesimiaan.

"Sometimes in the mornings, when I'm still in the twilight zone, I have flashes of feelings that I should be living on a small land surrounded by water, under a most incredibly strong light. I can almost smell the place. But how is that possible! I come from a dark world with hardly any water or light at all."

Saija listened, recalling how this wasn't the first conversation she'd had with an AmbSim along very similar lines. It became abundantly clear their hosts had not been honest with their own people, let alone with their guests. She let Lefe continue uninterrupted.

"I speak two languages as though I was born with the knowledge of both, but my mind goes blank when I try to think in Vesimiaan. Why is that Saija! Why is that?"

"The situation looks very bad out there Lefe. Tell me what is happening."

Saija knew exactly what Lefe was talking about, and she realized, as well as Tumma, that peace amongst the people had become extremely fragile, mostly because of Valokvantti's handling of rising tensions. If matters didn't improve significantly and Valokvantti continued his despotic handling of the unrest, there could indeed be bloodshed and perhaps even mutiny. These consequences Saija and Tumma discussed at length, and knew they could ultimately result in the end of human life on Earth. Tumma had suspected for some time the Dokks were technologically capable of engineering species extinction and perhaps would have no reservations in doing so if they had no alternative.

"They will rebel," Lefe said. "I cannot placate them any longer. The AmbSims and the Vesimiaans have joined forces in a common cause, driven mostly by their fear of what is going to happen to their children. They cannot conceive of life on an alien planet like TC-E. It's too far away; it's too abstract an idea. And let me tell you this - they are also driven by their growing hatred of Valokvantti. Is there nothing you can do?" Lefe pleaded with Saija. "They are ready to explode, and they are armed."

Saija had no idea it had become so volatile. From what Lefe said she feared the people would resort to force as the only solution. Having weapons would embolden them to recklessness.

"How can I go to Valokvantti to deliver an ultimatum and threaten mutiny? He will not listen to any demands! What do you think will be the consequence? And if I tell him anything less, nothing will change! He will continue exactly as before!"

"I've been talking to you as a friend, Saija. That may not be possible for much longer. I know how you feel. I know you've tried to help all of us. But if you can't do something very, very soon there will be bloodshed." With those last words Lefe left after embracing Saija, perhaps for the final time.

Saija followed her friend until she could see the crowd through the inner shell who gathered to meet Lefe. They were loud and vociferous as Lefe tried to make herself heard. A man, another AmbSim from the mob called out, "We Want Action!" … words supported by acclamations from all who gathered there. Lefe had to work hard to quieten the crowd.

"I can't make any promises. Saija will do everything she can to help us!"

Whatever else Lefe had said to them settled the gathering, at least for the moment. She watched them disperse down the main road to the fields before retreating herself, feeling extremely concerned about the energy in the crowd.

During the entire interview between Saija and Lefe, Tumma sat and listened from another room, thinking. Circumstances had changed considerably since his first encounter with Langur and Dr.Qilaq, and not for the better. *The entire project to save Langur's people is on the verge of collapse because of Valokvantti. He can't have been acting purely on his own volition. He's got to be following a plan, forcing its details on everyone more and more stringently – but it's not working!*

How could Tumma know? - His only trustworthy contacts were off Synty. He hoped it wasn't an abandonment; more likely a mission to reaffirm the details and strategies of saving their own race from extinction – he hoped. Tumma had misgivings about those very strategies, not just from the nature of Valokvantti's edicts, but also from snippets of conversation he'd had with Langur. *We need Langur and the others to return and take control. The people need reassurance. There's got to be a more sensible way of dealing with the difficult transition both species have to go through.*

"Saija, what can we realistically do?" he asked when she'd returned.

"Whatever it is, we had better do it quickly. Not that you've been much help lately … Sorry … I didn't mean that." The tension brought out the snitchy side of Saija.

"You're right, I haven't spent enough time with the people. I've been too absorbed with the 'big scheme'. We should go out there and see firsthand what's really going on."

In the next few weeks Lefe happily accompanied the two 'first citizens', as they came to be known to the masses, on their visitations amongst the people. Valokvantti was dully advised of the ambassadorial expeditions, to his consternation, because he wanted to keep close scrutiny on the first citizens. He'd become suspicious of their many meetings with the AmbSims and aliens and frustrated by Saija's constant representations on behalf of the experimental breeding couples. Although at first he'd developed a degree of tolerance towards the aliens, mostly under Langur's and Eili's influence, that tolerance turned hardline in their absence. The people were purely experimental subjects; Vesimiaans and the AmbSims. He saw no reason to trust either group. Whether he liked it or not Tumma and Saija were out there. He dared not interfere with them … not just yet.

Saija and Tumma traveled from village to village, sometimes meeting smaller, sometimes larger groups of the mixed bonded couples and sometimes meeting with the AmbSims who had not yet bonded. The two of them joined in the work in the fields or the maintenance of livestock, or helped out in the various small cottage industries that had sprung up. After one such hard day's work Saija and Tumma discussed the circumstances they'd encountered.

"It must be as obvious to you as it is to me, Saija. There's a well-developed social structure out here."

"It's no wonder they expect a high degree of autonomy from their masters." Saija concurred.

"This craft is so large and so well designed for life to flourish within its belly that I don't wonder the people have developed a sense of separateness between themselves and those living in the shell. I can understand if they resent any interference, especially direct interference; like having their children taken from them without prior arrangements, only to be subjected to who knew what kind of inhumane treatment. We don't really know what's going on behind the scenes." Tumma opened up after all the time he'd been withdrawn into himself.

Saija explored another problem. "There are also the atypical AmbSims who are experiencing increasing levels of disassociation within their dual psyches. Obviously the total memory wipe of the host body's previous life on Earth has not been entirely successful. Their lives on Dokkheim and their lives on Earth are bleeding into each other, causing a great deal of confusion. From speaking with Lefe I can see a serious conflict of allegiance emerging."

"What exactly does that mean?" Alarm bells rang for Tumma.

"It seems to me their inclinations are in our favor - their partners being from Earth. As far as the Project is concerned, the Dokks are becoming more Vesimiaan than the other way around. If Valokvantti got wind of this, he would do something drastic to reverse the trend."

"You'd think it would be the other way around given the highly biased education system putting exclusive emphasis on Dokk culture," Tumma mused.

"You're forgetting the parents. Their influence has been completely underestimated. The situation is getting very complicated."

What Lefe observed lately pleased her enormously. Firstly, a little improvement in the mood of the people resulting from the engagement of the 'first citizens' with them. Not much, but enough to buy a little time. She was also pleased to see how Saija understood the critical aspects of the situation, which helped to put their friendship back on a solid footing. As for Tumma; well, she wasn't sure about him. She'd met him on many occasions at his home, and found him to be pleasant enough. But after seeing his initial interactions with people she felt a tension developing between the two of them. He no longer looked directly into her eyes when he spoke to her, as if he was thinking of things other than what he was saying. No matter. Saija was a more important ally to have.

All had not been going well between Tumma and Saija either. Over the weeks of their encounters Tumma had become more and more guarded in his communication with people; more 'professional', more formal in the kinds of questions he asked. Obviously the research scientist in him assumed the prominent role. But was there more to it than that? So far Tumma still believed TC-E to be the target planet on which the hybrid population was to evolve into the 'saved' species of the Dokks. Perhaps because he had carried Langur in his head for so long and absorbed some of the man's actual beliefs. Perhaps it was his scientific training that dictated that the plan had scientific validity. And most importantly … he had no idea the human race was even then being gradually exterminated in order to accommodate the new hybrid race at some time in the not too distant future.

"Yes, the situation is getting complicated," Tumma stated after some thought. "You cannot pander to every wish and whim and minor discomfort of these people. I actually think more stringent controls need to be taken with the AmbSims and our own people if the race of Dokks is to be saved from extinction."

"You can't be serious!" Exclaimed Saija. "We have rights just the same as everyone else! Ultimately, we have the right to exist!"

"OK. I agree. We do. But it's premature to be talking about that now. The hybrid race is not yet fully formed. The process has barely started. We're only beginning to see the first generation of hybrids. Who knows how many generations it will take before they call themselves Dokks, Dokks who have attained mortality." Tumma said all this in a quiet, considered tone realizing Saija had become overly emotional about the whole situation.

"I cannot believe what you're saying! These people are not guinea pigs in a laboratory!"

"Well, actually … I think they are. All of them. They have all willingly sacrificed themselves to save an entire species of sentient beings from extinction. They are still experimental subjects, and to some extent have to be treated as such. From the Dokk perspective, this experiment must not fail." In spite of wanting to remain neutral, Tumma couldn't prevent himself from emphasizing the last point.

Neither Tumma nor Saija were aware of The Jarl's unshakable resolve that the aliens didn't deserve to keep their home planet, and that they did not deserve life! Perhaps that may have ameliorated Tumma's seeming loyalty to the altruistic idea of saving their species from extinction. Another little problem had yet to find its way into their consciousness; the solution to their personal immortality. There was only one possible solution for that. It lay in the degree of success of the mixed race progeny. What would Tumma and Saija have to do for themselves in the future, to become truly human again? It was something they didn't need to think about for the time being. Saija's immediate concern was how to present yet another case to Valokvantti for the better treatment of Synty's people.

"I want you to come with me, Tumma. You seem to have a better empathy for the Dokks' dilemma." She decided. "Perhaps if Valokvantti sees he's not alone in his thinking it might ease the vehemence with which he pursues his style of control. Perhaps you might be able to make him see that intimidation and forceful coercion doesn't work."

"True," Tumma agreed, "none of us want to see the growing discontent turning into riots and mutiny."

The Captain had become more withdrawn with time and not particularly interested in speaking with any aliens, especially not the troublesome Saija. Nevertheless, he acquiesced to an appointment, if for no other reason than for his own future accountability. It had dawned on him that his particular brand of discipline may have worked reasonably well with the crew, but definitely not as effective in controlling the hoard of experimental specimens. If the Project failed - not that he'd entertained too many thoughts about that - he had to be seen to be proactive in trying to ensure its success and not contributing to failure.

Perhaps these two annoying aliens could be useful in the future. "If you've come to tell me the … er … people are … if there is unrest, then don't bother. I already know."

"It is more than unrest Captain." Saija was careful to put sufficient emphasis on the degree of agitation. "Tumma and I have just spent several weeks amongst the society of our travelers …" She started to say.

"Yes I know that as well. Good news I trust." He interjected almost barking his words. Saija hesitated, for she had to pick her words with care to prevent any unnecessary reprisals resulting from the representation of their case.

Tumma cut in at this point because as a scientist he couldn't cope with beating about the bush.

"Their attitude has coalesced into uniting them towards a common goal. As much as I find it surprising to agree with you Captain, in the best interests of the Project, to which we are all dedicated, the anomalous behaviour of the people needs to be controlled more effectively. I believe the problem to be quite simple. A confusion has emerged as to why they are actually aboard the vessel. It may only be the passage of time that has dulled their memory."

Saija was quite surprised by the diplomacy, and accuracy of Tumma's words. He presented the situation in such a way as to point towards a reasonable solution, without actually instructing the Captain as to what he should do.

"Do you think a timely initiative to re-educate the people, to re-awaken in them the extraordinary value of the altruistic sacrifice they are making, could well hold the solution to the unrest?" In the tensions of the moment Saija forgot the real basis of all the problems. She wasn't a diplomat after all, just a nurse.

Valokvantti had no delusions about the severity of developments since his last edict. *Why couldn't they just do what they are told! Yes, Tumma is right. They have become confused. It's because I've been too lenient with them.* He was just the Captain of a space vessel, not a Psychologist - How could he have realized his own AmbSims were as much a part of the problem and not a part of the solution as was their intended purpose. The more he thought about it the more convinced he was of what he must do. But at least he'd learnt this much … don't tell these two aliens everything he was intending to do … *Wipe the memory of every alien of everything other than their existence aboard the vessel. That will ensure they have no recollection of their origins and it should obviate any basis for future unrest - and declare Martial Law of course.*

Valokvantti said to Tumma and Saija, "I will consider your suggestion and advise you of my decision."

On the way home Tumma voiced his concern. "I don't like the sound of that at all. It's most unlike Valokvantti to be anything but confrontational."

The very next day Martial Law was proclamation. Restrictions were placed on how many people could gather in the one place at any one time. Freedom of movement was curtailed for inhabitants of every village. They were not to go beyond the boundary of their fields and not to go into the immediate proximity of the neighbouring village. To ensure compliance with these and other restrictions, armed bi-ped slave clones made their appearance all over the interior of the craft.

The following day, under armed clone escorts, two hundred aliens were taken into custody for a comprehensive memory cleansing.

Reaction to the proclamation came swiftly, as any reasonable person could have anticipated. Lefe made sure Saija was immediately informed of the imminent uprising. Not that Saija could have done anything about it, for she and Tumma were placed under guard in their own home. The next courier, attempting to bring news to Saija of the results of the returned two hundred people, couldn't deliver his message because he was detained.

For a further week Saija and Tumma were completely isolated from any news of events in the bowels of the artificial moon. The next person they did see was Langur himself, accompanied by Leuhta. At first they were unrecognizable at the door. Neither Tumma nor Saija had met the two AmbSims standing there.

"Hello Tumma. It's me, Langur … and Leuhta." Stunned silence greeted them for several moments before Saija had the presence of mind to invite them into their home. Tumma just stood aside, hostile. He'd met Langur in several manifestations, but he'd never expected to see him as an AmbSim.

"A rather serious problem has developed …" Langur began. His Vesimiaan shell must have been selected with some forethought; youngish but not so young as to be dismissed as a person without life experience, tall, olive skinned and with friendly accessible eyes.

"I knew it! Lefe tried to warn me. What happened? We've heard nothing. We've been locked it!" Saija interjected throwing a defiant glance in Leuhta's direction.

Langur tried to diffuse some of the obvious angst by introducing his partner. "This is my bonded partner, Leuhta. I asked her to join us here because she has – well – a very clear perspective on our enterprise and may be able to help."

Leuhta's simulacrum was of a compatible age to Langur's and not much taller than Saija. Because Saija's glance was driven by anger she failed to register a certain sympathetic aspect to the woman.

Leuhta wanted to explain, "Yes we know about your detention. That is regrettable. The Captain …" But Langur cut her off.

"There's been a riot." Tumma and Saija exchanged a worried glance. "No deaths, but some injuries. The people tried to storm the shell near the Administration Centre. Valokvantti repelled them, regrettably with too much enthusiasm.

Leuhta added, "We arrived back on board before the second attack from the mob. The Captain concurred that alternative actions might have been more appropriate, after understanding our Jarl's wishes." She tried to smooth things over in an attempt to ameliorate the severity of the event.

More appropriate - I bet! Who are they trying to kid! Although she felt utterly disgusted with the situation, Saija let her go on without interruption. Tumma also remained quiet, forehead furrowed, pensive.

"The people withdrew to tend to their wounded. Valokvantti then brought in more reinforcements, which fueled the determination of the crowd."

"The three of us; Eili, Leuhta and myself, felt that the only way to control the situation was to go out and meet the mob ourselves in our AmbSim mantles. Apparently the condition of the detained two hundred individuals triggered the riot. They were returned confused, unable to remember their own names and unable to recognize their partners. The reaction from their families was immediate and violent." Langur made the situation as clear as he could. There was simply no point in misleading the two 'first citizens'. "By the time we met with some of those returned people they'd regained some semblance of normality, but they could remember nothing of ever having been on Vesimaa. I wanted to tell you personally what I've done so far." Langur took a moment to gauge Saija's reaction before continuing. "As well as introducing new 'health checks' for the children, with parents being permitted to attend, other restrictions were removed as well. The teaching staff have to remain. But as a compromise, I've allowed an equal number of Vesimiaan teachers to work with each of the AmbSim teachers."

""What are you not telling us?" shot back Saija, to which Langur didn't respond.

"How long are you going to keep us locked up?" Tumma asked quietly.

"We apologize for this misunderstanding. You are free to go about your business," said Langur.

*

The people were not told that the monitoring of their 'activities' would continue as before. Nevertheless, a measure of peace returned relatively quickly. It seemed that what wasn't blatantly obvious to the people, without immediate effect on their personal daily lives, didn't worry them unduly. Mixed pair bonding continued to be encouraged with incentives for those who complied. Some intra-species bonds were still being formed, but children were only born to the mixed couples. That in itself wasn't a sufficient irritant to cause anything more than some superficial discontent.

Langur and Dr. Dr.Qilaq had yet to confront the problem of the 'confused' AmbSims; those with memory bleeds from their Vesimiaan other selves. Although Lefe had raised the issue with Saija, as did many other women, she didn't pursue the situation for fear of further unpopular action from Valokvantti, unaware his authority had been considerably curtailed after his inept handling of the Project in Langur's absence. Perhaps if she knew she may have more vigorously pursued a solution to the rising anomalies.

*

In the Dokk conference room six individuals took up their random positions at the round energy console. Langur opened the discussion.

"So far there's no need to concern The Jarl with our minor problems. You've received his directive, Captain. I am now in total control of the Project. Your specific and only sphere of activity is to ensure this vessel arrives safely on TC-E. The individuals you see before you are wholly responsible for the Project in all its facets, under my direction. That includes all security matters related to AmbSims and Vesimiaans."

Valokvantti made no contribution for it wasn't actually a conference; more a censure of his actions. He couldn't go against the directive. He made no excuses for his actions. However, that didn't prevent him from having certain strong feelings. These showed clearly in his demeanor, which didn't go unnoticed by either Dr.Qilaq or Langur.

"Unless anybody has something to add, that is all." As the others left he called Valokvantti back. "Captain, could we talk?" Langur assumed a friendly, though businesslike attitude. "How do you think I look in this Vesimiaan body?" The Captain ignored his weak attempt at levity.

"Look Langur," Valokvantti began blustering, "I know what this is all about. They outnumber us now! What's going to happen when we pick up the next batch of aliens? I had to show strong resolve to maintain discipline!"

"Did it work?" Langur asked quietly. Valokvantti didn't respond. "The Project is the only thing that matters. We need to work together on this, my friend. You are the best man to get us to TC-E. Let me worry about the aliens."

Langur tried his best to maintain a good working relationship with the Captain, who was in no mood for a lengthy discussion. He was well aware his strategy didn't work. He was also well aware Langur could have caused him a considerable amount of anguish, possibly even the loss of his life if he had confided any of the details of the near-mutiny to The Jarl. For that he felt indebted to Langur, and he didn't like it. On the way out he locked his visual sensors with Langur's eyes, just for a moment. That short glance conveyed his feelings to the man now in charge.

Vesimaa Modifications Well Advanced

Many years flowed past the artificial moon as it made a wide sweeping change of course. To the Dokks the passage of those years seemed inconsequential. Everyone else felt the ageing that came with the relentless passage of time, except the 'first citizens'. Tumma and Saija were not getting any older. Every time they brought up the subject with Langur or Leuhta they were evasive, always finding a perfectly good explanation for putting off the procedure to reverse their condition.

"The two of you are critical to the success of the Project," Langur would say, "without you the people would lose their sense of continuity. They feel secure as long as the generations can see you looking after them," Leuhta would say.

She was right. Absolutely right. As Tumma and Saija moved and lived among the people they could feel the reliance they placed on the two of them. They couldn't betray that by dying! But longevity was a double edged sword. There were those who had begun to see them as not 'one of them' any more. How was it they didn't age like everyone else? Tumma tried to explain, with little success. The explanation seemed too far-fetched, too convenient. Who were these 'first citizens' really? The rumours and conjectures continued to ebb and flow with the passage of time. Questions were also asked why they didn't have children. It's been over thirty years since leaving Earth. Surely they wanted children. That's what the whole enterprise was about. Why was it they had not made their own contribution to the Project? Wasn't that the whole point of the expedition.

Yes, they did want children, but how could they? The only way possible would be to split up and form pair bonds with AmbSims. What if they didn't split up and still formed the other bonds? Could that possibly work. Tumma tried to convince himself Life was no longer normal. It had become downright strange and unconventional. Eili, now his very good friend and a common sight in their home was always welcome and he and Saija enjoyed his company.

Eili took Tumma aside during one of his visits. "We have to return to the Earth temporarily. This is just between us, not even Saija must know, and especially not Lefe."

"Any special reason?" Tumma became agitated.

Eili was vague about that. "Just a few minor issues to sort out."

All sorts of mixed feelings bubbled to the surface for Tumma. His previous suspicions about possible interference in human affairs by the Dokks resurfaced at the news. It had only been a few decades since he left Earth. Surely not much could have changed.

Aboard Synty, after some upheavals their society settled into a routine of life that assimilated the AmbSims almost seamlessly. A very large majority of pair bonds were a mix of the two species. Their offspring were growing into adulthood, soon to be ready for bonding of their own. They were not visibly different from their parents, except perhaps their skin colour discernibly more orange than amber. Both the humans and the AmbSims could envisage a future for their hybrid children on the new TC-E world. If not them, then their grandchildren.

Without exceptions the AmbSims especially felt the effects of ageing. Their shells were being corrupted by an incompatibility between their psyche and their physiology; an unforeseen emergent problem. The rate of deterioration more or less matched the ageing of the Vesimiaans. From within the society in the belly of the spacecraft there were no particular social concerns. However, Dr.Qilaq had become increasingly more alarmed. In itself, so far as the demise of the first wave of AmbSims were concerned, he saw no problematic issues. They could be replaced with new Dokk volunteers. Of greater concern to him was the reason behind their deterioration.

If the purging and replacement of the alien psyche had such a dramatic effect on the host body's physiology, then that eliminated a possible future control methodology for the troublesome Vesimiaans. He had at one point, during the middle of the riots, considered neural override, the way Langur had infiltrated Tumma's brain, in order to control the alien bodies' breakdown. Now there was no way of determining just how drastically their bodies would react to such intervention, or if they would remain healthy breeding stock.

Perhaps the team may not have to deal with that issue. For the moment they needed more live Vesimiaan host bodies, younger ones to be inhabited by a new lot of Dokk volunteer psyches. The new wave of AmbSims were destined to form pair bonds with the first issue of hybrid progeny, and so produce the second generation of hybrid Dokks. That process would have to be repeated an indeterminate number of times, until there were positive changes discernable in their DNA ageing characteristics. It was hoped some progress would appear by the third generation hybrids; at about the time of their scheduled arrival on TC-E. Dr.Qilaq and Langur considered two generations of Vesimiaans might be sufficient to initiate the evolution of a new line of DNA for their own species. Any more interbreeding might have the opposite effect of turning their own people into Vesimiaans, due unfortunately to weakened Dokk genetics; a consequence of an eon of over-engineering.

***

Unknown to the general population on the spacecraft, they had arrived back at Vesimaa to harvest another intake of aliens for the continuation of the Project. The efficiency of the process didn't require the expedition to linger for long. It was however long enough to allow Tumma one last look at his world. He appealed to Leuhta for the opportunity.

"This may be the only chance to see my world again, in spite of my little problem."

Leuhta, with a different emotional makeup than Langur, saw no reason to refuse Tumma. "It will have to be a very short stay, perhaps no more than a day."

Through Leuhta's intervention he visited briefly, with an escort, near his old research facility.

There didn't appear to be much change on first sight. Perhaps the grounds of the facility were not as well maintained as Tumma remembered. And perhaps some of the buildings appeared to be unused. Certainly no vehicles could be seen parked around them even though it was a normal work day. The Café he used to go to was still there; looking shabby and poorly patronized in spite of the summer season. He stopped at the open entrance surprised by the amount of cigarette smoke wafting out through the door. Nevertheless, he settled himself at a table for a coffee and glanced around the establishment. *Not many people,* he thought to himself. *Food must have much become cheaper. So many of the people are bordering on obese.* As the coffee was served he started watching the news on a flat screen hanging on the back wall.

War - war and more war. He couldn't hear the sound very well but the images told a terrible story. *What could they all be fighting about? I can't remember it to have been on such a global scale when we left.* The news stories were also full of the huge investments in the machinery of War. Individuals and companies invested heavily, reaping a considerable profit from the enterprise. Unemployment was no longer an issue, but rather the opposite. There were not enough people who could, or who wanted to work. Not because the war industry was so labour intensive, but because so many people had been killed. There wasn't enough manpower available. Tumma looked around the Café – *They don't seem to be overly concerned by this situation. I wonder what's going on.*

By the time Tumma finished his coffee the last item of news bemoaned the fact that population growth had plateaued out. Apparently it was a mystery to the scientists of the day. Fewer women were fertile. Hospitals had an overabundance of empty beds in their maternity wards. This also appeared not to worry the people. It all seemed somehow surreal thinking about what he had just seen. On further rumination among his most recent memories, he dredged up images of Earth as Synty approached it.

At the time he didn't notice anything unusual at all. Earth was extraordinarily beautiful. More beautiful than he remembered it - probably because for the last thirty odd years he'd been living on an artificial structure. Yes, he did notice there were areas of desertification, fire and smoke. But they didn't register in his mind as being significant. What he did notice more specifically was that some countries, like Australia, parts of Africa, the Amazon and great stretches of North America appeared be much greener than he'd remembered seeing them from past satellite images.

Tumma couldn't reconcile the images of a planet at War with itself, and the abundance of green and blue at the same time.

The visitation ended all too soon. Back aboard Synty he tried to get clarification of his confusion from Langur.

While Tumma was occupied on the planet, Langur, Eili, Leuhta and Dr.Qilaq had conducted their own investigation. It seemed mandatory given the circumstances following their most recent interaction with The Jarl. They took note of everything Tumma saw, and more. Yakiv's plans, put into effect by the three special Companies, were working with unexpected success. Being already a belligerent, warlike species the aliens obviously felt comfortable in engaging in global war 'games', with the added excitement of real deaths. As an added bonus they were reaping all manner of benefits; the fewer that remained alive the more comfortable their life styles became. Housing ceased to be a problem, food was in plentiful supply, good jobs were to be had at high pay rates and if you invested in war stocks then the dividends just kept rolling in.

Langur made the obvious observation. "They have no central governing body with the ability and the infrastructure to have a centralized overview of themselves or their planet. It's no wonder they're out of control."

"True," Eili agreed, "but they weren't entirely like this when we left."

"Our drones have reported startling changes to their ecology as well." Leuhta noted.

"Looks like we'd better meet with these people from Yakiv's supervising Companies." He knew of Jarl Haakon's position regarding the Vesimiaans and their planet, he just wasn't aware that the plans were put into effect so expediently. Although Langur had no responsibility for the preparation of the planet for their eventual permanent return, he was nevertheless given the security clearance to be made cognizant of progress. The Jarl must have been pleased with the reports.

Company A Supervisor addressed Langur's gathering first:

"All planetary water reserves have had their fluoride levels increased to the maximum. All bottled water and all soft drinks have had anti-anxiety drugs added; dosages sufficient induce a sense of general well-being. The side effects are as useful for our purposes as is the symptomatic behaviour from the initial effects of the drugs. Even those who exhibited manic, hostile or aggressive behaviour were valuable. They are even now used by the war efforts as exceptionally effective combatants. Levels of conflict around the planet have increased sufficiently to have an acceptable impact on reducing population numbers. War is becoming a desirable career path for the aliens, a means of accumulating wealth, a system of entertainment and a catalyst for innovation. This last phenomenon, though unexpected, has proved to be most useful."

The gathered individuals, except for the Supervisors, had already begun to feel uncomfortable by the scenario unfolding before them. They glanced at each other, trying to maintain neutrality as much as possible under the gaze of the Supervisors. Valokvantti's reaction remained seemingly non-committal. The next report was tendered without a pause. The last statement from Company A supervisor gave her the perfect lead-in to her area of responsibility ... Eco-rehabilitation.

Company C - Supervisor:

"Initially we thought we would need to sequester a great quantity of carbon dioxide and methane to re-establish more stable climatic conditions. We will still need to increase the ozone percentage in the atmosphere. The process is under way. However, the alien War effort has created innovative technologies for the production of renewable energy. Coal and Gas mining has stopped almost completely. Nuclear energy production is being scaled back in every country. An almost immediate effect of all that has been a dramatic decrease in the pollutants in the atmosphere, reducing the effects of the hot-house gases. The air is cleaner, and the ocean waters are already becoming less acidic. The good news is that the planet's ecology had not quite tipped past it's event horizon before we were able to intervene."

Langur thanked the Supervisor without commenting on her report. If they had not known that the end strategy was to completely exterminate the aliens in order to colonize their planet with the hybrids, perhaps they might have shown more enthusiasm about the encouraging progress in rehabilitating the ecology. Valokvantti knew some of the strategy directly from The Jarl. But the latest news nevertheless took him by surprise. Without a break in the proceedings Company B Supervisor continued. His report being the briefest, although his area of activity was the most critical for the colonization strategy to succeed.

"Population growth is now almost zero. With continued, or even escalating conflict it will become negative. Smoking is on the increase again. It seems to calm the aliens, as well as achieving a greater degree of sterility among the two sexes. It appears that a side effect of chemically enhanced smoke is causing abnormal cellular growths in their bodies, for which they have no cure. Many die as a result. With the reduction in population more food is available to the remaining aliens, of which they take great pleasure in consuming as much as possible. Their increased levels of obesity have had a detrimental effect on their fertility as forecast by our original research. At this stage it seems an STD pandemic may not be necessary: Perhaps only as a last resort if the planetary leaders realise their species is in danger of extinction."

With the last report concluded the Supervisors remained attached to their respective energy consoles, waiting for a response from the team. There was complete silence in the conference room. The team knew full well what to expect following on from their latest encounter with The Jarl, and Leuhta's bold alternative action plan. But this was actual reality hitting them hard.

Langur's voice broke the silence after an uncomfortably long time. "Thank you for your reports – You may go."

Oblivious of the tensions in the room generated by their reports the Supervisors promptly returned to their respective areas of responsibility on Vesimaa.

Valokvantti, who had very firm views about the limited intrinsic value of those exasperating aliens, taken aback by the clinical efficiency with which the extinction strategy progressed, said, "I'm disturbed by what I've just heard. You all know my attitude to the aliens, but," he paused to concentrate his words, "I need to think about what we are doing here."

Langur made no attempt to stop the Captain from leaving, feeling somewhat the same himself.

Leuhta voiced her thoughts openly first, while she fixed Langur with her stare. "What we have to remember is our original mission. You convinced all of us Langur, that there was only one way to save our people. Nothing has changed. Go down on the farms, look at all the AmbSims and their scions. We are succeeding. That's all we have to think about." Obviously she felt compelled to reaffirm their focus following the cold efficiency with which their own race went about exterminating their cousin species.

No one spoke for a while, deeply absorbed in troubled thoughts. Then, as always, Eili spoke softly and with considerable authority. "Our racial memory will now have woven into it guilt for a crime that should not have been committed, a crime that is in the process of being perpetrated right now. We ... we have the power to prevent that crime. Make no mistake – this is a crime of the greatest magnitude."

"The future inhabitants of TC-E who will represent our survival and who will claim this planet as their home, do not have to know about the ... the ... process." Dr.Qilaq couldn't believe what he just heard himself say. Nor could Langur. *What's Qilaq up to? I would have expected a comment like that from Valokvantti, but not Qilaq!*

Langur didn't feel he could contribute anything useful to the discussion so soon after the shock they all just experienced, other than to quietly say, "I don't have a solution. We are faced with an impossible situation. It is only our ethics making it so. Perhaps it is that small part of us we have inherited from these aliens that now creates this dilemma for us."

Eili ventured to voice his private thoughts openly. "You will all agree that not every individual on Dokkheim will be suitable, or will want to be involved in what we are trying to achieve." Affirmative nodding from his audience encouraged him to continue, though without knowing where exactly his thoughts would lead. "Not every alien individual is suitable, or would want to take part in this project either." More nodding. "I want to emphasize a most important point ... their extinction at their own hands ... Just cast your minds back to when we first encountered these people. What were they doing to each other? What were they doing to their planet? How much longer could their planet sustain their lives? Their extinction even then was imminent and assured. Let me again emphasize this ... Their total extinction was already guaranteed."

The room went quiet again as Leuhta asked Eili, "What are you saying?"

Dr.Qilaq volunteered, "what Eili is trying to tell us is that the aliens' only hope of survival is exactly what we are doing - interbreeding with them."

"That is exactly what I'm saying!" Eili exclaimed, pleased he got his message across. He had dedicated his life, what was left of it, to a cause he wholeheartedly believed in and no minor jittery scruples was going to undermine the great Project.

Langur needed to terminate the discussion before it went into realms of improbable fanciful or dangerous thinking. "We'll stop right there. We all have a great deal to think about. This discussion, and the report from the Supervisors stays between us. Understood?"

Perhaps he didn't need to say that, yet worth pointing out the delicacy of the situation. To his mind they couldn't countenance the salvation of their own people at the expense of the total extinction of another species. That's where the problem lay; but not for The Jarl, not for Yakiv, not for the Dokkheimiens back on their own world and possibly not for Valokvantti. It would certainly not go down well with Tumma and Saija or Lefe, if they knew all the finer details of what's happening so far.

Valokvantti returned to his post to prepare for departure as soon as they met the quota for young, healthy alien specimens. Langur found him there, fussing about obviously not his normal efficient self. He needed to clarify the Captain's feelings for himself about the reports. Langur didn't want a loose cannon if circumstances came to a head. Perhaps just as well Valokvantti wasn't privy to the post presentation discussions. Langur waited, quietly observing Valokvantti until being noticed.

"Langur! You startled me. I'm quite busy getting ready to get back to our original trajectory. Whatever you want ... can't it wait?" Langur could see Valokvantti was just maneuvering for time and that he had something pressing on his mind ... and he had a pretty fair idea what that was.

"This won't take too much of your time. I need your opinion."

The Captain was always willing to make time to give his opinion, about anything, especially giving advice. Langur's ploy worked and the Captain turned to him. "The report from the Supervisors - you've been able to digest it?" He'd chosen the word deliberately as the action unfolding on the alien planet was more than unpalatable. Valokvantti grunted. *A good sign*, Langur thought. "What do you make of it?" He tried to keep his approach casual.

"Efficient ... very efficient ... effective, most effective ..." Valokvantti paused, looked directly at Langur before coming clean. "Brutal! Absolutely brutal! It's not right! So the only aliens that will remain are the ones we have on board. That's what it amounts to, doesn't it?" Obviously there were some serious conflicts going on inside the Captain. Langur didn't want to react prematurely to the outburst.

He asked after a pause, "How many could we store on board?" Without actually stating the obvious the Captain had demonstrated, at least by his initial reaction, that he was in complete concord with the feelings of Langur's team.

"Twice as many as we have at the moment. That would make about ten thousand individuals. I'll organize it." Having got the emotion out of his system Valokvantti resumed his activities more purposefully.

Langur left the conversation drift at that point. hopefully Valokvantti would not be troublesome in the near future. The extra aliens would at least give Langur enough specimens to experiment with, should the need arise. There was no need to discuss the wellbeing of the inhabitants on Vesimaa. It was self-evident to everyone that Vesimaa's ecology, bio-diversity, climate and so on, had to be rehabilitated regardless of any other plan that may have been in progress. Langur decided that was the best line of approach to take the next time he met with Tumma, which appointment he scheduled for the following day.

"We are doing what we can to stabilize the situation on your planet," he said to Tumma.

Lefe and Saija were absent. They didn't know about the meeting. Langur's and Leuhta's transformations to AmbSims would prove to be most valuable in improving the relationships between themselves and the aliens. Already Tumma didn't seem as confrontational as on previous occasions. 'Appearances' seemed to make such a big difference to these primitive people.

"Already our scientists have achieved some remarkable results. You have noticed how the air is clearer and your planet is greener in many parts."

Tumma ignored Langur's attempt to steer the conversation away from the big issue. "I don't understand what's happened. There is so much conflict. Everybody seems to be at war with everyone else," Tumma tried sorting out the situation in his mind. "I was only there for a day, but I could see so much has changed in just a few years."

Langur used a conversational tone. He could sense Tumma's apprehensions but he didn't want to tease out Tumma's thoughts just then. "You know, probably better than us, that your people are a warlike species. There isn't a period in your history without there being conflict to a greater or lesser extent in many areas on your planet. You've already had two global wars. Perhaps your people are heading for the third."

Langur could say all these things with complete comfort in his mind. It was all true. The consequences of these aliens' nature were inevitable. There was no reason for him to dwell on the fact that the Dokks had simply accelerated the inevitable.

Tumma wasn't to be put off. "Everywhere people are smoking as if being paid to do it! So many of them are overweight! And what about the birth rates. Maternity hospitals are almost shutting down for lack of business. What is going on!"

"War has its inevitable consequences." Langur tried to speak in general terms about Tumma's observations. "People become anxious. They need to do things to make themselves feel better. But you can see that our scientists are already there to help restore the health of your planet. More will come, and we ourselves will return … to help."

Tumma didn't notice the slight hesitation. His thoughts were in too much confusion for the moment. Instead of digging further into details, he just made an offhand comment, "But will I still be alive to see it?"

"That could be arranged," Langur said immediately, perhaps a little too quickly. He knew the solution to Tumma and Saija's immortality wasn't easy, and he didn't have a workable one just yet. In some ways he would have preferred that Eili had not mention their return to the planet to Tumma, or that Leuhta had not permitted Tumma to land there. Yet, in the long term, it could prove to be advantageous to keep the two 'first citizens' in closer confidence with the progress of the Project, and at more of an arms-length from the discontent of the general population on board the spacecraft.

Many weeks later Tumma still ruminated over his visit to Earth and his unsatisfying discussion with Langur. By that time Synty had returned to its previous trajectory and a fair way out of the Solar System. Because of his position as a 'first citizen' he had privileges others didn't. For example, he could go almost anywhere he liked on the vessel. The really critical laboratories and 'alien' storage facilities were well hidden from his scrutiny. He wasn't even aware they existed. However, he was starting to hear and see things that were at odds with what he had been given to understand, either by omission or by deliberate misdirection. He confided his troubling thoughts to Saija for the first time in a very long while.

Deception Discovered

Tumma wanted to share his recent visit to Earth with Saija.

"And you didn't think to include me! What is your problem!

She hit him on the shoulder with the palm of her hand, furious at having been left out. It took considerable effort to bring her around. Only when he started discussing his misgivings, his unfulfilling discussion with Langur and the things he'd discovered on his travels around the vessel did she begin to listen to him more attentively.

"There is some kind of conspiracy we know nothing about. It's got nothing to do with another potential riot – something even more serious - something to do with the way the Project is being carried out."

"So what do you think is going on? I never really trusted these weirdos!" Saija said, pleased to see Tumma coming out of himself, though still upset about being left out of the chance to visit Earth. "You are unbelievable. You make me so angry sometimes."

"I've spoken with Langur and the others. He didn't say anything very helpful. He spoke in evasive generalizations without really saying anything at all. I kept getting the feeling he was hiding something. But first tell me more about the children taken away for examinations, and the children who are dying."

"Well, initially I thought it was perfectly normal for the young kids to have medical check-ups. After all they are hybrids. But they've had one examination after another. It all seemed too much after a while. And they appeared to change a little, as if they were becoming a bit aloof. I can't really put my finger on it, but it's got many people upset. Then lately we've started to have a high incidence of child mortality. I know I was only a psychiatric nurse, but that doesn't mean I'm stupid. I know from my training what normal infant mortality rates could be expected in any given population. What's happening here is just not natural. Look

Tumma, I hate to say it because you have shown such dedication to the plight of these odd-balls, but I think some kind of 'weeding' is going on - as if the kids are being vetted and some found not to be up to scratch, and their deaths are being engineered somehow."

He became pensive for a while, absorbing what Saija had said and trying to fit the pieces into the jigsaw puzzle that had formed in his mind. He kept coming back to the same starting point ... *The problems on Earth didn't start until the Dokks appeared. True, there was conflict on Earth and everything else Langur said was true. But thirty years can't explain the scale of changes I saw.*

Eventually his mind came back to Saija. He revealed his thoughts, no longer conscious of being monitored. They'd lived with the surveillance for so many years without there being any form of persecution that could be tied back to it, that it was inevitable to lose awareness of it. Every individual was under constant scrutiny, especially the first citizens.

Security personnel alerted Langur to the nature of the discussion to which he now listened, becoming highly alert.

Tumma launched into it. "When I spok with Langur, and I don't know why but I got the feeling he was being evasive. He said they would be back. Now why would that be if we are supposed to colonize TC-E? When I mentioned I wouldn't be alive to see that, he had a very strange answer. I thought he was supposed to restore our mortality ... but it may be contrary to his plans."

"What do you mean," Saija asked.

"Let me finish before I lose my track of thought. Langur said they were doing everything they could to make Earth healthy again. Now why would that be do you think? Why would they feel the need to interfere with our planet if Tau Ceti-E was the new planet for them? He said 'stabilize the situation' on Earth. Why interfere at all! When I asked him about TC-E. He became most animated. Things were going so well he said; they had the majority of their twenty bio-domes constructed, needing only atmosphere and buildings. No word about the terraforming of the planet to make it suitable for life.

It just seems to me the work is on an insufficient scale if they're going to truly colonize TC-E. It appears to be more like a holding pen until they're ready for the next stage."

Saija had already developed a healthy skepticism towards the Dokks. Tumma's thoughts did nothing to change that attitude.

"Do you mean what I think you mean?"

"Exactly! I think Earth has become very attractive to them, but there are too many people on it already – and they've realized it!"

"You can't mean they're trying to … to … I can't even say it Tumma!" Saija was outraged.

"I tried asking Dr.Qilaq about what I saw back home. He lost his usual composure. He didn't know, he said. He said he was only concerned with matters here on the ship. The more I dug the less helpful he became. He just kept talking about the AmbSims not acclimatizing to the environment, whatever that meant. It's more what he didn't say when I asked him how the Project was progressing. When I pushed him about Earth again, he kept changing the subject to talk about TC-E and how close we were."

"That's odd. What else did he say about the AmbSims? Did he say anything about the children?"

"Please don't interrupt Saija, let me get it all out."

As Langur listened to the conversation he knew what he had to do. These two had become a serious security risk to the Project. *They are proving to be far more intelligent than I gave them credit for.*

"When I asked Eili about the riot and the way Valokvantti handled matters he just said nothing bad would happen to the people on the vessel. Well, that was reassuring to a point. But by omission I felt he was indicating something bad was going to happening to those back on Earth. So what do you make of that? Here's another important individual running the show and who's also doing a little dance around the whole issue when we try to speak to him seriously. So as a last attempt to get some clarity on this mess, I tried Leuhta. She may seem like a pretty hard nut to crack, but I thought she would be more direct and less evasive. The first 'batch' of 'chosen' hybrids, she said, would soon be ready to bond with the second wave of AmbSims. Everything was under control and we didn't need to worry about anything."

"Whatever did she mean by 'chosen' hybrids?" Asked Saija with renewed interest, as it was a subject of particular concern to her and Lefe.

"Well let's have a look at what she said. Obviously some of the children were not found suitable."

"What has, or is going to happen to them?" Saija caught her breath … "The increased mortality!"

Tumma continued. "She used the word 'batch' instead of group or whatever. Now doesn't that suggest something rather experimental to you? As if she was dealing with, dare I say it, lab rats! She had said it so naturally, so unguardedly. Makes me wonder just where we stand with these Dokks. Ok … now this business of the second wave of AmbSims. Wouldn't you say it was the natural progression to use new rather than recycled DNA if you wanted to dilute the base genetic structure. Well I do! It means they want to bleach out as much of humanity as possible in order to achieve their goal."

Saija simply stared wide-eyed at Tumma, scarcely able to comprehend everything he'd been leading up to. A knocking at their door interrupted her response. Even before the conversation had concluded between them, Langur, Leuhta and Eili arrived at their enclosure, with several security personnel.

**

The Jarl had been busy at home while changes were taking place on Vesimaa and aboard Synty. He was more than satisfied by the reports he'd received from the three Supervisors on Vesimaa. The cleansing, in all respects, of the alien planet was progressing ahead of schedule. Within three of their generations he could expect the majority of the aliens to have been terminated. Valokvantti's reports were brief, terse even, but the message clear. The last of the suitable specimens had been taken aboard Synty, so the rest left on Vesimaa were expendable. There were enough of them in storage even if there were large losses during the genetic transition on TC-E. As for the hybrid population … Valokvantti had carried out The Jarl's directive to the letter. He was just the right kind of man to do that sort of job.

The hybrids were being satisfactorily vetted. The strict quality control parameters established by The Jarl proved to be adequate to ensure that only the genetically advanced, and the appropriately psychologically oriented individuals were retained to produce the next generation of hybrids. The illness from which the unsatisfactory hybrids died seemed 'natural', to those who didn't know better. Genetically, The Jarl only required those whose DNA showed a modification to the telomeres without having taken on too many Vesimiaan characteristics. Anyone who showed a bias in their thinking towards the aliens was also considered to be a malfunctioning unit, and disposed of efficiently. Valokvantti was doing a good job in The Jarl's estimation.

Yakiv was in attendance with The Jarl when the latest shorter than normal report arrived. It indicated two original aliens, their first contact specimens, had to be taken into custody. They became a security risk to the Project. *I'll let Langur deal with them. They are superfluous to me now.* There was no particular reason for The Jarl to share that with Yakiv; he was after all, just a means to an end.

Instead he demanded, "Yakiv, update me on your volunteer program."

Yakiv no longer behaved like the self-assured businessman Langur originally knew. Under the yolk of The Jarl's demands he'd resigned himself to being told what to do and when to do it, most of the time. Receiving handsome remuneration for his efforts certainly didn't cause him any distress.

"We don't have enough," Yakiv said.

When The Jarl decided on the best method of enlisting members of his species for the Project, a method that would cause him the least amount of complications, he settled on a volunteer program; not enforced secondment but a free choice process. The preparations on TC-E were well under way. It was no small matter to establish living centers for several hundred thousand individuals, but certainly much less aggravation than trying to change their entire planet's ecology to support life well into future millennia. The arrangements on TC-E had to be ready for Synty when it arrived. The project time line didn't allow for an eon to make a planet suitable. Just another reason why the water planet was such a good option. In practical terms, it only needed minimal attention to make it work.

"I told you to round up an adequate number of breeding stock using the volunteer program. Did you make it clear to them the sole object was to save our species from extinction by re-engineering mortality back into our genetics? Did you happen to mention that they would be most generously compensated for shorter life spans?" Asked the Jarl.

"Yes - Yes."

"Then why are there not enough volunteers?" As The Jarl pondered the problem he recalled what Dr. Dr.Qilaq had said about a particular sector of their community, he called them Temporals. They were already under a sentence of shortened life expectancy. Surely many of those would be suitable and willing to undertake the adventure. "Get the Temporals. Vet them. Take the youngest only. Think you can handle that?" So much for volunteers. What needed to be done, had to be done. There was no room, or time for procrastination. It wasn't part of The Jarl's makeup, from his point of view anyway.

Yakiv couldn't afford to disappoint their Jarl too often. The Leader had his sights set on one thing only. Nothing would stand in his way. Yakiv knew about the Temporals but not who they were, or what conditions had brought them under the classification. Eili knew and he provided access to more individuals than Yakiv actually needed. He combed through their global society to find those with the right backgrounds, the right education, the right attitudes, and those whose longevity was curtailed without affecting the health of their already compromised genetic code.

Well into this round-up, news of further unrest reached The Jarl. He'd had just about enough from his unruly people. The violence again escalated rapidly. Their magnevid news media began asking obtuse questions about The Jarl's intentions in selecting from only a limited sector of their community for the Project; a sector considered by most to be 'damaged', though tolerated by their culture. The Jarl responded with a heavy hand.

"Use force if you have to Yakiv to make up the numbers. While you're at it, make it clear – Non-compliance will be treated as a crime against our people – punishment will be severe."

He'd already made up his mind only a very small percentage of the population would be used. The others just had to remain on Dokkheim and take their chances. There was still the option open to them of resurrecting their desire to live enriching lives to the fullness of time, although a very slim chance of that happening – and they would have to do it without him. *My destiny is to rule the new Dokkheimien civilization on a healthy new world.* He could see no reason why He, the supreme ruler, should become mortal. *An immortal among mortals – that has a certain appeal to it. Yes indeed - Vesimaa will be most suitable!*

As the unrest continued and the population chose civil disobedience The Jarl's ideas crystallized concerning his position in the greater scheme of things, which involved having a competent, loyal individual by his side. *Valokvantti is doing an outstanding job aboard Synty. Yakiv has also proved himself to be competent enough here. He's succeeded in getting the full quota of Dokks together and has sent them on their way to TC-E.* It had taken the man many years to do it, but a very short time from the Dokkheimien perspective.

People had come to fear Yakiv as well as respect him, or at least respect his position of power. He took the initiative to slave clone every individual who openly opposed the Project, and enlisted them into manufacturing the vessels that took the Temporals to TC-E in much less time than originally anticipated. Yakiv had potential - It was worth The Jarl considering the unprecedented step of appointing his own successor. Valokvantti might have been next in line by virtue of his past association with The Jarl, but he would be of much greater value otherwise occupied. It was unfortunate Haakon wasn't informed of the way Valokvantti handled emergent situations while he was in sole charge aboard Synty. The Jarl may have been able to avert some of the disastrous events of the future.

**

Lefe hurried around the corner of the main corridor leading to Tumma's rooms. She stopped suddenly at the sight of a small group of AmbSims assembled outside his door because several of those individuals were armed security personnel. She stepped back out of sight as some of the group entered.

She had come to the two 'first citizens' to discuss a most worrying matter. In the past, those two had always been able to somehow help sort things out for the Vesimiaans, AmbSims and the hybrid children. Too many of those children had become ill and died in the last six months. There appeared to be no explanation for the phenomenon, no foundation for the illness, which by all accounts was the same for all the deceased. Not as many of the second generation had succumbed to the mysterious illness, but it was of course still a major issue to the parents. It aggravated the unrest amongst an already agitated society.

Influx of large numbers of new AmbSims, without a corresponding number of Vesimiaans, agitated apprehensions. Something was definitely happening about which they were being kept ignorant. These issues fled from Lefe's mind as she watched events unfold at Tumma's door.

"Do you see the picture that's emerging," Tumma asked.

Instead of responding Saija answered the door. Her mind was still in an uproar about the implications of all Tumma had said. She greeted Langur, Leuhta and Eili.

"Come in," she invited flatly not noticing a security guard stepping in behind Langur.

She led the visitors to the sitting room and sat beside Tumma. Langur, Leuhta and Eili sat opposite to them on the other couch. *How come they've arrived right in the middle of our conversation? –* though Saija, still not making the connection to the surveillance system. Langur appeared unusually preoccupied as he greeted them. Leuhta and Eili just nodded. Tumma and Saija glanced at each other, both thinking something serious was going on. Without any preamble Langur came straight to the point.

"We have been listening to your conversation." He stopped there for a moment - in that moment they were aliens, not the 'friends' he'd been interacting with over the long years as their craft sped towards Tau Ceti-E.

Saija's eyes flashed anger and hostility. Tumma set his jaw and his pupils dilated.

It's easier to deal with an emotional alien out of control, than a self-composed one, Langur thought to himself and half glanced in the direction of the door where the guard had stepped in to wait. Saija followed his glance and saw the guard. Thrusting her pointing finger out in his direction, she demanded,

"Why do you need him!" She shouted.

Leuhta waved at the guard to wait outside. Ordinarily Saija wasn't given to such demonstrative outbursts, but everything Tumma had been saying suddenly came to the surface – and she was livid!

George joined Lefe, still around the corner, watching; a Vesimiaan man who'd also come to advise Tumma. The two continued to wait in silence, hidden from view of the guards.

"Anything else?" Tumma asked Langur slowly.

This could turn out to be difficult. Langur could see the rising tension in Tumma in spite of his calm voice. He decided again to be straight forward, ignoring Saija's question.

"You knew from the very beginning why we came to your planet. It wasn't for the benefit of your species. We did not make war against you. We asked for your help, and you gave it willingly. For us that was most expedient, and we thank you for your ... altruism ... I hope that is the right word."

Saija made a superhuman effort to control herself. "We didn't ask for anything in return. It is true. But by your implication we had come to ... to look forward to ... certain benefits. Specifically, for those of us aboard the vessel." Saija was about to add something else but Tumma put a soft restraining hand on her knee.

"Come to the point Langur," Saija urged between clenched teeth.

So far Eili just kept his eyes on the two aliens without saying anything. They could be unpredictable.

Langur stated the situation as clearly as he could. "Our primary intention was to colonize another planet with the hybrids of our two species, in the expectation ours would become mortal, hence prevent our extinction."

Then Eili continued for Langur. "Our leader, Jarl Haakon, after considering the nature of your people and what you were doing collectively to yourselves and to your planet, decided on a slightly different course of action."

"Which process has now been fully implemented," Leuhta added.

With teeth gritted Tumma raised enquiring eyebrows. It seemed all his suspicions were correct. Saija had started to fidget and perspire.

"Tau Ceti-E will be a temporary place for us; for our regenerated people until there is a sufficiently large population that could sustain itself and grow."

"Then you intend to colonize our Earth!" Saija shouted, not being able to contain herself any longer.

"Yes," said Langur.

Still in a quiet tense voice Tumma ventured the obvious, "Without us on it."

"Preferably," Langur softly confirmed.

Langur was now committed to having to tell these two everything; as much as he knew himself. They were only two individuals, and as such expendable now that they had made their major and most critical contribution. But it wasn't that simple. Over the years they had become the main mechanism through which the Dokks were able to maintain order and control amongst the experimental subjects. All the Vesimiaans and all the AmbSims and all the hybrids trusted them. That was a double-edged sword. It worked for the Dokks, but could equally work against them. Unfortunately, and this little matter was overlooked in their initial planning, the Dokks on the vessel were greatly outnumbered by everyone else. A major armed conflict could well mean the permanent termination of the Project. If these two aliens decided to lead such a revolt it could prove disastrous. Even if the people only thought they were under threat, that itself could initiate the unthinkable.

Tumma and Saija were in an unenviable position for themselves, and a most awkward one for Langur; but only because Langur was a reasonable man, and only because he could see the consequences of making the wrong decisions. If Valokvantti had still been in charge that could well have precipitated a catastrophic disaster. The man wasn't blessed with diplomacy. This situation had to be sorted out with great care, without undue haste.

"We need to come to some arrangement Tumma, Saija. Would you come with us, now, somewhere where we would not be disturbed?"

What alternative did they have? They were aboard a vessel in deep space, under the control of these extra-terrestrials, with no one to look to for help.

Tumma was about to acquiesce when Saija spoke out. "You would not be looking for our cooperation unless you felt it was essential to your noble plans."

Eili nodded slightly, Langur and Leuhta showed their acknowledgement with their silence. "We two are not enough. You need another, Lefe, to 'cooperate' as you say. She's one of yours. I don't need to tell you how important she is, being one of your leading AmbSims. If you have been spying on us you've been spying on her too." Although Lefe was essentially a Dokk, Saija felt she was on the side of the Vesimiaans. Having her with them could prove to be a trump card.

Langur considered this and looked to his two companions for their thoughts. They nodded assent. "Yes." That's all he said as he led them to the back door.

Lefe didn't have to wait too long for her friends to appear. They were not restrained, but the guards were obviously at the ready. Tumma and Saija seemed to be going with them willingly, but she saw in their faces something to instantly put her on alert. That was no ordinary gathering. She had to get back to her people immediately. After a brief discussion with George each got ready to run.

The group in front of her proceeded down another corridor. She and George took off to return to their people to alert them to imminent action. George ran ahead and turned another corner. He didn't see Lefe being intercepted by several security guards. Langur knew about Lefe. He had been under surveillance for some time.

Negotiations

George got away.

Although a fairly prominent citizen he wasn't tagged as a potential problem. With their limited resources the Dokks couldn't keep track of all their experimental subjects all of the time. George was one of those rare, level headed individuals whose first reaction wasn't to panic, but to think. He put the word out and the grapevine went into action. The people began to organise; more accurately, they put their existing plan into action.

Lefe arrived with her security escort at the same time Tumma and Saija were being ushered into an interview enclosure. The three of them represented the main obstacle to the Dokks getting carried away with their ill treatment of the people. Langur, Leuhta, Eili and Dr.Qilaq went to the adjacent observation room when Lefe arrived. The bare interrogation chamber with its light coloured walls offered no seating of any kind and the dull, diffused lighting created a dead zone. The walls swallowed up the sound of Tumma's words as if they were floating in a sensory deprivation chamber.

"Glad you could join us Lefe," he tried not to sound as concerned as he felt.

Langur first wanted the three of them to exchange thoughts. Then he could better decide when and what to do with them. *I want to know what's happened to Lefe. She's a Dokkheimien, except for her physical appearance. Why has she formed such a strong alliance with the aliens?*

"Why are we all here, Tumma?" Lefe asked the moment she saw him. She wasn't anxious, just upset and angry at being forcibly detained.

"We have become aware of certain things, that your people would rather not have us know."

"What do you mean 'my people'? I'm Saija's friend ... your friend, Tumma. I have made my life among the people in the Great Valley. I've dedicated my life to the same cause you have. So don't shut me out. What's happening here?"

Langur and his team listened with dismay at Lefe's words.

Saija explained the situation, now somewhat calmer than she was at home. "You have come to me on many occasions with various issues that made you think about your situation. Things that appeared to be out of the normal; things that made everyone anxious. It seems there was a good reason for all of it; as much among my people as yourselves and the hybrids." This time Lefe threw a challenging glance at Tumma. She was always ready to face any situation head on.

Tumma went on, "The Dokks intend to exterminate the people on my planet ..."

He stopped suddenly, jumping forward to prevent Lefe from falling to the ground. She'd immediately turned deathly pale on hearing Tumma's pronouncement, reached a hand out towards Saija and began to fall. Tumma just managed to catch her, lowering her gently to the floor. They sat beside her waiting for her to recover. The blood rushed back into Lefe's head quickly enough and as her eyes refocused on his face, Tumma continued with the bad news. He didn't know how long they would be allowed to be together, and there wasn't a moment to be lost.

"I'm sure they're listening to us, but I have to tell you this Lefe. They want to return to Earth from TC-E once there's a large enough population of hybrids with the corrected life span parameters. They never intended to colonize TC-E permanently. The people on Earth are expendable, but it seems those of us trapped aboard this ship still have our uses."

Lefe cried out, clearly distressed, "How do you know all this Tumma? Who told you? It can't be true!"

As the conversation continued it became clear to Langur, whose body had slumped in depressed resignation, and to the others, that there was much more to deal with than just the Vesimiaans. Their own people may have become alienated from their own race. Whatever was causing the AmbSims to change allegiance had to be stopped.

While Langur and his team retired to confer, the three potential mutineers were given beds, food and water. They remained incarcerated for several weeks before meeting Langur and the others again. Valokvantti accompanied them for the interrogation, looking dark and extremely somber.

Lefe learnt everything Tumma and Saija knew, guessing what she wasn't told directly. She in turn had information as well, telling them quite openly, knowing all their conversation would be monitored, "The population has been increasing exponentially. I think the combined population of AmbSims, Vesimiaans and hybrids outnumber the Dokk personnel. More and more AmbSims are being brought in, and some of the first hybrids are having children of their own. And here's something I don't understand – more and more Vesimiaans are miraculously appearing, as if they had been taken out of storage. These people couldn't remember any of their past."

Then Lefe gathered Tumma and Saija close to whisper to them. "You know about George? He was with me just before I was detained. He got away. He's got a lot of connections and knows what to do in case of an emergency. Ever since the first riot we've been getting ready to defend ourselves – or if necessary – take control."

Tumma and Saija tried not to look surprised. Their shock wasn't at this clandestine activity but that Lefe had not trusted them enough to confide in them earlier. On reflection perhaps it was just as well. What they didn't know couldn't be coerced out of them.

"We had no idea such a strong movement had developed. It seems the people are in more of a position of strength than we could have imagined," Saija glanced at Tumma as she whispered her reaction, conflicting thoughts rapidly emerging.

At the first interrogation Langur initiated the conversation by giving the three an opportunity to make themselves comfortable in the new chairs and to accustom themselves to the idea of having Valokvantti present.

"I think it is unwise to include the Captain, given the bad feelings he'd generated in the past," Eili voiced his opinion.

Langur insisted. "It's not just the Project that's in danger, yet again. The security of the vessel has to be considered. All our lives could well be at stake. It is essential to have the Captain of the vessel here."

As was his custom, Langur went directly to the heart of the matter. "As I said before Tumma, we need to come to some arrangement," glancing at Saija and Lefe as he made the statement.

They want some 'arrangement' – hmm, Tumma almost said aloud.

The three of them must have been thinking the same thing, as they looked at each other in silent communication.

Leuhta immediately put Lefe on the spot, "Where do you stand in this, Lefe?"

A very good question indeed, one Langur wanted to know the answer to as well. During the course of the last week Lefe regained her composure, and her courage. She not only knew where she and a good many others stood, she'd made up her mind exactly what she was prepared to do – how far she was prepared to go.

"If everything Tumma has told me is true then I'm not exactly proud to be a part of the same race as yourself Langur. I can also tell you that there are many who feel that the treatment they and their children have received is reprehensible, to say the least. Now you tell me, what is the truth about what's going on! Are you intending to kill all the people of Vesimaa?"

"Our intention has only ever been to prevent our species from extinction. We will do everything it takes to achieve that," Langur indicated quite firmly.

"Even it means global genocide?" Interrupted Saija.

"Yes, but I would not call it genocide."

"WHAT would you call it?" Lefe shot back.

This time Valokvantti stepped into the fray with his own personal opinion.

"It isn't genocide to prevent a living planet being destroyed by a primitive, aggressive, brutal species." He turned to Tumma. "You are raping your planet. You're sucking it dry of all its resources when you have perfectly viable alternatives. You are killing every other species on it. You're even killing each other with your wars and every other way you can imagine! THAT'S the truth! What would you call that?"

Langur waited a moment for Valokvantti to settle, then summarized quietly, "This is the situation as it stands Tumma: The cleansing on your planet is almost complete even as we are nearing TC-E, which will be ready for us by the time we arrive. Our breeding program is progressing on schedule. The results so far indicate success in what we are trying to achieve. It is up to you if you want to continue to be a part of the Project."

"Will there be no one left on Earth? Surprisingly, Lefe asked the question.

Leuhta made no excuses about the situation. "In time, no. However, when we return there may still be some small areas of habitation."

Tumma wanted to know the details of this 'arrangement' they had in mind. "You still need us, otherwise you would have disposed of us by now. You want an arrangement you say. What kind of arrangement?" It was time to come back to reality. Tumma has had to deal with a great deal of unreality in his life, so he knew the difference between the two.

Of them all Eili was probably the most diplomatic. And he knew it was critical to reach TC-E with a live and healthy seed population. "There is agitation and unrest which could become problematic. It would be helpful if the three of you could prevail upon the people to settle down. They will obviously not do that if you give them too much information out of context. They will panic and put all of us in danger; not just us on board, but the future of all Dokks, and ultimately the future of your own people."

So, they want to bargain. I'll give them something to bargain with! "Here's what We want." Saija became the impromptu spokesperson for the people, taking the opportunity to deliver their 'arrangement' demands.

"One: Our people are to be allowed to have children.

Two: Stop the killing of *any* children on the ship.

Three: Stop the genocide on Earth!" The manner of her delivery allowed no room for negotiation."

The Dokks immediately left the interrogation chamber, not even bothering to acknowledge what Saija had just said. All niceties and formalities were off the table. This was fast becoming a fight for the continued existence of the two greatly divergent sapient species.

Tumma or Saija could do little to help people on Earth. What was happening to them was an outrage, an unthinkable, impossible nightmare. Everything Valokvantti said about them was true - they acknowledged that. But did these strange beings have the right to decide humanity's fate? Between the three of them, even with Lefe in agreement, they decided on a plan of action that might benefit everyone. But they needed time. They had to get to TC-E as much as the Dokks. And they needed to make sure, absolutely certain nothing would happen to their spacecraft. It was as critical to their plans as it was for the Dokks.

Saija had delivered the ultimatum, fervently hoping Lefe was right about what George was organizing while they were in detention, it being their only hope. Outnumbering their masters wasn't enough. They had to demonstrate strength and conviction. They had to show they were a serious threat, otherwise delivering an ultimatum could easily make life much more difficult than it had already been. If Valokvantti had his way, they would all be treated like laboratory animals.

There was no way they could find out what was happening on the outside. They need not have worried for when Langur returned two days later he told them.

"It seems we have another situation on our hands Tumma. To prevent us being forced to take the lives of many individuals, you have the chance to ensure the rest of the journey to TC-E is peaceful. The people have delivered their own ultimatum. They want the three of you released immediately. They want us to stop all interference with the children. They want the freedom to bond with whomever they wish, and to be allowed to have children with whomever they wish." Then with a tinge of disappointment in his voice Langur turned to Lefe. "It seems you have organized them well, Lefe."

George deserved most of the credit - best Langur didn't know about that.

Tumma had become quite bitter about the situation. "Why not just take over everyone's minds, like you did with mine, Langur. Then you would have a completely compliant population to work with."

"We considered that option," Langur explained, "before we found the AmbSims shells were having an adverse reaction over time to the Dokkheimien resident psyches. Anything that could interfere so much with normal genetic function has to be avoided. This is our one opportunity to survive."

Langur had no choice but to be quite candid with Tumma. Their best chance to gain time was to placate the people as much as possible. They were only one generation away from TC-E. Once there, everything would change dramatically. The aliens would no longer be needed. Besides, there were enough of them in storage if and when the need arose to use them.

"Vesimaa's regeneration will continue as planned," Valokvantti cut in, "the removal of its people will continue as planned. The process has now advanced to the stage where it cannot be reversed."

Before the three captives could react to the rather inflammatory delivery of an untenable situation, Leuhta explained their position to the prisoners.

"Provided we have a certain undertaking from you, the three of you will be released today. There's only one possible way we can all benefit from this situation. The people must remain calm. They must continue to have the children. You have to realize that once the Vesimiaan generations die out, they cannot be replaced. They can only continue on their evolutionary path through their children … the progeny who will be representative of both our races. That is the only future possible. After the third generation of hybrids, we will permit free bonding pairs, and free procreation. However, the health of the offspring will continue to be monitored to ensure only healthy traits are passed from generation to generation. This is, after all, a controlled breeding program."

Langur made no attempt to soften Leuhta's delivery. The resolution to the impasse was going to happen on their terms or not at all. That was the message Leuhta tried to get across.

Although armed with primitive weapons, the people made up for that with their numbers. At the four primary entrance points from the valley into the shell of the spacecraft, large crowds gathered numbering in the several thousands. Dokk guards, though outnumbered, were ready to defend their positions to the death. Not being a warmongering people themselves without appropriate training, the situation had deteriorated to the point where many of the guards could easily have lost control to fire upon the insurgents with very little provocation. Once the conflict started, there was only one foreseeable outcome. Either the people prevailed through force of sheer numbers or they would not be able to withstand the firepower of the Dokks.

George addressed the crowd at the main entrance urging them to restraint. They had delivered their ultimatum for the release of Tumma, Saija and Lefe, but the crowd grew restless. They'd been waiting for several days without results.

Someone in the crowd, finally overcome by impatience and anger, shouted, "They've killed them!"

Another voiced his discontent, "They're killing our children and they're not going to stop!"

Others began shouting and the surge of feeling spread like fire from person to person, from group to group. George looked at his closest companions with apprehension realizing he would not be able to hold the mob much longer. Just as he turned back to the unsettled throng a missile struck him in the chest and knocked him off his feet. It may or may not have been aimed at him. The target was probably the guard directly behind him, protected by a tall barricade. As George fell the mob surged forward.

A Dokk guard fired the first shot. The soundless weapon made no explosion on impact. The victim had no opportunity to scream his anguish. He just froze and began dropping to the ground in pieces. Even before all of him could hit the ground he had turned to a white ash, demolecularised in an instant. Instead of the shot stopping the surge of the mob it spurred them on. The crowds at the other entrances also turned into attacking mobs when they heard what had happened. A full attack began in earnest.

Some way above the barricade to the main entrance, a door slid open and the three figures appeared on a balcony; Tumma, Saija and Lefe, unaccompanied. Their words were broadcast throughout the vessel, to the mobs, to the Dokks in the shell and to those who remained in their homes. Tumma's loud voice could be heard above the tumult, his group of three individuals clearly lit so they could be seen by the attacking forces.

"Friends!" He said aloud, without shouting.

"Friends! Friends!" He had to repeat himself several times before the three of them were noticed.

"We are free!" Saija added, "We … are … FREE!"

The surge of the attacking mobs was abruptly halted before it could gain deadly momentum. All eyes turned in the direction of the light and the sound. At the same time, the guard who fired the first shot was quickly taken into custody by the Dokks and secreted away.

Langur and his team watched anxiously hoping they had averted the worst possible outcome. Their weapons could have, would have, destroyed the vast majority within just a few minutes.

Valokvantti decided the offending guard had forfeited his existence, and if necessary would be held accountable publicly in front of all the people. As irksome as that was to him, he realized at once considerable value could be gained from the guard's execution. In the greater scheme the guard was expendable, as were many others for the good of the Project.

Not wanting to lose the impact of the moment, Lefe also spoke out, "We are free to choose our own partners!" She had to repeat it several times, before the crowds understood what she said. Suddenly an explosion of cheering filled the air. They'd realized their demands were successful. During a lull in the cheering, Lefe continued, more loudly than before, "We can all have children! We can *All* have children!" she reiterated.

Just those two concessions were enough to arrest the blood lust of the mobs. The cheering continued for quite a while as people and AmbSims hugged each other, jumping up and down, shouting, doing everything a happy crowd usually does. As they settled Lefe extended an invitation, "I will meet with your representatives to explain everything in detail."

Those last few words worried Leuhta and Langur. Eili noticed and quickly commented. "I'm confident Lefe understands the situation and all its implications if she doesn't abide by our arrangement."

Valokvantti felt they'd gained a tactical advantage. "Look how easy that was. With just a few minor compromises we will regain the allegiance of the AmbSims!"

Leuhta disagreed. "All we've gained is time – enough perhaps to get us to TC-E. The AmbSims and Vesimiaans will now be feeling they've won a victory – together. I think it will bring them even closer to one another. From everything Saija and Lefe said, their attitude is most probably that they've won a major battle against their oppressive masters." Langur just listened, getting more worried with every word he heard.

The people were not told about the changes on Earth - they were not told the breeding program was to continue as before. In any case Lefe didn't know what to tell them about that. She couldn't tell them the Dokks already had a solution to make the unexplained disappearance of unsuitable progeny appear more natural. She couldn't tell them, because she didn't know about the fatal illness that would overcome the 'below standard' children. She could also not tell them what the strategy was once the ship arrived at TC-E. The AmbSims were no longer taken into confidence by the Dokk hierarchy. Their sole purpose was to procreate. Afterwards they were just as expendable as the Vesimiaans. If, by living amongst the aliens they developed a kinship with them, a deep familial loyalty to them, then they could no longer expect to be kept aware of how the Project was progressing.

Journey's End

Hurtling through space Synty carried the hopes of salvation for an entire species, and the death of another, as it sped its way to Tau Ceti-E. After many decades in its belly the people lived as if there was no other existence, no other meaning to life, no other aspirations possible than the daily routine which consumed their physical energies, their thoughts and all their desires whilst surviving in the Great Valley. They knew, but only because it was taught at their schools, that their greater purpose was to prevent the extinction of an entire species. But after so many difficult years, it was hard for them to conceive of that as a reality. The story of 'Species Salvation' had begun to take on the semblance of a myth.

After the last great uprising, which had gone into the chronicles of their history, life again settled down to daily routines. People were dying and children were born. Parents developed aspirations for their children; hopes for their lives that didn't include the myth of a planet revolving around a star system in space. The memory of space dimmed over the many years. Contact between the people and their masters living in the shell became almost non-existent.

Some people lived much longer lives than others. Many children died of a mysterious illness not long after birth. Their 'first citizens' didn't age. They had become almost God-like figures. Once there were people who had fair or chocolate complexions. Now the majority had an amber, amber-orange hue; the hybrid generations. No one took much notice. It just seemed to be how nature intended it. Once there were those who claimed they used to live on a planet they called Earth - probably just a story for children. What was a planet, anyway? Although there could still be found the odd individual, aged around a hundred years or more who claimed there was a blue green planet floating in space, whatever 'space' was, populated by billions of individuals. Billions? What was – billions? It was a quantity beyond comprehension for the population of Synty. That couldn't possibly be true. This Great Valley that gave them life, was all there was. There was nothing else. Mysteries did exist, but they were mysteries of the Great Valley not strange unbelievable stories told to entertain children.

One great unexplainable mystery, which had come to have the title 'reincarnation', baffled the amber-orange people. Many AmbSim adults would appear suddenly without any record of them having been born, to become part of society, forming relationships, eventually bonding and producing children. Then after a time they would become ill and just disappear. But then some of these new AmbSims would claim to be the deceased people. How could that possibly be? They certainly possessed the mannerisms and the character and the skills of the deceased individuals - and all their memories, but they looked completely different. Most of the time they would seek out their old partners and try to resume life as if nothing had happened.

But as with all things mysterious time created an explanation, and with repetition the strange phenomenon lost its strangeness and became part of normality. There even emerged an expectation that a lost loved one might very easily reappear unexpectedly, looking completely different, to resume life with their families. Twice already Langur, Leuhta, Eili and Dr.Qilaq had needed to change Vesimiaan shells.

With the passing of time first generation hybrids became adults and bonded with new AmbSims; some with Vesimiaans, but that was in the minority. Their children were well on the way to adolescence. It would be their children who would step out onto the surface of TC-E. The biased education towards Dokkheim continued to drum home the undesirability of immortality, as if it was a deadly plague, while extolling the virtues of a short, productive and vigorous life.

"I know the experiment is succeeding," Langur said to Leuhta, "but it seems to be taking too long."

"Yes," she replied, "but we do have time to see the Project through to its conclusion, and there are still many complications to be resolved. One of which is the unpredictability of both the aliens and our AmbSims. Perhaps the hybrids will not be as troublesome." She tried to find something positive. "Soon the second generation will be ready for pre-selection."

Langur had other problems as well, on which he worked with Valokvantti. "You realise, don't you Captain, that our original crew cannot drive the Project indefinitely. There's just not enough of them. We'll have to select new recruits to train."

"We can get them from the first generation hybrids. If we are to make a break from Dokkheim it has to be a complete break."

"You're right, Captain. I've had my eye on one promising youngster for some time."

The people who would eventually colonize Vesimaa had to be viable hybrids. They had to be people of the light guided by their own principles, by their own destinies. Those who remained on Dokkheim had to change under their own volition or die there. But the future of the new Dokk civilization was in the hands of the hybrids.

"His name is Kirkas Valo," continued Langur. "He's the most successful example of a new generation with telomeres that have shown every indication of deterioration during replication. It looks like he's going to have a shorter life than you or I but still long enough to make a significant contribution to the fulfillment of the Project in the median term."

From The Captain's 'security' perspective Kirkas was a good asset for another reason. "He's formed a strong relationship with Lefe, and he's become prominent within the AmbSims' society. He's gained their trust."

"True," Langur seemed slightly reserved, "the matters he's dealt with were reasonably mundane, but I have to admit, the people seem to have developed respect for him. I'm not sure that's entirely to our advantage. Kirkas has become an intelligent, diplomatic leader, with an air of authority about him, a sense of self-confidence and honesty."

Valokvantti was quick with a solution to Langur's uncertainty. "Recruit him. Put him through our training course. Then we'll see if he can be trusted with reality."

None of the four; Tumma, Saija, Lefe or George had as yet taken Kirkas into their confidence, although they all liked the tall young man. So the plans they were making remained unknown to Kirkas. From the moment of reaching a compromise in the interrogation chamber, the three champions of freedom resolved they would have to find a way, a mutually beneficial way if possible to save the people of Earth from total extinction. First their lack of privacy needed to be resolved. The people were being monitored, especially the enclosures occupied by Vesimiaans domiciled in Synty's shell. They were not sure how much of The Great Valley was under surveillance or how comprehensively. It was also entirely possible they themselves were implanted with tracking devices that could perhaps even transmit visual and audio data.

"We cannot plan unless we have security. We'll have to come up with some kind of shielding device that won't arouse suspicion. Any ideas Tumma?" Saija's impatience clearly showed how much she may have been regretting her decision to accompany Tumma. But then again, she had the opportunity to play a major salutary part in the whole sordid affair.

"Perhaps," Tumma said, "but we must establish some kind of routine of getting about and meeting people that would also not be suspicious."

"We've done it before. You and I'll go down regularly into The Great Valley, visit the villagers in their homes – keep them settled and at the same time keep the peace for the Dokks. They can't complain about that."

Tumma though Saija had a good workable idea there. He had one of his own. "I think there may be a solution for a shielding device. Perhaps I can put all those years of research into the properties of light to some practical use."

He knew that Dokk technology, particularly communications, was based on the quantum encryption of photons allowing for the emission of single photons in data transmission wavelengths. "All I have to do is to intermittently block transmissions without arousing suspicion. What I have in mind will not need sophisticated equipment or tools. It's a device that has not received much attention on Dokkheim because the planet is too dark for it to have worked."

"How will you test this device?" Saija was just a bit wary. "If it fails people could die."

"We need someone who would definitely have been bugged. That's the only way to make absolutely sure. I've got two people in mind."

"You can't mean George - perhaps Kirkas?"

"Probably George, if he'll do it. Kirkas shows the greater potential to infiltrate the Dokk leadership and gain their trust. We must keep him in reserve. If we don't manage to have an inside man our plans have no hope."

**

For over half a century Synty had been ploughing through the dense soup of space towards its destination. Construction work on TC-E advanced ahead of expectations due to Yakiv's various innovations, and concentration on bio-domes at the expense of hauling more ice meteors to the planet's surface than was immediately needed. As far as The Jarl was concerned, if TC-E wasn't the final destination then best to concentrate on short term essentials. It would be many more years yet before Synty arrived with its living payload. Time enough to initiate regeneration of the biosphere after the domes were completed.

**

Cleansing of Vesimaa had slowed. The ecology continued to improve, but the aliens came to their senses. Constant wars with ever increasing casualties, unprecedented natural disasters and declining population growth eventually focused the minds of the world's warmongers. With great difficulty they brought the war machine under control, without being able to stop it altogether. The leaders may have become aware of the greater implications of wars; of rapidly diminishing populations, but the people themselves had developed a liking for the aggression. A blood lust seemed to have pervaded Earth's population to a point where life expectation dropped to below thirty years. The only way to die was in combat! The only reason to live, was to fight! The best form of entertainment was violence!

Of the seven billion aliens only four billion remained. It was time for Company B to implement the back-up strategy. There were two useful methods to further reduce the population. Over the course of the last fifty years the Dokks learnt that the planet's tectonic plate movements could be stimulated. The advantages of generating tsunami were considerable. Such events didn't damage the ecology because they didn't pollute the atmosphere. Their effects were fast and reliable. They not only eliminated aliens but also substantially damaged their major cities, demolished unnecessary infrastructure and introduced such devastating health problems that the aliens could not recover. The greatest advantage was the locations at which these giant waves wreaked their havoc; at the highest population density areas situated by ocean-land boundaries.

The Dokks also took advantage of the alien species' predisposition for coupling. The fervor with which they engaged in this activity, seemingly without the least desire for procreation, offered the perfect opportunity to introduce a few 'natural' diseases. The aliens called these Sexually Transmitted Diseases. The beauty of the program was that their sexual activities were being encouraged by world leaders in an attempt to recover from the population decline. Hence the more coupling occurred, the more the STDs were spread. Population numbers continued to fall exponentially as the global mortality rate continued to increase.

However, the Universe in its infinite and inscrutable wisdom, did feel obliged to contribute to the concatenation of events threatening to throw chaos into balance. The Dokks aboard Synty began experiencing problems of their own. Of the two major emerging issues, neither could have been foreseen by them.

Dr.Tulok, Langur's chief Bio-Engineer, had been kept busy over the years after he'd initiated the Amber Simulacrum program. Langur had him in his office to try sort out yet another major issue.

"Tulok, what are we going to do about the crew's exposure to visible EMR? The effects seem disastrous."

"I've been studying the phenomenon. Most unexpected. The changes to our physiology are – dangerous."

"Yes, I know that much, but do you have a solution?"

"Here's what we know," Tulok did his best to put the issue in layman's terms for Langur, "EMR in the visible light spectrum consists of photos at the lower end that are capable of causing electron excitation within molecules. Such exposure leads to changes in the bonding chemistry of the DNA molecule, in particular at the tail end of each chromosome. The telomeres are under attack from the very source you thought would be the main contributor to our salvation."

"Please come to the point, Tulok."

"Right - although the changes became discernible only when the hybrid young were being examined, the effects of those changes would not be known for several generations. To further complicate matters, the expected changes to telomeres resulting from the alien DNA contribution couldn't be readily distinguished from the effects produced by the EMR." Langur didn't like where this was heading.

Tulok continued, "By comparing observations between the hybrids and ourselves I found many DNA differences. As for the structure of the telomeres, although marginally altered, it has not been possible to determine if the changes have been benign or otherwise. Only time would tell."

"Under normal circumstances time would not be an issue, but these are not normal circumstances. We're working to a deadline. You don't have a solution?"

Dr.Tulok remained silent. There was nothing more he could say. Perhaps in a few more generations. He wanted to get back to work, but Langur had more on his mind.

"This other problem is somewhat more urgent."

"I know. I've had many AmbSims complaining about it. You've already had a couple of new shells yourself Langur. It seems there's an incompatibility between our own psyches and the alien physiology. There's no need to find a permanent solution to this. As long as we have enough alien stock in storage we can update ourselves periodically as needed."

The issue was related more to the confusion within the body caused by interference from an alien mind. That confusion could affect the health of the sperm being produced in the male AmbSims and the eggs of the female AmbSims. Although their technology had advanced well beyond the capabilities of the aliens, they could still not completely unravel the incredible complexity of networking between all the elements of the chromosomes. Their own historical predicament was a testament to that failing. The only solution appeared to be to change Vesimiaan shells at regular intervals.

"We have solid data of the effects on the crew from exposure to visible EMR, although only for a short time while the ship was in proximity of the alien sun. It's not encouraging. They are becoming ineffective at their jobs. Continued exposure to the artificial sun necessary to maintain life for the passengers on board has just made things worse," Dr.Tulok explained.

"Indeed. We've already had to replace much of our pure Dokk crew with hybrids. We're going to need to transition people like Kirkas Valo out of the society of Vesimiaans.

Overall, the Project could have been in a better state. Langur had an ailing crew, some of whom could no longer do their jobs; an ageing and unhealthy AmbSim population; a Captain undecided about his loyalties, and an alien population on the verge of mutiny if Tumma gave the game away. *What I won't need for much longer are Saija and Tumma. That will be relief.*

**

Jarl Haakon left Dokkheim.

He put his personal agenda into action. The lure of a new world became overwhelming. Not only could he be at the beginning of a new chapter in the history of their race - not only be the only immortal amongst a species of mortals, but to be able to leave behind the greatest disappointment of his very long life; a people who could no longer control themselves and who seemed incapable of saving themselves.

He appointed Yakiv as the new leader on their home planet.

Yakiv had great ambitions, but becoming the Jarl wasn't one of them. No matter how successful, how rich or how popular a man might have become on Dokkheim there was no possibility for him to become The Jarl; not unless the incumbent leader appointed him into the position. Against all probability it happened to him. The appointment was sudden and unexpected. Yakiv now had power, unlimited power. He was soon to realize that unlimited power carried with it unlimited responsibility.

The Jarl of the new Dokks on TC-E, henceforth to be known as The Ensimmainen, a title he chose for himself, became the supreme controller on the new planet. He installed himself at the centre of the largest bio-dome. He had no intention of TC-E being the final world for his rejuvenated species. Nevertheless, now that all the domes were almost completed and fully capable of supporting life; the life that was aboard Synty, he initiated the first major stage of establishing the external biosphere.

258

A benign outer world could only be of benefit to those evolving inside the domes – perhaps essential if his people were to acclimatize successfully to life on Vesimaa. Besides, The Ensimmainen didn't relish the thought of placing all his hopes on survival purely on the domes. It was essential to have a contingency environment.

Already several hundred ice barges had resumed collecting ice comets carrying them to every part of TC-E where large depressions could accommodate liquid water. Solar collectors had been positioned around the planet to concentrate light heat from Tau Ceti onto those same areas. Space dust orbiting TC-E was being harvested to be used to start the soil layer of the biosphere.

There would soon be an atmosphere; soon, if one was a Dokk with an unlimited lifespan. All this wasn't his original intention, but as circumstances evolved upon Synty he had to have contingency plans on top of contingency plans. Staying on Dokkheim was out of the question if his species was to survive well into the future. Langur was definitely right about that.

Aboard Synty Valokvantti became deeply depressed on learning of The Jarl's migration and that he himself was to continue being the second in command on the spacecraft … just a superseded secretary with no power whatsoever. Not only was he to play second fiddle, but he was robbed of the opportunity of his rightful 'inheritance' on Dokkheim. He should be The Jarl there now, not Yakiv. Even his responsibilities as Captain aboard Synty had greater status than what he was destined for on TC-E. Langur's commiserations did nothing to alleviate his brooding discontent - a discontent which would eventually manifest itself as anger, paving the way to thoughts he couldn't imagine having entertained even a few years ago. *At the very least I should have been given the opportunity to run things on TC-E until The Jarl took over - if at all.* Valokvantti stood at the crossroads of loyalty. Now, first and foremost there was himself. Then there was Langur. That man always treated him fairly and with respect. The only other individual who had any impact on him at all was Tumma Varjo, surprisingly. But Tumma was an alien. If anything, the fate of the aliens as a species had more of an impact on Valokvantti's sensibilities then the future of his own people.

Although still facing numerous challenges in bringing the Project to a satisfactory conclusion, Langur enjoyed the extended period of peace aboard the spacecraft.

"You've earned both recognition and a little peace after all your efforts," said Leuhta, pleased to see her mate a little more relaxed. "Not since our departure have our experimental specimens settled down to a good working routine for any reasonable length of time."

"People – Leuhta – call them people. At the moment there are no major issues with the breeding program. Our first generation of vetted hybrids are almost all breeding themselves. The Vesimiaan population is diminishing in proportion to the AmbSims and hybrids. I don't mind a relatively few aliens breeding amongst themselves."

"They're not causing any problems lately. Besides – we can easily dispose of them when they're no longer needed. It's really only a minor concession to allow them to breed if it keeps them under control until we get to TC-E." Leuhta tried to keep the situation in perspective.

Tumma and Saija were not making waves. Their ally, Lefe had scaled down her anti-Dokk activities and even George seemed to be doing nothing more than helping to keep order amongst the people. All in all, Langur wasn't at all displeased with progress on board their cosmic ark.

"Do you know of the youngster, Kirkas Valo, a first generation hybrid?" he asked Leuhta. "He's showing promise of being exactly the kind of individual I've been working towards. I'm going to spend more time with him; involve him a little in activities in the shell to get a feel for his dedication to the Project."

"He seems pleasant enough. I haven't met him, but he's building a reputation. It's worth a try." Leuhta expressed the same opinion.

Eili urged caution. "Kirkas is too well liked in The Great Valley. He's become very good friends with Tumma and Saija. There's also his obvious interest in Lefe. She could yet prove to be an undesirable influence on young Kirkas."

"If we could train him those connections could be most helpful to us." Langur maintained.

Eili didn't press the point. "I'll just wait and see. We should be vigilant with this one."

Leuhta listened patiently as Langur spoke his mind later in private. "It's getting too complicated, Leuhta. It's not just about us aboard Synty. What about the people on Vesimaa? We can't just kill every single individual there." Langur stated this not as an opinion but as a self-evident fact. "My conscience will not allow such an abomination. Necessity may be driving us to take extreme action but it doesn't mean we have no obligation to consider the greater implications of those actions."

The fact that he sat opposite someone who looked every bit like a Vesimiaan, because Leuhta was actually inhabiting the body of one, made it even more difficult to think of the aliens just as a means to an end. He'd become used to seeing his mate in the alien body, several alien bodies over time, and he had to admit to himself that she was attractive. She was attractive to look at and attractive in … other ways as well. Certainly more attractive and functional than their dual plane bodies back on Dokkheim, which seemed such a long time ago. A century more or less was no time at all for them. But so much had happened, their involvement in life had been so comprehensively accelerated that it seemed a long time ago indeed.

He'd made the statement and let the sound of it fade while he observed and enjoyed Leuhta's presence. She was relaxed sitting there, smiling at him. There were no emergencies for some time and lately she had even begun to entertain the thought of perhaps planning to have a scion of their own. Langur's statement managed to interrupt those pleasant thoughts. She didn't want to respond. But Langur's pregnant silence insisted on it.

"We've been through this before. None of us likes the idea. You know where our loyalty lies. You know very well what kind of creatures these aliens are. We may have a common ancestry, but that was much too long ago. We have no obligations whatsoever towards them. They will wipe themselves out even if we don't interfere - themselves and their planet. At least this way some of their genetics will endure into the future."

"How can we be their judge and executioner?" Langur couldn't help voicing his reservations.

"We are neither of those," Leuhta said calmly, moving closer to him. "We are trying to save our own species, and we can only do it by using their pure DNA, and - by taking their planet."

"But what if there was another way? What if ... what if ... we could change worlds?" Langur struggled for an impromptu idea to present itself. As soon as he expressed the idea it immediately gathered the momentum of a possible reality.

Leuhta had to take a few minutes to digest what he'd just said. *Is he joking, is he actually suggesting ... No ... it's too far-fetched.* She slid right up beside him. She had to make sure Langur wasn't losing his capacity for logical, judicious thinking.

"What exactly do you mean - change worlds?"

It was the only prompt Langur needed to let his thoughts cascade into a flood of unimpeded words.

"Give them TC-E when we move to their planet. How much simpler could it be! By then TC-E will be habitable outside the bio-domes. Why shouldn't they be given a chance! They are giving us the opportunity we were so desperately looking for."

Leuhta responded quietly and with utter conviction, "Because they don't deserve it." He'd suddenly become weary of the whole subject. Leuhta's close proximity must have helped to take his might off such weighty matters. Her reality check had killed the conversation, but not his admiration of his mate, resulting in a little impromptu action of a much more pleasant nature.

For many weeks neither one of them revisited the subject. It was too outlandish, too unrealistic. There were too many factors against such a course of action. For one, the amount of energy it would take away from their own priorities. And for another, there would probably be no one left on Vesimaa by the time it was possible to even think seriously about it. When they eventually decided to take Eili into their confidence he seemed even more skeptical than Leuhta.

"I cannot think of a single altruistic reason to consider such a plan even as a remote possibility. The cost would be prohibitive," he said. "Besides, they are a belligerent, violent species. Even the aliens aboard Synty have caused too much trouble," he said. "They could also become a threat to us some time in the distant future."

That didn't exactly ignite Langur's enthusiasm. He could think of no other way to help the aliens and ease his own conscience. The whole concept was left right there, unresolved, dead in the cosmos. Langur could trust Eili not to mention the discussion to anyone else. A few days later the Captain sought a meeting with Langur.

"Langur, I need to speak with you – in private – about the fate of the aliens." Valokvantti sounded extremely worried.

Surely Eili hasn't told Valokvantti about the planet exchange idea.

From the moment Valokvantti stepped into Langur's quarters he was ill-at-ease. Langur suspected he'd been struggling with something for some time. He could almost read the man's thoughts. His brooding discontent had turned to anger and frustration. Valokvantti had come to question where his loyalties lay. *If The Ensimmainen doesn't need me anymore and all I'm good for is to be a lackey on a ship, how can I contribute to the Project. Why should I care what happens to the Dokks?*

Thoughts of that nature chased each other around in an endless loop in his mind. Valokvantti didn't know exactly what he wanted to say, but he had to vent his feelings and Langur was the only individual who had consistently treated him with respect and consideration. He was no longer the self-assured authoritative figure who saw himself in control of the expedition. He had been reprimanded, his authority questioned and his range of responsibilities greatly curtailed. So when he finally spoke, Langur could barely recognize him as the man who was a Captain of their spacecraft.

"He should not have done that." Valokvantti began the conversation, omitting all small talk, even a simple greeting.

"Who and what?"

"The Ensimmainen, promoting Yakiv to be The Jarl on Dokkheim." Langur waited. Something strong was brewing inside this man. "That position was rightfully mine!" Valokvantti exploded.

Under normal circumstances that would have been considered a treasonous statement punishable by the severest of penalties. Langur realized Valokvantti had put considerable trust in him just by uttering the statement.

"Who does he think I am to be treated like that! And another thing … just look at the way he's treating those aliens, like they were no more than savages. Even animals are treated with more consideration."

"What are you getting at my friend?" Langur took the chance to pull Valokvantti further into his confidence by calling him 'friend'. He'd not done that often.

"I – I don't know where my loyalties lie any more. I'm the Captain and I know what I have to do. But I'm beginning not to agree with what others are doing. And I know you have your own reservations about the genocide on Vesimaa."

"So what do you intend to do?" Now Langur became cautious. There was no reason to suspect Valokvantti might have been a plant by The Ensimmainen to report on the continuing dedication of his 'Temporality Nexus" team to the Project. There was absolutely no foundation for that … but still he had to be careful. He had said things to Leuhta that could just conceivably be used against him, not that Leuhta would ever betray him.

"I intend to do exactly as planned and get this ship and all its passengers safely to TC-E."

"Highly commendable. But what about the aliens on Vesimaa?" Langur wanted to push a little and see just where Valokvantti stood. The question hung in the air. Valokvantti moved about the room making noises to himself not looking directly at Langur. Then suddenly he stopped, looked right into Langur's eyes and declared, "If there was anything I could possible to do to help them, I would." Then hurriedly he added, "but nothing that would jeopardize our Project!"

Langur wasn't sure just how far he could take this man into his confidence. Most assuredly a man who had taken such a bold risk could be most useful to him. The outlandish, impossible concept he'd discussed with Leuhta suddenly became a possibility. A very distant but distinct possibility.

"Let me just say this, my friend. You are not the only person whose conscience cannot come to terms with mass murder. I too, if an opportunity presented itself, would be prepared to do something for the aliens."

There was nothing else the two could say to each other. Valokvantti had unburdened himself to a man he thought he could trust, and that trust had been confirmed. He wasn't berated for his feelings about his loyalties, and furthermore, Langur trusted him with his own misgivings! He walked out of Langur's quarters feeling much relieved and with a new sense of purpose. Yes, he would do his utmost to ensure the safe arrival of all those under his care – and yes – if Langur needed his help regarding the fate of the aliens on Vesimaa he would not hesitate to give it.

*

The tunnel of time stretched into the cosmic distance. With each passing year Synty neared its destination, and the Earth retreated further into the past in distance and in memory. Tumma and Saija knew they had to do something to try and save their planet. There was no more time left for procrastination. While they took the first tentative steps to put a plan into action the people of Earth were in a state of extreme distress. Sixty alien years may not seem like a long time to a Dokkheimien, but to the aliens it represented at least two generations of their species. In terms of their technology it was the same time span between their first air born flight and landing a man on their satellite moon. In that short time the Dokks had reduced the Earth's civilization to complete chaos. There were still aliens alive, but relatively few; no longer seven billion souls, not even one billion. They had been reduced to small isolated warring tribes fighting for survival.

Communications, commerce, the rule of law, had all broken down. Long distance travel became non-existent. The remaining population consisted mainly of ageing individuals living in tribal village units. There were still a few million left scattered around the planet, however they were isolated from each other. Those in closer proximity continued fighting. Subsistence farming barely sufficed to keep them alive. Although a few children were still being born, it had become a rarity. Children were one of the 'treasures' the tribes fought over. The Dokk extinction engineers left the remaining aliens to their own devices, not bothering to continue with spreading the STD's among them. It was only a matter of a few short years before they could be considered an extinct species. Not everyone had to die, but sufficient numbers of them so the species would not be able to recover.

*

The Ensimmainen on Tau Ceti-E received the news with a great deal more enthusiasm than Yakiv. Yakiv's future and that of his people on Dokkheim seemed to be much more predictable than that of the relatively few that his former boss now ruled on TC-E. Yakiv was still not entirely independent and had to continue to support both the expeditionary spacecraft and the planet regeneration workforce on TC-E. That support had become a considerable drain on his resources. Yet The Ensimmainen continued to demand more manpower and resources to try and push the Project ahead of schedule. The more Jarl Yakiv grew into his power the more he became resentful of those demands.

Yes, he was without question loyal to his species and wanted them to have every opportunity to survive. But things were not going as badly on Dokkheim as Langur had predicted. As time passed he felt increasingly isolated from those who had 'deserted' Dokkheim - at least that's how he saw the situation. The pioneers had made their choice. They had everything they now needed to create a new model of their species. Why did The Ensimmainen keep escalating his demands? He felt the time was coming soon when he would cast them adrift from Dokkheim; cut the umbilical and let *them* look after their fate.

Kirkas Valo

Tumma had no way of knowing how bad the situation on Earth had become. Perhaps just as well. The utter hopelessness of any chance for humanity's survival would most probably have reduced him to a state of inconsolable depression from which suicide may have been the only escape. He didn't know, so he had put into effect the plan for the salvation of his species. It would be at least another generation before they arrived on TC-E. Time enough to do what had to be done aboard Synty.

Within his small group of conspirators many options were discussed until all but three remained. Tumma tried to caution Saija against acting rashly.

"There's obviously no point in trying to convince the Dokks our two peoples could co-exist peacefully on Earth. That's no longer possible since their plan is genocide the effects of which I have personally witnessed. We could take over Synty, but to what end? What could we possibly do with the vessel except wander about in space till the end of time? That wouldn't save Earth."

He paused, seemingly exhausted by the enormity of the situation facing them. Saija, Lefe and George accompanied them from one village to the next. They let him take his time, Saija watching him intently. Tumma had run out of options.

"We can't even take over TC-E and kill all the Dokks. There's still a planet full of them on Dokkheim. They'd come and attack if we tried colonizing TC-E ourselves, and we simply don't have the technology to survive there. They walked on in silence. Their decision had already been made some time ago. Tumma was just torturing himself going over old ground.

Saija seemed to have the only workable alternative. "We carry on as we planned; take control of Synty, wipe out the Dokks on TC-E and return to Earth, salvaging what resources we can." Lefe wasn't the only one of the group troubled by such an act of desperation.

Tumma's plans began with several years of careful preparation beginning with mirrors. Photons bouncing off mirror strips disrupted the photonic communication tracking devices implanted into Vesimiaans, AmbSims and even hybrids. It took a year of surreptitious activity to bring mirrors into fashion amongst the people of The Great Valley. Once established as an acceptable addition to people's homes it wasn't difficult to create children's toys using mirrors. Those very quickly became popular. Strips of thin mirror hanging in concentric circles created light reflecting mobiles that could be found in almost every home. Some of these toys were small things, several centimeters long. Others between one and two meters tall, hung from ceilings almost touching the floor.

"This is a good plan," George said, "it has to be done. We must have a secure way to communicate. I found another volunteer to test the device and see if photon beams could get past the constantly moving reflective apparatus."

"You're certain he can be trusted?" Asked Tumma.

'We both know the consequence if the device fails. He's been against the bastards since the first abductions. I'm certain I've been bugged after my part in the last great riot, so if they twig to my fictitious plan to engineer an insurrection – you'll just have to find something else." George made light of his fate in the event of discovery. But that was George – a man without fear and great dedication. "All we have to do is sit in the middle of one of the large mirror mobiles and discuss the plan … then go home and wait."

No one on the Security Team in the Shell of the spacecraft took much notice now of Tumma and his close companions going out to visit people regularly, and staying for extended periods. Initially Langur was alerted to the new activity, but over time, as nothing happened other than the continued peaceful existence of the people, he lost interest. As long as peace prevailed he was satisfied and didn't feel threatened.

George going on a visitation with a friend didn't register on their radar as being suspicious. Of course they knew where he was. They always knew where he was but no longer bothered to maintain close surveillance. The few breaks in the transmission from his implanted device was of no concern. A day passed, then several days, then several weeks. The two pretend conspirators were not arrested.

Tumma and Saija were now free to plan without fear of detection. They only had another ten years, perhaps twenty at the most to bring their plan to fruition. A lynch pin in the plan was to have an insider in the shell; a hybrid insider completely trusted by the Dokks. It became Lefe's responsibility to cultivate the loyalty of such an individual, while others slowly assembled everything else for the mutinous scheme. If Tumma had bothered to reflect on what they were contemplating he would have realized it had all the hallmarks of the very reason the Dokks thought humanity unworthy of special consideration.

Lefe had taken up residence in the shell many years ago. Langur had invited this AmbSim to live in closer proximity to himself. She had become an influential member of Tumma's little group and it was easier to keep an eye on her activities by keeping her close. Lefe had two changes of alien bodies so far, but each time she selected individuals very similar to her original. Having similar bodies gave her a greater sense of continuity. She wasn't due for another change for at least fifteen years. At each neural cleansing of her alien hosts her Dokk persona and that of the alien had gradually blended. The cleansings were not entirely successful. Gradually she became more alien in her thinking than Dokk.

Lefe and Kirkas made a good looking couple.

They met soon after the first uprising. Kirkas still quite a young man. Tall, with masculine handsome features, an outstanding physical example of the breeding experiment. His mother was an AmbSim and consequently it was expected he would have a stronger disposition towards the Dokk culture than the alien one. Nevertheless, he identified very strongly with his alien father and had a healthy relationship with him. Despite all the biased conditioning during his education, through his father he identified unusually strongly with his Vesimiaan ancestry. Until he met Lefe his loyalties had never been tested.

At age twenty-five, far too young to be considering a relationship with a woman whose psyche was several thousands of years old, and who in addition was an amalgam of three personalities, he nevertheless felt a strong attraction to Lefe. Such pair bondings between AmbSims and hybrids was encouraged. However, there were complications with these bondings, too complex for even the Dokkheimien expert psychologist Dr.Qilaq to fathom. It wasn't a simple brew of the right DNA constituents to provide the expected outcome to the recipe. There were the complexities of the conjoining of unique minds. Putting together two such complex entities and expecting to know the outcome was the height of arrogance.

Langur may have been pleased to see this particular pair slowly develop a bond, but he had no idea what the result would be either. He liked Kirkas, liked him very much. He even liked Lefe in spite of her activities and obvious bias towards the aliens and hybrids. She caused him a great many problems, but she was a person of integrity and clear intent. He could work with such people. Tumma on the other hand also saw only advantage in the Lefe and Kirka's relationship. He didn't initially feel he could place any great trust in Kirkas. Lefe on the other hand had amply proved her loyalty.

Neither he nor Langur were in the least disturbed to see Kirkas calling more and more regularly on Lefe, who was at first indifferent to the youth. He was nice enough but really excite her imagination. When Tumma indicated to her the long-term value there could be in having Kirkas' loyalty, through her relationship with him, she wasn't averse to at least exploring the possibility of such a relationship. His confident personality did attract her a little.

Some years before, when Kirkas first met Tumma and Saija he was awed by their 'immortality' and the fact they were the immortal aliens. They were the 'first citizens' who represented the critical first contact. The meeting was his first experience of the reality of the 'legend' taught at school about Dokkheim, TC-E and the Project. As his relationship with Lefe developed he became a regular visitor to Tumma and Saija as well; a most welcome visitor.

Kirkas also made a very positive impression on Langur, who found opportunities to be with Tumma and Saija as often as he could whenever Kirkas visited them. Eventually Kirkas had private audiences with Langur.

"Come in – come in my young friend. You are always welcome."

"Can I speak to you in confidence?"

"Of course – of course. Anytime. Anything you like. I have to say you do some excellent work among the people. Perhaps you don't realise what a valuable contribution you are making to the Project."

"Thank you. This is more of a personal nature."

Perhaps neither Tumma nor Langur considered the intelligence of the young man, being much too concerned with their own agendas. Kirkas was indeed highly intelligent, with an innately diplomatic bent and above all, perceptive. He had a mind of his own. That mind was undiluted, and had not undergone neural cleansing or implantation of pre-prepared data. It was a balanced mind quite capable of understanding the mechanizations of both Tumma and Langur. Although he wasn't privy to the intimate plans of either, Kirkas knew there was a great deal more going on than just a breeding program to save a species from extinction.

"Oh yes?"

"It's about Lefe."

Kirkas had not confided in Lefe where his loyalties lay. He had ambitions of his own and wanted to make the best of both worlds. To that effect he did a bit of cultivating of his own, although his emotions on a personal level for Lefe got in the way of the clarity of his ambitions. He was certainly no fool and could see that the Dokks controlled the lives of the people from the security of the Shell. His future career may possibly be there.

"I like Lefe. She's become special to me. She's a good person, don't you think?" Without betraying confidences the two men discussed Lefe, agreeing about their high regard for her.

"There's something I want to talk to you about as well," continued Langur. "Have you thought seriously about your future?"

"I'm aware of the future we're all working towards. And yes, I have had thoughts about how I could contribute more meaningfully to it."

"Good lad. Would you consider taking part in a special training course?"

The short conversation ended to both their satisfactions, particularly to Kirkas'.

"Hi Lefe!" he said as he burst through her door. "You'll never guess … go on … have a guess what's happened," he prompted after an affectionate greeting. Lefe disengaged herself from his embrace to better take in his beaming countenance. She squinted her eyes, screwed up her nose and tilted her head to one side.

"I can't … Come on tell me! You'll burst!"

"I've been invited to be in the next Intake." Kirkas tried to calm himself and assume a nonchalant attitude. It was a big deal for anyone to be selected. Although it happened every year now, but only for a handful of special hybrids.

"What do they want *you* for?" She asked, teasing.

"Don't be like that. You know the work I've been doing, and you know that Langur is … well, his like a good friend. I think they want to recruit me to the Liaison staff. You know, keep things cool between all the peoples of The Great Valley and themselves. From what I've heard we're getting close to TC-E. Only a few more years. They probably need more staff for the big disembarkation."

"Come here handsome," Lefe successfully distracted him from talking, no doubt to reward him in the nicest possible way.

Kirkas was much too pleased with himself. Normally displaying a more reserved personality, he'd let his ambitions loosen the grip on his self-control. As it turns out, he was right on both counts. Langur did want Kirkas 'on the team', but first had to test the young man's loyalty. Kirkas had formed a strong bond with Lefe, and had been taken into Tumma's confidence, or so Langur thought, so was perfectly positioned to ferret out any clandestine activity possibly brewing under the seemingly calm surface of life among the people. He was to be trained as a Diplomat. If that worked out, then Langur contemplated taking a bigger chance by promoting him to a much more responsible position.

Unfortunately the original Dokkheimien crew were ailing. Particularly those who had not taken on an alien simulacrum. It would have been possible for the entire crew to undergo the change, but alien shells had become very valuable, and had to be kept in cold storage to be used expressly for their initially intended purpose of creating AmbSims capable of breeding. The best solution was to replace dying members of the crew with trained hybrids.

As Eili had said, "It is the perfect solution. The hybrid generations have to eventually take control of the destiny of the new race of Dokks anyway. Why not start training them while we're on final approach. The trainee intakes so far processed have proved to be successful. True, they were not required to do complex tasks and are not involved in any of the critical aspects of running the ship. But the time will come when that will become inevitable."

"That is simply fantastic!" Saija exclaimed when Lefe told her the news. "Tumma will be so relieved. He'd been hoping there would be some way to infiltrate the crew with our own people. You know we consider him to be one of us despite being a hybrid.

"Yet you still keep him at arm's length," said Lefe.

"You are fully aware of how much is at stake. We need to take extreme caution."

"I know what the plan is and I know Kirkas could play a critical part. But I don't want him to be forced into dangerous circumstances." Being one of the innermost circle of trusted conspirators she knew the potential dangers.

In spite of her initial reticence regarding Kirkas, she couldn't help becoming seriously involved with him. Apart from being a genuinely good person, he was such a handsome devil. "I just don't want him to become part of a plan involving the killing of people. The hybrid children have all been taught from the very first, both at home and at school that the very reason they all existed was to save lives, not to take lives. How could I possibly reconcile myself to having my man become a murderer? Whatever the reason he might have for killing, doesn't matter; killing is murder. That's all there is to it. I don't know if I can keep doing this," she said to Saija, "I can't involve him in … in … in killing his own people."

"What do you think they've done to us! Can you think of any other way to save what is left of the people on Earth? … Well … Can you?" Saija shouted these last few words, before falling on Lefe and giving her a furious hug. Saija started crying, as did Lefe.

"What are we going to do Lefe?" She pleaded. When they'd both calmed down, they went to find Tumma to talk to him about the situation. Part of the plan had worked, perhaps a little too well. Lefe wasn't supposed to fall in love with Kirkas.

"Yes I know about the training. Kirkas has already spoken to me," Tumma said, "He's the one element we were missing. If you've done your job well Lefe, and it seems to me you have, we have a chance. Kirkas could be the perfect person to have on the inside. It just remains to maneuver him into the right position. Now you and I Lefe, will have to …"

At this point Saija interrupted Tumma's train of thought, "We have a problem with all this. Do you want to explain, Lefe?"

Tumma looked baffled. What could possibly be the problem. It had finally started to work out for them. There were only a few years left. The first generation of hybrids was fully grown. They were having children of their own. The third generation would be upon them before they realized it. The humans were getting grossly outnumbered, and they were now dying out fast. They, unlike himself and Saija, were not immortal.

While these thoughts passed through his mind, Tumma nevertheless listened as Lefe agonized over her conundrum. She could see no way out of the situation. Tumma let her finish, and gave Saija time to unfold her thoughts as well. Saija had always been the hard-liner, but even she could see murder couldn't be considered an ideal solution to their dilemma. The three of them went to visit wise old George, putting the scenario to him. Although he'd spent most of his eighty-five years on Synty didn't mean

George was any less matured in the wisdom that a long life of experience brings to a man. He listened patiently to the two girls, and he listened to Tumma's well-argued case to stick with the original plan.

"Firstly," George began, "we don't know exactly what the Dokks want to do with Kirkas. He may end up being of very limited use to us. Secondly we still have a little time, so there's no need to panic. And thirdly, consider this ... There's no actual need to kill the existing inhabitants of TC-E. Talk to their leader. Ascertain how successful they've been in changing the planet. Maybe they don't have to use our Earth. Don't let yourself get emotional about the already great loss of life back home. What's done is done. It cannot help our cause to be vindictive. There's no room for revenge. It will achieve only more death."

"We can't see any other way, George. We must act decisively," Tumma didn't think George had any other option in mind.

"Consider this alternative ... we take the ship as hostage, and all of its crew. If the Dokks on TC-E play along, we'll leave only the AmbSims and hybrids and return to Earth with a minimum team to manage the craft. If they don't play along, we take the craft anyway, and use it to defend ourselves against them back home should they decide to invade." No one spoke for a moment after George finished. He made a lot of sense.

It could just work. If we have control of Synty ... Tumma started to see the possibilities.

"But what if fighting breaks out?" Asked Lefe.

"It probably will. We won't be the ones to start it. And anyway, if it does, it would only be while we try to take over the ship." George said. "A lot depends on how well we're organized and where Kirkas ends up."

Tumma was already thinking ahead of the rest. "We need someone high up in Dokk's security, and also someone in Weapons."

"How about we let Kirkas organize that part of it," George suggested.

"Lefe …" George turned to look Lefe directly in the eye and held her gaze for a moment. He knew this was going to be incredibly difficult for her. "Lefe, you know what has to be done. We have to know if we can count on Kirkas."

Lefe left the meeting crying. She did know what had to be done. She knew it all along, but she hid it from herself as she became more involved with Kirkas. He was hers now, yet she also knew she would do what had to be done. If there was the slightest doubt he would betray them, then he had to … the threat had to be neutralized. She cried all the way home.

*

In a small discussion room within the shell, the closely packed ten hybrid candidates felt intimidated, as was the intention.

"Make no mistake, any of you! You are here for one reason only. If you cannot do your jobs, you are of no value to us. There would be no reason for you to continue using our resources - Do - I - make - myself - clear!"

On the very first hour of the very first day of the training session for the new intake the Instructor laid it out for the recruits. They were all destined for Administration, including Kirkas. One aide-de-camp for Valokvantti, one Quartermaster, three Communications, four Liaison Officers and one possibly for Security. Attrition rates were high. So most of them were expected to drop out … lack of aptitude or lack of loyalty or because they would prove to be a high security risk.

Kirkas wasn't one to be easily intimidated, but he got the message loud and clear. He was also under no delusions about his already precarious position. From a career point of view, it wasn't particularly smart of him to have such a strong affiliation with the aliens, or with Lefe because of her known loyalties to them.

For the first week of the two months stint they were bombarded with the same kind of rhetoric they'd all received at school.

277

"Our race is dying. The only salvation is in The Project, of which all of you are now an indispensable part. There is only one aim in your lives … you must ensure the survival of the hybrids and their safe passage to Tau Ceti-E." Kirkas found the same litany, repeated every day, to be unnecessary. They just went on and on. "Whatever job you are assigned to is critical to the success of The Project. Our species must survive … at any cost!" 'At any cost' became almost an hourly, daily mantra during the days of that first week. Kirkas had little time to sleep, to eat or to communicate with anyone outside the shell. He had no time for his own thoughts even. Every long day started and finished with the same thing … Survive at all costs!

It all started to sound very strange to Kirkas. Apart from the manic brainwashing obviously going on, he couldn't understand why survival was so intimately linked with mortality; and especially why they couldn't manage the whole thing on their own home planet. He wasn't a scientist, so how could he understand. So he put it to the back of his mind. It was something to ask his friend Langur when he got out of the crazy training facility. Kirkas also wanted answers to a whole lot of questions he'd discussed with Lefe … about the children who were dying so often, for example … about the harsh treatment of the people by their Captain … and the reason for the Great Uprising. He asked these questions of his instructors. None of these were answered during his training.

Already after the first week their numbers were down by two individuals. The recruits were given a break for a week before the resumption of training, during which time they were under constant surveillance. Kirkas thought as much, and made sure that when he met with Lefe to discuss some important things it would be private. Perhaps she knew how that could be arranged. But first he went to see Langur. The Head of Temporality Nexus was expecting him.

"You have done very well, my boy," he said, being unusually friendly. "I was hoping you would come and see me. Tell me, how do you feel about the opportunity to join our team?" Langur's method of operation had not changed a great deal over the length of the journey so far. His attitude to some things may have softened, but he was still the same come-to-the point person of the past.

"Over the last few years I have come to look upon you as a friend," Kirkas started in a round-about sort of way, "and I hope the feeling is mutual." He watched Langur as he spoke to gauge his reaction.

I like this boy. I like his mind. Langur decided.

Kirkas waited for a reaction...

He has courage and he has patience.

And Kirkas waited. So did Langur. He was enjoying this little game immensely.

Finally, Langur responded with a smile, "Of course my boy, of course. You know that. I recommended you for the training. You should be grateful. It is indeed a privilege. I'm proud of you. You have survived the first and most difficult part." Then Langur waited and watched Kirkas.

Kirkas said nothing, biding his time.

Smart boy!

"Tell me, what's on your mind. I can always tell when you're troubled."

That immediately put Kirkas on alert. If what Langur just said was true, that he was easy to 'read', he would have to work on it. In the career he had in mind for himself he couldn't afford to be an open book to anyone who happened to look at him.

"There are some things I don't understand. For me to do the best job I can, I feel I need to fill in those blanks. I was hoping you would be able to help me." Kirkas put the onus back on Langur.

"Don't stop now my young friend. We have plenty of time. Unless you're in a hurry to go and see someone else?" Langur added with a smile. Kirkas reddened slightly, but didn't respond to the implication. Instead he put forward the matter uppermost on his mind.

"The training so far held nothing new for me, but it did raise some questions; questions which I felt would be best answered by –

shall we say – a higher authority. The business about so many hybrid children being taken away from their parents, and then soon dying ..." Kirkas left the rest unsaid and waited patiently for a response.

Langur weighed up how much he could confide in this smart young man. Kirkas had not shown any worrying signs of a bias towards the Vesimiaans. He'd even chosen an AmbSim as a mate. *Perhaps ... perhaps it's worth taking a chance with him.*

"They were found to be genetically flawed and we couldn't take the chance of contaminating any future generations."

There. He'd said it. It wasn't really such a big risk. A risk yes, but not one that couldn't be fixed with a bit of 'memory cleansing' if absolutely necessary. And it was worth taking the risk to see the young man's reaction. To Langur's considerable pleasure Kirkas didn't react. He waited a moment to assimilate the answer before asking his next question. As soon as he began Kirkas knew that was the crux of what had been worrying him for a long time, not just during the first week of training.

"While we are going through the breeding program on board, what is happening to the aliens back on their own planet?"

Oh, now that's a big one. Where did that come from? Langur caught his breath. *Interesting. Very interesting. This Kirkas is no fool.* With considerable composure and a cool, calm voice Langur answered, "We are rehabilitating their planet after centuries of their abuse of it. We are also cleansing the species of their defective characteristics. Now let's have a little refreshment before you go. I know you're anxious to be on your way."

Again Kirkas didn't react and didn't seek elaboration. As far as he was concerned Langur had not answered the question to his satisfaction. The last thing Langur said didn't quite match the things he'd heard around the place down amongst his friends in The Great Valley; amongst them Lefe and Tumma. *He's being too general, and too evasive.* Instead of asking for details he thanked Langur.

"You've been forthright and honest. Thank you for your trust." He had the refreshment and left.

Langur didn't feel as much at ease as he would have liked after the brief conversation. The last question was completely unexpected and should not have been asked. For the first time he felt the need to keep a closer eye on his young protégé. Langur determined to follow his training very closely indeed.

"You look troubled," Lefe said as soon as she saw him.

There it is again. Damn. I really must work on that.

Lefe had been obsessing about how to approach Kirkas with the subject of her mission. "There's something I have to talk to you about – but first, what's on your mind?"

"Oh, don't worry about me. How about we say a proper hello," Kirkas said as he led her to a more comfortably furnished room. Her heart wasn't in it just then, but she did love him. Afterwards, as they lay exhausted from their proper greeting, she asked, "What would you do for me Kiri? Would you do anything for me?"

"Whatever do you mean. You know you're the most important thing in my life." Again he was put on alert, for the second time that day.

"It's just that you seemed so worried when you arrived," she said evasively. Kirkas was in the mood for talking. He'd held everything back for a week, and he had an unsatisfactory conversation with Langur.

"I've just come from seeing Langur."

"Oh yes?" She explored while stroking his chest.

"You would not believe the week I've had," he said, suddenly realizing that privacy was an issue, which it had not been in the past. His previous personal freedom no longer existed he realized. Everything changed because of the last week – and because of his conversation with Langur.

"Let's go out for a walk while I tell you how exciting it's been." The sudden mood change didn't fool Lefe one little bit. Something was up, and she would just have to go along with it till he opened up.

"Alright. Where shall we go?"

"Let's go down to The Valley and get some fresh air." So the two lovers; lovers to all intents and purposes to any prying eyes, were simply going out on a lover's tryst. Neither spoke during the long ride out into the open landscape.

Kirkas suddenly asked, "Is there somewhere private we can go?"

"How private exactly?" she responded grinning.

"Very private," he replied with a cheeky grin of his own.

The nearest 'safe house' was several kilometers away. They took the only available means of transport; horse, although there were low energy vehicles available but not at that location, and arrived soon enough at a largish house well known to Lefe. Fortunately, the occupants were all away working for the day, and it was free for the two lovers to use as they wished. Lefe led him into the house through several rooms to one resembling a nursery. It had an enormous child's toy dangling from the ceiling. She led him gently through the concentric circles of long, narrow hanging mirrors to the mattress in the middle.

"What's all this?"

"It's a very, very private place. No one knows what happens in here and will never know. No one can hear or see us in here. Private enough?"

"If you say so."

He trusted Lefe; the only person in his entire life he really trusted, apart from his deceased father. He took Lefe by her shoulders and turned her to face him. For a few moments they stood there together, looking into each other's eyes. Then he made up his mind and told her everything.

"The training is terrible. It is nothing more than brain washing. It's as if they're preparing us to do something terrible. And I think I really don't want to be a part of it. But how can I stop it. They made it quite clear that if we were not with them all the way, then we were the enemy and would be dealt with as such."

Lefe caught her breath and clung to his arms. He went on. "I went to see Langur today. I thought he was my friend. But now I have serious doubts. Lefe, if anyone finds out about this conversation we are both dead!"

Lefe didn't hesitate with her response. Her clarity of mind returned and she saw an opportunity opening up for what she had to do.

"Don't stop Kiri, go on. We are safe in here. I will tell you why, later."

"I asked him about the children who were dying. Do you know what he said, without any feeling, without any show of compassion? He said they were disposed of because they were defective and he didn't want them to contaminate his experiment. Well, not in those words exactly, but that's what he meant."

Kirkas and Lefe took a big breath and remained in the middle of the mirror mobile as he continued. "Then I asked him what was happening to the aliens on their home planet. He said they and their planet were being cleansed. Now what in the Great Valley did that mean? I think they're doing something despicable and they don't want any of us to know about it. How am I going to get myself out of this mess Lefe? I am certain I'm in a heap of trouble because of those questions I asked him."

For several minutes Lefe just stood in front of him, clutching his arms as he held her shoulders. Kirkas started to break out in a sweat. She looked deeply into his eyes, "When we leave this place put your arm around my waist and smile. You know, like we've been … you know."

It brought a smile to his face. Then she asked her big question again, "What would you do for me Kiri? Would you do anything for me?" His smile disappeared as he looked at Lefe's deadly serious expression.

"Well, yes – of course, Lefe. What's the big mystery?

"Would you be prepared to - to - join us?"

"However do you mean – join – you. Oh – OH! You mean Tumma and Saija and George - don't you?

"Yes my dear Kiri. There is something we must do, and we desperately need your help. If I said it had everything to do with the children who were killed and the people on Vesimaa, would you join us and help?" She was pleading now, desperately pleading – not manipulating or cultivating – just pleading for all the lives that had been lost and all the lives that could still be lost – or possibly saved. "We don't want to harm the Dokks, or the AmbSims or the hybrids. Would you join us?"

Kirkas watched his love pleading for something far greater than both of them, something greater than all the people in The Great Valley. He made up his mind - yes, he would do anything for Lefe, anything – for Lefe. All his suspicions surfaced – the evasive answers from Langur – the brainwashing during the training. There was something definitely seriously amiss.

"Yes. Just tell me what you want."

They embraced, standing there for what seemed like a long time. Before leaving the safe house she ruffled his clothes and hers, and said, "There's only one thing we can do. We have to make the Dokks believe they can completely trust you. During your next training break we'll come here again. It is a very, very safe place. They cannot receive signals from the implants. We have both been implanted with bugs, but perhaps you know that already. Now, put your arm around me and grin." The two lovers walked quietly out of the house, grinning, their clothes thoroughly untidy, looking as guilty as lovers do.

Kirkas returned to his training course, and Lefe returned to meet with Tumma and company. She said to them, before they could quiz her, "He is beautiful and I love him – and I'm very happy."

They got the message. At their next safe meeting a plan was devised to commend Kirkas' loyalty to his Dokk masters. Langur also received a message some time later, from Kirkas, but a totally different one about a plot.

Several months later six aliens died as a result of a plan devised by Lefe. They were leaders of a fictitious group discovered hatching a fictitious plot to assassinate Tumma and a number of key AmbSims, as well as numerous other important hybrids. The martyrs were all volunteers, prepared to give their lives to save what was left of humanity. Langur was very relieved to have nipped another potential disaster in the bud. *Kirkas is going to be a perfect plant amongst the aliens. We can trust him completely.*

No wonder. The Dokks had no idea such altruism could exist among the primitive peoples of Vesimaa. Such a characteristic certainly didn't exist among their own people. Most of them weren't even prepared to shorten their own lives to make it better for themselves, let alone for the survival of their own species. How could the Dokks on board Synty even conceive of such a heroic deed, let alone work out it was a devious scheme against them?

Without any shadow of doubt the conspirators were guilty. And it was only through the astute investigation carried out by a young trainee, by the name of Kirkas Valo that made it possible to apprehend the would-be assassins.

It was a brilliant plan. It didn't implicate any of Tumma's group, it consolidated Kirkas' loyalty to the Dokks and even brought Langur and Tumma a little closer by having averted the threat of a common enemy. Tumma made very certain not to give the game away. The ruse also tightened the grip he had on Kirkas and Lefe. Now they were both irretrievably entwined in the intrigues of life and death, aboard Synty.

Langur was very pleased with himself: Pleased with the excellent sense of judgment he'd shown in recommending Kirkas for the training program: Pleased with having further subdued any undercurrent of unrest among the people. Yes, he'd made an excellent choice - and he made sure everybody knew it.

At a large ceremony, Kirkas received a medal in recognition of his service to The Project and to the people of Dokkheim. Langur knew it would make a most favourable impression on The Ensimmainen. He had to get as much kudos out of this as possible. He needed to build his own reputation, for he was hatching a plan of his own, which needed good people around him to put into effect. He needed the likes of Valokvantti, his mate Leuhta, Eili and people like Kirkas. He was even hoping to somehow get Tumma on side. After all, he'd managed to get the alien scientist to help him back on Vesimaa, and look at the outstanding results so far.

Arrival at Tau Ceti–E

After almost a century in space Synty finally approached TC-E.

The great artificial moon carried in its belly a strange mix of creatures originating from two planets. Their journey had not been without incident. Its peoples were exhausted with the strain of the experiment and overcoming its accompanying problems. The third generation of Hybrids was just emerging out of infancy. Already their DNA showed their lives would not last forever. That generation was no longer immortal; long lived, yes, but not immortal.

Very few were left of the aliens not in storage and of the children allowed to them during the journey. They were mortal after all, except for the 'first citizens'. They were both immortal, and no cure had yet been found for their condition. There were some octogenarians and very few centenarians, and those thousands of other aliens still aboard Synty, in cryogenic stasis destined to be used to continue The Project on the transitional world of TC-E.

The original alien travelers still didn't know that so many of their species still existed in storage on the ship. Back on Earth barely enough were left worth counting.

On TC-E, a small colony of Dokks thrived in their bi-ped manifestations, under the domes constructed by the guidance of their Ensimmainen with Jarl Yakiv's help from Dokkheim. A few years still remained before the arrival of the travelers. Enough for all the domes' interior preparations to be completed, but nowhere near long enough to have a stable life sustaining external bio-sphere.

Valokvantti kept The Ensimmainen informed of progress aboard Synty. He wasn't going to neglect his duty despite his strong feelings against his leader. He saw his responsibility more towards his species survival than any single Dokkheimien individual.

The Ensimmainen felt oddly ill-at-ease about The Project. From all the reports, which were factual but by no means detailed, he believed everything had gone exceptionally well, despite the few necessary changes. The latest news about an outstanding hybrid individual confirmed his hopes, no less than Langur's, that his species was well on the road to survival despite the extraordinary risks he'd taken. Perhaps it was the unusual brevity of Valokvantti's reports that had put Haakon on edge.

Time had come to move The Project into a much more sustainable development phase, and out of the experimental one. Jarl Yakiv had supplied all the breeding stock Haakon needed from Dokkheim, and Langur was going to provide all the aliens, AmbSims and hybrids to ensure a good cross-section of genetic material. There was really nothing left for him to worry about; all was going according to plan. *I'm even looking forward to having Valokvantti by my side again.* He believed Valokvantti to be a good, loyal individual. Efficient, reliable and without ambitions of his own. *But something is not quite right. Why do I feel apprehensive?* He couldn't shake that sense of unease.

*

An unusually large crowd gathered for the Intake graduation ceremony on Synty. Langur wanted to make an example of Dokkheimien superiority, highlighting the success of his breeding program with the promotions of hybrids to positions of prominence. He invited his entire inner circle, all officers of consequence aboard the spacecraft, a large contingent of the first and second generation hybrids, including Tumma, Saija, Lefe, George and some of his contemporaries who were still able to travel. Keeping your enemies close was a motto not lost to Langur.

Inevitably Kirkas Valo would be the celebrated outstanding graduate. Of the ten original intakes only six managed to complete the course, more than the previous year. Each of them received their Commissions according to their talents and security risk clearances. Each had the opportunity to address the crowd, and each uttered the usual platitudes.

'So many have made great sacrifices to save their species from extinction … blah, blah, blah …'

'So much work is still to be done... blah, blah …'

'The outstanding dedication of all hybrids guarantees the Project will succeed to its maximum potential … blah … blah… blah …'

Even Langur had had enough by the end of the second last speech. Finally the spotlight came on Kirkas. Langur and Lefe waited in anticipation. Kirkas had been assigned as 2IC of Liaison between the Dokks and the inhabitants of The Great Valley. He wasn't nervous in front of the crowd. Being a double agent had polished off the corners of his insecurities and fears. At age thirty, though very young in some respects he was much experienced in many others. He stood at the podium and looked around at the gathered throng, making a mental note of all the individuals who mattered and assessing why they were invited. He made eye contact with some and nodded in the direction of others. When he felt he had everyone's attention, he began.

"I am not here because I want to be here." That wasn't strictly true coming from such an ambitious individual.

"I am not here because I want to make a lot of friends and to be popular." After each statement he waited a few seconds.

"I am here because I have to be here. There is a job that must - must be done and I - aim - to - do it."

Langur understood what he meant. Tumma also understood, but to him it meant something different. The assembled general crowd understood only what crowds understand, and that wasn't very much. They just enjoyed looking at him, for Kirkas had a good presence – he stood straight and confident. He commanded respect and attention. He had that indefinable air of authority about him, something Langur lacked and was envious of. Standing there in full uniform, addressing the gathering with complete composure, he looked like a leader – spoke like a leader and Lefe couldn't have been prouder of her man. He finished his speech with an open-ended statement.

"Make no mistake, The Project is still in its infancy and many challenges are still to be faced. Soon, very soon we will be arriving at Tau Ceti-E." Kirkas let that sink in, for it was the long awaited culmination of the difficult journey all had endured.

"Tau Ceti-E will be home for some of us, but not for others."

He finished on that last sentence, waited a moment while he scanned the crowd with his intent eyes then stepped down to resume his place amongst the other graduates. The last sentence almost made Tumma jump out his seat.

What exactly did he mean by that? Langur asked himself.

After the general round of congratulations, hand shaking and back slapping abated the crowd began to disperse. Langur and Tumma found each other in the milling throng.

"He's a good man," Langur said while carefully watching Tumma.

"That he is – a rare individual who can be trusted." Tumma replied, unable to resist a dig. Both knew the other had high hopes for Kirkas. Both were aware Kirkas had a foot in each camp. Only

Tumma knew where the new Diplomat's true allegiance lay. Langur only thought he knew.

Then Langur sought out Kirkas to have a private word with him. "I'm proud of you my boy. Because you have already proved yourself, I think a short period in the Diplomatic Division for twelve months should be enough training for you. Then we'll see." *That will be enough time to give him plenty of exposure in the shell and out in The Great Valley,* Langur calculated. "What did you mean TC-E would not be a home for everyone?" He didn't intend to ask. The question just pushed itself out.

"Isn't it obvious?" stated Kirkas. "I look forward to the challenge," Kirkas replied noncommittally.

*

He used the time well, establishing his network amongst the Dokks whilst Tumma and his team ensured the continued peaceful existence amongst the people so Kirkas could concentrate his efforts. The strategy also worked well for Kirkas' promotional prospects.

Even before the twelve-month period lapsed, Langur gave his protégé the good news. "I've been following your activities. You've worked well with Tumma in maintaining the peace. If there were any other conspirators I'm sure you would have found them."

"There's been no unrest that I could discover," Kirkas replied truthfully, neglecting to mention the plans under way to destabilize the established authority aboard Synty.

"I have a more important job for you, for someone who is loyal to out Project." Kirkas raised a questioning eyebrow, not showing any undue eagerness. "We will be arriving at TC-E quite soon. I expect there may be some – say we say, unrest. We need a strong, trustworthy individual in Security." Langur's personal ambition wasn't just to get his protégé established in Security, he needed a strong ally he could rely on, should the need arise – and he had a growing expectation it would, if he had any hope of putting his own plan into effect. "What do you say?"

Kirkas already behaved like a man in charge. "I will, of course, need to be taken into full confidence by yourself and Captain Valokvantti. Hidden agendas behind my back will not do."

Langur slapped him on the back, acknowledging his astuteness. The two men parted with satisfied smiles. Langur liked the idea of his man being in regular close contact with the alien encampment. It kept him abreast of all the latest news that couldn't be captured by their surveillance system; like changing moods that might be indicative of unrest.

Before speaking with Tumma and Saija, Kirkas hurried home to tell Lefe the good news. "Guess what?" He asked in a jovial mood.

"You'd better tell me before you turn green again," she encouraged him, hoping for something spectacular.

"I've been promoted!" He stretched it out.

"No! Langur's gofer?" She teased.

"Better – Security." He tried sounding nonchalant about it without succeeding.

"Have you told Tumma and Saija?"

"Soon, after we celebrate."

"And just how do you intend to do that?" she asked sounding suspicious.

"Let's have a baby." Kirkas suggested quietly.

Lefe suddenly plastered herself against him almost knocking him to the ground, smothering him in kisses. Their child would be a second generation Hybrid, destined to live out its life on TC-E, contributing to the greater good of its parents' species.

The following day, a tired looking Kirkas met with Saija and Tumma.

"At last!" They cried in unison, "and not too soon," elated on hearing the good news.

Kirkas immediately took control of the situation. "It's a long and difficult career path for me," he sighed, "there's a lot of work to be done in the shell."

Because of his specialized duties Kirkas had to move his day-to-day living quarters further away from Lefe. Nevertheless, the two lovers found plenty of time to spend together. They were still five years out and a year before deceleration had to be initiated. Kirkas concentrated his first efforts on working himself into the Captain's confidence. It became inevitable they would form a close working relationship as his duties required close liaison with Valokvantti. Security in the shell itself had become as much of a concern as it was in The Great Valley. When not engaged in professional exchanges the two men had time to get to know each other.

"Congratulations," Valokvantti grudgingly acknowledged Kirkas' promotion. The young man's success made him even unhappier than he already was. It didn't take long for Kirkas to work out Valokvantti wasn't an entirely satisfied man.

"Thank you. It seems not everyone is recognized for the efforts they have made in ensuring the success of the Project." Kirkas knew the rumours about Valokvantti's thwarted ambition to be the Jarl. His words made an immediate impression on the Captain.

"True – very true," Valokvantti responded, taking a moment to give Kirkas a long hard look. In spite of his suspicious nature, he liked what he saw, and what he just heard. Kirkas was astute enough to behave as a colleague in whom the Captain could trust and to whom he could open up a little from time to time.

It was Kirkas' discussion with Tumma and his team about the Captain's state of mind that finally convinced Lefe that her mate could be trusted with the fullest disclosure of their plans - necessary now they were so close to TC-E. The remaining short years were needed to prepare everything for the arrival. A great deal depended on Kirkas and his ability to enlist the Captain's help, or at least to be able to seriously compromise the Captain's position at the critical time.

It was agreed that Lefe could tell Kirkas the full story, and everything they expected of him. To prying eyes, the now famous Security man and his pregnant sweetheart were just out on another one of their secret trysts. Everyone knew by then exactly what the two were up to, and everyone enjoyed their clandestine activities. Ensconced in the middle of another mirrored safe house the conspirator's most important conversation of the entire adventure since leaving Vesimaa was taking place.

Kirkas became incredulous at what Lefe suggested. "What! You can't be serious! You actually want to take the entire ship hostage! And you want me to provide your 'army' with weapons! How long has this plan been in motion?" He was shocked. "You were just using me, that's what this amounts to!"

Although he'd raised his voice Kirkas had not lost his composure. It was too much for him to take in, coming out of the blue like that. He knew very well he'd become an important element in the aliens' attempt to save their species. To have it stated so bluntly right to his face, by the only person he'd ever truly trusted – it was just too much. He just wanted to turn and leave as the full impact of the request hit home. His mind reeled with the realization of all the years of intricate maneuvering he himself had been subjected to.

Lefe saw the struggle on his face. She touched him softly on the cheek, took his face between her two hands, then took hold of his hand and placed it on her belly.

"This is our child. I wanted to have this child with you. I want him to have a good life among good people."

Kirkas let his hand linger on the warmth of her fullness. He could feel the child moving under his touch, as if responding to him. He kept his eyes in Lefe's tummy, saying nothing for a long while. Lefe could feel his struggle – the struggle of his loyalty to his own people, his love for Lefe and his child, and his disgust at the fate of the aliens on Vesimaa.

"What do you need?" He asked eventually. Everything else was too complicated. He could only think of Lefe and his child.

"We need weapons - and we need you to set up a communications link between Tumma and The Ensimmainen."

*

Arrival minus three years:

Tumma had his conversation with The Ensimmainen without Langur or Valokvantti's knowledge.

"I am Tumma Varjo, the …" He was almost immediately interrupted.

"Yes, I know. What do you want?" In spite of a new world he had to rule Haakon remained true to his character.

"I want to talk about the future of the people on my planet."

"They have no future." He displayed zero empathy for the species being sacrificed so his own could continue to exist.

Tumma tried another tack. "What about our people on Synty?"

"They have served their purpose. Anything else?"

It became clear very quickly that The Ensimmainen had his mind firmly set on exactly how and when everything was going to happen.

Tumma tried one last time, "Is the environment on TC-E ready for my people?"

"Why?" Without waiting for an answer Haakon terminated the communication link-up.

Tumma found out what he wanted. The leader of TC-E was a hard, uncompromising individual. There could be no negotiation with that man. Tumma realised he would have to deliver the ultimatum with a firm resolve and an exactitude that would exclude any possibility of misinterpretation.

George, despite his advanced years, managed to gather a formidable, albeit small militant group to carry out the coup. They didn't need to present overwhelming strength, only efficiency, speed and the element of surprise. Under the guise of sporting competitions of ingenious design, he forged the group into a team as well coordinated as a starling murmuration under attack by a hawk.

Kirkas provided a few sample weapons for familiarization by the attack team under cover of the mirror baffles. The rest of the weapons had already been gathered in readiness for distribution.

Saija managed to get herself reconciled with Langur - actually, more with Leuhta. She built on Leuhta's soft spot for Tumma, remembering how she allowed and arranged for Tumma to revisit Earth so long ago. She found the woman pleasant enough, although somewhat harsh in her attitudes; a phlegmatic personality on the surface who nevertheless found it difficult to diverge from a predetermined path. Putting all that aside, Saija did get the information she wanted. Tau Ceti-E was ready to accommodate the influx of a large population. The bio-domes had been ready for the past six months, and most of the effort went into consolidating progress in the setting up of a viable biosphere for the planet. Within the next five hundred years the external environments would be able to support vegetative life, and soon after, animal life.

Based on all her information Saija had no doubt about the possibility of an alternative future. *There is no reason why the Dokks need go anywhere else. TC-E will be perfectly suitable for their use. They don't have to have Earth as well!*

Arrival minus two years:

Langur continued to cultivate Valokvantti's friendship, seeking more opportunities to interact with the Captain in private.

"It's been a long and difficult journey, especially for you, my friend. But we are almost there. I'm certain all will work out for you. You have my support."

"You've been a good friend, Langur. I will not forget what you have done for me. I have many friends from the past, on TC-E. I will tell you this about The Ensimmainen ..." Langur didn't interrupt the Captain, as he rarely spoke more than a dozen words, "... I've been in regular communication with him. He seems to be constantly worried about relatively minor operational matters. Why do you suppose that is? A Leader should not be concerning himself with such details of The Project. It tells me – and I'm telling you this in strict confidence - that The Ensimmainen is feeling vulnerable.

Perhaps the sheer logistics of our enterprise has begun to unravel him."

"How very interesting. I thank you again for your trust. This will remain between the two of us." Then Langur moved closer to Valokvantti, speaking in low conspiratorial tones, "I'm certain we can count on each other – should the need arise."

As he left the Captains quarters he was quietly elated - *A vulnerable leader can be used to advantage!*

In small installments Kirkas provided detailed schematics of the labyrinth of the shell's administrative areas for the attack team to study. The conspirators became fully cognizant of all the key locations; Engineering, Communications, Life Support Systems, Weapons, The Bridge; and which key personnel to target to ensure success of their coup. Security was already under their control through Kirkas.

Lefe gave birth to a boy. "He is exceptionally beautiful," Lefe crooned to Kirkas.

"He is indeed, and healthy, and he meets all the requirements of the Dokks." Kirkas no longer felt any loyalty to those murderous beings. From his position of authority he could ensure *his* child didn't experience any intervention from the Dokks. The child grew quickly, adored by both his parents.

"I have to tell you, Lefe – I will do everything possible to make sure we take control. If after disembarkation, you and I and our son are not welcome on TC-E, we will return to Vesimaa with all the other aliens and make our life there."

Arrival minus one year:

Synty delicately positioned itself in orbit around TC-E, carefully balancing all the gravitational forces in order not to upset TC-E's path around Tau Ceti; a time consuming operation because of the sheer size of the moon sized spacecraft.

Kirkas had progressed quickly through the ranks to be promoted to Security Commander of Synty. It was only a matter of time that he should become aware of the large number of aliens in cryogenic storage. Unfortunately, the mechanisms had started to gradually fail over the years. Although Tumma and all the conspirators were distraught at the possible loss of those people, they couldn't change their well advanced plans. If they succeeded in taking over the ship, the fate of the souls in suspended animation would be in their own the hands, not the Dokks. It became critical they be thawed out and either taken to TC-E or back to Earth if they were to have any chance of survival.

Valokvantti and Langur couldn't oppose The Ensimmainen's insistence that he should be the one to officially promote Kirkas. Valokvantti considered the move just another example of the Leaders interference. He was in two minds about the appointment. *Haakon is definitely feeling insecure for some reason. Why else would he want to be personally responsible for choosing the Head of Security on Synty? It's my prerogative as ship's Captain to make such an appointment! Again he's undermining my authority! But Kirkas is a good man.*

Almost immediately after the appointment The Ensimmainen contacted Kirkas.

"I want to come aboard. Arrange it."

"With respect my Jarl, for what reason?" Kirkas asked.

"That is not your concern. Just do it." He had no specific reason to visit other than a personal desire – perhaps an attempt to pacify his apprehensions, perhaps to consolidate his position as ruler of TC-E.

"Because of our imminent arrival, there is a considerably tense situation here. Your visitation, though most welcome by many, would cause further instability, especially among the still living aliens who had been denied permission to procreate with their own kind for so long. Many young alien adults are fearful of their and their children's future, making a potentially volatile situation."

Ordinarily The Ensimmainen would not countenance any opposition to his will. "I will re-schedule my visit when it better suits me," he harrumphed.

Valokvantti noted the supreme ruler's back-down. The more the new Leader of the hybrid civilization exposed his growing weakness, the more it fanned a growing ambition in Valokvantti's heart. He decided to take the Security Chief, Kirkas Valo, into his confidence. The young man had shown every indication of his sympathies with him.

"I've arranged everything on TC-E. All I need is to have The Ensimmainen aboard Synty." He didn't wish to be too explicit with Kirkas. If the man was too thick to work it out for himself then he would be of no help at all.

"Now why would you want to do that, friend? Are you plotting something I should know about? Don't forget, we've just convinced him not to come on board."

Kirkas had a great deal of power, and he knew it. He'd also learnt how to use it. Having spent a few years as the Captain's confidant he was aware of his 'disappointments' from the past and his desire to set things right for himself. It only remained for Kirkas to determine if having Valokvantti as the Ensimmainen would be more advantageous to the imminent execution of their plans; his own and the aliens. Without hesitation Kirkas decided in the affirmative.

"Give him a few months then send him an invitation. I'll back you up. Tell him it's to welcome his new, healthy civilization when we arrive. That will flatter his wounded ego. Tell him we have resolved the previous worrying unrest."

Disembarkation minus one month:

Langur directed the people to prepare for disembarkation. His order went out, without explanations, disappointing many after years and years of anticipation:

"You are permitted only your essential belongings. Everyone is to disembark, except for the alien-alien bonded pairs and their families."

This didn't exactly fit in with his plan, but he had to be seen to be 'patriotic' and to be following The Ensimmainen's orders. Shuttlecraft were made ready at TC-E's spaceports to ferry thousands of souls off the interstellar vessel, while Kirkas finalized all the security arrangements. He had to take extra precautions in light of the preclusions in Langur's directive.

"About time you sorted those people out, Valokvantti." Instead of showing appreciation for the invitation Haakon remained obnoxious.

"He didn't even bother asking why I invited him. For whatever reason he must be feeling a lot of pressure," the Captain confided in Kirkas, "quite out of character with the person who once ruled Dokkheim with an iron will."

"You seem relieved. Just what are you up to?" Kirkas asked half jokingly. As part of his increased security measures for the visitation, Kirkas brought the majority of his guards to the immediate vicinity of The Ensimmainen's designated quarters. Such measures were totally expected and unquestioned.

Disembarkation minus one week:
The fully armed attack team took up their pre-determined positions. They encountered minimal resistance when they entered the shell as most of the guards had been taken from their usual posts. Engineering, Weapons and the Bridge were all taken by surprise. No deaths ensued. Nobody expected anything like a well organised armed assault simultaneously at all three locations. All previous surveillance had been focused on the immediate area of The Ensimmainen's arrival. The takeover was achieved quietly and swiftly, which reassured Kirkas of being able to maintain both order and full control, and Tumma of being able to advance his strategy.

For the welcoming ceremony the many essential personnel filled the large auditorium to capacity. Subdued applause greeted The Ensimmainen as he stepped up onto the raised podium in the front of the invited guests, with the two bodyguards on either side and a little back. Standing directly beside him on the left Valokvantti seemed agitated, and on the right the Head of Temporality Nexus, Langur Skuggi, appeared a little apprehensive. Behind them stood a self-composed Kirkas close to Valokvantti, flanked on either side by Eili, Dr.Qilaq, Leuhta and Tumma then Saija, Lefe and George. Behind them, another row of security guards all under the total control of their Security Chief, Commander Kirkas. Kirkas pulled back Haakon's two personal guards to stand with the others at the back.

The Ensimmainen expected a more enthusiastic reception, the lack of which put him in a particularly unpleasant mood.

A group of select people from The Great Valley, mostly AmbSims and hybrids sat in the front rows facing the dignitaries, waiting expectantly for some great announcement. None of the pure aliens were permitted in the auditorium. All activity in The Great Valley stopped to enable the people to watch on large screens the address by their new Leader.

They watched The Ensimmainen take two short steps forward. He used an alien shell to present himself as an Amber Simulacrum for the occasion. He wore a costume faintly reminiscent of the type worn by past dictators on Vesimaa. Just as he was about to speak Tumma stepped up beside him.

Haakon stared at Tumma, annoyed at the interruption. "What do you think you're doing? Get back in your place!"

The annoyance soon turned to incredulity as Tumma prevented him from addressing the audience by pushing in front of him to deliver his bombshell message to the entire gathering.

"We have taken control of this vessel."

Haakon jerked his head around to Kirkas, receiving a nod in affirmation. It would seem that amongst the company gathered there, only Kirkas was self-composed and unruffled. He, and only he was in full control of the entire situation; he controlled Synty, the people, Ensimmainen, the crew and the two factions all vying for dominance, though no one realized that little fact.

Tumma continued. "We will take Synty back to our home world and use it to defend ourselves against you."

"WHAT! YOU WILL DO NO SUCH THING! NO – NO – NO!" Anger, and the frightening realization that he had lost control burst out of The Ensimmainen.

Tumma delivered the rest of the good news. "If you attempt to interfere, we will take all your AmbSims and hybrids with us." He addressed himself directly to the crowd gathered in the auditorium, and all those in The Great Valley, rather than to the Leader, which further infuriated Haakon.

"NO! ABSOLUTELY NOT! - "I AM THE ENSIMMMAINEN. YOU WILL OBEY ME!"

Haakon lost his composure. Never in his entire existence has anyone dared to confront him in such a fashion! He was entirely uncomfortable wearing the alien body shell and now he had a full blown mutiny on his hands. He jerked his head from Kirkas to Langur to Valokvantti in rapid succession. None of them showed the least sign of support.

Valokvantti couldn't have been more pleased with the turn of events. Circumstances were working in his favor; better than he could have hoped or planned. He was ready to act.

Langur just stood there, stunned. *What the hell is going on here? Why isn't Kirkas doing something? Tumma should be dragged off the podium. Why is Kirkas letting him continue?*

"If you do not oppose us, you can have your AmbSims and hybrids. We will only take the operating crew and our own people, including those in storage."

"YOU ARE OUT OF YOUR MIND!"

The Dokkheimien, no longer acting or looking like a Ruler, stood there shouting and shaking. A deep red colour rose to his cheeks and perspiration broke out over his face. His simulacrum body behaved exactly as it should under the extreme stress of the experience. It became obvious to everyone The Ensimmainen had stopped listening. He'd certainly stopped hearing the message.

Leuhta kept a calm head and thought the proposition through. *This has merit. If the aliens are truly in control best to take the offer. TC-E is in good shape. Our genetic engineering experiment is working. We can invade Vesimaa any time in the future. It has no population left to speak of. They wouldn't be able to defend the planet against even a modest force.* She glanced at Langur and gave him a nudge. She'd assumed he followed the argument and had come to the same conclusion as herself. It was up to him as Head of Temporality Nexus to make the appropriate recommendation to The Ensimmainen.

But by then Langur, instead of listening to Tumma was thinking about his own ingenious plan; the creation of three distinct civilizations that could forge an alliance and be of benefit to each other into the future. To achieve that, they only had to swap planets. With those thoughts in his head he took Leuhta's nudge to mean he should go ahead and put his idea out there.

He took a step forward trying to attract The Ensimmainen's attention. Haakon was in no condition to hear anything, let alone be expected to make any rational decisions. Nevertheless, he was still the Leader. He heard the sound of words coming from his right and automatically turned his head to face the source. But the eyes were glazed and unfocused. Langur had to deliver his concept, right then and there, or never. The Ensimmainen heard only the inflammatory words he was capable of hearing.

" ... Swap planets," Langur concluded.

"WHAT! ARE YOU INSANE! WHAT ARE YOU SAYING MAN!" He looked to Kirkas again for support. "ARREST THESE MEN!" Haakon commanded.

Kirkas didn't move. He issued no such order, instead giving Valokvantti an almost imperceptible nod; his cue to step out in front of The Ensimmainen. With so much unexpected action going on everyone else was rooted to the spot. Of all of them, Eili was the only one to catch onto what was actually happening. He could see the bigger picture. There was no need for anyone to panic. The Project was still on track. The few remaining aliens could have TC-E. No reason why not. And Vesimaa was ready for the Dokks, only a question of nuts and bolts to make it happen. He watched Valokvantti to make the coup d'état official.

"Haakon, you are no longer fit to rule. I, as your rightful successor, now take full responsibility for the leadership of our people."

He delivered the measured words with the gravity befitting the occasion. He looked around in front of him before turning to Kirkas. The Ensimmainen's wild eyed stare followed Valokvantti's. "Commander Kirkas, take this man into custody!" Valokvantti ordered.

Kirkas nodded to two bodyguards beside him to carry out the order. There ensued a temporary easing of the highly charged atmosphere. The entire population of the vessel watched the drama unfold, not sure what was actually happening. It wasn't over yet.

Valokvantti, The new Ensimmainen unopposed, officially and legally because the mutineers had not played a direct part in the Coup d'état on stage, was looking exhilarated and thoroughly pleased with himself, though somewhat prematurely. He was still not in control - Kirkas was. The new Ensimmainen had temporarily forgotten he stood in the middle of a mutiny.

Tumma, the first to fully grasp the drama as it unfolded, knew of Valokvantti's ambition from Kirkas. He also knew Valokvantti wasn't entirely unsympathetic towards the plight of the aliens. Langur had also shown his hand. Without the time to confer with his team Tumma had to make the decision on the spot. Which option would work best for the people of Earth? While he contemplated and hesitated, Langur moved up to his side and quietly spoke to him, within Valokvantti's hearing.

"What makes more sense? Having our two civilizations at war with each other, or at peace for mutual benefit?"

Langur was certainly no fool. His people had done their best to exterminate Tumma's species. That was in the past. That action couldn't be undone. But the aliens could recover, with help. The choice was obvious; a solution the new Ensimmainen could live with. Valokvantti achieved everything he had personally wanted. He now had a civilization to build, complicated enough without engaging in interstellar conflict. More importantly, he couldn't take any chance of losing the seed population on which the new civilization would be founded. The new Ensimmainen had to remember that the aliens and Kirkas still had the upper hand.

As Langur and Tumma approached him, Valokvantti had already made up his mind as to the best course of action.

The aliens and their children were instructed to prepare for disembarkation to join all the others.

Survival On Tau Ceti–E

It was hot on TC-E. At seventy degrees centigrade at least four times the temperature of Vesimaa out in the open and at least ten times the mean temperature on Dokkheim. No one could exist outside the bio-domes. But the planet was changing, responding slowly to the terraforming efforts of its settlers. It was far too hot for the Dokks, even if they could bring the temperature down over the next several thousand years. Vesimaa was a far better prospect.

Shorter days and nights on TC-E meant the temperature spread was more even, and the weather patterns more predictable. Already weather had begun to manifest. Tumma and Saija went in protective suits on many excursions to all parts of the planet over the next few decades. The water from ice meteors had melted creating large oceans, from which rain had forged the beginnings of great rivers. It wasn't Earth, and could never be Earth. But life could have a future there. Blue waters and smudges of green were an excellent start.

Of the twenty initial dome complexes, made up of interconnecting smaller domes, looking like groups of soap bubbles, the aliens only had two entirely to themselves. Their average ground diameters of thirty kilometers was large enough to support the existing population of just several thousand. The people acclimatized well to both internal and external conditions. Clustered in rural villages under the protection of the domes and a larger rural city, life was good for a while, with clean air, water and healthy food. As good as if not better than in the belly of Synty.

It would have been easy for Tumma and Saija to succumb to a sense of false security after years of comfort under the domes.

"You know we can't stay here," Saija said to Tumma after one of their excursions. "Although we managed to cope with Valokvantti's unpredictability while he was a Captain aboard Synty, he's changed a lot here on TC-E. I just don't trust him anymore."

"There is that, yes," replied Tumma, "and another thing – Langur has not kept his promise."

"You mean about restoring our mortality?"

"Yes. I'm just waiting for the right opportunity to make a move. I agree with Kirkas – as soon as soon as our population in the two domes approaches the critical mass to hold their own against the Dokks, it'll be time for us to leave. Preparations are well under way. The cryogenic equipment on Synty has been repaired and our people can be maintained in stasis. They will help to regenerate the population on Earth. It won't be long now."

Kirkas remained on Synty with Lefe and their five children. The skeleton crew maintained all systems to allow a considerable population of aliens to continue existence within the artificial moon. Trust wasn't easily earned between the civilizations of Dokks and Vesimiaans. Many with large families chose to remain on Synty instead of disembarking to TC-E.

Four of the largest dome complexes on TC-E were occupied by AmbSims, biped slave clones, Pure Dokks, laboratories, factories and life sustaining agriculture. It was still a precarious existence for the Dokk civilization, as many unresolved issues still needed attention before the Project could be declared a complete success. Valokvantti was immortal, but he grew tired of waiting for the aliens to leave so the next stage of The Project could commence; preparing the exodus of his new hybrid species to Vesimaa. Nothing had changed in their plans despite the temporary misguided attempts of the aliens to save themselves.

They agreed to adopt Langur's proposition. They would swap planets. Instead of completely annihilating the aliens, they could have Tau Ceti-E. Synty would soon become a shuttle, transferring the people between the two planets. In the long term that was the only way the aliens could have a future. They were too few in number to defend their home planet. It was either a case of being wiped from the memory of the cosmos, or start again somewhere else.

At the time of the original disembarkation the Dokks, AmbSims and the hybrids eagerly stepped onto the new world of TC-E believing it to be theirs and their children's in perpetuity. The new Ensimmainen had not told his people about their ultimate destination. He didn't tell them what had to be done to secure a perfect world for their species. His experiences aboard Synty during the long journey taught him to keep people in the dark. What they didn't know would not upset them; would not depress them, and most importantly, would not incite them to another mutiny. They had a big enough challenge still ahead to survive on the inhospitable world where they had arrived. In time, his people would know – but not until the last minute when they would have no choice but to leave TC-E.

For now, The Ensimmainen had to face the emergent problem of overpopulation. Valokvantti chose to discuss most issues with Langur. He was the one individual he could trust implicitly.

"We have a new problem to deal with, Langur." The telomeres of each new generation of Taucetians are being progressively modified. "I don't care about the hybrids referring to themselves as Taucetians – inevitable after thirty years on this rock."

"They are not going to be immortal," Langur agreed.

"No – but they are still going to live a very long time. They are not dying fast enough for me to keep control of our population growth."

"You don't have many options," Langur came to the brutal reality quickly, "There will not be enough room under the domes. I've been working on accelerating the ageing process, but we have to be cautious."

"So what I'm left with is either to create more space or cull the growing population."

There were times when The Ensimmainen almost looked back to the old days with longing when he only had a ship and a few rowdy people to worry about.

Langur had no illusions left about the aliens. They'd proved themselves to be undependable, devious and untrustworthy. "Unfortunately, Synty is in the hands of the aliens," he reminded. "Whether you like it or not they still hold the balance of power, in the hands of Tumma and his loyal followers, including Kirkas."

"An extraordinary betrayal by Kirkas. I cannot understand how his mind could have been twisted like that. Those aliens are dangerous in the extreme! If we only had another spacecraft like Synty. Who could have anticipated we'd ever need two?"

"Until they relinquish control of it, you have only three options to work with." Tumma told Valokvantti.

"I will dispose of the aliens eventually." It made The Ensimmainen feel better just to say it, "they're too much of an unpredictable, troublesome, annoying and above all, highly adaptable species." The Ensimmainen looked forward to the day when Tumma would eventually make that first journey to begin the process of migration. "I'll keep some of the resident aliens in their domes as hostages. That'll make sure Tumma returns, with whoever is left on Vesimaa – and I'll be ready to strike!"

As part of the bargain struck with the aliens, he had to maintain the terraforming of TC-E. Fortunately, the need for more resources for the process had diminished considerably. The greatest effort and expense had been spent in bringing water to the planet. Initiating the water cycle was the beginning of creating life. Flora and fauna could be seeded into the environment from the alien's dome. It didn't matter if the aliens didn't survive, as long as The Ensimmainen had another planet ready when it was needed.

Unfortunately, he didn't have all those thousands of aliens in cryogenic storage to enable Langur to continue the dilution of alien characteristics in his hybrid generations. Without a scientific background The Ensimmainen wasn't equipped to foresee the consequences of the process. He was also not aware of the leaching of alien psyches into the Dokks' minds inhabiting their neural network. Dr.Qilaq had been studying the phenomenon for a decade. He and Langur now knew enough to have serious concerns.

The day finally came for Tumma and Saija to depart. Only a small, subdued crowd gathered at the spaceport on TC-E to see off the voyagers, whom they would probably not see again for another two hundred years. It was best not to publicize the event. The inhabitants of the alien domes had found out anyway. Saija made no secret of their departure, although she didn't give them the real reason for the expedition back to Earth. From among the new generations of aliens on TC-E many volunteered to go on the journey, relieving the overpopulation problem for Valokvantti.

If they were lucky, they would still be alive on arrival on Earth. It gave them a new reason to live; a career, an adventure, a chance to become part of the new history of the human race.

There was a very clear understanding between the leaders of the two races. It was a truce of necessity. Both had evil intentions towards the other, but - both had much to lose by failure, and much to gain by success. As much as Tumma needed to leave, he had to return. He and Leuhta had become pawns of fate in the game of survival of their species.

The twenty shuttles left without any ceremony. Langur, Leuhta and Dr.Qilaq remained behind. Tumma and Saija were accompanied by the new generations of humans who had never seen Earth. Kirkas had previously decided to stay aboard Synty. He remained in command of Security, and by default, second in command to Tumma. They had a new Captain and some of the old crew to control the craft. All were loyal to either Kirkas or to the two immortal aliens. Also on board the full load of humans waited in suspended animation. They may be the only source of uncontaminated DNA left in existence other than the few people remaining on TC-E. And from what Tumma had seen on his short visit on Earth, the people there were in very poor health. The humans on Earth had been subjected to all manner of interference from the Dokks. They couldn't be relied on to produce a healthy seed population for the continuation of the human species.

*

Without having to break their voyage Synty didn't take as long on the return trip. The Ensimmainen received updates from Kirkas, all indicating an essentially uneventful journey. So uneventful that the frequency of reports thinned out so much that Valokvantti began to worry. His own communications to Kirkas were mostly ignored. *I cannot afford to alienate those damn … those damn …* he couldn't even find the words to describe them, he'd become so angry. *I must have that vessel! Everything depends on it.* Many times he tried to grasp this new reality. It was so different as seen from the eyes of a man who had the responsibility for the lives of an entire species, than it was from the perspective of a spaceship's Captain. And the greater reality was that the aliens could still prove to be dangerous to their survival in the future if they were allowed to survive themselves.

Relationships with Jarl Yakiv on Dokkheim had deteriorated to such a point that TC-E no longer received help from them. He couldn't understand why, and Jarl Yakiv refused to elucidate. *They could have built another craft for us, even if it wasn't as large as Synty, they could have managed that. We just don't have the resources on TC-E to do it ourselves.* All their effort had gone into establishing the bio-domes. *At least the terraforming is progressing well. We just might have to stay here longer than planned. Vesimaa is the best place for us. I've seen it with my own eyes. It has regenerated to be the most absolutely perfect jewel in all of known creation. The aliens are reduced to insignificant numbers. I could exterminate them with very little effort when we arrive.*

Langur had many lengthy discussions on numerous occasions with The Ensimmainen about his many apprehensions. As still the nominal head of Temporality Nexus, Langur continued to have primary responsibility for the yet to be completed Project. An incredible amount of progress had been made in a relatively very short time.

"The priority, the absolute priority, is the re-engineering of our species' DNA in order to achieve mortality. It is not about invading the home of another species," Langur often had to remind The Ensimmainen. "Don't forget that an integral part of the plan in its original form was to colonize Tau Ceti-E. You yourself found it for us. We are here and we are doing exactly that."

'Hrumph,' was the general response Langur received for his logic. Valokvantti then went on to express his thoughts aloud.

"If Tumma decides not to return, which I doubt, unless there's something which prevents him from doing so, we would still not have a problem. Yes, he does have our back-up stock of aliens in storage aboard Synty. But we have live aliens right here under our noses, ready to use. I'd like to exterminate the lot of them. They've been nothing but trouble. And now they are breeding faster than we are. It would be so easy. Their entire life support system has a bypass control directly to me. The fumigant is already loaded and primed!" The Ensimmainen had no secrets from Langur. They had known and trusted each other for far too long.

Langur chose not to respond directly to that line of thinking. "Our fourth and fifth generation hybrids are doing well, but we still need to further dilute the alien characteristics. It's not the telomeres that are a problem. There is something else happening that Dr.Qilaq and I have been studying for some time now. You need to know the situation, and why we might have further need of the aliens."

"Y-e-s. Should I be concerned about this – something else?" The Ensimmainen suddenly became quite alert to what Langur had to say.

"No, not unduly, but best if you are informed of the phenomenon, and the possible consequences." Langur kept his voice and his manner subdued, in spite of the seriousness of the matter.

"Does anybody else know about this other than Dr.Qilaq? No? Good. Keep it that way. Right - out with it."

"It concerns the neural cleansing of the alien brain matrix prior to uploading it with the psyche of our own breeding volunteers. We have made some progress in refining the process but ..." Langur hesitated.

"Just exactly what have you done, or not done Skuggi?" The Ensimmainen only called him that on the rare occasions when he became particularly upset.

"It seems the resident alien psyche has always managed to somehow evade the full effects of our bleaching, and the residuals have been able to infiltrate the minds of our AmbSims," Langur said more quickly than he normally would have. His Leader noted his slight loss of composure. Langur very rarely came off the level.

"And – the consequences?" Valokvantti hissed, behaving more and more like their old Jarl, probably due to the pressures of his high office.

"Severe." Langur said, finally admitting even to himself how precarious the survival of his species had become from such a simple, unforeseen side effect of his plan.

"Yes? Just how severe?"

"They begin to think more like aliens than Dokkheimiens."

"AND YOU ONLY THOUGHT OF TELLING ME THIS NOW!" The Ensimmainen burst out, no longer able to contain his anger.

"I believe we have a solution." Simmering silence washed over Langur from The Ensimmainen, as the Leader waited for an explanation. "Use only our females for artificial insemination of healthy alien and hybrid sperm."

"Have you tried this?"

"Yes, but the females have been reluctant."

"DAMN THE FEMALES. They will do as they're told. They are not here on a holiday! And while you're at it, get Leuhta to intensify the re-education of the scions and begin Dokkheimien conditioning data uploads as soon as their neurons can handle it."

Langur had a feeling this particular interview would be a difficult one. He wanted to introduce the problematic subject more gently, but at least now it was done. As much as he tended to be considerate of the aliens in the past, he was certain their future didn't look too good, at least not on TC-E. Perhaps it would be better for Tumma to stay where he was. Langur had become tired of all the problems. He'd given up the idea of having a scion of his own with Leuhta. That was impossible now. The child would be immortal and would be out of place on a world of mortal hybrids, all with substantially differing life spans. How long would it be before the whole mess was resolved? How many generations? How many more unforeseen problems? If he was going to be honest with himself, he would have to admit that the alien neural leaching was going to have a dramatic effect on the minds of future generations of Taucetians. They might even disinherit their ancestry. The complexities generated by his initial 'simple' concept had worn him down.

His internal dialogue further depressed Langur. *I'm so tired of all the challenges. I just want to be free of all the intrigues, all the pressures - free of that cursed planet. If I could just go to a place of eternal rest!* That, he realized sadly, would only happen if he brought it about with his own hands.

Perhaps in another four or five generations the external world of TC-E would be ready to welcome its new parasitic inhabitants. Whether they be the Dokk hybrids or the aliens didn't matter to TC-E. It was a dead world coming back into the maelstrom of existence. It had rested long enough. It was time to come back to life and suffer the pain of evolution again. For the time being TC-E enjoyed a peaceful interlude in which it was learning to breath and perspire and listen to its new heartbeat. Langur waited, he had no option. He knew Leuhta would not let him find release, not that he'd mentioned the unmentionable to her.

Ensimmainen Valokvantti also waited; fuming, rumbling, planning; life for some and death for others. *Surely in the next few generations Synty will arrive. All I want is the ship, just the ship –I can do without the people in it – All of them!* Valokvantti had his own disturbing self-talk. Like the first Jarl on TC-E, he too started losing his clarity of thinking. Priorities of survival seemed adamant of establishing their own order of importance. In all likelihood it would be Tau Ceti-E to decide who it cared to host. Valokvantti was more angry than afraid, because he knew that the aliens were a far more adaptable species. They were already outbreeding the Dokks and inhabiting more of the available bio-domes. They'd even begun to establish small satellite colonies in other parts of TC-E.

Survival On Earth

Tumma and Saija became grandparents during the journey to Earth. Without interference from the Dokks, the human population aboard Synty grew exponentially. Kirkas and Lefe became great grandparents as well; though Lefe had to inhabit several new shells. They had visibly aged, but were still vibrant in their extended youth. The experiment had succeeded well. It appeared they might not outlive their great-great-great grandchildren.

When Tumma and Saija's children looked at their parents they knew, because they had been told, that they could be considered immortal. But that was a hard concept for a child to understand. Other than a little wear and tear during the many long years of travelling the two 'first citizens' remained much as they were when Synty left TC-E. Oddly, as their children developed into young adults, signs of their ageing seemed not to be as prominent as that of the other human children.

Lefe and Saija took the education system into their special care whilst in transit. There were certain priorities every teacher had to adhere to strictly. Above all, there was to be no mention of deity. The Universe, the great Cosmos was all there was – God did not exist. If there was anything at all humanity had learnt from the Dokks it was one single great truth; they were entirely and solely responsible for their lives, for their future and responsible for all their actions. Accountability was only to themselves and to those they affected with their actions. They had to be strong, unshakeable in these beliefs because soon they were going to experience a soul shattering shock – there was more to existence than the inside of a spacecraft.

Teaching the difference between right and wrong proved to be more difficult. How could the ultimate fate of two species be considered as a foundation for such a concept, when each tried to exterminate the other in order to survive? It was easier to teach children to have respect for themselves and for others, and how to manifest that respect in reality. So no rules were taught to differentiate between right and wrong. There were no ten commandments - there were only consequences – both pleasant and unpleasant. And the last high priority item on the education curriculum began and ended with history. Taught as if history was a series of events recorded on a string, where the two ends were joined. There was no beginning and no ending; just a stretching and an unfolding and an overlapping. With each child, their perspective started with themselves and where they were at that time. They could look to the left, or look to the right along the string. One direction had more clarity than the other. One had more certainty than the other. To look to the left, into the past and to understand it was just as difficult as looking to the right and trying to guess how the events would coalesce into realities in the future. Saija's idea of the Uncertainty Principle of History evolved out of her extended life of experience. There is no beginning, there's no ending – our continuum propagates itself in those who survive after us.

The uncertainty principle of history perspective meant that one could construct history ahead of its happening but couldn't be certain the past had been understood and verified accurately. Hence the future's fluidity. However, certain things were always known about the elements making up the two segments of the string.

Lefe invented a game to create a new story out of the uncertainty of those elements, a story taking into account all the known facts of the past and possible future parts. Wonderful presents were given to the best stories. It became a game played by children of all ages. A game also played by the leaders at all levels of Synty society, though much more earnestly, to bring future possible reality into ultra-sharp clarity. It was from expectations constructed on the Uncertainty Principle perspective of History that parents, their children and their grandchildren were going to meet planet Earth and its inhabitants.

*

Excitement aboard Synty overflowed into many celebrations as it neared Earth preparing to park in orbit just past the moon. How strange it must have been to see a large multitude celebrating a homecoming. Other than two people none of them had ever actually seen Earth.

"I don't know what to feel, Tumma. It's too overwhelming."

"It saddens me to think what we'll find."

Tears of joy flowed freely in spite of her sadness. "It's been too long."

"Almost two centuries, Saija. Could you possibly have ever imagined such a thing?"

"So much has happened. I found it difficult to keep track of the passage of years."

"Yes," Tumma agreed. "I knew we had to come home one day."

"You are a good man, my love. You tried to help save those people and ended up fighting for our own survival."

*

Several tribes had come together, fully armed with weapons, though lacking in technological sophistication, to greet the extraordinary flying structures descending from the thick clouds. No point trying to forewarn others of their coming - there wasn't enough of a population to warn.

Viewed from the moon the 'water world' was extraordinarily in its magnificence. Tumma knew what it was like when he left, but the visual memory of it eroded with time. He just gazed at the spectacle as they neared. Tears welled up in his eyes unable to contain themselves, cascading freely down his cheeks.

Saija cried so copiously her tears blurred the vision of her home. Lefe couldn't help herself either and sobbed in sympathetic rhythm with Saija. No extraordinary flight of her imagination could have prepared her for the splendour before her eyes.

She tried looking at Kirkas, who was struggling with his own emotions. He wanted to shout to give expression to the overwhelming experience he was going through. He couldn't even breathe or blink for fear the jewel that entranced him would disappear. *It is not possible – just not possible! The myth is real – and more beautiful than any story could have described! It is a living being in a garden of the Cosmos.*

The entire population of the ship was awed by the emerald planet. It looked so frail, so delicate in the vastness of nothingness around it. How could it possibly exist? How was it possible for anything to be so magnificent? Was this treasure truly what they had travelled for, for so long? How could anyone even contemplate abandoning such a paradise?

Synty moved ever so slowly towards the blue green world.

It moved much too slowly. The pace of existence shrank to allow the few privileged ambassadors of sentient life emerging out of the cosmos to absorb the miracle in front of them.

No one saw what Saija and Tumma saw from within themselves as they tried to reconnect with their home. Others had to dig deep into their synaptic labyrinths to find shadows of memories they could relate to, because what was revealing itself to them wasn't a world they had known in the past. It was a new world.

As the planet slipped from day into night the image in front of their eyes went dark. Completely, unbelievably dark. Something was wrong. Very, very wrong.

The two of them stared and stared uncomprehending until suddenly it dawned on Saija,

"There are no lights!"

There were no cities where brilliant necklaces of light intertwined with each other. There were no hubs of sparkling diamonds. There were no cities with life pulsing through their towers and their highways. Some great calamity must have befallen their beautiful home world.

"It is worse than I could have imagined," Tumma whispered almost inaudibly.

The Earth continued its slow revolution as the ship approached cautiously nearer. The light of the sun once again washed against the shores of its darkened continents. In some places tall white mountain beacons caught the first rays of the Sun and cast its reflected photon spears into the void, lighting up the world below them.

Silence dominated aboard the vessel. How else could one assimilate into oneself the symphony of perfection?

"I can't see any cities – where are the highways?" Saija sobbed through tears.

Where once there were long narrow grey ribbons crisscrossing each continent, wrapping them into presents of fossil fuel fed technology, there was only a carpet of green, or the gold of wind swept sands or the blue of shimmering oceans. Where once great fields of wheat and corn crops waved in over-abundance, there were only forests. Deserts and plains of dead soils had been attacked by armies of verdant intruders. Where once flowed arteries of the oceans suffering the atherosclerosis of pollution, brown and pungent and oil-slicked, now flowed crystal clear life nurturing waters of the great rivers.

"This wasn't the planet we left behind, Saija. This is paradise." Conflicting thoughts surged into Tumma's mind. *The Dokks have resurrected our home from the ravages of the plague of human exploitation. Was the price too high? What is the value of human life if all it can create is destruction?* He had to stop himself. The future had suddenly become clouded by too many uncertainties. Fortunately, Saija interrupted him from spiraling into maudlin introspection.

"Where are the people? There's no sign of civilization anywhere. Surely they couldn't all have died out already! There hasn't been enough time. There were seven billion people when we left. They couldn't all be gone!"

Lefe and Kirkas could only listen, gradually realizing what the Dokks had done. They saw only genocide, and a magnificent world that surely must be worth any sacrifice. Survival of the Dokkheimiens paled into insignificance.

Only one landing craft searched from below the clouds. It carried the crushed hopes of the only two people left alive who used to call this place their home. Once again they crossed the boundary of light and dark, and as the craft flew low over the land mass they knew to be Europe, the faintest glimmer of hope flickered within the two human beings; within the creatures who had become so used to being called 'aliens' they almost forgot they were humans.

They saw little shimmerings of sparkling amber-orange here and there, far apart from each other.

"What's that?" Saija pointed in their direction. "Could they be forest fires?"

"No, too small for that. Perhaps a lightning strike - no, there are no storm clouds over the continent."

They flew on and turned north away from a great inland sea that lapped on the shores of the boot of Italy. They flew towards the land where they used to sleep at night, and make love and have children and families and birthdays … And Birthdays. How many birthdays have Saija and Tumma had they should not have had! Myriad conflicting emotions played out their drama on their faces as they stared with rapt attention at the forests below them.

They hovered over the lands of the Vikings. They were almost home. The light of the winter sun led them towards the East. Lower and lower the craft descended, and as it slowed they could see an occasional clearing in the land of the Suomi.

"There! There!" Saija shouted, "we have to land!"

Tumma looked and he saw them. People! Not many, but there were people.

They touched down without the cloaking shields, the ramp extending itself onto the soil of this strange, unfamiliar world. Saija and Tumma walked out slowly together, hand-in-hand. They stopped for a moment at the end of the ramp. The overwhelming unreality freezing them to the spot. The aroma of Earth, their Earth awakened them to courage. Slowly, reverently placing one foot, then another onto the soil of their home they stopped again after a few steps.

Unable to speak, for words for the emotions of that moment had not yet been written into the language of any living being, they looked upon the people they came so far to find. What happened here? Why are they wearing dirty animal skins and rags? Why are they waving spears at us?

One individual from the small gathering, more ornately clad than the others, a female, stepped forward towards them. She held a thick long stick with what looked like a lump of raw glass on the end and shook it at them. Tumma and Saija couldn't move. The woman came closer, glancing back to her tribe, then at the two arrivals from the sky. She held out her wand and pointed it at them. They remained motionless, silent, holding each other's hand. What could they say? They felt they were somehow intruders, unwelcome strangers, aliens.

The woman uttered some strange words, inviting words, unafraid yet keeping her distance. Saija and Tumma slowly moved forward, still clutching each other's hand. The Shaman beckoned, moving away from the craft towards a fruit laden tree. They followed. She pointed them towards the tree so they moved to the tree, stopping below its branches. All this time the tribe watched in silence.

The spears had stopped their threatening dance. The savages observed with large saucer eyes and looked in expectation upon the two sky-people standing under the fruit tree. The Shaman, a show woman certainly, stopped her movements of dramatic effect for a moment. Suddenly she thrust out her wand towards Tumma and shouted just one word,

"ARDM!"

The shock of the sudden movement and the unexpected bellow emanating from the lips of the fragile old woman almost made Tumma lose his footing on the damp uneven ground. Before he had time to comprehend what she shouted, she did it again. This time the glass adorned wand thrust towards Saija, simultaneously the Shaman shouted,

"EVR!"

In a smooth continuous movement, the Shaman then turned to the tribe and shouted again, even louder this time, raising both hands high into the air, thrusting the wand towards the heavens.

"ARDMJAEVR!"

Immediately the voices of all the tribe erupted into cheering and shouting and stomping of feet. It seemed all fear had fled at the magic words uttered by the old woman. They continued shouting, hugging each other, dancing and circling around Tumma and Saija who were still standing rooted to the spot under the fruit tree. The whole event had been so bizarre neither of them could understand what had just happened.

Many times they heard the word "ArdmjaEvr" shouted over and over again. They had no idea what was going on, but they were relieved the threatening encounter had turned into something less so, albeit incredibly strange.

Eventually the impromptu celebration abated. An invitation was extended to the two sky-people to move towards another part of the clearing where a large fire had been burning, and a great variety of food appeared; an invitation they couldn't refuse - they didn't want to refuse. They wanted to know – everything! Who were these people? What was that strange thing the old woman had said? Tumma and Saija wanted the answers to a thousand other questions that clamored to be asked. Tumma's mind was already working on the problem of whether they would be able to speak to these people? *What was it the old woman said? Ardm ja Evr* – Tumma turned it over and over in his mind until one word of the three stood out like a beacon – 'Ja'.

He knew that word!

Tumma and Saija sat for a long time on some crude stools listening to the conversations going on around them. The Shaman argued a great deal with those near her, as did other groups around the fire ring. It seemed the energy of those vehement discussions would never abate, until the old woman suddenly disappeared giving Tumma and Saija a chance to bring their thoughts back to each other.

"I don't know what's happening here," Saija said, "but I have the strangest feeling they are using a language I should be understanding."

"So do I!" Tumma agreed. "Do you know where we are? Can you remember how we got to this place? I was too busy trying to take it all in."

"Wait, wait … yes … Yes! I know exactly where we are! - Tumma," she grabbed his arm with two hands and squeezed, "we are in Finland, Tumma. We Are In Finland!"

"Good God! Yes! That's it … 'ja' means 'and'! What has happened here?"

The old Shaman reappeared from the shadows carrying what looked like a book; an incredibly old, tattered leather bound thick book. No bigger than a large sheet of paper, she carried it reverently with two hands holding from underneath. She placed it gently on the table in front of the sky-people and with great care she lifted its pages, turning each page with infinite tenderness.

The tribe folk gathered around to look at the pages of that revered book. Each time a faded half distinct image appeared on a page they made appreciative noises of recognition. Obviously they all knew this book intimately. At about the tenth page the Shaman paused for a second to savor the flavor of the moment before turning the page once more. A hush came over the gathering. Breaths were held within chests for fear of letting out the beasts of heresy. Tumma looked around at faces frozen almost in rapture.

Saija pulled his attention back to the table. They examined the image more closely.

There, on the much thumbed page, faded, partly torn, almost damaged beyond recognition Tumma gazed upon an illustration of two people standing underneath a fruit tree. He couldn't stop the words escaping from his mouth under their own volition, like the first soft breeze of the very first languid evening of a summer day,

"Adam and Eve … … … … …" His whispered statement, exhaled rather than spoken, drifted to mingle with the smoke of the fire, permeating the souls of every individual standing around the table, transfixed by the transcendent moment.

Ardm had spoken to them.

The days following the great revelation degenerated into disorder in spite of everything Tumma and Kirkas tried to do. When the people of the tribe realized the sky-people were just like themselves, all notion of hostility disappeared. First, they met and welcomed the other members of the landing craft. Initially the amber-orange skinned ones fascinated them, but that soon gave way to much greater fascination for the vehicle they were allowed to inspect. Such wonders!

"Can you believe these people? They actually believe we're Adam and Eve." Tumma couldn't get over it. "So much more has changed than I could ever have imagined."

"From now on just think of me as Eve," she gave him a cheeky look. "They're a society that's completely reverted to a primitive state. They've kept many artifacts from the past, like the book. But life must have become very difficult. And the language - to have evolved so quickly in such a short time."

Saija found it hard to think they were amongst descendants of the Finnish people. Although techno-speak had disappeared and almost all of the original Suomi, communication wasn't at all primitive. The language had 'evolved' as all languages do over time.

There were complexities and nuances of expression just as there were so many hundreds of years ago.

Yet the passage of so much time had its effects. Saija decided it would be best to establish some measure of mutual understanding between themselves and the tribe before introducing the Society of Synty to them. It took several months before Ardm and Evr were able to find common ground with their hosts. All the tribes' folk had decided to call them 'Ardm and Evr' despite Saija's protestations that they were not the people represented in the illustration.

Obviously not only language had evolved but also myth. Tumma couldn't work out how the confusion arose for them to think the biblical stories of the past somehow related to the future. It made more sense to Saija, who had created the Uncertainty Principle of History. To her it became a prime example of how the 'theory' could find application in reality. She was discussing that very phenomenon with Lefe, when the Shaman walked in on her in mid-sentence.

Well, the cat was out of the bag. The Shaman heard all the references to their space craft. "What this place – Synty? People inside, live?"

The sky-people tried to keep the existence of Synty quiet until they felt the tribes' folk were ready. Many months had elapsed and relationships with them were excellent. So there was nothing for it but to tell them everything. One night Saija took the Shaman out under the cloudless sky.

"Tell me about your yötaivas – your night sky,' The Shaman asked. She was, in their own fashion an educated individual who pondered deeply about the mysteries of the sky.

The moon was a particularly fascinating subject for her. She explained the old myth. "Special tribe – very smart – live long way - across meri - great waters."

These people had special powers for they could fly through the air, she said. A group of them had decided one day they must visit the light of the night sky. She pointed at the moon – 'kuu'. So these people flew higher than any other of their tribe had ever flown before, flying so high that they reached the 'light of the night'. "They return not," she explained.

As the Shaman completed her tale Saija also pointed into the night sky. "See those little sparkling lights slowly making their way across the heavens? They are called 'satellites'. They were made by the same tribe who could fly in the air."

The Shaman would not believe her at first, but she looked and thought about it for a little while, then examined the sky more closely and began discovering other moving shinning lights.

"Look over there. Can you see anything different? Look closely. Is there anything there you haven't seen before?" Saija prompted her. When she spotted it the Shaman's eyes strained wide open, her mouth formed itself into a great round OOH, then looked questioningly at Saija.

"Yes," Saija confirmed, "that is where we come from."

Within days every one of the tribes' folk wanted to go into the sky to where Evr had come from. She discussed it with Tumma and Kirkas.

"We don't have much choice. These are the only people we know so far, and at least they are friendly." Kirkas provided the level headed, unbiased thinking. "It would be best to bring these folks into our confidence as much as possible. They might be able to help us search for other remnants of alien – oops, sorry - human life on the planet. It might make it much easier to convince them to abandon their primitive lives and come with us to another world, if they can see we have made 'friends' with the 'Finnish' tribe people.

The tribes' folk at first made many visits to Synty, meeting everyone and seeing all the wonders. They were told the story of the sky-people and how they were abducted so long ago. It wasn't necessary to discuss the genocide of the human race. It would have achieved nothing but anger, distrust and resentment ... perhaps even a desire for revenge. After the novelty had worn off, many decided to stay on Synty for a while and live there. Civilization had returned to their lives.

Crystal clear waters continued flowing down the rivers of the new Earth into oceans brimming with all manner of life as time continued on its impersonal path to plough deep furrows into the history of human existence. Several years passed without the sky-people making any progress with their mission. The time had come to take as many landing craft as they had, and search the Earth for more survivors. Each craft's crew included members of the Tribe who had spent some time living with the sky-people in The Great Valley of Synty. Their mission was to gather as many people as they could, as would willingly join them to go to Tau Ceti-E.

They told the same story to everyone they found. People learnt their Earth was soon to be invaded by a species who would annihilate them completely. Many isolated tribes were found on all the continents, numbering in the hundreds of thousands. Children were still a rarity, but life found a way to repair the damage done by Dokk extinction engineers. Many more years passed, yet, in spite of all the proofs presented by the sky-people to verify their stories many of Earth's survivors refused to believe. They couldn't comprehend that their entire species would disappear into cosmic oblivion if they didn't do something to help themselves.

The Shaman, who became Saija's very close friend, was taken into confidence about what had happened on Earth. She believed most of the things she learnt about the history of her people but couldn't believe the story of the abduction and the genocide. She had one compelling reason for her skepticism.

"You are my dear Ardm ja Evr. You have eternal youth for a reason." She had noticed, as had the other tribes' folk that those two sky-people never changed, they never aged. They never became ill, and all their injuries healed miraculously quickly. "It has been foretold; Ardm ja Evr will return from the sky to populate the Earth again, to look after us and safeguard us against all harm. You have even brought the magnificent second moon to make certain the people would survive."

Strangely, the story isn't all that farfetched. We're doing exactly as was prophesied. We've even brought back many people who were abducted and stored 'for future use'. Who would have thought we would be using them? Reality had become very fluid for Saija.

Inevitably the old Shaman aged over the years to ancient-hood. She wasn't immortal. Her time had come.

"I die a happy woman," she said to Saija on her death bed, "I've seen you with my own eyes, knowing you will save our people. It is why you were given back to us."

Many had come to believe as the Shaman believed and therefore refused to abandon their home to go with the sky-people.

To show their good intent, the Society of Synty did a great deal to bring some semblance of civilization back to the survivors. They improved living standards, established the means for simple necessities like hygiene, ready access to water, power generated by the sun and improved living accommodation with better shelters – houses that could be kept warm and would protect them from the elements.

Kirkas and Tumma even brought large groups out of cryogenic storage, reintroducing them to the areas where they were abducted from. Genetic diversity was maintained, and with time the human species could regenerate. To achieve all these things cost a great deal more time for the sky-people. But their good intentions and hard work backfired. The more comfortable the people of Earth became, the more they resisted the idea of leaving that comfort. Life was becoming good again. The air was clean, food was healthy and plentiful and the water truly life giving. They were living in the garden of Eden.

Tumma, Saija, Lefe, Kirkas and a number of the new hybrid leadership, one of whom was Kirkas' eldest daughters, had many discussions about the conundrum they faced. Lately, at the end of each such session they arrived at the same inevitable conclusion.

"Abduction. There is no other solution."

Tumma found it unnervingly strange that he should say such a thing, but he felt that the future of the human species depended on it; especially if the Dokks returned and finished the job they'd started. If they were able to 'volunteer' people, then Tumma could do it also. It would only be a matter of time before the Dokks did return in force, and without any reticence put their original plan into full and devastating effect.

"Is there no other way?" Saija and Lefe were dismayed, hoping there might be.

Kirkas, their level headed Captain agreed without any reservations. "There is no other way if they refuse to come willingly. Abduction, and cryogenics for those unwilling to live life in The Great Valley. The next time we bring shuttlecraft down they will be fully cloaked." The matter was settled. Humankind would have to try and survive on Tau Ceti-E.

"How much longer do we have to live as immortals?" Saija asked Tumma. "I want us to die before our children. I want to have a normal life. When, Tumma - when will we be normal again?" A shadow passed over the surface of his mind, as Tumma thought back to the less complicated times, when he first lost his shadow.

The time had come to harvest passengers for the long journey back to Tau Ceti-E. Perhaps there Langur will keep his promise to Tumma and Saija.

Survival On Dokkheim

Another milestone had been passed in the long history of Dokkheim and its inhabitants. Unlike the planet, its inhabitants were experiencing only a semblance of immortality. Some had abandoned their home. Others unwilling to follow.

The facilities of Temporality Nexus were still as Langur Skuggi had left them. His personal office remained undisturbed. Things changed very slowly on Dokkheim. Many of the employees continued working on projects Langur initiated but with a slight difference; without the urgent imperative of survival. It had only been a few hundred years since the business of a 'light' universe and an alien planet with strange life forms had become the focus for their energies. In proportion to their life expectancy it was almost like a flicker of the visual receptors.

Temporality Nexus had a new CEO appointed by the new Jarl, Yakiv. Vertical Systems remained under Yakiv's control, but he no longer needed the income from it. He had the resources of the entire planet under his control, and he had plans requiring a great deal more of those resources. When Yakiv first took control, he cleaned up the troublesome dissidents, those opposed to The Project, by making them into slave-clones to build spacecraft for the colonization and rehabilitation of Tau Ceti-E. As a result the entire population of the planet learnt to fear him and his absolute power. Like his predecessor Jarl Yakiv no longer had any qualms using his power to its absolute limits – which he did without hesitation.

The people also respected him for a time, after he had introduced measures that alleviated some of the ennui they were suffering. Those strategies were only a temporary measure. Too much time remained the enemy. Unrest continued, not because the people were afraid their species would die out as Langur had predicted, but because of an ever growing sense of meaninglessness.

Riots became more frequent necessitating rigorous reprisals from Jarl Yakiv. His heavy handed actions only resulted in eroding his hard earned respect.

As a pattern emerged for the behaviour of the populace, frequency of audiences with The Jarl also increased. The single common theme was uncomplicated; that is uncomplicated in itself but not in its ramifications - unrestricted breeding. Consequently, Yakiv stopped all requests for breeding indefinitely. He needed time to think things through. This wasn't a situation where he could call upon advisors. The solution had to come from him.

Haakon and Langur may have thought they'd resolved the issue of the demise of our species. Perhaps. But they still left me with a planet full of immortals who are not happy! Their future still hangs in the balance. At least I still have my army of slave clones I'd used to build Synty.

A vague idea began to coalesce into feasibility.

They don't have the option of being disloyal. I could enlist many more from the frequent rioters who are still active all around the planet. Perhaps build an armada to explore the universe. I need to get away and think about this.

The notion had some merit, also a high element of risk. He wanted to consider it in depth away from the trappings and responsibilities of his position, even if only for a day.

He hadn't been The Jarl for very long. Most people didn't know his markings, they wouldn't recognize him in public, so it was still safe for him to move about outside of his power base. In the very early hours of one morning he took his personal magnemini and went to the energy bar Langur had recommended to him not so very long ago.

It was indeed a magnificent location. He'd almost forgotten how beautiful his world was, being weighed down by the unlimited responsibilities that accompanied unlimited power. He settled at one of the energy outlets and plugged himself in. He gazed out across an expanse of iron red rocky landscape from the edge of the plateau at the river of mercury flowing far below, barely visible.

Yakiv let his mind wander and absorb the mystery of the coming dawn.

His world gradually emerged out of pitch blackness into blackness then into a deep, deep orange-red black glow as he lost himself in thought. The mercury river flowed and played with the tantalizing promise of light, which never came. Their sun wasn't capable of producing 'light' in a dark matter universe. The light they did experience was a fugitive from another universe.

Yakiv thought back over the beginnings of his association with Langur. At first he couldn't accept Langur's idea their species was doomed to extinction. Even less could he accept the fact that it was, according to Dr.Qilaq, because of their immortality. But so much had changed in such a short time. So many of his people wanted to procreate freely. They wanted scions to give meaning to their lives. It was as simple, yet as complicated as that. A rioting mob does not think with its head; thousands of rioting mobs even less so.

Complete personal freedom to procreate at will cannot become a reality. We simply don't have the resources to sustain a larger growing population indefinitely.

We have reached the limit.

Yakiv reeled at the thought of every available square metre of space being taken up by enormous throngs of people. The planet itself wasn't big enough. No planet would be big enough to support an immortal species breeding uncontrollably with no effective natural means of balancing its hordes.

As a consequence, breeding had already been strictly controlled. So strictly in fact, that if a bonded pair produced a scion without authority, they were immediately terminated, including the scion. Yakiv brooded on this unacceptable foundation for their civilization.

He contemplated the harsh measures he'd initiated.

For a bonded pair to gain authorization to produce one scion, the planet had to show a corresponding reduction of two individuals in the population count. There were other requirements as well, but that was the primary criterion without which every application automatically failed.

One for two. That is the rule. Nobody must break the rule!

But now the people had gone completely crazy. It seemed their memory had been wiped clean of that one critical condition if they were to have any hope of surviving as a species. Yakiv couldn't fathom the reason for the revolt against their survival imperative.

One for two.

Yakiv kept turning that over in his mind.

One for two.

What if it was two for three, or a thousand for a two thousand! What if I could control the dying instead of … ?

We have outstanding genetic engineers! …

His gaze never left the river as night turned into day; the pitch black melting into utter darkness. Dawn had arrived, and with it a Jarl who knew the answer to the dilemma. It was such a simple solution, such an elegant solution. Much better than Langur's complicated, expensive and above all, divisive plan.

Why couldn't our wise old Jarl with millennia of life experience conceived of such a simple plan!

Now it was his plan, Yakiv's plan – the man who was once CEO of Vertical Health now supreme ruler of Dokkheim.

It will solve the problem of immortality. It will ensure the maximum of health and vigor amongst the population, and they will have unlimited freedom to produce scions at will.

His excitement grew as he realised Temporality Nexus could create the technology he needed. Just a little genetic manipulation – just a little clever engineering.

LST-DNA. That's the answer. A programmable Life Span Terminator DNA, with a maximum upper limit life span and a zero lower limit. I could set the upper limit myself!

He would maintain absolute power, and immortality. No one would know their finite limit. They would have to live life accordingly. Yakiv couldn't remember ever being so excited in his life. He had the answer, and he would not share it with The Ensimmainen or Langur or any of them.

They have abandoned us; left us here to die! They can survive on their own.

Yakin continued to recharge at his energy terminal while enjoying the spectacle before him, relaxing. For the first time in his very, very long life he was actually enjoying being alive.

I'll get the procedures started tomorrow … perhaps the next day … no, next week would be better, perhaps. There's no hurry.

We have time.

***

Zsoall, born in Hungary, was brought to Australia by his parents after the 1956 uprising in Hungary.

He currently lives a creative life with his wife and animal family in the Northern Rivers area of New South Wales, Australia.

His life has changed direction a number of times. Starting as a Secondary Teacher then becoming an Administrative Officer in a large national organisation. Neither offered much in the way of creative involvement. That began when he embarked on a career as a computer programmer. Whilst in that profession his continuing compulsion to create made it inevitable that his life would change again. Completely giving up programming he immersed himself in creativity as a Sculptor and Painter. Much of his time is now dedicated to creating glass paintings and sculptures, and to writing.

Another change is looming on the horizon as the art of recording visions of the future in the form of Science Fiction novels takes a firmer hold of his creative energies.